HEART QUEST®

PRAISE FOR DIANE NOBLE'S
HEARTWARMING NOVELLA:
A PLACE TO CALL HOME

"Beautifully written and told with poignancy and conviction. Diane Noble has once again delivered an unforgettable story. Sure to brighten the holidays!"

› **Lori Copeland** ›

author of the Brides of the West series and A Case of Bad Taste

"A charming glimpse into 19th-century Boston where two people from opposite ends of society open their hearts to others—and find true love. Curl up with a cup of tea, some cookies, and snuggle under a warm throw— and prepare to enjoy this heartwarming tale."

› **Kathleen Morgan** ›

author of Embrace the Dawn *and* Consuming Fire

romance the way it's meant to be

HeartQuest brings you romantic fiction
with a foundation of biblical truth.
Adventure, mystery, intrigue, and suspense
mingle in these heartwarming stories of
men and women of faith striving to build
a love that will last a lifetime.

May HeartQuest books sweep you
into the arms of God, who longs for you
and pursues you always.

HOMECOMING

Diane Noble
Pamela Griffin 💠 Kathleen Fuller

HEART
QUEST®

Romance fiction from
Tyndale House Publishers, Inc., Wheaton, Illinois
www.heartquest.com

Visit Tyndale's exciting Web site at www.tyndale.com

Check out the latest about HeartQuest Books at www.heartquest.com

HeartQuest is a registered trademark of Tyndale House Publishers, Inc.

A Place to Call Home and *The Heart of a Stranger* edited by Kathryn S. Olson
Christmas Legacy edited by Lorie Popp

Designed by Zandrah Maguigad

Scripture quotations are taken from the *Holy Bible*, King James Version.

Library of Congress Cataloging-in-Publication Data

Christmas homecoming / Diane Noble, Pamela Griffin, and Kathleen Fuller.
    p. cm. — (HeartQuest)
    ISBN 0-8423-3576-5 (sc)
    1. Christmas stories, American.   2. Christian fiction, American.   I. Noble, Diane - Place to call home.
II. Griffin, Pamela. Heart of a stranger.   III. Fuller, Kathleen. Christmas legacy.   IV. Series.
PS648.C45 C4466 2003
813'.54—dc21   2003005689

Printed in the United States of America

09   08   07   06   05   04   03
 9   8   7   6   5   4   3   2

C · O · N · T · E · N · T · S

A PLACE TO CALL
Home

FOR AMY AND MARK

*A story with a wee bit of Irish and a whole lot of love
can only be dedicated to a young couple
whose hearts hold both.*

May God hold you in the hollow of His hand.

I LOVE YOU.

DROGHEDA, IRELAND
CHRISTMAS EVE 1890

RORY O'KELLY trod through the winter brown grasses to his grandm'am's cottage at the edge of the sea. The wind sliced across his face, causing him to shiver and hunch his shoulders forward. Foam-laced waves hurled toward shore, seeming as angry as the ashen, storm-laden skies; and the wind moaned, as shrill as a poor woman about to bring a wee babe into the weary, cold world. Not unlike Ireland herself, struggling to give birth to freedom, struggling to rid herself of the English tyrants who bound her with unbreakable chains.

Rory shook his head slightly to rid his mind of such a fierce image. He would arrive at the cottage soon enough, and she would tell him straight out there was no room for such dark gloom in his heart on this Christmas Eve. Straightening his shoulders, he lightened his step, knowing her well. Sure as one Irish dawn followed another, she would be watching him through the small window by the front door.

He let himself through the picket gate and glanced up to see that he was right. His grandm'am stood, tattered lace curtain pulled to one side, a smile lighting her thin and weary face. Warmth filled his heart at the sight of the one who had raised him, raised both him and Eamon, his wild little brother. Though truth be known, they both were still as wild as the howling wind, each in his own way. Had been from the day they came to live with their dear departed da's own ma, Nuala O'Kelly, after their parents died back in seventy-one.

Grandm'am opened the door and drank in the look

of him, her eyes watering. "Heaven be thanked," she said, reaching to draw him into her arms. She seemed not to care about keeping the chill wind from whistling through the cottage. "Haven't I been praying I'd wrap my arms around ye this day?"

Rory grinned and scooped her close, delighting in the feel of her birdlike arms wrapped round his waist. She smelled of fresh-baked bread and smoke from the peat fire. For a moment he rested his head atop hers.

"It's been too long, Rory-mine," she said, craning her neck to look up at him. "What's the business that's kept ye away? As if I dinna know." She shook her head and stepped back so he could enter the small, dim room.

"'Tis just as ye brought me up," he said. "A greater business, as ye've called it, than life itself, this fight for freedom."

"'Tis," she said simply. "'Tis." She nodded to the chair by the fire. "Sit, lad. And I shall fetch ye some tea. Then I'll listen gladly to the news from Dublin."

"Don't go wasting such preciousness on the likes of me." He knew tea cost her dearly in such times, and she meted it out so she could enjoy one cup every Sunday.

She turned, her hands resting at her waist, bony elbows pointed outward. "On the morrow, we celebrate our dear Lord's birth. But wasn't it during the night before that the wee Babe was born? Don't ye see, lad? Now 'tis the true time to lift our hearts in gratitude." She paused, peering at him from across the room. "Besides, my dear Rory himself has come this very night. Isn't it time to warm ourselves by the fire with a hot cup of tea?"

He nodded then, feeling a tug at his heart at the familiar way his grandm'am ended her sentences with a questioning lilt. "I'm glad I'm here to share it with ye."

She looked pleased.

"Have ye heard from Eamon?" he asked.

Bending low over the hearth, she dropped in more

peat, poked at the fire until it flamed high, then with a thick towel at the handle, set the iron teakettle atop a flat stone to one side. The worried crease of her forehead caused his heart to catch. "Ach, now, Rory," she sighed. "Isn't the lad the cause of me wakeful nights?"

"Ye have news then?"

As if she didn't hear the question, his grandm'am moved across the room to the shelf near the corner table. For a moment there was no sound but the sizzle of burning peat and the clink of pottery mugs, saucers, and teapot as she set them on the tray beside a hunk of dark bread. She didn't speak until she settled into a chair across from Rory, the tray on a crooked-legged table between them.

"True enough, Eamon was here a fortnight ago," she said, studying her work-worn, folded hands.

Rory leaned forward. He had been waiting to hear of Eamon's whereabouts. "Did he say where he was going next?"

"Dublin."

He frowned. "Eamon's in Dublin, is he?"

She nodded. "Aye, lad. Said he was going straightaway."

"Then why didn't he come to me?"

"He's in some kind of trouble. I think he might've been wanting to protect ye—to keep the English from nabbin' ye as well as himself."

"Doesn't he know I would give me very life to help him?"

Her look was sharp as she met his gaze. "'Tis well the truth, Rory-mine. But Eamon also knows ye want a war fought with words not swords. Perhaps he wonders how a pen might protect him now."

"He's joined forces with dangerous men, these who call themselves the Society of St. George."

The water had risen to a boil now, and his grandm'am stood to fetch the kettle. "Don't I wonder at the truth of that?" she said as she poured the water into the readied teapot. A weak but fragrant steam rose. "If Ireland is ever to throw off her shackles of oppression, will a pen make the same point as a sword?"

"'Tis not the English I aim to stir up." He watched as she sliced a hunk off the hard loaf of bread. There was no butter or jam to spread, and it hurt him for her sake, knowing how she enjoyed such sweets. "'Tis me own countrymen who need the stirring with my pen."

She cocked her head at him, her eyes birdlike bright. "Ach, but Rory-mine," she said, "isn't it true that Irishmen canna read or write?"

Most could not. He and his brother were among the fortunate. His grandm'am had seen to their education herself, sitting by the fire in this very room, painstakingly instructing her grandsons, word by word, from the only book in the cottage, the *Holy Bible.* "They will read someday," he said stubbornly, taking his mug of tea from her thin fingers. "And until then those who can read will tell the others." But his heart was not in his words. He feared his grandm'am was right.

She smiled then, and lifting her cup, closed her eyes to savor her first sip. "Isn't it freedom we want?" she said after a moment. "No matter whether it comes by pen or sword or both, isn't it freedom?"

Rory stood and moved to the hearth to stir the fire. It sparked and crackled. As he sat again, she spoke, her voice dropping almost in reverence. "They aren't such a bad sort, these young men of the Society of St. George."

He sat forward with a start. "Ye know them then?"

The corner of her mouth curved upward. "Entertained them in this very room." Her shoulders lifted in pride, and her smile widened. "And didn't I enjoy it?"

Rory slammed the mug down, caused the crooked table to wobble. "The *amadain* had no business putting ye in danger."

"Don't be callin' yer brother an eejit, lad. Surely ye know by now that I'm not afraid of the English."

"They bring troubles to all who cross them. To young and old, man and woman. Dosna matter. Surely ye see that. . . . "

She lifted a hand and laughed. "Don't ye remember 'twas I who taught ye about those same troubles . . . also about the cost of freedom?"

Rory knew the story well. Nuala O'Kelly had lost her husband, Rory's own grandda, during the great potato famine. She had witnessed the English burning the potato fields; she'd watched neighbors and friends, the children, the old, the sick, die of disease and starvation. She had never forgotten. She had taught her grandsons about oppression, pounding into their hearts and minds the glory of freedom, the honor of fighting for it no matter the cost. The boys had caught hold of her spirit; it burned bright in their hearts.

Eamon was headstrong and impulsive. Ready to march off to fight the English without provocation. That reckless spirit caused Rory to fear for his little brother. It also caused him to take a more cautious path, one that he was certain Eamon thought lacked courage.

No matter what Eamon thought of his methods, Rory would fight. Oh yes, he would. But in his own way. In his own time.

His grandm'am was watching him over the rim of her mug. He saw the corners of her eyes crinkle and knew she was smiling even before she set down her tea.

"Haven't we concocted a plan for ye," she said, "if it's truly a war of words ye want to fight?"

"A plan?" He choked. "'We concocted a plan'? Who is 'we'?"

She took a long draught of tea, sighed with contentment at the taste, and placed the mug on the table again. "'Tis the wrong shore ye're fighting on, Rory."

"Ye've been waiting for my visit to tell me Ireland is the wrong place to fight for freedom?"

"'Tis for ye, lad."

Her look was one of smug satisfaction, having delivered such a surprising announcement. She met his gaze with a small, crooked smile. "Won't ye soon be sailing to America?"

He laughed. "Impossible."

"Won't ye be sailing within a fortnight of Epiphany?" she said, not laughing with him.

Rory leaned toward her. "What good would going to America do for the Irish cause—even if I could afford passage?"

"We have cousins in Boston. Young Quigley O'Kelly sells newspapers on a corner. He'll see ye settled. 'Tis there ye'll sail. 'Tis there ye'll take yer war of words— to the Irish in America." She settled back, her mouth in a rigid line. When it was set like that, there was no arguing with Nuala O'Kelly.

He took hold of her hand. "I canna leave ye. Surely ye know that." The lines in her face seemed more pronounced this visit, the tiredness beneath her eyes darker than before. The price of leaving her might be greater than money.

Nuala O'Kelly drew her thin shoulders tall and fixed her bright eyes on his. "I have something for ye." She turned to look out at the deepening gray of the skies. "I have the means to see ye sail to America."

"Don't ye know that even the price of steerage is dear?" he said gently.

She reclaimed her hand from his grasp. "'Tis possible." She rose and walked to the shelf on which the thick *Holy Bible* rested. Next to it stood the chipped, pottery sugar crock he remembered from his childhood. Lifting the lid, she withdrew a tightly bound package. When she returned to Rory she handed the fat roll to him.

It lay heavy in his hands. He almost feared loosing the twine. She seemed to sense his reticence and nodded. "Go on, Rory-mine," she said. "Go on."

He pulled one end of the thick string, and the package fell open in his lap. He stared with amazement at the neatly rolled bills, then back to his grandm'am's face. "How . . . ?" he began.

Again she fluttered her hand, dismissing his question as if this astounding gift was an everyday occurrence. "'Tis not important," she said. "Don't ye know it's to fight for freedom? Don't ye know ye'll soon be fighting with all the passion in yer Irish heart?" She sighed. "Don't ye know where it came from surely canna matter?"

"Eamon . . . " He narrowed his eyes as he leaned forward. "He's behind this—and the blackguards from St. George." He met her steady gaze and knew he was right. "I fear thinking how they came by such a sum. And now I know why ye looked so worried when I asked about Eamon. He's in trouble because of this." He felt his jaw working hard. "The English are after him." He tossed the roll to the table, making its crooked legs shake again, causing the mugs to rattle in their saucers.

"Have ye not guessed there is something in return, Rory-mine, we ask of ye?"

We again. "I'll wager there is." With a dark sigh, he rose and walked to the fireplace, stoked it, and turned again to his grandmother.

She set her chin in a stubborn tilt as she peered up at him. "'Tis funds we need as well as words, lad. Ye must talk to the Irish—our cousins and brothers and sisters— in the New World. Tell them about our plight. Don't ye know they need reminding of why they left their homeland? Don't they remember the deaths of their wee ones from famine, the burning of the fields and homes? Tell them we need their help. Tell them to reach into their pockets and send what they can."

Rory looked away from her intent expression, the pleading look in her eyes. "Eamon is for me going? I figured he still thought me a coward for being unwilling to bear arms."

She smiled. "Eamon keeps to himself. But don't ye know he believes in yer heart's passion as surely as he believes in his own?"

"I fear for the lot of them, Eamon and the brutes he's running with."

His grandm'am laid her hand on his forearm. "I pray for my boys each morning, lad, asking the dear Lord to keep ye in the palm of His big hand. For 'tis God, not we ourselves, who knows the number of our days. He's called ye and Eamon, true. But to use different treasures from yer hearts. Treasures like unto gifts from Him more precious than gold itself."

Rory turned from her gaze to stir the fire once more and to keep the water from filling his eyes. Why did the Irish always weep at tender words spoken by someone they loved? 'Twas a bain. 'Twas.

After drawing in a deep breath, glad his eyes were still dry, he turned to see that Grandm'am was sitting again in the rocker. "Sure, don't I have other words ye must hear?" Her eyes were brighter than before and, like wet stones, caught the glow from the fire. She nodded to the empty chair across from her, and he sat. "I fear ye'll not be returning soon, Rory-mine. Because ye're the firstborn, I have something that belongs to ye."

She reached for the worn gold chain that graced her thin neck. Then sliding her fingers to the clasp at the back of her neck, she unfastened it and reached for his hand.

"I canna . . . " he began, then saw the warning in her expression and closed his mouth.

Grandm'am dropped the locket into his palm. "This is not for ye . . . " she smiled at his surprise. "Don't ye know 'tis for the lass ye will someday marry?"

He threw back his head and laughed at that. "Finding a wife is the last thing I'll be thinking about." He smiled. "Nah, my dear grandm'am, 'twill be a long while ye must wait for such a day. And I reckon 'twill be in Ireland herself that such a maid will be found. Not in America."

Still smiling, she quirked a brow. "That's something else I pray about every morn. Whether in Dublin or Boston that yer lass may be awaitin', I pray our dear Lord is keeping her in His big hand as well as He does ye."

"If I go—and I'm not saying for certain I will—my travels will take me across dangerous seas. Your locket might be lost or . . . worse." He studied her face. "Grandm'am, couldn't you keep it safe until I have found the one I love?"

His grandm'am's expression was gentle now. She seemed not to have heard his words about not sailing for America. "Rory-mine," she said softly, "dinna yer grandda give me this locket on the day we wed? Ye canna see it, but a wee bit of Irish family love is tucked inside. 'Twill see ye safely home . . . perhaps with a bride at yer side." She smiled. "Besides, before ye go, I'll give ye a small velvet box to keep it in. 'Twill keep it from harm, tucked inside. 'Tis the same as yer grandda gave to me."

He moved his gaze from her face to the worn gold design on the locket case. "Hands holding a heart," he mused. "A loved one giving his heart to his beloved."

"'Tis a lover, sure enough, but the lover is God Himself holding yer heart. Can ye not look closer and see 'tis true?"

"Still, I canna—"

She paid no attention to his protest. "That's why ye must take it now, lad. No matter if ye go—or if ye stay. No matter if ye fear my being gone when ye return . . . don't ye know ye're in yer heavenly Father's care?" She closed his fingers around the locket. "Don't ye know," she said, her voice as soft as the Irish breeze in summer, "that ye must never forget all I've told ye?"

Rory felt the weeping begin in his heart and move to his throat. This time he gave in to the water filling his eyes. He placed the locket on the table, and then he wrapped his big hands around the small parchment ones belonging to Nuala O'Kelly, freedom fighter and beloved Grandm'am. "Ye needn't worry about me not comin' home again. 'Tis Ireland—and ye—I will long for all me days."

Her lilting voice took on a low and serious tone when she spoke again. "Ye're mistakin' me meaning, lad. Me meaning of that place called home." She removed her hand from his and settled back in her chair, wearing the look of fierce pride and loving expectation he'd known all his life. "Dosna matter where yer feet trod—here in Drogheda or somewhere across the big ocean." She studied him while the fire snapped and popped.

The locket caught a flicker of firelight, and Rory picked it up again, holding it by its delicate chain.

His grandmother's gaze settled on the worn gold heart, on the carved image of hands around it. "Home is that place in yer heart, that place that God holds fast," she said softly. "Whenever ye worry about finding yer way, lad, look to Him, yer heavenly Da. Look to Him who made ye. For 'tis He who holds ye fast. 'Tis He who will see ye home."

I

BOSTON, MASSACHUSETTS
JUNE 1891

I N THE NEWBORN NURSERY at Trinity Settlement House,
Dr. Olivia Endicott-Jones bent over the middle bassinet in a row of five and tucked a flannel cloth around
the infant's small body. Nurses bustled around Olivia,
caring for the four other babies born this week, each fussing to be fed or changed. But Olivia's attention didn't
stray from this feisty one.

At seven days old, the baby had defied every principle
in Olivia's medical books. Born well below the average
birth weight, the scrawny little miss was healthy and
determined to live. Even though down the hall at the far
end of the clinic—in a ward set aside for the most seriously ill—her mother lay dying.

This little one is Yours, Father, Olivia prayed silently,
resting her hand on the baby's back. *Keep her close to
Your heart.* As the infant sighed in her sleep, a feathery

contented sound, the threat of tears stung Olivia's eyes. Oh yes, it would take God's help to see this precious one through the hard life ahead. She was poor and Irish and soon to be an orphan.

She left the infant in the care of a nurse and returned to the ward with a dozen beds set aside for the most seriously ill. Olivia checked the baby's mother's temperature with her palm, then dipped a cloth in a pan on a nearby table, squeezed out the excess water, and dabbed it across Nell's forehead to cool her.

Nell's eyes fluttered open, bright with fever. Olivia bent her ear close to the young Irish mother's lips as she struggled to speak.

"Madeilein . . . " Nell McGrail's breathing rattled. "Where is me wee one . . . ?" Her voice broke off as a fit of coughing racked her thin chest. She held a cloth to her mouth.

"Your baby is healthy and well," Olivia said when Nell once again lay quiet on her pillow. She gently patted the young mother's hot forehead with the damp cloth. "She's tiny. And beautiful, oh so beautiful. Her eyes are the color of violets—just like yours. You must rest, regain your strength so you can hold her in your arms and see for yourself." Though even as she spoke, Olivia wondered at the sad truth. Nell was dying.

Nell's breath seemed more shallow and rapid than before, but a weak hint of a smile played at the corners of her mouth. "Aye," she said softly. "An Irish beauty. Oh, that her da could see his wee babe . . . " Her eyes fluttered closed. "Lost at sea, he was, returning to Ireland," she wheezed. "Last spring . . . just when the wild roses were a-bloomin'." Her words ended as another fit of coughing overtook her.

Olivia rinsed the cloth again, twisted it until the last drip fell, then laid it folded on Nell's hot forehead. When she had finished, she reached for the woman's hand and squeezed it gently.

The young woman—likely close to Olivia's age but seeming so much older and wearier—fixed her gaze on Olivia. "There's no one else. Just Liam and me. I took work in the factory soon after his passing to put food . . . on me table." Another violent fit of coughing interrupted. This time there was blood in the handkerchief. Olivia's heart quickened, and a stinging fear rose to her throat.

From the room's single window, sounds from the street mixed with Nell's coughing. Horse hooves clacked along the cobbled road, pulling their creaking wagons and carriages.

"You must rest now," Olivia said.

"I have something to ask ye first, miss."

"Please call me Olivia."

Nell smiled, sinking deeper into her pillow as her eyes closed. "Aye," she said. "Liv, I bet ye're known by."

"My mother and father call me Liv. Sometimes Livy."

"'Tis a name meanin' life. Bounteous life from God Himself." Her eyes were still closed. "Liv . . . ?" she said after a few minutes.

"I'm here, Nell."

"Could ye take me babe? Take wee Madeilein and raise her as your own?" Nell turned her head to fix her gaze again on Olivia's face. "I want to get well . . . for me babe. But I must be wise . . . if I . . . " She didn't finish.

"You must try to live," Olivia said firmly, but her eyes stung with the truth of the young mother's words.

"Please." Nell then coughed again. "I need to rest in knowing me Madeilein is with someone I know . . . with you. Someone who will love her." She reached for Olivia's hand and held it fast with both of hers. "Promise me now, will ye, Liv? Promise me?" She fell into her pillow, obviously exhausted from talking. But she didn't let go of Olivia's hand. "Please," she breathed with a voice so soft it almost disappeared in the evening air.

Olivia swallowed hard. Her life was already complicated. The clinic took nearly every ounce of energy and so much time that often she stayed for days on end, caring for the sick, the poor, those who had no home. How could she take on the burden of a child . . . a child she promised to raise to adulthood?

Nell's eyes were abnormally bright.

Olivia nodded slightly, biting her lip. *Oh, Father, You ask us to let our hands be Your hands, our eyes Your eyes, our ears Your ears, our hearts Your heart. You ask us to care for others as if caring for You . . . but this, Lord? Are You asking me to take this child as my own . . . when my hours are already full to overflowing? Is it You who is asking me . . . as well as this precious mother?*

"'Tis not an easy thing I ask of ye." Nell's voice, little more than a whisper, echoed Olivia's prayer.

"And your request deserves a thoughtful answer," Olivia said quietly after a moment. "I don't take your words lightly."

"I knew ye wouldna."

Olivia considered her mother's and father's antagonism toward anything related to her clinic, related to the poor Irish children and families in her care through Trinity Settlement House. What would they think if she brought home a wriggling newborn . . . an *Irish* newborn?

Oh, Lord, she breathed heavenward again, *surely You can't be asking this of me!*

"Are you certain there is no one else?" Olivia hesitated. "Your daughter might be better off with your own family . . ." She swallowed hard then added lamely, "perhaps someone in Ireland. I could see that she receives safe passage."

Nell didn't speak for a moment, and Olivia thought she had fallen asleep. "'Tis too much for ye. I'm sorry,

Liv. Aye, there might be someone else after all." Her sad expression said otherwise.

Since childhood, Olivia had loved a small illustration in her Bible of Jesus holding a lamb cuddled in His arms. The image came again to her mind. Her arms were His in this world. She had become a doctor so she could be His instrument. Healing hearts was even more important than healing bodies. How could she say no?

She swallowed hard and reached for Nell's hand. "Nell," she said softly, "I will do it. I feel honored you asked me."

Eyes still closed, Nell gave Olivia a weak smile. "Aye, 'tis as it should be," she said. "God be with ye, Liv. And bless ye for what ye're undertakin'."

"And you, dear Nell," Olivia whispered. "May our Lord carry you close to His heart."

Nell McGrail died just past midnight, Olivia sitting beside her.

⋅⋅⟨◈⟩⋅⋅

THE NEXT MORNING Olivia clutched the baby close as she stepped from the streetcar near her family home. At the clang of the streetcar bell and the clack of the wheels on the track, a tiny fuss erupted from the flannel folds. Olivia stopped in the shade of an elm to peer at the tiny face inside.

Two bright blue eyes gazed back at her. Babies this young were unable to focus, but Olivia smiled anyway and cuddled her closer. "There, there, wee Madeilein Mary McGrail." She adjusted the baby in her arms and the nappy bag at her side. "We're almost home."

Home. Her stomach turned a somersault at the word.

Home was a place filled with happy childhood memories. Her parents had lavished her with their love, taken pride in her achievements, quietly cheered her on with each step Olivia took toward adulthood. Even before she was old enough to understand, her father had cuddled her into his big lap and read to her of faraway places, his voice rumbling and low. Her mother had played games, sung, and laughed with Olivia in the sunlit gardens, even as she patiently taught her only daughter reading, writing, and deportment. And at Olivia's bedside at twilight, she sang lullabies in a sweet, loving, lilting voice.

It seemed Olivia could do no wrong; that is, until she grew older and her hopes and dreams no longer matched those of her parents. Then that same home, once filled with laughter and song, turned silent and cold.

Home. How Olivia longed for it to be once again the cheerful place of her childhood. How she longed to feel again her parents' love and acceptance.

She tucked the blanket around Madeilein, gently brushed her cheek against the down soft head, and started walking. With each swish of her long skirts she prayed that she would find the words to express to her mother and father this little one's need for shelter.

Her parents traced their blue-blooded ancestry—on both sides—to families who arrived on the Mayflower. When they packed her off to Rockford Female Seminary and allowed her to continue her education at Women's Medical College, her life—and her views of the world—had changed forever.

It was at Rockford that she heard Jane Addams speak about the need for settlement houses to give loving care and medical help to children and their families. The same passion caught hold of Olivia's heart, and one year ago she opened a small two-story settlement house on the edge of Back Bay, donated by Trinity Church where generations of Endicott-Jones families had worshiped.

Many of the parishioners helped get the clinic ready, donating time and money to the cause. Olivia's parents were not among them. It saddened her that they refused to cross the threshold. She wanted them to be proud of her, but more than that, she wanted them to take joy in the education they had given her.

Just once, she wanted to see a flicker of pride in her father's eyes, feel his arm around her shoulders as his gravelly voice whispered, "I'm proud of you, Liv." Just once, Olivia wanted her mother to stand at her side as she brought a baby into the world, to share the miracle of new life.

But instead, the disapproving silence between her parents and Olivia grew cooler by the day. No matter how she tried to cheerfully ignore their indifference, it remained.

She glanced down at the child in her arms. Now she was bringing home a baby. An Irish baby. With a heavy sigh, Olivia lengthened her stride. Her heart caught as the tall, brick family mansion loomed at the end of the street.

Within minutes, Olivia stood quietly at the sitting-room door, the gramophone playing scratchy music in the background. Her father and mother were lost in conversation, their attention on each other.

Olivia cleared her throat and smiled as Hazel Endicott-Jones looked up. "Why, Livy, I didn't hear you come in—" Then she frowned and her voice broke off.

Olivia's father lifted the needle arm from the gramophone and the baby's fussing filled the room. Her mother's alarmed gaze slid from Olivia's face to the bundle of blankets in her arms. "Whatever do you have there?" She rose elegantly to her feet. Hazel Endicott-Jones was seldom in a hurry, even when warranted.

Olivia tried to calm her racing heart, worrying that the tension in her arms might distress the baby.

She was right. Madeilein filled her lungs with air and wailed again.

Weston Endicott-Jones, his forehead furrowed in disapproval, followed his wife across the thick Chinese rug where Olivia stood rooted.

"What in the world . . . ?" her mother said again, raising her voice above that of the crying baby.

"Whose is it?" her father demanded at the same instant.

Olivia ignored both questions. Drawing back a blanket corner and murmuring words of comfort, she rocked Madeilein in her arms. The wailing stopped abruptly, and Olivia lightly rested her cheek atop the baby's head.

Hazel frowned. "What *are* you doing with this baby, Liv?"

"Madeilein's mother died last night," she said, keeping her voice low. "But before she died, she asked if I would care for her baby." Olivia prayed for wisdom. "I thought—that is, if you don't mind—"

Her father's neck was stiff, his words clipped when he spoke. "Keep the child here? Absolutely not," he said, keeping his gaze off the baby. "It's quite out of the question."

"Of course I agree with your father, Liv," her mother added. "It's bad enough that you're working down at that . . . that clinic, among the dirty, the poor. It's quite another to bring one home with you." She paused. "It's a good thing to help the poor, the defenseless. But there are people we can hire to do the work." She gestured elegantly.

Olivia turned away from their aloof, hard-eyed expressions, fighting tears of anger and disappointment. She had hoped for a miracle. But it didn't seem it would happen. "All she requires is a cradle," she said quietly, "and a little table for changing nappies and bathing and such. Perhaps you might let her . . . let us . . . stay until I can make other arrangements."

"Quite out of the question. It must go." Her father

might as well have been speaking of a stray kitten Olivia brought home.

"Her name is Madeilein Mary McGrail."

"Irish!" Her father's words were quietly angry. "That's worse. You must make other arrangements."

"Then I will leave as well."

A cold silence filled the room. "Surely you can't mean that . . . " her mother finally managed. She glanced uncertainly at Olivia's father, then back to her daughter.

"I will move my things tomorrow," Olivia said. A memory, warm and lovely, filled her mind: Her mother's arms wrapped around Olivia, her cheek resting gently on Olivia's head. And from across the music room, her father beamed at them both, leading them in a song with his big, booming voice, while he plunked out a tune on the piano.

There came to my window
One morning in spring,
A sweet little robin;
She came there to sing.
The tune that she sang
It was prettier far
Than any I heard on the flute or guitar.

Her wings she was spreading
To soar far away,
Then resting a moment
Seem'd sweetly to say—
Oh happy, how happy
The world seems to be;
Awake, little girl,
And be happy with me!

Be happy with me? Oh, Papa, Olivia wanted to cry, looking now at his angry face. *What has happened to our home? What has happened to our love for each other?*

Her mother's voice interrupted Olivia's sad thoughts. "Where will you go?"

"To the clinic." She tried not to think about how much she wanted Madeilein to know the love of her family, to be surrounded by those who cared for her. And as she grew older, toddled, and walked, to know the freedom of giggling and exploring lawns and gardens—not to remain cooped up in the settlement house.

Her father stared hard into her eyes. "After all we've done for you . . . you would choose to throw everything—your standing in the community, your opportunity for a decent match, all of it—you would choose to throw it away?" His face was red, his words harsh. "Throw it away on the ungrateful poor?" He made a sputtering sound. "That's like throwing pearls before swine."

"The Irish aren't swine, Father. Neither are the poor."

But he wasn't listening. "The decision is yours," he said. "You know what you must do." He turned abruptly and strode from the room.

THAT SAME AFTERNOON in Charlestown, an Irish settlement near Boston, Rory O'Kelly furrowed his brow in thought and moved his paper and pen to one side of the ancient, scarred oak desk, the only piece of furniture in the room besides the sagging iron bed.

His young cousin Quigley stood before him, shifting his weight from one foot to the other in obvious agitation. The light in the room was dim, barely filtering through the tattered curtains at the room's single window, but he could make out the distress in the boy's face.

Rory let out a sigh of impatience. He was but two paragraphs into his next fiery essay for *The Liberator*, the weekly pamphlet he printed and distributed to the Boston Irish.

"I tell you, Rory O'Kelly," Quigley said, interrupting Rory's thoughts, "'tis a travesty and a sin." He shook his head. "We take care of our own, from wee babes to the long in the tooth. We dinna need help from those who revile us."

"Who was this woman . . . this Nell McGrail, God rest her soul?"

"A poor young thing, Nell was," the boy said, working his jaw. His thin face showed more freckles than skin. "Worked herself to an early death, she did. Then up and died after delivering her wee one. Dinna tell anyone here she was about to pass. The folks at the do-gooder house—"

"Trinity Settlement House, yer meanin'?" Rory had heard plenty about the place since his arrival in Boston six months earlier.

"Aye, the same," Quigley said impatiently.

"How did ye find out about the woman? this Nell McGrail?"

"One of the blue bloods running the place sent word to Smiling Joe Callahan just this morning. Said since Nell McGrail's husband was lost at sea and there was no next of kin, no one to take her baby, the poor infant had been given to her. A doctor. A fussy Brahmin, nose stuck in the air so high she'll drown when it rains."

"'Tis true enough, though, isn't it?" Rory raised a brow. "About the next of kin?"

Quigley ran his fingers through a shock of flame-colored hair that hung over his forehead and slumped into a nearby chair. "Aye, 'tis," he said with a frown. "But blood kin or not, we take care of our own. Ain't no reason for some Boston Brahmin to take a wee Irish babe home with her." He stood to pace the floor. "Likely to turn the infant into free labor down the road. Couldna be out of love for the Irish." His laugh was bitter.

"Do ye know where this one—this doctor might live?"

"I do," Quigley said. "Did some sleuthing on me own, nosin' around Trinity Settlement House. She lives in a section of mansions where the likes of you and me canna tread."

Rory leaned back in his chair, studying his young cousin. The boy wasn't yet twenty and still full of youthful passion tinged with bitterness. He reminded Rory of his brother Eamon.

"I've never allowed meself to be pushed from a place I care to tread . . . especially if I'm certain God wants me on that path," Rory said. "And I dinna intend to start shyin' away from such places now. But keep in mind, God says there is a time under heaven for everything . . . but He expects us to not go bargin' in ahead of His own good time."

Quigley grinned, looking considerably happier than when he first entered Rory's walk-up. "Who's to say that time ain't now?"

Rory laughed. "There's one small problem," he said. "Who, dear Quigley, will take care of the child?"

Quigley glanced around the room then pointedly looked back to his cousin.

Rory held up a hand, palm out. "There isna room for anyone but me. Besides, what would I do, carin' for a baby? I wouldna know where to st—"

"Ye yerself keep spoutin' about the collective Irish heart and how it needs to grow," Quigley interrupted. "Why, just last week in *The Liberator* ye said that we must be our brothers' keepers, take care of our own no matter the cost. We need hearts big enough to spread across the Atlantic Ocean, ye said."

"Aye," Rory said with a half smile, "that I did. But carin' for Irish infants wasna what I had in mind."

Quigley came around to Rory's side of the desk and leaned back against it, a look of triumph glittering in his eyes. Arms folded across his chest, he said, "I promise we'll find a family who will take in the wee babe if ye'll come with me to retrieve her."

With a sigh, Rory stood and wrapped an arm around his cousin's thin shoulders. "All right then, Quig," he said. "How difficult can it be to take away something that is rightfully ours in the first place? What did ye say this doctor's name is?"

"I dinna. But it's Endicott-Jones." He drew out the words with disgust. "Dr. Olivia Endicott-Jones."

Rory pictured the snooty, gray-haired Boston blue blood Quigley had described. She might be a harder match than he imagined.

·⁙·

OLIVIA'S HEART was heavy as she folded her clothes and stacked them in her satchel. She was glad her clothing needs at the clinic were simple. Her usual dress was a gored gray skirt, a white blouse covered with a long pinafore, and her upswept hair fastened with simple combs. It wouldn't be an easy life. She was used to indoor plumbing and bathing in the privacy of her own room. Worst of all, her heart ached for her parents' sadness and lack of understanding. Even as she packed, she hoped one or the other would step to the door and ask her forgiveness, tell her they had been mistaken, and she could stay. With little Madeilein Mary.

But the house remained silent.

The baby lay sleeping in the center of the tall four-poster bed as Olivia packed the last of her toiletries then moved to the bedside table to pick up her Bible. Madeilein sighed in her sleep, moving her rosebud lips as if sucking on her bottle. A wave of affection rose in Olivia's heart, and she touched the infant's whispy hair, curling a feathery tendril around her finger.

She opened the Bible's worn leather cover to the

illustration of Jesus with the lamb and, gazing down at Madeilein again, she whispered a prayer for God's guidance. After a moment, she tucked the Bible into her satchel and snapped the clasp closed.

She settled onto the window seat overlooking the back garden to wait for the baby to wake. *Heavenly Father,* she breathed silently, *be with little Madeilein and me. My heart aches for my parents and their bitterness. Soften their hearts.*

But even as she prayed, she knew that it would take a miracle. A sense of lofty superiority had befuddled the thinking through generations of Endicott-Jones families. Her parents were no different than others in her father's riding club or her mother's garden club. Some openly touted the Irish as subhuman, and now that the Irish were active in politics, worse accusations than that were being bandied about. Accusations based on unreasonable fears that their way of life was about to be lost.

Her parents were wrong, but that didn't stop her from loving them. Tears threatened as she gazed around the bedroom that had been hers since babyhood. She wondered if she would ever set foot in it again.

A soft rapping at the door interrupted her thoughts.

"Come in," she called, praying it was her father.

The knock sounded again, and she crossed the room to open the door. The Endicott-Jones houseman stood before her, looking troubled.

"Miss Liv," he said in a whisper, casting a worried look at the baby, who had just begun to fuss. James had been with the family since before Olivia's birth. He adjusted the black patch he wore on his left eye. "You've got visitors, Miss Liv. Two men from Charlestown, they say. But if you ask me, one sounds like he's straight off the boat from Ireland." He grinned. "A handsome fella, too, miss. That he is, all right."

Olivia flushed slightly as she went to the bed to gather Madeilein into her arms. "Did they say what they want?"

"No, Miss Liv. Only to speak with you."

Figuring they wanted to see her about the settlement house, she nodded. "Show them to the garden, James. I'll meet with them there."

He nodded, and after another tender glance at the baby, left to do Olivia's bidding.

She had just stepped into the shade of the gazebo, Madeilein in her arms, when she heard footsteps crunching on the gravel walkway. She turned to see James heading toward her, two men lagging slightly behind. The first, with a shock of flame red hair, appeared to be little more than a gangly, overgrown boy. Maybe eighteen if he was a day.

The second, the one who seemed to be taking the lead, judging from his towering presence and confident demeanor, was older. Perhaps thirty. It was hard to tell, because as soon as his startlingly blue-gray eyes met hers, she forgot all her musings about his age.

"May I help you?" Her eyes were still riveted to his.

He surveyed her kindly. "Aye, lass, 'tis indeed why we've come . . . to seek your help now." His lyrical voice reminded Olivia of Nell McGrail's. Music like an Irish harp. Or birds calling as they wheeled above the Irish Sea. Not that she had ever seen the seas of Ireland . . . or heard an Irish harp, of course. "Me name is Rory O'Kelly," he was saying, "once of Drogheda, Ireland, most recently of Charlestown." He dipped his head in a slight bow, then elbowed the younger man to do the same.

The boy doffed his hat, scowling. "That ain't why we're standin' in front of the blue blood, Rory. All these niceties and such." His whispered growl was loud enough for Olivia to overhear.

Her heart beat more rapidly with sudden fear at his tone. She stared at the younger man. "Tell me, then," she said and instinctively hugged Madeilein closer to her heart, "exactly why you are here."

Rory O'Kelly's Irish-sea gaze didn't leave hers. "'Tis about the wee one in your arms."

"We ain't leavin' here without her," the younger man snarled, stepping closer. "She's ours, and we've come to take her home."

T HIS RUDE LAD is me cousin Quigley," Rory O'Kelly
said. "Our grandm'am in Drogheda sent me all
this way to teach him his manners." He smiled
apologetically. "Ye can see he needs me lessons."

Olivia didn't answer. Her heart still raced with fear
for the child in her arms. She cast a look toward James to
reassure herself of his presence. He too seemed alarmed
and had moved closer to the small group.

Olivia kept her voice calm, clutching Madeilein closer.
"Perhaps you should tell me why you're threatening to
take my child."

"'Tis your child?" Rory O'Kelly stood directly in front
of her. "Or would her mother be one Nell McGrail
now?" His expression remained honest, caring, gentle.
Unthreatening. It didn't match the threat of his stance,
the soft challenge of his tone.

Olivia took a few steps backward, her arms tightening around the infant. She looked from one man to the other. The men had come to take her baby back to the Irish community. The slums of Charlestown. She met Rory's gaze with a challenging one of her own. "This is Madeilein Mary McGrail."

"It's the one—I told you we'd find her here!" Quigley's voice was triumphant. "She belongs with her own kind."

James stood next to Olivia now, arms folded at his chest, looking as mean as she'd ever seen him. He was the gentlest of souls, but because of his size—when he wanted to make sure no one bothered the Endicott-Joneses—he looked like a pirate who'd as soon knock a person to kingdom come as look at them.

"I must ask you to leave," she said. "James will see you out."

The big houseman drew himself up even taller, his face set in a menacing scowl. The tension in the summer air was as thick as potato soup . . . or *Irish stew*, she thought wryly, *in this instance.*

Then the beginning of a smile tipped the corners of Rory's mouth, that same disarming, eye-lighting smile that had unnerved her from the first moment she saw him. "Aye, lass," he said. "Forgive us for bargin' in on ye this way. But surely ye can see our dilemma. Our people are used to carin' for their own. They take great pride in havin' hearts big enough to do it—even if their pocketbooks do not match their big hearts."

Squaring her shoulders, she stared unblinking into his Irish-sea eyes. "Nell McGrail asked me on her deathbed to care for her baby as if she was my own. I gave her my word."

"Do ye have any proof—of the poor dyin' woman's request, then?" Rory O'Kelly was looking down at Maddie, his expression soft. He didn't seem an evil man. Just misguided. He moved his gaze once more to Olivia's eyes, his own crinkling at the corners. "How do we know ye're telling us the truth, then?"

Olivia cleared her throat, forcing her thoughts back to the infant and her mother. "You'll have to take my word for it." She paused, breathing a prayer heavenward. "I wouldn't lie about such a thing."

Rory O'Kelly kept his eyes on her for at least three more beats of her heart. Though it could have been a dozen. She wasn't counting, so distracted was she by the look of him.

"I think ye wouldna," Rory said at last. His voice was soft, and he looked down at the baby again with that gentle expression. "I think our Nell chose well."

There was a sputtering sound behind him. "Is this what you want for the Irish? Is that why you came to us— to let babes be robbed right out of our cradles, taught Brahmin ways . . . ?"

Rory laid his hand on his cousin's arm. "Look at the life this wee one will have, lad." He gestured widely, taking in the house and grounds. "Can we be providin' anything close to this for the wee lass?"

"She'll be makin' a servant outta the bairn," Quigley muttered. "You wait and see."

"Madeilein will get the best education I can provide," Olivia said. "The best of everything." How she would manage it she didn't know. She would be homeless by the end of the day.

Quigley was still muttering under his breath, but Rory's smile was gentle. "Madeilein Mary McGrail," he said and touched the baby's down soft head with his fingertips. "'Tis a fitting name for one so pretty."

"Should there be any doubt about her care," Olivia said, surprising herself, "you're welcome to visit." Her cheeks warmed when he raised his eyes to smile into hers. She knew she must tell him the truth. "Though it won't be here you'll need to come."

He frowned. "Where, then, might it be?"

"I–I will be moving to the clinic . . . so I can better care for Madeilein while I work."

He glanced around the estate, his gaze resting briefly on James before meeting hers once more. It was obvious what he was thinking. Here, there were servants to care for the child. She should be free to come and go, work at the clinic, care for the infant in the morning and at night. His expression softened. "'Tis a fine thing ye're doin', Dr. Endicott-Jones, givin' up a home like this to care for wee Maddie."

For the first time she smiled. "Maddie?"

"Aye, Madeilein Mary seems much too long a name for such a mite." He looked down at the baby again.

She nodded. "Maddie," she said, pleased. "You and Quigley, or anyone else from your . . . your community— I mean, anyone who might want to check on the child's well-being—are welcome to come to the clinic anytime."

"Aye," he said, still smiling. "'Tis a fact Madeilein Mary McGrail should be watched over."

"I want her to know her people," Olivia added. Though she hadn't thought of it until just now. Perhaps it was a good thing she and the baby were leaving. She pictured her father's face as a parade of Irish made their way to the Endicott-Jones door and almost laughed.

"Aye," Rory said, keeping his gaze steady on hers as if reading her mind. "I will see to her well-being meself. I'll be her guardian."

Behind him Quigley sputtered. "I tell ye, man, we should grab the wee bairn and—"

"And I'll see that no harm comes to Maddie," Rory said, ignoring his cousin. "I give ye me word."

Quigley was still muttering. "As if ye fancy yerself some sort of guardian angel or somethin'." He shook his head in irritation. "Come over from Ireland itself to teach us all to fight for the homeland. Some warrior."

Olivia barely heard the boy so caught up she was in the kindness in Rory's face. "Thank you."

"We'll be on our way then." Rory moved away from her as he spoke. "We're sorry to have bothered ye."

She nodded, watching as he headed to the side gate, wondering when she would see him again. *If* she would see him again.

As if reading her thoughts, he stopped and looked back. "I'll be seein' ye again, lass . . . 'tis a promise."

The words had no more left the Irishman's mouth when Weston Endicott-Jones rounded the corner and stopped dead still. Staring after Rory and his cousin, who were now heading through the garden to the gate at the other side, her father frowned then turned to Olivia.

His face was as white as the prized Queen Victoria rose in his garden. "'Tis a promise?" He spat the words, imitating Rory's Irish brogue. "I'll be seein' ye again, lass?"

Near the garden gate, Rory and Quigley had turned toward where Olivia stood with her parents. She had no doubt that they could hear every word. Her heart caught at the ridicule her father had just dished out.

"His name is Rory O'Kelly, and he was talking about Maddie. He's to be her Irish guardian."

"You have disappointed your mother and me with your headstrong behavior. We admire the work you're doing, Liv—to a point. But you've gone way beyond what is reasonable for a young woman of your social standing. I must insist that you give up the child—" He held up one hand, palm out, when she started to protest. "I'll even help in any way I can to see that she's placed in a proper home."

"We've just come from speaking to the proper agencies downtown," her mother said, "people who handle this sort of thing. You'll be relieved to know that we are providing funds to oversee the child's welfare." She touched Olivia's arm. "You don't need to worry your head over this whole . . . affair, Liv. Think about it rationally."

Olivia shook her head, lifting a now-fussing Maddie to her shoulder.

Her mother's eyes filled. "Please don't cause this rift in our family, Liv. You're not just hurting yourself. You're hurting us . . . deeply hurting us."

"You're making me choose," Olivia said sadly. "Choose between you and the child I promised to raise."

Her father nodded and let out an exasperated sigh. "You *will* be caring for her—by giving her a family, a proper Irish family, and money to see to her needs."

"I gave my word to her mother," Olivia said. "But more than that—" she smiled at the little one in her arms— "nothing can make me give her up now." She glanced up again, looking from her father's face to her mother's, then back to Maddie. "I love her."

Her father made a choking sound and shook his head slowly in defeat. Her mother's face was now white with pain, but she said no more.

Olivia cuddled the baby closer. "I'm packed and ready to go," she said sadly then turned to James. "Will you drive me to the clinic?"

He waited until Olivia's father gave him a nod of approval then said, "Yes, Miss Liv, but I'm surely going to miss you."

"And I will miss you, James."

Her parents said nothing as they turned to walk toward the house. A movement by the gate caught Olivia's attention. Rory still watched from across the expanse of lawn and garden. His gentle expression told her he knew the real reason she was choosing to leave her home. With a small salute, he disappeared through the gate.

QUIGLEY O'KELLY MARCHED to the entrance of Trinity Settlement House exactly one week later. He doffed his hat as he entered the front door and disappeared into the building. A moment later he trotted back to the street, leaned against a lamppost, arms folded across his chest, and kept a watchful eye on the door.

All this Olivia observed from her second-story office as she stood by the window, plain muslin curtain pulled to one side. One of the nurses had taken Maddie for a walk in the pram, and Olivia was between patients. So when her assistant handed her the envelope, Olivia sighed at the luxury of having a few minutes alone to read the missive. Not that she expected it to be anything out of the ordinary. Not in the least. Or romantic. Then why did her fingers tremble as she pulled the small folded paper from its encasement? The decidedly male cursive began:

> Dear Miss Endicott-Jones,
> 'Tis my great fortune to have made your acquaintance a week ago today. And such a delightful child, this Madeilein Mary McGrail. Truly, she would bring delight to the hearts of her ma and da, God rest their souls, if they could see her. As you suggested, I would like to visit you and the child. I also have some important information about Madeilein Mary McGrail from the Irish community leaders. With your blessing, I would like to visit you this Saturday afternoon at four o'clock. I have instructed me cousin Quigley to await your reply. Until we meet again I remain
> Yours very sincerely,
> Rory O'Kelly

Olivia frowned at the letter, her eyes riveted to the phrase about Irish community leaders. Her worries of late returned, thoughts that had nagged her since meeting Rory O'Kelly: The man was a newcomer to Boston, so why would the Irish bosses bow to his desires? Even his cousin Quigley's disagreement with the decision to leave the baby in her care had been obvious. Why should any of the others feel differently? A chill spidered up her spine. She might lose little Madeilein Mary after all.

She quickly moved across the room to her mahogany secretary, sat down and dipped a pen in the inkwell, and wrote her answer on a small fold of parchment. Slipping it into Rory's envelope, she scrawled his name across the front and headed downstairs to deliver the missive to Quigley.

Moments later, Quigley trotted down the street, letter in hand, to catch a trolley to Charlestown.

• ⌇∧⌇ •

RORY GRINNED as he read the curt note from Olivia Endicott-Jones. He had sized her up quite nicely. A decisive woman, this one. In a scrawling, decidedly feminine but bold handwriting, she had written:

> My dear Mr. O'Kelly,
>   I regret that I cannot meet with you this Saturday afternoon at four o'clock as you suggested. Rather, my desire is to meet you tomorrow morning at ten o'clock here at Trinity Settlement House. Until then, I remain
>   Yours sincerely,
>   Olivia Endicott-Jones

Faith, the lass didn't even give him the opportunity to disagree! Chuckling, he stared at the note, picturing its author the last time he saw her, standing with the wee babe in her arms, eyes blazing like a mama grizzly's protecting her cub. Not that he had seen either. Nor had he even been close to where these animals roamed in the Western wilds. But those snapping, deep-feeling eyes of hers . . .

Ballinderry and Killybegs, their fiery, intelligent beauty was enough to make an Irishman weep. Rory wasn't a man prone to oaths; his grandm'am had taught him better than that. The only thing she allowed, when he and Eamon were lads, was to let the names of Irish villages roll off their tongues with a touch of spirit and merriment. It was a habit he had never broken.

Aye, sweet lass, he breathed as he stood to walk to the room's only window, *methinks ye will not be as happy to see me as I will be to see ye, especially with the news I have to bear.*

He gazed down at the street below: the storefronts, the milling clusters of women shopping and calling out to one another—some with heavy brogues, others with only a hint of their motherland tongue. Little children yelled and played; da's trooped home from factories and fishing boats. Trolleys clanged and wagon wheels rattled along the cobbles.

'Twasn't a bad life, this. Ma's and da's and lads and lasses with their hoops and sticks. But the clamor and confusion of the city made him long for the cliffs by his grandm'am's cottage, for the broad sky and unfathomable sea where a soul could get lost in their immensity, in the sounds of the gulls and crashing surf, the smell of peat smoke and saltwater.

He turned from the window, glancing back to the note from Olivia Endicott-Jones. Wasn't he an eejit to have allowed himself to be captivated by the lass? And after but one meeting? But what a gap between them. Herself with the fine upbringing of a Boston Brahmin. Himself just a poor lad from the old country and soon to return at that.

Holding the missive again in his hands, he scanned the curt few sentences and grinned. What was he thinking to allow himself such dreams about the fiery-eyed Miss Endicott-Jones? As he'd told his grandm'am often enough, 'twould be a fine, upstanding lass back home in Ireland who would one day win his heart. A lass who wanted to cook and sew and raise at least seven wee bairns. Not a placard-bearing, suffragette-marching, woman doctor who seemed willing to take on the troubles of the world whether they were hers to bear or not.

Killarney and Carraroe, what was he thinking?

THE NEXT MORNING, Olivia gently settled Maddie into a bassinet beside her desk, tucking a square of flannel around her. The infant fell asleep, and Olivia turned to finish a report about the latest patients to be admitted to the clinic.

At ten, she heard footsteps approaching from the hall. When they halted, she looked up. There, lolling against one side of the doorjamb, stood Rory O'Kelly. He studied her with a bemused expression, one brow raised, a half smile curving one side of his mouth.

Flushing, she stood and extended her hand in the most professional manner she could muster. "Mr. O'Kelly," she said, keeping her voice low because of Maddie. "Please, have a seat." She nodded to a chair opposite her desk.

"Miss Endicott-Jones," he said, tilting his head respectfully. "'Tis a pleasure to see you again."

Why did his eyes seem to say more than his words did?

She swallowed hard and seated herself at the same time he did. "You said you have news for me. I'm assuming it's about Maddie." She glanced down at the sleeping baby and held her breath as Rory O'Kelly dropped into his chair. He seemed in no hurry to answer her. A curious shadow of something akin to reluctance fell across his gaze.

From the nursery down the hall a baby cried, and farther away a woman called for a nurse. Footsteps approached the door, and a moment later, Olivia's friend Eliza Hale stuck her head in. Grinning, she gave Rory a wide-eyed appraisal, then looked back to Olivia with a curious sparkle in her eyes.

"Good morning," she said, giving Olivia a wink that her visitor couldn't see. "I have some admitting papers for you to sign."

"Eliza, this is Rory O'Kelly," Olivia said, narrowing her eyes at her friend in warning, then continued briskly with a nod toward Rory. "Mr. O'Kelly, my colleague, Eliza Hale. She's in charge of the mother and infant ward here at Trinity."

As he stood to take Eliza's hand, Oliva noticed again the tapered shape of his fingers, the masculine, square cut of his nails. Embarrassed that her mind had momentarily wandered, she looked back to Eliza when her friend spoke again.

"As I was saying—" Eliza was still grinning—"these papers need your signature, Liv. But I can stop by later to get them." She placed them on the desk in front of Olivia, winked again, then disappeared through the door.

She hadn't been gone for more than a half minute when there was another tap, and Vicar Preston looked in. He was the pastor at Trinity Church where Olivia attended. He and his wife had worked tirelessly to convince the vestry members to help fund Trinity Settlement House. "I'm sorry," he said when he spotted Rory O'Kelly. "I'll return when you're not busy."

Behind the vicar, his wife, Charlotte, peeked around his shoulder, her gaze also lighting on Rory. "We just wanted to give you some ideas for keeping the wards cooler on these hot nights," the vicar continued. "Gorman's been working on a plan."

Olivia laughed as she considered the elderly volunteer. "Gorman's always working on some plan. Last time it was to paint the hallways a cheerful yellow. He mixed three paints together, only to have the lot of them turn the color of mud."

"I think he's got this one figured out," Charlotte said, entering the room to stand next to her husband.

Obviously, the word had gotten around Trinity Settlement House that Olivia had a visitor. She wondered how many others on staff would drop by her office for one reason or another. With a sigh, she stood and once more made introductions. Rory O'Kelly's expression was gracious and his words kind as he shook the vicar's hand and grasped Charlotte's in greeting. He didn't seem to notice he was the object of curiosity.

As soon as the two had stepped back into the hall, Olivia closed the door and turned to Rory O'Kelly. "Now," she said, sitting down again. "You were about to say . . . ?"

He laughed lightly. "'Tis a busy place, this Trinity Settlement House. And ye seem to be at its heart."

The words had no more than crossed his lips when Maddie stirred. First a small snuffle rose from the small basket bed, then a chortle, followed by a sucking sound as the infant stuck her fist in her mouth. Before Olivia could lift Maddie into her arms, the baby let out a wail and, red-faced, waved her tiny fists in the air.

"I believe the wee bairn is hungry," Rory said with a worried frown. "Shall I hold her while ye fetch a bottle?"

The room was silent for only a heartbeat as Maddie filled her lungs with air then wailed again, this time even louder.

"And I might say, the sooner the better," Rory said, reaching for the infant.

With a laugh, Olivia gently deposited the small noisy bundle in Rory's arms. "I'll be back in just a moment . . . you're sure you don't mind?"

He jostled Maddie up and down against his shoulder, crooning something that sounded like an Irish lullaby. Wonder of wonders, he seemed perfectly at ease with the baby in his arms.

Olivia stepped to the door, then hesitated and looked back. She wondered briefly if she could trust this man. What if he disappeared with the child while she was gone?

But the look of him bent over Maddie, rocking her gently against his heart, made Olivia relax. The little one would be safe with him. Olivia didn't know how she knew it; she just did. She smiled, and for an instant she watched the two of them together. Words of a blessing from the Holy Scriptures came to her: *"The beloved of the Lord shall dwell in safety by Him; and the Lord shall cover him all the day long, and he shall dwell between His shoulders."*

Between His shoulders . . . precisely over his heart . . . just as Rory was holding Madeilein Mary right now. Just as Jesus held the lamb in her Bible's picture. The thought gave wings to her feet as she headed to the house kitchen for milk.

When she returned a few minutes later, she paused at the door, one hand on the worn crystal knob. From inside, soft singing drifted toward her. She pushed the door open a few inches and stopped again to listen.

As I was a-walkin' one mornin' in Spring,
For to hear the birds whistle and the nightingales sing,
I saw a young damsel, so sweetly sang she:
Down by the Green Bushes he thinks to meet me.

Rory's face wasn't in her line of vision, but the baby's was. Maddie stared up into his face, her round eyes unblinking. Her crying had ceased. Only the gentle resonance of his Irish brogue filled the room.

I stepped up to her and thus I did say:
Why wait you my fair one, so long by the way?
My true Love, my true Love, so sweetly sang she,
Down by the Green Bushes he thinks to meet me.

Olivia waited for him to pause before she entered the room. Even then, she wished he would keep singing, so filled with merriment and light-hearted melody it was.

When Rory saw her he stood, and when she approached, he gently transferred the bundle to her. His hand brushed hers as he laid the child in her arms. Olivia had the wildest urge to jump back, but instead, met his gaze evenly as if she hadn't noticed.

"You've watched over her well," she said, ignoring the strange, heavy rhythm of her heart. "I expected red-faced wailing by the time I got back."

"By me or the babe?" he said, grinning.

Swallowing hard at his merry look, Olivia did back away finally, seated herself behind her desk, and, supporting Maddie's head in the crook of her arm, popped the soft bottle top in her rosebud mouth. Tiny murmurs accompanied the sweet, soft sighs and sucking sounds.

Rory seemed to be watching her carefully. "This wee one has the soul of an Irish lass. Quieted right down when I began to sing."

"Perhaps she knows you're here to watch over her," Olivia said softly, moving her gaze to the curve of Maddie's cheek. She stroked it lightly with her fingertips. Her eyes moistened, just as they always did when she held the little one. After a moment, she looked up again and smiled. "Now maybe you can tell me the news from the Irish community leaders." She held her breath and waited for Rory to speak.

"AYE," RORY SAID with a sigh. "'Tis something that may trouble ye altogether." It broke his heart to relay what the Irish bosses had decided. For a moment he considered not telling her. But as he looked into her clear, honest gaze, he knew she had a right to know.

A shadow of alarm fell across her face and, almost imperceptibly, she drew the baby deeper into her embrace. "Tell me," she said, her brow furrowed in worry.

He drew in a deep breath and prayed for the right words. "The word has gotten around Charlestown, and many folks are up in arms. The bosses have met to decide the child's future, thinking she would be better off raised with her own kind. A family who wants to raise wee Madeilein Mary has come forth."

A small gasp escaped Olivia's lips. For a moment she just stared at him, almost as if trying to comprehend. Down the hallway, the clatter and noise of the busy settlement house continued. Finally she said, "You've come to take her from me then?"

"There is a group who's planning to visit yer parents' house and take her away. I dinna tell them ye are no longer there, but it willna take them long to find out. Right now they're working to get others to join them— in case there's . . . ah . . . resistance." He could not bear the look of pain that filled her eyes at his words.

Her voice was low and filled with passion akin to anger when she spoke again. "You've come to warn me, then? So I'll have Maddie's little things packed and ready when the time comes? Is that why you came today?" Clutching the baby who now had begun to fuss, Olivia stood and glared at him. "Tell your Irish bosses I don't care what they've decided," she said, putting the baby to her shoulder and patting her back. A tiny burp erupted, but Olivia didn't smile. "Tell them Maddie stays with me."

"Please, lass," Rory said quietly to Olivia, sitting down in his chair. "Please sit down and hear me out. There's more."

III

RORY SETTLED BACK in his chair as Olivia leveled an unblinking stare at him. If ever there was a proper guardian for the wee Maddie McGrail it was this ferocious woman with a heart the size of Boston Harbor. Fiercely protective, this one.

"There's more?" Olivia held Maddie encircled in her arms.

"Aye," Rory said softly. He moved his gaze from Olivia's face to the child then back again. "Aye, there's more to me tale."

If she was worried, she didn't show it. Olivia sat back down in her chair and kept Madeilein upright. The wee lass sighed and snuggled against Olivia's shoulder. Outside the closed door, the hubbub of the clinic continued, people marching by, voices calling out, the clatter of dishes on a tray as someone wheeled a cart down the hall.

But Maddie seemed not the least concerned, so comfortable she was in Olivia's arms. Her eyes drifted closed, and her breathing slowed to a peaceful, sleepy rhythm. Olivia briefly laid her cheek against the baby's head. "Go on," she said to Rory, her voice low. "I'm listening."

For the life of him, his eyes misted. Oh, the luck of the weepin' Irish! Blinking, he fixed his eyes on the window for a moment to regain his manly bearing, then looked back to Olivia. "Ye want to keep the baby," he said gruffly. "Ye have the means, the heart for it. Raisin' her, I mean."

Olivia frowned. "Perhaps not the means," she said, and he knew she referred to her leaving her family's estate. "But I have the heart . . . and the determination."

"She belongs here—" he cleared his throat—"here in your arms."

There was a flicker of surprise in Olivia's eyes. "I thought you just said . . . "

Rory held up a hand. "'Twould take a blind man not to see it." He paused. "Faith, I came here to tell ye what the bosses are plannin'—what they think would be best for the bairn." He leaned forward. "But after thinkin' it through I have me own plan to propose."

She tilted her head, her expression skeptical. "A plan?"

"Aye. These bosses, they need to see with their own eyes what a fit ma ye are for Maddie." He smiled. "I say we go to them together. Let them see yer . . . tender heart toward her."

"Take Maddie with me . . . with us, you mean . . . into Charlestown?" A flicker of alarm crossed her face. "After what you've said, that could be risky." She was looking down at Madeilein Mary now. "What if they disagree . . . take her from me?" Her clear-eyed gaze held surprising trust when she tilted her face back to him.

Swallowing hard, he nodded. "I will protect ye. And the little one. I give ye my word. Will ye come with me tonight?" For a moment he considered what it might be like to walk into the meeting with Olivia at his side, the babe in his arms, and he was surprised at the lovely warmth that filled him. "Will ye, then?"

·✧·

Before Olivia could answer him, a knock sounded at her office door.

Maddie still nestled in the crook of her arm, Olivia rose to open the door. Her friends and coworkers at Trinity, Eliza Hale and Rachel Newbury-Smyth, stood before her, each with a wriggling child in her arms. The women looked harried, first glancing down at their little charges, then to each other, and finally to Olivia. Their long starched aprons were smudged and wrinkled from holding the squirming children.

"We've got twins on our hands," Rachel said. "Identical from the top of their curly heads to the bottom of their tiny toes."

"Is their mother in the clinic?" Olivia looked out into the hallway, halfway expecting to see a worried parent marching down the corridor. But only the usual staff and patients milled about.

Eliza shook her head. "Someone left them here. Dropped them off and disappeared. This little one—" Eliza touched her cheek to the top of the child's head— "had a note pinned to her collar." She gave the folded paper to Olivia to read for herself. "Their names are Katie and Keara. This one is Katie." She hugged the child close.

Without being asked, Rory O'Kelly moved to Olivia's side and reached for Maddie. Olivia smiled her gratitude and handed him the infant with the bottle. As their eyes met, Olivia remembered her manners. Flushing slightly, she turned back to her friend. "Rachel, this is Rory

O'Kelly. He's from the Irish community—and Maddie's self-appointed guardian."

"I'm happy to meet you." Rachel smiled over the top of Keara's head. "You're a welcome addition to this place—what would we do this minute without your extra pair of hands?"

It seemed that all of Trinity Settlement House was taken with the Irishman. Olivia shot her friend a warning look, figuring another wink and knowing look would follow. But Rachel merely gave her an innocent smile then turned her attention to the toddler in her arms who was wriggling to get down.

Rachel stooped to place the child's feet on the floor, and the little girl raced to the window, jabbering in a musical language that Olivia couldn't understand. As if on signal, Katie squirmed out of Eliza's arms and followed her sister. They pointed and jabbered and pointed again, looking back to Rachel and Eliza—then to Olivia—with questioning eyes.

Olivia's heart went out to the little girls. The note could wait. She stuffed it into her pocket and knelt beside the twins at the window. "What do you see?" The little girls spoke again, this time to each other. Katie's bottom lip pooched out, and tears filled her eyes. "I'm sorry," Olivia said. "I don't understand . . ."

Then Rory spoke up. The children turned from the window and looked at him in surprise. Smiling gently, he said a few more words to them. Katie and Keara brightened noticeably. "Gaelic," he said to Olivia. "'Tis a wonder to be speakin' it again meself."

The twins raced to his side, jabbering louder than before, now inspecting the baby's fingers, patting her tummy, and gazing up into Rory's face with frank adoration. Cradling Maddie with one arm, he knelt and drew Katie close with the other. He smiled and spoke again, his voice calm and low.

Olivia felt the smart of tears behind her eyes. "Tell me what they're saying."

"They're asking for their ma and da," Rory said. "That's why they ran to the window." Keara squeezed between her sister and Rory, and he reached to draw her closer. "They think they were brought here to be reunited."

"They're old enough to understand . . . to explain all that to you?"

"I asked how old they are, but they don't know," he said. "But I would say they're almost four. Possibly older." He paused, frowning. "Parts of Ireland are so poor the people don't get enough food even if they're trying to grow it themselves. Sometimes the wealthy landowners—the English—require such high taxes there's not much left for the family. These two may be small because they haven't had enough to eat."

"The note will explain what's happened," Eliza said quietly, her sad gaze resting on the twins.

With a nod, Olivia pulled the note from her pocket, unfolded it, and frowned as she read:

Doctor, ma'am,
 We hear tell yer takin in infants. These here are two mighty fine girls, but orphans without livin kin in the world. There names are Keara and Katie. (The one I am a-pinnin this note to is Katie.) There folks are from the Old Country, most recent, but died in the crossing. Some kind old folks took care of the twins on the boat but seein as how there older, they cain't care for them any-more now there in America. God bless you, kind doctor, for what yer doin.
 An admirer of yer work

P.S. The old folks seein as how there gettin fergetful and all could not remember the childrens family name.

Olivia's eyes were watering when she looked up. One on either side of Rory, the twins had fallen silent. Katie popped her thumb into her mouth, and Keara sucked on her first two fingers. She twisted one wispy curl with the thumb and forefinger of the opposite hand. Both children watched her solemnly, almost as if they knew their future was in her hands.

"Surely you're not thinking what I think you're thinking." Eliza looked worried. "You've just taken on an infant . . . " Her voice trailed.

"You know our Olivia better than that," Rachel said to Eliza. "You don't dare tell her she can't do something."

"Something tells me she always finds a way," Rory said, giving Olivia a crooked half smile.

"Katie and Keara will stay with me. We'll set up a nursery here at Trinity—three beds instead of the one I'd planned for Maddie. I will be personally in charge." She knelt before the little girls, her heart full as she looked into their eyes. Lifting her gaze to Rory, she spoke to him. "Because they speak only Irish—do you think they didn't understand that their parents died?"

"Or maybe they were just overlooked in the hubbub. Steerage isn't an easy place for folks to stay while crossing. There were likely many others who fell sick."

"You'll have to help me tell them," she said.

He shifted the now-sleeping Madeilein Mary and nodded. "Aye, that I will."

"And about tonight . . . " she began.

He smiled, clear understanding in his eyes. "'Tis very busy ye'll be, I fear—with three bairns to care for."

"'Tis," she said.

"I'll speak on yer behalf, to be sure. I'll tell them all about ye, Dr. Endicott-Jones, why ye should be trusted with these lasses, all three." He settled the sleeping infant into her bassinet and looked down again at the twins. "Such sadness and change they've suffered in a short time. Now they'll be settlin' into a new home. We should wait to tell them . . . about their ma and da, I mean."

Olivia nodded.

"Until then, there are just three things I'll teach ye to say in Irish."

"And it will suffice for . . . everything?" She pictured trying to get the children to eat . . . to climb into a bathtub . . . to squat over a chamber pot . . . to get dressed—without any words they could understand. She swallowed hard. "What are the words?"

He smiled into her eyes. "The first is 'Look to me now.'" He repeated it in Gaelic.

The children watched, wide-eyed, as Olivia tried it.

"With this, ye'll get their attention when ye need it, especially in cases of danger," he said, looking pleased at her efforts. "The next is 'I'll be caring for ye now.'"

Again she repeated it in Gaelic after him, grinning at the lyrical sound of the Irish language. She reached for the little girls to come into her arms. They walked toward her reluctantly. "I'll be . . . caring for ye . . . now," she said in halting Gaelic. "And the third?" Though her eyes were on the twins, her question was for Rory.

"Aye," he said, "'tis the most important of all."

She waited.

He knelt beside her, his attention fully on the toddlers. "'Tis ye I love," he said in Gaelic. "Tell them this every day, lass. No matter what else they can or can't understand, just tell them this. Tell them 'Tis ye I love."

His eyes were bright with compassion when he turned to Olivia. "Think what it must be like for them. No one understands their words, knows where they came from, or even what their mama's face looked like."

Olivia didn't speak. She didn't think she could with the sting in the back of her throat.

"Just tell the wee bairns ye love them," he said, standing. He gave her a gentle smile. "And pray the Irish bosses in Charlestown listen to me tonight." He looked down at her, sitting there with Keara on one side, Katie on the other. He mussed the girls' curly heads and grinned into their upturned faces. "'Tis ye I love," he said again in Gaelic.

With a tilt of his head to the wide-eyed and unnaturally quiet Eliza and Rachel, Rory left the room, closing the door behind him.

Olivia gathered the twins close, and they laid their heads on her lap.

"We'll help you find a trundle bed and collect some things for their nursery," Rachel said. "They'll need toys and books . . . a rocking chair . . . bright blankets and cheery window curtains."

Olivia nodded in gratitude. "The storage room will make a grand nursery—if we clean it out. And the side room is big enough for a larger bed," she said. "Mine." She drew Katie and Keara close. "We'll find a way to make this work." *With God's help,* she added silently. "I'll visit my parents tonight and ask if I can bring some toys and books from my childhood." She pictured their faces the last time she saw them and wondered at the reception she might get . . . especially with three children in tow.

Katie wrapped her fingers around Olivia's hand, looked up at her with solemn eyes. "Da?" she said softly. "Ma?" Gaelic words followed, and Olivia understood the sorrow in her voice.

"'Tis ye I love," she said in Irish. "And I'll be caring for ye now."

"ABSOLUTELY NOT!" Weston Endicott-Jones fumed an hour later. "We will not aid you in any way." He shook his head. "The sooner you come to your senses, the better."

Olivia stood in the foyer, Madeilein Mary in one arm, a twin on either side of her clinging to her skirts. "I thought if you met the most recent additions to my little family, your hearts might soften."

Hazel Endicott-Jones gasped audibly. "Additions to *your* family? Surely, Olivia dear, you can't mean that." She stepped closer, avoiding the inquisitive faces of the twins. "You have no idea how the neighbors are talking. They're concerned—as well they should be—about the decline of the neighborhood by all this coming and going with . . . well . . . children, Irish children, such as these." Still, her mother didn't look down at Katie and Keara.

Olivia swallowed hard and met her father's gaze, her own unblinking. "God has given me these little ones to care for, and I intend to do exactly that."

For a moment no one spoke. Then with a small coo and a big yawn, Maddie opened her eyes. She looked at Olivia's father and smiled. All Olivia's medical books said that babies this young couldn't smile, that when lips upturned it was caused by a gas bubble in the infant's stomach. It was merely a tiny grimace that looked like a smile.

But Olivia's father didn't know that . . . or if he had heard it somewhere he seemed to have forgotten. He cleared his throat and blinked, frowned, started to speak again, then looked back to Maddie, who was still smiling. He sighed heavily, cleared his throat, and finally said, "You may take whatever you wish from the nursery."

He seemed to be struggling to keep from looking at the faces of the children. "But you are not to bring these . . . children . . . into this house again." He set his lips in a straight line and muttered, "And that is my final word on the subject."

Then he turned and strode from the foyer.

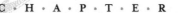

IV

THE SUMMER SUN was on its downward slope and the shadows long as James helped Olivia and the children into the family carriage. She settled back against the plush seat, Maddie asleep in her arms, Keara cuddled close on one side, Katie nestled into her skirts on the other.

James flicked the reins and the vehicle started forward. The twins' little heads bobbed in rhythm with the turning wheels on the cobbled streets, and before they reached the end of the boulevard their eyes closed. Olivia snuggled them closer, suddenly weary from the added work she had taken on with the children and from the emotional turmoil of being in her family home . . . and being ordered once more to leave.

Ordered to leave. She tried to put aside the tiny seeds of anger that were threatening to take root in some deep and hidden place in her heart. They reminded her of weeds sprouting unbidden in a garden. Each time she thought of her parents' unreasonable attitudes and actions more seeds were sown. She rested her cheek lightly on the top of Maddie's head and closed her eyes as she listened to the soft breathing of the sleeping toddlers at her side. How could her mother and father turn these little ones away?

Perhaps, she told herself, what she felt wasn't anger. It was righteous indignation. Her parents were wrong, and someday they would be sorry. Lifting her chin with new courage and determination, she pushed the unpleasant emotions back into the dark depths of her heart. She had a family to care for, a clinic to run. She had no time to devote to the rift in the family. After all, it was their doing, not hers.

⁂

A SHORT TIME later, James carried a trunk of Olivia's childhood treasures up the stairs at Trinity Settlement House. Tucked inside were dolls, stuffed toys, and books of nursery rhymes once read to Olivia by her father. Two nurses helped carry the children from the carriage to their newly scrubbed room near the kitchen. It would take some time to make it cheerful with curtains and quilts, but it was clean and comfortable-looking with a double trundle at one end for Katie and Keara, Olivia's larger bed at the other end, and the bassinet nearby.

As soon as James opened the trunk, the wide-eyed twins dived into the toys with abandon, squealing and giggling and chattering.

He smiled across their heads at Olivia. "It's good to see them happy," he said, "playing with the same toys I remember seeing in your hands." His big face was sad when he stood to leave. "Your mama and papa love you, child. You know that, don't you?"

She nodded. "They have a strange way of showing it."

"Be patient, Miss Liv. And don't ever give up . . . just like your heavenly Father never gives up on any of us."

"But they're so wro—," she started to say.

But James stopped her, shaking his head slowly. "Maybe so, maybe so, child. But that doesn't mean they don't love you." He stepped through the door and was gone before she could comment.

When the children were bathed and fed, Olivia read to them from one of the books of nursery rhymes. They couldn't understand her words but seemed to take comfort in the cadence of the words. They'd had a busy day, and it was no surprise when they fell asleep in her arms. She stood and lifted first Keara, then Katie, into the trundle.

Eliza and Rachel stopped by the room shortly after. "We've made a decision," Eliza announced. "You must go to Charlestown. Rachel will stay with the children. I'll go with you." She drew herself up tall and added with a laugh, "To protect you, of course."

Olivia laughed and shook her head. "Keara and Katie might wake while I'm away. . . . I can't bear to think of them being afraid again. I should be here."

"You're the only one who can make an impassioned plea on their behalf," Rachel said. "You really must go." She smiled gently. "Besides, I can hold them and sing and play with them."

Eliza put her hands at her waist, elbows akimbo, and frowned. "You really shouldn't allow them to pop out of bed once they're tucked in for the night. It will build bad bedtime habits, you know."

Olivia grinned at her friends. "I think you both need to stay—you'll bring the right balance of order and love. Besides, I think these little ones are worn out from their day. They'll probably sleep the entire time I'm gone."

"But you shouldn't go down to Charlestown by yourself."

Olivia held up one hand. "You've convinced me I need

to go. I'll feel better if you'll both stay with the babies. There are three you know, and it will likely take both of you to handle them—if they do wake. Besides, Mr. O'Kelly will be meeting me."

Eliza laughed and tossed her head confidently. "How hard can it be to keep three little babies calm and quiet?"

Rachel smiled. "And we've been practicing the Gaelic words that your Rory O'Kelly taught us, especially ''tis ye I love.'"

"Though his eyes were only on you as he taught us what to say," Eliza said, "it was as if no one else was in the room." She raised a pointed brow in Olivia's direction.

But Olivia was stuck on what Rachel had said. "*My* Rory O'Kelly?" She felt her cheeks flush.

"Aye," Eliza said with a knowing look. "Yours."

IT WAS NEARLY DUSK when her streetcar rolled down the boulevard, passing horse-drawn buggies and bicyclists ringing their bells. The streets became quieter as she reached the Commons, and only a handful of strolling couples were visible in the deepening twilight. The tall, ornate lights that flanked the street flickered on as the streetcar entered the central terminal and she boarded the streetcar for Charlestown.

Soon the clatter of the wheels mixed with the clamor of the Charlestown peninsula, the summer-warm stench of seawater and sewage, as the streetcar headed to the waterfront. Narrow cobbled streets shot off the boulevard, and clusters of milling men and women made their way along dreary walkways. Storefront windows were dull with dust and grime, and scantily dressed women lolled in doorways and leaned from upper-story windows. On every corner, and sometimes on the blocks between, lewd drinking songs spilled into the streets from seedy saloons.

Olivia's heart ached for the families who lived in this place. So many were new arrivals, expecting the grand land of America to welcome them. Instead, they landed here and in other wards just as dismal. Wards run by Irish bosses whose word was law, whose integrity was questionable, whose retaliation against those who opposed them was swift and sure. Olivia shivered in the heavy summer heat, wondering if what they found here was worse than the famine and lack of freedom at home.

She'd heard of the kingpin of Charlestown, Smiling Joe Callahan, and her heart was heavy at the thought of facing him. When the streetcar screeched to a halt, she squared her shoulders and gritted her teeth as she stepped to the ground. A man like this shouldn't be too hard to find. She would recognize him when she saw him from caricatures she had seen in the *Boston Globe:* his massive bald "dome" of a head, gold-rimmed spectacles, drooping black mustache that framed a perpetual toothy smile. A smile that wasn't reflected in his eyes.

She only hoped that when she found the boss, Rory O'Kelly would be with him. Her step lightened at the thought. Even being jostled and pressed and almost tumbled about by the milling, noisy crowds around her, she stopped and smiled.

Rory O'Kelly. His name alone caused her heart to dance. She pictured his broad shoulders, his kind face with its strong jawline, his Irish-sea eyes, and she sighed as her heart quickened to an Irish jig.

Her smile widened as she hoisted her skirts above her ankles and strode along the cobbled street.

·⚜·

RORY O'KELLY APPROACHED Smiling Joe. The man stood to one side of the cleared floor in his saloon, a place called the Gilded Shamrock. He was leaning his back against the bar, elbows back, supporting himself. Tables had been shoved against the walls, and around the makeshift ring a boisterous crowd was gathering. Within minutes two bare-fisted boxers would take their places inside the clearing, and there would be no way for Rory to make himself heard above the jeers and cheers of the crowd. He elbowed his way toward the grinning politician.

"New here, aren't ye?" Smiling Joe said, once Rory was standing in front of the man. He eyed Rory up and down as if measuring him for the ring. "Come to fight?" His big-toothed grin never dimmed.

"Not this Irishman," Rory said with a shrug. "Come for another reason altogether."

"To lay a wager, then?" The grin was wider. "Or perhaps a loan . . . so's ye can lay a wager?"

"Name's Rory O'Kelly." He stuck out his hand. "I'm not here to place a bet."

"O'Kelly is it?" Smiling Joe narrowed his eyes. "Same as the one writing those scathing leaflets about our responsibilities to the motherland?" He spat on the dusty floor beside the bar. "Something called *The Liberator*?"

Rory nodded. "Aye, 'tis me."

"You said that we're our brothers' keepers . . . need to take care of our own."

"Guilty as accused," Rory said.

"So ye're here to solicit funds?" The big man took a swig of dark beer and set the mug on the bar with a bang. "Get me to send me hard-earned cash to the fightin' Irish?"

"That's not why I came to see ye, but it's not such a bad thought. Helpin' us out, I mean." Rory tried to look friendlier than he felt.

Smiling Joe nodded, his expression not quite as harsh. "Maybe someday, lad. But ye said that's not why ye're here. Tell me why ye are."

"I've come to speak to you about the sad plight of a family of orphans."

The man gestured broadly, his smile fading for the first time. "Orphans. The ward is too full of them. What could ye possibly want to discuss?"

Rory scrutinized the man, wondering for the first time if there might be a glimmer of hope for Olivia Endicott-Jones. If the ward had too many orphans already, didn't it stand to reason that someone outside the ward who cared would be a good thing? "I've met a woman doctor at a place called Trinity Settlement House who's carin' for poor—"

Smiling Joe held up a hand. His eyes were cold. "A young man came to see me about this woman . . . told how she's stealin' our young right out from under our noses."

"There's no stealin' going on. She's just lovin' our bairns, carin' for them like they're her own. First there was an infant lass named Madeilein Mary McGrail—"

"Aye, I remember now . . . the young man's name was Quigley. Quigley O'Kelly, as a matter of fact."

"The lad's me cousin."

"He was of a mind that the infant should be kept in Charlestown."

"Even without kin to call her own, then?"

"Ye yerself have called upon the Irish to care for their own. How is it that this case is different? Young Quigley made the point—and I heartily agreed—that we don't want to have our bairns stolen only to become the servants of the Boston Brahmin. That was me judgment, and I'll be stickin' to me final word on the subject."

"This good doctor wouldna do that," Rory said, picturing the gentle face of Olivia Endicott-Jones. "I've gone to her home—and to Trinity Settlement House—to see for meself how she treats those she's carin' for." Behind him the fighters were taking their places in the makeshift ring. Cheers went up, loud and bawdy, causing Rory to raise his voice as he continued. "'Tis my opinion . . . " he yelled above the din.

Smiling Joe had lost interest. A roar rose from the crowd as the fight began. He pushed Rory backward, then shoved past to get to the edge of the ring.

Rory followed, and against his better judgment, grabbed Smiling Joe's arm. "Ye must listen . . . ye must hear me out."

Smiling Joe turned abruptly, his eyes looking like two flat river stones. "And ye hear *me*. Ye're barely off the boat, and ye're trying to tell me all we're doing wrong—from the money we're keepin' from Ireland because we're tryin' to care fer our own—to advisin' that our laddies and lassies would be better off raised by the blue bloods instead of by their own." He leaned close to Rory's face, grabbed him by the collar, and shook his neck with each word. "Ye tell yer blue-blood do-gooder that she's to bring back the bairns of ours she's harborin'. Ye tell her if she don't, we'll come after them ourselves."

"We'll see about that," Rory growled, shaking himself loose from the man's grasp. Smiling Joe was still staring at him with hard eyes when Rory turned to leave.

He took a few steps then turned to call out to the man, loud enough to be heard above the din of the boxing match. "Smiling Joe Callahan, ye havena heard the last of this. Ye're wrong to judge this woman who's helpin' those God's given her." He paused, drawing himself up tall.

"God's given her?" Smiling Joe shouted back. "I'd say she stole 'em right from under our noses. That makes her a thief. Worthy of arrest, if ye ask me." He laughed and spat at the floor.

"Ye're wrong about Olivia Endicott-Jones!" Rory shouted back. "The woman's got a heart purer than gold. I'd trust her with me own grandm'am's life. Why won't ye trust her to care for the babes in Charlestown who have nothing but bleakness ahead?"

With that, Rory spun and headed to the door. He had taken only three steps, when he halted, dumbfounded.

· ❧ ·

OLIVIA SCANNED the crowd, dismayed. The policeman on the corner had said this was where she would find Smiling Joe Callahan, but she hadn't expected this raucous crowd. Swallowing hard, she searched for Rory O'Kelly. But the smoky air made it almost impossible to see across the room.

She took a deep breath, coughed, and started forward, weaving her way toward the greatest cluster of men. They seemed to be gathered around a sporting event of some sort. Cheers and whistles joined the din of voices and bawdy laughter. She shivered, whispering a prayer for her safety and reminding herself why she had come.

It was for Madeilein Mary and the twins. She blinked against the sting in her eyes caused by the stench of cigar smoke, willing herself forward one step at a time.

A figure emerged through the smoke, stopping her forward stride; she halted, startled, and looked up. When Rory smiled into her eyes and took her elbow, she sighed with relief. "I'm glad to see you," she said as he steered her to the door. "I had no idea your meeting would be in such a place."

Rory didn't answer. He hurried her through the double saloon doors and along the street with giant strides, looking back from time to time as if to see if someone followed. "'Tis not a place fit for ladies," he said when they turned the corner. "Ye shouldna have come here tonight."

She halted midstep. "I thought you wanted me to come . . . "

He still looked worried, his eyes on the street behind them. "That was before I knew what kind of place—what kind of people—I'd be dealing with." He nodded the direction of the saloon. "Ye saw fer yerself, lass. This is no place for a lady . . . " His face softened. "I'm just glad ye dinna bring the babies." He looked stricken. "I would never have forgiven meself, should something have happened to them . . . or to ye."

He took her arm again, and walking briskly, they headed to the streetcar stop. The narrow cobbled street was now dark and nearly empty. Olivia shuddered, glad she wasn't alone. "You're fearful we're being followed?" she breathed, trying to keep up with her companion. Her heart was sinking with each step they took away from the saloon. Rory wouldn't be whisking her away like this if Smiling Joe had agreed to let her keep the children.

"Aye," he said, "and I'll explain later. Right now, we just need to see ye into a safe place."

Without speaking further, they hurried through the darkness. They reached the streetcar stop a few minutes later, and Rory seemed to relax. Taking a deep breath, he reached for her hand. His grip was firm and warm. Down the track the coming car rattled and clanged, and for an instant, Olivia didn't want it to arrive. She didn't want to let go of Rory O'Kelly's hand.

"I'm sorry, so sorry, lass," he was saying. "But Callahan's mind is made up. He threatened to have ye arrested. Said ye're breakin' the law by takin' babes from the ward."

Squaring her shoulders, Olivia stood a bit taller, dropping Rory's hand at the same time. She tilted her face upward, looking directly into his eyes, barely visible in the ashen darkness. "Do you think I fear him?"

For a long stunned moment, Rory stared at her without speaking. Then his whole face spread into a smile. "I'm thinkin' I should've known otherwise."

She lifted a brow. "It's not been by accident that these little ones have been given into my care. I will fight to keep them." She paused as the streetcar rattled to a halt in front of them. "I don't care who . . . when . . . or where. I will fight." She raised her chin and turned to step into the car.

Behind her, Rory's laughter held a full-hearted sound. "Strikes me, lass," he said, stepping into the car with her, "that ye should've been Irish—with such spirit, I mean. Not to mention heart."

Feeling the warmth of his laughter fall on her like sunlight, she smiled at him. She sighed deeply, enjoying his company. When he took his seat beside her, she asked, "So you think only the Irish have spirit and heart?"

He chuckled and took her hand again. "Me grandm'am always ends her sentences with a questioning lilt . . . just like ye did. Just now."

Olivia quirked a brow. "I remind you of your grandmother?"

"Not altogether an unflattering comparison, lass." He sobered. "'Tis not yer comely looks I'm meanin'—but yer spirit . . . and heart."

She saw the same in him, and it startled her to realize it. She stared at him in the dark of the streetcar, conscious of nothing except the kindness in his face.

"Aye, her tender heart," he said softly and looked out into the streets as they passed by. "And her spitfire will. No stopping that one." He turned back to Olivia. "She has no patience for the word *no*. Not at all."

A warm glow flowed through her at his words.

As they rode, Rory told her about the conversation with Smiling Joe, his troubled expression telling Olivia more than his words could. When it was time to step from the streetcar, Olivia thanked Rory for seeing her back to the clinic. But he stood and escorted her from the car, obviously with no intention of letting her walk alone the short distance from the streetcar stop to Trinity Settlement House.

As the streetcar rattled away, he tucked her hand in the

crook of his arm. "I have another plan," he said with a grin. "An even better one than the last."

She sighed as they walked up the boulevard. "Tell me."

"It has to do with your tender heart and spitfire will," he said, smiling. "And how ye haven't patience for hearing anyone tell ye no."

She stopped and looked up at him. "I'm listening." Around them a balmy summer breeze rustled the elm leaves.

He sobered. "But there's something ye ought to know . . ."

"I'm still listening," she said.

"What I plan . . . won't be easy. Yer name will be spread throughout Charlestown . . . and beyond."

"Will it bring danger to Maddie and the twins?"

"I will keep them out of it—and write only about ye."

"Write?"

"I intend to tell all of Boston about what ye're doin' at Trinity Settlement House. If we can't show them yer heart in person, then we'll tell them about it." He was holding both her hands now, his smile boyish and sure.

She nodded, wondering about this man standing before her. "Write?" she repeated.

He laughed. "Aye, 'tis something we Irish are prone to do. Handed down to us from the ancient Celts. Of course we have our limericks and ballads. Poetry seems to come to life in each Irish heart at birth." He placed his hand at the small of her back and turned her toward the sidewalk at the side of the boulevard. His hand stayed around her waist. "But this is something else altogether."

As they walked, he told her about his grandmother, about Ireland, and at last, about how the Irish—through their writings in ancient days—had preserved the Holy Scriptures. They reached the front door of the clinic, and Olivia turned to Rory, reluctant to say good-bye.

He touched her cheek as he gazed into her eyes. She thought he might kiss her, but the door squeaked open, interrupting the moment, and a frantic voice called out. "Liv! Is that you?" Eliza cried. "Come quickly!"

C · H · A · P · T · E · R

V

O LIVIA SHOT RORY a frantic look, lifted her skirts ankle high, and bounded up the stairs and through the clinic door. It brought her comfort that he sprinted behind her.

"It's Katie," Eliza said. "She's inconsolable."

Without hesitating a moment, Olivia gestured for Rory to follow. The parade made their way upstairs, Olivia in the lead, Rory next, and Eliza bringing up the rear, urging the others to move faster.

At the nursery door, Rachel stood with Maddie in her arms, jiggling her up and down. The infant fussed but hadn't gotten to the red-faced stage yet. At her side, wide-eyed Keara sucked on two fingers, grasping Rachel's skirt with the tight wet fist of her other hand.

A deafening wail carried into the main hallway from the nursery, propelling Olivia through the door to the trundle.

"She wouldn't let me hold her," Eliza said as Olivia knelt beside the child.

"Katie," Olivia said softly. "Katie . . . I'm here. You're safe." The child wailed on. Taking a deep breath, Olivia tried to remember the phrases Rory had taught her. But in her worry over the child, her mind went blank.

Rory knelt beside the bed and touched Katie on the shoulder. He spoke Gaelic in a firm but calm tone.

Katie stopped crying and turned to face him, eyes wet, face red. Tiny droplets of tears glistened on her long lashes. She answered him in a small shaky and scared voice.

He spoke more soft and gentle words. Katie sniffled while Rory translated what he had said. "I told her we've all come to be with her. Her sister Keara is here, the baby she loves is here . . . you are here . . . and I am here. She doesn't need to be afraid."

Remembering the Irish phrases that had eluded her, Olivia reached for Katie's hand and said gently in Irish, "'Tis ye I love."

Katie stared at her, unblinking.

Olivia tried again. "I'll be caring for ye now."

Still, no reaction.

Katie moved her gaze to Rory's face and lifted her hands up to him. Standing, he gathered the little girl into his arms. She popped her thumb into her mouth. "Is there a place I can rock her?" he said.

Eliza quickly showed him to the rocking chair in the corner of the room. "We borrowed it from the newborn nursery," she explained.

With a smile, he sat down and beckoned to Keara to join them. The toddler almost flew across the room and into his arms.

A relieved-looking Rachel followed and handed Maddie to Olivia. A hush fell over the nursery, until from the corner where Rory sat with the twins, an Irish lullaby, soft and sweet, floated on the air. Smiling at the sound of it, Olivia laid Maddie on the wicker baby-dressing table and unfastened her nappies. When fresh diapers were in place, she lifted the baby against her shoulder and swayed gently back and forth, humming along with Rory's lullaby. Then she laid the baby in the bassinet and knelt on the floor nearby, gathering up the scattered toys.

Across the room, Katie yawned and cuddled against Rory's chest. Keara reached up and touched his cheek before popping her fingers into her mouth. With heavy sighs, their eyes closed, but Rory continued holding them close.

Above the twins' curly heads, he met Olivia's gaze and smiled.

THAT NIGHT RORY O'KELLY headed back to Charlestown, lost in puzzling thoughts. He wanted to court Olivia Endicott-Jones, but feared it was an impossible dream. Why would someone of her genteel upbringing pay mind to him? There was no doubt that the smile in her eyes seemed to linger on his whenever they spoke. Just as her strong fingers lingered in his grasp when twice he dared to hold them. And watching her humming along with his lullaby tonight, faith, he could have sworn the loveliness in her ivory face and rose-hued cheeks contained something he'd never seen in her before. Love.

He grinned. Could it be? Glory, what a thought! Surely she was thinking of someone else altogether. She couldn't have been thinking of this poor Irishman with such a look in her eyes.

He was still smiling when the streetcar reached Charlestown and he stepped off. Try as he might while walking to his room on the waterfront, he couldn't get Olivia out of his mind . . . even when considering the scathing open letter he planned to write to Smiling Joe.

The same letter that would be published in the next issue of *The Liberator*.

Aye, but that was more important than a young man's fanciful, impossible dreams, he told himself as he headed up the stairs to his walk-up. Considerably so.

He wasted no time in sitting down at his desk, lighting the lamp, and picking up his pen. He wrote furiously, his heart full of images: the children sleeping in the Endicott-Jones nursery; Olivia's face as she watched over them; the utter sorrow of hearing wee Katie and Keara cry again if they were packed off to another family.

It was nearing dawn when he finished writing and high noon when he left for the typesetter down the block. The clerk frowned as he glanced over the piece; then he looked at Rory with a scowl. "'Tis Smilin' Joe's wrath ye're bringing on yerself, lad—don't ye know?"

Rory merely lifted a brow and nodded. "Dinna I now, indeed? Dinna I?"

The pamphlets would be distributed by week's end—by himself and Quigley. He hoped every Irish man and woman in Boston would rally behind him. But he shuddered to think what Smiling Joe might do when the open letter of defiance reached his eyes.

One thing Rory knew: he couldn't wait until the end of the week to show Olivia the letter. She needed to see it now, so together they could face what was ahead.

Together. For at least the hundredth time since leaving her last night, he smiled.

OLIVIA LEFT the nursery with its jumble of toys, rumpled beds, and chirping children's voices at Trinity Settlement House only long enough to see her most acutely ill and injured patients, then hurried back to spend time with Maddie and the twins, leaving Eliza and Rachel in charge of the hospital admissions. Throughout her busy days, whether with the children or her patients, she couldn't stop thinking about Rory O'Kelly. He filled her every thought. What was it about the man that had captured her attention so?

One afternoon she took the children to a small patch of grass at the rear of Trinity Settlement House. As soon as Maddie was nestled snug in the pram, Olivia settled onto an old wooden bench, worn smooth from years of use, beneath an ancient elm tree, and scooped the twins up onto the seat, placing one on each side of her. Then she opened a big book of nursery rhymes and, in murmuring tones, read the verses and pointed to the illustrations. Katie and Keara chattered in Gaelic, seeming unconcerned that they couldn't understand her words. Little *oohs* and *ahs* escaped their lips as they poked at the pictures, their eyes wide with wonder.

Olivia laughed, hugged them both, and turned the page. "Ah," she said, rolling her eyes expressively. Katie copied her and giggled. Keara tried it, only to cross her eyes and make Katie laugh harder.

Olivia read the next verse:

Pat-a-cake, pat-a-cake, baker's man,
Bake me a cake as fast as you can;
Roll it, and prick it, and mark it with a B,
And put it in the oven for Baby and me.

The twins watched her solemnly as she read, their brows furrowed as they tried to understand.

"Look to me now," she said in Gaelic.

Katie gazed up at her with expectant eyes. Keara popped her fingers into her mouth.

"Pat-a-cake, pat-a-cake," Olivia said, smiling. She patted her hands together, and the twins did the same. "Pat-a-cake," she said slowly.

"Pat-a," Katie said.

"Kay," Keara said.

Olivia clapped her hands together. "Let's try it again!" It took only two more tries for the girls to say the words clearly. Within a few minutes they could say the entire verse, complete with hand motions. Olivia marveled at their quick minds.

She pointed to the baby in the drawing and said, "Baby." Then standing, she led the twins to the nearby baby carriage. First she lifted Katie so she could peek in at the sleeping infant. "Baby," she whispered. "Baby."

"Baby," Katie whispered back, pointing to Maddie.

Beside the carriage Keara jumped up and down in anticipation of her turn. Olivia scooped the child into her arms and turned her toward Maddie. Before Olivia could get the word out, Keara whispered, "Baby," and pointed to the infant.

Katie had already run back to the book of nursery rhymes. She stuck one tiny finger on the illustration and said clearly, proudly, "Baby!"

A low rumbling chuckle carried from behind the gazebo. "'Tis a schoolhouse ye're runnin' I see."

Before Olivia could speak, Katie squealed and ran to Rory, and Keara wriggled out of Olivia's arms to follow her sister. They chattered in Gaelic, pointing to Olivia and then to the nursery rhyme book, and finally to the carriage.

"Baby!" Keara pronounced.

"Baby," Katie squealed, which woke Maddie with a start.

Grinning at the pleasant hubbub, Olivia lifted the infant into her arms. When she turned around again, Rory was sitting cross-legged under the tree, a twin on either side. Carefully, Katie turned the pages, speaking in Irish about each picture. Keara leaned her head against his arm and stuck her fingers in her mouth.

The afternoon passed pleasantly. Rory and Olivia sat together on the bench while the twins played on the small patch of lawn. By three o'clock they were sleepy and ready for their naps. Olivia took them upstairs to their trundle bed, leaving Rory with Maddie, who had again fallen asleep in the carriage. Rachel stepped in to watch the twins when Olivia returned to Rory and the baby.

As she stepped from the back of the clinic, she looked out to where Rory sat leaning against a tree trunk, his legs stretched out in front of him and hooked at the ankles. The dappled sunlight filtered through the elm leaves and partially shaded his profile, but the slant of his jaw, the line of his nose, the rich outline of his shoulders, gave him a look of strength, even from this distance. Yet she knew that strength was coupled with gentleness.

She walked across the grounds, thinking about this man who had so suddenly appeared in her life. It seemed she had known him forever . . . as if there had been a space in her heart just waiting for someone like Rory O'Kelly to come along and fill it.

He stood as she approached. Again she noticed the hint of merriment around his mouth and near his eyes. She flushed and smiled in return as he waited for her.

"I brought ye something." They sat together on the bench. He reached into his pocket, produced a folded paper, and handed it to her.

A wave of apprehension swept through her as she unfolded it and read the heading at the top of the page:

An Open Letter to Smiling Joe Callahan:
    'Tis not a sin to let others help our children.
    Here in Boston there is a very loving and capable woman who has opened her heart to those less fortunate. She trained for years to become a doctor, not to serve the rich and famous—or even the Boston Brahmins, as ye call them. She opened a settlement house where she now cares for the poor, no matter their need,

whether from injury or disease, or even lodging and food. With no thought to her own health, she gives of herself tirelessly to the families and children of Boston.

Mostly, she gives of herself to the Boston Irish, because we are the most recent immigrants. We have the most pressing poverty.

We could all take lessons from Dr. Olivia Endicott-Jones.

Our Lord once said . . . and I quote:

"Then shall the King say unto them on his right hand, Come ye blessed of My Father . . . for I was an hungred, and ye gave Me meat: I was thirsty, and ye gave Me drink: I was a stranger, and ye took Me in: Naked, and ye clothed Me: I was sick, and ye visited Me.

"Then shall the righteous answer Him saying, Lord, when saw we Thee an hungred, and fed Thee? or thirsty, and gave Thee drink? When saw we Thee a stranger, and took Thee in? or naked, and clothed Thee? . . .

"And the King shall answer and say unto them, Verily I say unto you, Inasmuch as ye have done it unto one of the least of these My brethren, ye have done it unto Me."

Who are we—any of us—to set ourselves up higher than God Himself? to take away the gift of caring, when it is given as if to our Savior? to take away food and shelter and medicines from the "least of these," our own children?

I ask ye, Smiling Joe Callahan, Political Boss of Charlestown: Do ye want to be the one to rob our children of good health and well-being when it is given with such love?

I ask ye, citizens of Irish Boston: Do ye think that we should take away Dr. Endicott-Jones's clinic, put her out of business—as Smiling Joe recently threatened?

I invite ye all to see it for yourself—Trinity Settlement House in South Boston—where the doctor serves with such diligence and ability. I invite ye all—including ye, Smiling Joe Callahan—to stop criticizing her for helping. I invite ye all to pitch in and help her care for our wee bairns and their mas and das.

And if ye do, remember our Lord's words: "Inasmuch as ye have done it unto one of the least of these My brethren, ye have done it unto Me."

VI

J UST AS RORY EXPECTED, the families of Charlestown
rallied round him after they read the latest issue of
The Liberator. He was stopped on the streets, slapped
on the back, and congratulated for his courage in standing up to the political boss.

Every evening he visited Olivia after her work at the
clinic was done, to play with the twins or push the pram
as they all strolled along the tree-lined boulevard near
Trinity Settlement House. But he had no news about
Smiling Joe to report. There was deep concern in Olivia's
eyes now that her family name—and that of the settlement house—had been broadcast all over Boston in *The
Liberator*. There was also pride shining in her eyes as she
beheld him.

Each time he was with Olivia, her quiet strength and
tireless spirit for serving others drew his heart closer
to hers. During his morning prayers, he sought God's

wisdom in speaking to Olivia about courtship. He wanted to ask her father, as was proper, but he knew the estrangement between Olivia and her parents would prevent such a conversation, at least for now.

One night three weeks after the pamphlet's publication, Rory joined Olivia in the nursery at Trinity Settlement House for the children's playtime. First he read them a Bible story, a lively account of David and Goliath told as only the Irish could. Then while Olivia changed Maddie's nappy, he let the twins ride on his back, yelling giddap in Gaelic. So lost he was in the altogether wondrous clamor of giggling and yelling and his own heart prayer, he nearly missed the sounds that carried from the downstairs waiting room.

But as soon as he recognized the speaker's gruff voice, Rory gently let the twins down from his back and stood in alarm. He'd taken just two steps toward the door when hurried footsteps sounded in the hall, and Eliza burst through the open door. "There's a man here to see you," she said breathlessly. "Says his name is Joe Callahan. Smiling Joe, I believe he said."

"Ye've got it right, miss." Smiling Joe pushed past Eliza and headed into the nursery without invitation. His gaze took in the scene before him: the scatter of toys, the wide-eyed twins; Olivia, now protectively holding Maddie; the disheveled and gaping Eliza—before boring in on Rory's face. "I thought I'd find ye here."

"Ye have no right to roar in uninvited—," Rory began, but Callahan interrupted.

"Hear me out, O'Kelly." He stepped closer, quirking a brow. "Been lookin' for ye. Every night I've sent me men out on search. Finally was reported ye're spendin' time with the blue-blood do-gooder herself."

"Ye should've waited for my return to Charlestown," Rory growled at the man. "There is no need to trouble the fine folks at the settlement house."

"Ah, me fine Irish lad. There's all the reason in the world to trouble them." He narrowed his eyes. "Strikes me odd that ye'd say such a thing when 'tis ye who brought them to my attention in the first place."

Rory drew himself up and exchanged a glance with Olivia, who was now standing tall and alert near the twins. He measured the distance between them, should he have to tackle the man.

"Ye came alone, then?" He narrowed his eyes in what he hoped was a menacing way at the Irish boss. His grandm'am had always said he couldn't look fierce even if his life depended on it. Smiling Joe didn't blanch at Rory's menacing look. His grandm'am was obviously right.

"Ye should know better," Smiling Joe said with a shrug of one big shoulder. "Me men are outdoors."

"Why did ye come here then?"

Smiling Joe drew out a tattered and dog-eared copy of *The Liberator* and waved it in Rory's face. "This, me man. This, of course, is what brought me." A grin spread wide across his face. He hit the paper with the back of his fingers. "Ye have a way with words . . . ye've got everyone in Charlestown talking about this . . . and me."

"'Twas my intent."

The man laughed, then reached into his pocket again. "Ye smote me conscience, lad. Sure as Ireland's the Emerald Isle, ye did." He turned to speak to the astonished women, now holding a long envelope in his hand. "Ma'ams," he said, nodding again, "forgive me for bargin' in this way, but I wanted first to offer me apology. And as a token of me esteem . . . me gratitude, I'd like for ye to accept this." He handed it to Olivia, who shifted the baby to one arm to take the envelope with the other.

"Open it," the boss commanded, though not unkindly. She did, and a small gasp escaped her lips. "Will that help at the settlement house, then?" he asked.

She swallowed visibly hard and for a moment didn't

speak. Finally, still staring at the bank draft in her hand, she said, "Yes, Mr. Callahan, this will indeed care for many . . . of your children and families." There were tears in her eyes when she raised them to Smiling Joe. "Thank you."

Callahan cleared his throat awkwardly then turned back to Rory. "As for ye, lad, I admire the way ye have of convincin' even the most stubborn of us. Anytime ye want to come to work for me, ye've got a job." Rory held up a hand of protest, but Smiling Joe hurried on. "And if it's help for the mother country ye're still workin' for, I'm willing to see what I can do there as well." Callahan turned and was gone before anyone could say another word.

Olivia's eyes were shining when her gaze met Rory's. "You did it," she whispered as if no one else was in the room.

He grinned at her. "I believe it was God's words, not mine, that made all the difference."

"More powerful than a two-edged sword," she said, her smile radiant. She handed him the bank draft.

He almost stopped breathing when he saw the numbers written there. "'Tis a glory indeed," he said in awe.

"Thank you, Rory O'Kelly," she said, still smiling as if she'd never stop. "Thank you." Joy shone in her eyes.

For a moment they just stared at each other.

Rory's heart seemed to be speeding into an Irish jig. Without stopping to wonder if she would step into his arms, he opened them wide.

She didn't hesitate. Still holding Maddie, blankets and all, she stepped into his embrace. He laid his cheek on the top of Olivia's head, breathing in the wondrous bouquet of Maddie's baby powder and Olivia's lilac-scented soap.

After a moment Eliza cleared her throat and giggled. With a chuckle, Rory stepped back and gazed into Olivia's flushed face. It seemed she was as moved as he was by their nearness.

"It's a lovely evening for a stroll," Eliza said, her eyes bright with merriment. "I'll put the children to bed . . . if you would like to, ah, continue your conversation elsewhere." As if knowing there would be no argument, she settled to the floor and gathered Keara and Katie close. Soon they were chattering in a mix of Gaelic and English and pointing to pictures, demanding that Eliza keep her attention on them and the story. Keara leaned her head against Eliza's arms, popped her fingers into her mouth, and sighed with contentment. Katie played with a strand of Eliza's hair, twisting it into a curl around her finger, letting it unwind and twirling it again.

"I don't think they'll miss us," Olivia said, smiling into Rory's eyes.

He took the sleepy Maddie from her and gently laid the baby in her bassinet, straightening and tucking the soft pink square of flannel around her shoulders. With a sign, her eyelids fluttered closed. When he turned back to Olivia, she was watching him with an expression of warmth and wonder.

He crossed the room and ruffled the tops of the twins' curly heads as Olivia stooped to kiss them good night. Minutes later, they stood beneath the lamplight on the boulevard in front of Trinity Settlement House. A warm summer night's breeze fluttered the leaves above them, and somewhere in the distance a mockingbird sang out, followed by another farther away.

"There is something I've been meanin' to talk to ye about," he said after a moment.

Her gaze was gentle and contemplative. "About Trinity Settlement House? How you're planning to give us the gift of your time? You're awfully good at it . . . I mean you're especially skilled at working with the children, interpreting for the Irish who enter our doors."

He grinned. "That's not my meaning altogether, though I must confess 'tis an idea that has crossed me mind."

She tilted her head, looking up at him from beneath her eyelashes, her look now turning a wee bit mischievous. Behind her the leaves rustled again in the breeze. "What then, dear sir, might be the other topic you wish to discuss?"

"'Tis about a man and a woman, and well . . . er . . . about a kind affection they might entertain one toward the other. . . . "

Her lips curved up at the corners, and she arched a delicate brow. She looked amused.

He couldn't remember the last time he had suffered so acutely from a lack of words. But then, he hadn't any experience with this sort of thing . . . with a love that nearly burst his heart whenever Olivia smiled his direction, with a warmth that dropped his stomach to his toes whenever she spoke his name, with a sting that caught fast at the top of his throat when he happened upon Olivia cuddling Maddie, Keara, and Katie.

Ballybofey and Dunkineely, what was this Irishman to do? Here he was, just standing here, gazing at the moonlit upturned face of the most beautiful woman God surely ever created, wanting desperately to declare his love. Yet the very emotion had rendered him . . . well, speechless. And for a man who prided himself on his way with words, the unsettling condition he found himself in made his knees tremble and his heart thud so fast he nearly lost his ability to breathe.

"You were saying something about a man and a woman . . . ?" she prompted. "About kind affection?"

"Aye," he said, still lost in her gaze, "that I was." He took a deep breath and started over. "You see, when man discovers that he holds an affection . . . or perhaps I might say a deep and abiding fondness in his heart, so much so that he can't sleep at night for how the lass occupies his dreams . . . well, 'tis time for this lad to speak of, that is . . . to tell the lass—figuratively speaking, of course—"

She touched his lips with her fingertips to shush him with a mix of amusement and love—*oh, glory, could it be love?*—glistening in her eyes. He caught her hand and kissed her palm. She brought his hand to her cheek, laid her face gently against it, and murmured, "This lad, this Irish lad you speak of . . . ?"

"Aye?" His voice was hoarse. He cleared his throat and tried again. "Aye?"

"Would it help if he knew that the lass returned his . . . ah . . . deep affection—figuratively speaking, of course?" Olivia pulled back a step, looking up at him, a small smile playing at the corner of her mouth.

He chuckled, holding both her hands. "Aye," he said, his voice stronger. "'Twould indeed."

She was still smiling as if she found it impossible to stop. "Would it help if the lad knew that the lass was beginning to cherish him altogether?"

"Altogether?" he repeated, loving the Irish inflection she had adopted just for him.

"Altogether," she said with certainty.

"Cherish, ye say?"

She nodded. "Aye, treasure also."

"Treasure?" The word came out in a wondrous sigh.

"Would it help the lad to know these things?"

He stepped closer to her and, releasing one hand, touched her cheek with his fingertips. She blinked and swallowed hard. His voice was a little more than a whisper when he spoke. "It would indeed, lass." He let the backs of his fingers trail to her chin, then turned his hand to gently tilt her face upward. "Altogether," he said.

Her eyes were damp, and she blinked. "And what exactly might the lad say in return?"

He bent closer. "The lad might say—if he could be heard above the loud thumping of his heart—he might say that there's never been a moment the lass has been out of his thoughts since he first set eyes on her . . . that the glow of happiness that sweeps through him every time they meet is brighter than the noonday sun . . . that . . . " He stopped and gave her a sheepish grin. "'Tis time to stop speaking in riddles and tell you true, Liv, what's in this Irishman's heart of hearts."

He gathered her into his arms. Trembling, she buried her face against his throat. He tightened his grasp and rested his cheek on the top of her head, breathing in the lilac scent of her hair. "What I haven't said plainly is that I care for ye, Liv. The last thing I was looking for in America was love. I have too little to offer, only me heart, and with the differences between us—you being a blue-blood Mayflower descendent and me a poor Irishman—I'm sure ye would never agree to courtship, let alone something more, something lasting till eter . . . " He swallowed hard. He was making a bumbling eejit of himself. He wouldn't blame her if she turned around and hurried back to the clinic.

But before he could start over, Olivia pulled back and looked up into his eyes without speaking. The leaves above them rustled, and in the distance a mockingbird warbled again. The silence between them stretched too long, and he had almost decided she wasn't pleased to hear him speak of love. Then she placed her hand on his cheek. "'Tis ye I love," she said in Gaelic. She stood as still as a glorious statue in the moonlight, her lips parted, her eyes searching his.

Bending, he touched her lips with his and drank in the sweetness of her kiss. "'Tis ye I love," he whispered in English and drew her close. With a soft sigh Olivia slid her arms around his neck and laid her cheek against his chest.

After a moment, Rory turned Olivia gently, and arm in arm they strolled slowly down the street, the glow of streetlights twinkling through the leafy branches of the trees. When they reached the end of the street and stopped to let a carriage pass, Rory cleared his throat. "I don't take love lightly. I mean, when I tell a woman . . . not that I ever have before . . . " Here he was, turning into a rambling *amadain* again.

She grinned up at him and raised a brow.

"What I'm trying to say, Liv, is that I can't imagine spending the rest of my life without you. . . . I–I want to marry ye, but I daren't ask. I have nothing to offer, nothing of substance."

"*You* are substance, Rory O'Kelly," she said. "You offer me yourself . . . there is nothing better. Nothing more I want."

"You see, me brother Eamon and meself were orphaned at a young age, raised by our grandm'am—but I always missed the love of me ma and da. When I marry, I want to provide well for me family, make sure nothing will ever separate us, not country strife or poverty, such as the twins' poor ma and da. I want to make sure I can provide well—"

"You're thinking already of the built-in family I come with?" There were tears in her eyes now.

He nodded. "Aye. Young Keara and Katie, and our wee Maddie. And ye, Liv."

She reached up and touched his face with her fingertips. "You can't change life's circumstances, Rory. God is with us all—the children, you, and me. But that doesn't mean that country strife or family poverty . . . illness or accidents . . . any of it, won't happen. He just promises to be with us if those things do shake our world."

"I want to marry ye, Liv, I do," he said. "Perhaps not soon. There are things I must attend to, pledges made to me grandm'am and brother in Ireland . . . but I promise ye my heart . . . if ye'll have it." He was almost lost in her eyes when he added, "If ye'll wait for me."

"I'll wait forever, Rory. Do what you need to do." She studied him for a moment. "Your pledge," she said, "does it have to do with the strife in your land? I've heard about the uprisings in Ireland, the fight against English rule. Would you ever be involved in such a thing?" She paused, biting her lip. "Would you fight?"

He didn't speak for several moments, and when he did, he kept his words light to put her at ease. "Only if I had too. That's why I've come here, you know. I don't believe in takin' up arms meself. But I will fight a war of words. Sometimes—as we saw tonight—words can be more powerful than weapons."

She was earnest now and wore the same expression he'd seen at Trinity Settlement House. All business. No play. "If we were to marry," she said, "might you be called away to fight?" She paused. "Would it be expected of you?"

He shook his head slowly. "But I canna promise ye, Liv. I canna know tomorrow." He smiled at her gently. "But as ye said, our heavenly Father is with us always, in times of war and times of peace. We have to trust Him altogether with our tomorrows."

She didn't answer but studied him, her eyes dark with emotion.

"My grandm'am gave me a locket," he said softly. "It was a gift from me grandda to her." He caressed her face with his eyes, his heart nearly bursting from his chest. "I'd like to give it to ye, my love. As a pledge that some-day, God willing, we will be together—"

But as he spoke the words another voice interrupted. From a ways down the street, Eliza raced toward them. "Olivia," she called out breathlessly. "Rory . . . " Her voice carried through the dark night.

"Over here," Olivia called back with a frown. She glanced at Rory, worry written on her face. "The girls . . . ?"

Rory grabbed her hand, and as she lifted her skirt with the other, they ran toward Eliza.

"Quigley O'Kelly's here to see you," Eliza said when they reached her. Then she saw Olivia's pale expression and added, "The babies are fine. They're all sleeping, and Rachel is watching them."

Rory wondered what possible business Quigley might have that would cause him to come here this time of night. "Where is he?"

"Waiting at Trinity—in the lobby."

Minutes later, a worried-looking Quigley, lolling in a chair, stood to greet them. "'Tis bad news I'm bringing ye," he said solemnly.

Rory exchanged a glance with Olivia then laughed. "Ye've probably got wind of the fact that Smiling Joe is on his way here. I'm thankful for yer diligence, but in this case 'tis unwarranted."

Outside the window, the moon slipped beneath some buttermilk clouds, casting a strange pattern of shadows across the landscape. Quigley shook his head, his expression sad. "'Tis not Smiling Joe," he said. "Not at all."

Rory stepped closer, feeling his heart begin to pound hard. "What is it then, man? What have ye come to tell me?"

"News from Ireland. Just arrived minutes ago."

"Our grandm'am?" The words came out in a choking sound. Beside him, Olivia reached for his hand.

"Nah," Quigley said. "Not at all." He fell silent for a moment then began again. "There was an uprising. Against the English. Many were killed."

Rory nodded, feeling like he might never breathe again. He thought of Eamon, so like Quigley. He remembered carrying his brother as a child, lifting him over puddles too deep for his rolled-up pants, holding him close when riding their grandm'am's old mule before it died. Teaching his brother to read and write. It had been only the two of them . . . and their grandm'am's loving arms to keep them steady.

"'Tis Eamon, isn't it?" Rory said, willing himself not to weep.

The boy looked stricken. "'Tis."

Rory buried his face in his hands.

VII

OLIVIA DIDN'T SLEEP at all that night. She paced the floor of her bedroom, praying for Rory and his family in Ireland. Her heart was filled with the words of love they had spoken to each other and the memory of his kiss, but she also grieved for the sorrow Rory was feeling right now.

At two o'clock, Maddie woke fussing. As Olivia sat in the rocker and fed her, her thoughts were only on Rory. Surely he wouldn't return to Ireland to avenge his brother's death. Not after what he'd told her last night. He would go to his grandmother and help her bury Eamon; then he would return to her.

But even as she considered his actions, she understood that his responsibilities lay elsewhere, not here in America with a woman he'd known for such a short time. He had spoken of a pledge to his motherland. Rory was a

man of integrity. He would carry through with that promise. She shivered, thinking of his heart ties to Ireland.
Lifting the infant to her shoulder, Olivia rubbed her back
gently until a tiny hiccup sounded. She touched Maddie's
cheek and for a moment rested her own lightly against
the baby's downy head.

A few minutes later when she stood to lay the sleeping
infant in her cradle, her thoughts were still on Rory
O'Kelly. She understood his heart, and as sure as the
dawn, she would lose him to Ireland. His brother was
dead, killed by the English, and his grandmother was
alone.

How could he not go? She sat again in the rocking
chair, moving it slowly back and forth in the dark, quiet
nursery. It creaked on the floor, mixing its rhythm with
the soft breathing of the twins in their trundle and the
tiny, sleepy sighs of Maddie in her cradle.

Tears welled again at the thought of telling Rory good-
bye. She wanted to believe she was wrong . . . that there
was another way.

But in her heart she knew there was none.

HALFWAY THROUGH the night, a loud banging at his door
woke Rory. His sleep had been fitful at best, his dreams
filled with images of Olivia, his nightmares aflame with
memories of Eamon.

Rubbing his mussed hair, he stumbled to the door.
"Who is it?" he growled.

"Quigley," came the whispered answer. "I've got news."

He pulled open the door and let his cousin in.

"There's a freighter sailin' at dawn," Quigley whispered
hoarsely. "I've just heard they need an extra hand. 'Tis yer
chance to get back to Ireland . . . and quickly."

Rory rubbed his head again. Of course he needed to go

home. As soon as possible. To help his grandm'am.
To tie up loose ends with Eamon's troubles.

But not yet. He had to see Olivia. He couldn't leave
without telling her good-bye. "How long do I have?"

"Two hours maybe."

He sighed. "I'll go then . . . but there's something
I must do first."

Quigley put his hand on Rory's arm. "There's not time,
if it's heading to yer sweet love ye're thinking of. No
streetcars are running this time of night, and if ye wait
till they are, ye'll miss the ship."

"I must see her."

"Then ye'll wait another two weeks till the next ship
sails. And it's not a freighter. 'Tis the *Queen Victoria*. Ye'll
be payin' top dollar even for steerage on that one. Dosna
even go into Dublin Harbor. Ye'd be sailin' straight into
merry ol' England herself."

Rory sank to the edge of his bed and dropped his head
into his hands. "There's a task I need for ye to do then."

"Tell me what ye need," Quigley said, uncharacteristi-
cally agreeable.

"Come back in an hour. I'll have a small package for ye
to deliver to Miss Endicott-Jones. Will ye do that for me?"

"Aye," Quigley said. "I will this very morning."

"Ye said the *Queen Victoria* is sailing in two weeks?"

"Aye, but—"

"Not for meself. I just need to know, that's all."

Quigley left, and Rory sat heavily at his desk. He
pulled out a sheet of paper and began to write:

Olivia, my love,
    I have only just found that my ship is leaving before
dawn. It grieves my heart that I cannot hold you and tell
you of my love once more before I leave. And oh, the
sorrow it brings me this minute, not to tell you good-bye
in person.
    I am sending you money for passage—enough for

you and the wee ones—to come to Ireland. The *Queen Victoria* is soon sailing from Boston Harbor for England. I could meet you at the dock in Portsmouth and travel with you to Dublin and home.

Two reasons I ask that you come. The first is because I love you and want to be with you. My stay will not be long I hope. Only to bury my brother proper and comfort my grandm'am.

The second reason is this. 'Tis my grandm'am's locket I am sending you. She gave it to me with instructions to give it to the woman I marry, the woman I promise my heart to. I would like you to meet—you and my grandm'am. I know she'll take a deep likin' to you and the wee bairns.

You'll find the locket enclosed in this packet . . . and the bundle of money wrapped in it as well.

Forgive me, my love, for sending this instead of delivering it in person. 'Tis you I love and always will. I go now, knowing you hold the key to my heart in your hands . . . and my grandm'am's locket around your neck.

With all my love, I remain yours forever.
Rory O'Kelly

He opened his canvas satchel and pulled out what was left of the bundle of money his grandm'am had given him months ago. He wouldn't need it now that he planned to work his way back across the Atlantic. Rolling it tightly in a sheet of paper, he tied it with twine, then dropped it into the same heavy envelope that Smiling Joe had brought his gift of money in. Next he folded the letter to Olivia, propped open the small velvet box that held the locket, dropped the letter in, and snapped it closed again.

Quigley arrived on time, just as the first rays of light stretched across the ashen sky. Rory placed the two packages in his hands. "God be with ye, lad," he said, giving him a bear hug. "'Tis precious cargo ye have with ye."

"I'll deliver it before yer Miss Endicott-Jones is pouring

her breakfast coffee." He tucked the velvet box in his pants pocket, the bundle of money in his vest pocket, gave them a pat, and smiled at Rory.

Rory nodded his thanks and turned to grab his satchel. "Godspeed," he said as Quigley headed down the stairs two at a time. "Godspeed."

"And same blessings be with ye, me cousin," Quigley called up the stairwell. "Give me love to Grandm'am."

And he was gone.

Rory made his way to the waterfront, his stocking cap pulled low over his forehead, his canvas bag draped over his shoulder. Fog had rolled in during the night, and it hung in the air, damp and gray. The ship's horn blasted one long, loud, and mournful wail as Rory climbed the ramp. He turned for one last look at the city before heading into the midnight depths of the ship.

·⚜·

QUIGLEY RACED along the narrow streets of Charlestown. The *drip-drip* of moisture fell from rooftops onto the cobbles. He nimbly hopped over puddles. The air was thick and dank, still late-summer warm. It would be a day that caused a body to sweat with every move, he thought, as he headed to the streetcar stop.

He had just passed the Gilded Shamrock when he heard footsteps coming up fast behind him. Patting the bundle in his vest pocket to make sure of its safekeeping, he ducked into an alleyway, hoping whoever was following would pass on by.

The footsteps halted, and for a moment Quigley didn't breathe for fear of being heard. The footsteps drew closer.

He looked quizzically at the one who had followed him, surprised when they at last came face-to-face.

Then from behind him, more footsteps sounded.

Before Quigley could turn, a flash of pain struck the side of his head. He felt his knees give out; then blessed velvet darkness settled around him like a cloak.

He sank deeper into it until he knew no more.

· ✤ ·

"THERE, THERE NOW, boy," a female voice said somewhere in the fog. "Don't try to sit up."

"What happened?" Quigley groaned, struggling to open his eyes.

"You were robbed," the voice said. "And left for dead."

Quigley touched his head and grimaced.

"I had to stitch you up. I'm a sausage maker, but I sewed you up just fine. Needle and thread, just like I was making a quilt." She chuckled. "Found you right outside my door four days ago."

"Four days ago?" he whispered. He remembered something about Rory . . . something he was supposed to do . . . but he couldn't remember what it was. He would ask Rory next time he saw him.

He forced his eyelids open to narrow slits and squinted at the room. It was bare except for the single iron bed, a small table, and the woman sitting opposite him. He looked down at the strange nightshirt he was wearing and frowned.

"My husband's," the woman said, reading his mind. She was a pleasant-looking woman with carrot-colored hair and a face with more freckles than not. It gave her an odd, speckled look. "He's been gone now for years, but I saved some of his clothes. Makes me not miss him so much. I've got shirts and pants for you when you're able to get up again."

"Wh-what happened to me clothes?"

"Filthy dirty. Not fit for laundering if you ask me. But I saved them to let you decide." She shrugged as Quigley closed his eyes again. "I don't think it's right to throw away other people's belongings. No siree, not me."

Quigley lay quiet, willing the ache in his head to go away. He wondered how he could get word to Rory. Or maybe Rory was already searching for him . . . especially since he'd been laid up for four days.

"I need to get word to me cousin," he said. "He's . . . "

Then he remembered. Rory had sailed for Ireland. Four days ago . . . right before the ruffians attacked him.

"Was there anything in my pockets?" he asked, squinting at the woman again. "An envelope? Anything?"

She shook her head. "Nothing, lad. I'm sorry."

He lay back on his pillow and groaned. He didn't even know what the packets contained so that he could tell Miss Endicott-Jones. Not that he needed to tell her anything. He'd never really approved of Rory consorting with the Boston Brahmin anyway. Exhausted with pain and thinking things through, Quigley closed his eyes and fell again into a deep sleep.

·⟨✤⟩·

OLIVIA PICKED HER WAY along the cobbled street toward the Gilded Shamrock. It was the only place she knew to go for information about Rory. She didn't know where he lived or where to start searching. She only knew it had been too long since she'd seen him.

She stepped inside, letting her eyes grow accustomed to the dim late-afternoon light. The dirty gilded mirrors and tattered red wall coverings gave the place a tawdry look in light of day.

The place was nearly empty. Only a barmaid stood at the bar, polishing glasses. She looked up and gave Olivia a puzzled smile. "Are ye lost, lass?"

"I'm looking for someone . . . "

"Ain't we all?" The barmaid laughed raucously, set

down the shot glass and rag, and leaned against the bar with one elbow. "Ain't we all?"

Olivia moved closer to the woman, noticing the thick paint on her face, the drawn-on mole above her lip. "Have you ever heard of Rory O'Kelly?"

"Nah, can't say I have. Sorry." She shrugged.

"Then how about Smiling Joe Callahan?"

At the mention of the political boss's name, the woman's eyebrows shot up. "He owns this place. His office is in the back." Then she narrowed her eyes and stood up straight, stretching like a feline. "What business do you have with him?"

Olivia tried not to show her annoyance. "Like I said, I'm looking for someone."

"Oh yeah. Rory O'Kelly."

"Where's Joe Callahan's office?"

The woman pointed toward the back of the big room. "Over there. First door to your left."

"Is he in?"

"Been here all morning near as I know." She shrugged and turned to her polishing, her back now to Olivia.

Olivia swept past her to the office door at the rear of the room. Without hesitation she knocked. The door opened a moment later, and she looked across the room at Smiling Joe Callahan.

For a moment he didn't seem to recognize her. Then he rose and stuck out his hand in greeting. "It's Doctor Endicott-Jones herself," he announced. "What can I do for you, good doctor? Surely you haven't run through my funds already?" He threw back his head and laughed.

She didn't laugh with him. "I've come to find the whereabouts of Rory O'Kelly. He's—" she hesitated, embarrassed to be asking about the man she loved— "missing," she finished lamely. "He's been so good to . . . check on the babies. I'm just concerned. That's all."

"You didn't know then?"

She frowned. "Know what?"

"Rory O'Kelly sailed to Ireland over a week ago."

"A week ago?" She stepped backward to touch the wall for balance, thinking her knees might not hold her much longer.

"Aye, lass. At least that."

She shook her head slowly. "He didn't even say good-bye."

"His cousin Quigley is telling it all over town that Rory was fighting mad. Went back to fight the English, he did. Avenge his brother's death."

"He wouldn't do that . . . ," she began then let her voice drift off. How could she guess what Rory would do? Tears came unbidden to her eyes. Had he deceived her? She turned away from Smiling Joe and slowly walked to the door.

"I'm truly sorry, lass," he said. "But it's the truth as told by young Quigley, who said he was with Rory O'Kelly right up to the hour he sailed." He shook his head. "Poor lad, this Quigley. Got himself into trouble as well. Said he was standing up for Ireland when some English sympathizers took offense. I never thought the lad had it in him. But he's got the scars to prove it."

Unable to bring herself to speak, Olivia merely inclined her head. Minutes later, she boarded the street-car for the inner city. Weeping, she tried to think of anything but Rory, but he filled her heart and mind completely.

Through the shimmer of her tears, she stared out at the passing city, trying to forget the lyrical sound of his voice, the light in his Irish-sea eyes, the touch of his lips on hers. But she could not.

VIII

I N PORTSMOUTH, ENGLAND, Rory watched as the *Queen Victoria* docked and her gangway creaked to a halt just yards from where he was standing. The officers stood at attention as the first-class passengers disembarked then moved away with disinterest as the dozens of men, women, and children in steerage poured onto the dock.

He studied each face, looking for Olivia. He examined profiles, the slender curve of a cheek that could only belong to her, the twist of luxurious hair piled high. Women holding babies, curly haired toddlers squealing and laughing, infants in prams . . . women strolling . . . he didn't miss one.

As the knots of passengers thinned, his heart caught with the sinking realization: Olivia wasn't coming.

Even then the hope in his heart wouldn't die. He paced the length of the wood planks into the chill of the evening, hoping that somehow he had overlooked her.

During the hours he waited he imagined how she would run into his arms, laughing and crying at the same time over how they nearly missed each other.

But twilight fell, and still there was no sign of her. He couldn't bring himself to leave. Finally, as the frigid mists rolled in, he shivered and turned away, his hands stuck deep in his coat pockets, his collar turned up, and his shoulders hunched nearly to his ears against the cold. He had booked return passage for himself on the *Irish Gold*, a British boat that ran daily between Portsmouth and Dublin, as well as passage for four more—a lady and three wee bairns, he'd told the ticket agent proudly. Now he would be traveling alone.

Heavenly Father, help me accept what I canna change, he prayed later that night, staring across the cold, gray seas, as the *Irish Gold* made its way across the swells. *And help me keep me eyes on Ye, rather than dwell on the sadness in me heart.*

LATE THE NEXT AFTERNOON, Rory sat in front his grandm'am's fire warming his hands. She sat near him, waiting for the kettle of water to boil for tea. She watched him, her lined face drawn narrow with grief and now a touch of heartache on Rory's behalf.

"Maybe there's a reason ye havena considered," she said with a sigh. "Something givin' her great reason to stay."

He nodded slowly. "She could have sent word. I asked at the ship's manifest office if any mail had been sent with the crossing. Of course, there were boxes, already sorted and ready to post. But nothing for me." He didn't tell his grandm'am, but when it had been apparent she wasn't among the passengers, he had expected the locket to be returned with a letter of explanation.

"Might there be some good reasons she couldna make

the crossin', a dozen at the least?" She stood to lift the kettle from the fire. "I see yer deep disappointment, but don't let it choke yer love." She turned to smile at him as she warmed the pottery teapot with the water. "Dinna seein' the light in yer eyes when talkin' about her make me want to meet her?"

He stared into the fire. "I shouldna be thinkin' of meself at a time like this. We've just lost Eamon, and both our hearts are breakin' because of it. Not just mine because of love."

She walked slowly over to him and touched his cheek with her parchment hand. "Ye're a man in love. No matter about other tragedies or sorrow, isn't it love that holds yer heart steady in the end . . . the love of the woman God's chosen fer ye—and fer God Himself?"

He nodded, considering her words, the bright spirit in her eyes—even in her sorrow. The look of her reminded him of what he'd once told Olivia about his grandm'am. He studied her a moment then spoke again. "Me Olivia favors ye, and I told her so."

Grandm'am looked pleased, but she scolded him. "Don't ye know if I was young and beautiful—as I know yer Olivia is—that I wouldna want to be compared to a granny like me?" She laughed and went back to fetch the tea he'd brought her from Portsmouth. A moment later, she poured the fragrant liquid into two mugs, then set a bowl of sugar between them. A sack of the sweet brown lumps had also been a gift, but he waved the bowl away, wanting his grandm'am to enjoy every dear tidbit of sugar herself.

Rory took a long sip of the strong liquid, his eyes closed. "This is something I missed in America."

"They dinna have tea then?"

He chuckled. "Aye, they have tea, but 'tis weak as bathwater. And about as tasty."

Grandma'am sat back, watching him carefully. "Isn't

it time to tell me about yer plans. We've given Eamon
a proper burial. Yer young lady hasna yet come . . . what
is it ye're plannin' now, Rory-mine?"

He shook his head. "I don't plan to go back to America, if that's yer question."

"I dinna think so." She leaned forward, her lined face
earnest, her eyes bright. "There's a meetin' here at the
house tonight."

"Don't tell me. Society of St. George?"

"Aye."

He set his mug down with a thud and stood to move
to the fire. "Surely after what's happened, ye wouldna
entertain the blackguards here."

Her voice was strong when she answered him. "'Twasn't
their doing, Eamon's death. He wasna with them. Dinna
the English catch him alone, bringing in weapons off a
small boat?"

Letting out a long, noisy sigh, Rory studied the flames.
"I canna join them, if that's what ye want me to do. I
canna." The peat crackled and smoked.

Grandm'am pulled herself up from her chair with a
groan and moved to stand beside him. "Eamon was a
leader among them, lad," she said. "Canna they use yer
help now?"

"I have no interest in the kind of war they're fighting."

"Just listen," she repeated. She touched his arm, her
hand as frail as a leaf, her convictions as strong as iron.

He grinned finally. "I'll listen. But I can't promise ye
anything more."

"They need ye," she said again, then turned back
to her tea.

HE DID INDEED LISTEN. For three weeks the young men of
the Society of St. George tried to convince him to join in

their bitter ways of fighting a guerilla war. They told glowing accounts of what his brother Eamon had done— his courage, his leadership, his uncanny understanding of the tactics needed to fight the English.

The seven men appeared almost nightly, preferring to meet at the obscure thatched-roof cottage of Nuala O'Kelly instead of in town where they might be overheard. Always, his grandm'am sat to one side, knitting needles clicking, smiling and nodding her agreement, or openly disagreeing, but always a lively part of the group. It touched him that they showed her great respect, especially now that Eamon was gone.

It also became apparent that they expected him to take his brother's place.

"I'm not Eamon," he told them one night. "And I never can be. I believe in our cause—I'm as passionate as any of ye, and maybe more so."

"Ye think ye can fight a war with words," scoffed a man name Michael O'Greeley. "Yer brother told us all about ye—how ye think the written word's got a power all its own."

Rory smiled and lifted a brow. "He wasna far from the truth. I've seen it in action with me own eyes." He told them the tale of his fight with the political boss in Boston. By the end of his tale, which he relished telling, the men were laughing with him at the outcome.

"True, maybe, the written word's got power," O'Greeley admitted. "But not always."

The others agreed. His grandm'am nodded, looking up from her knitting.

"This same political boss said he might help us," Rory said, remembering the night Smiling Joe paid a visit to the Endicott-Jones estate. He tried to ignore the memories of what followed that evening with Olivia . . . the look of her in the moonlight, the feel of her in his arms, the glory of her kiss . . . but they flooded into his heart. For a moment he could not speak.

"Tell us about this Boston politician. What kind of help is he meanin'?" Greeley leaned back in his chair, his eyes brighter than before.

"Name's Smiling Joe Callahan," Rory told them, enjoying their grins and hoots at the name. "A tough, iron-fisted man. Runs a Boston ward called Charlestown. Surrounds himself with a group of ruffians who keep the Irish citizens under his thumb."

"Sounds good and bad," said a dark-haired man named Cashel Brady. "Also seems that ye should return— fight that war on our behalf. In America, I'm meanin'."

The others nodded their agreement.

"I canna leave just now," he said, glancing at Grandm'am. "Not so soon after Eamon's—"

The scarf she was knitting fell to her lap. "Understand this, me lad," she said sternly. "When it comes to our fight against the English—don't ye think I'm ready to sacrifice nearly anything—even sayin' good-bye to me Rory?"

"Even a greater sacrifice she's paid already," Michael O'Greeley added, his voice low. His eyes glistened. "The highest price our loved ones can pay."

For a moment no one spoke, then Rory's grandm'am gave him a hard, knowing look. "Don't be usin' me now, lad, as the reason ye don't want to sail the Atlantic again."

O'Greeley spoke again. "If this man, this Smiling Joe, is willin' to help—to get others in his ward to give—'tis no question that's where ye need to be. Ye were only there less than a year. Think of the arms and materials ye can supply from there if ye return." He paused. "We'll pay yer crossing anytime ye say."

Rory gave the men a steady look. "I'll weigh what ye've said, lads. For now, I'm not ready to leave, not certain I'll ever be."

"If ye're stayin', then," Brady said, "ye will come along on our next raid?" He grinned. "Maybe ye'll see how we work and change yer mind altogether."

Michael O'Greeley laughed. "Ye wouldna be the first. Not atall." Then his expression sobered. "And at the verra least, lad, ye can use the passion in our guerilla war in yer writings . . . especially when ye get to Boston." He leaned forward. "Will ye come with us?"

THE NEXT MORNING Rory walked alone to the cliffs outside his grandm'am's cottage. The day had dawned cloudless, a rare happening on the coast in late November, but held a bitter cold that stung his face and hands. The wind off the sea blew hard across the land, coming in a buffeting rhythm that mixed with the crashing waves below him.

He shivered and hunched his shoulders against the force of the wind, climbing farther up the rocky path leading to the topmost point of barren land. Once there, he sat on an outcropping of granite, facing the sea. In the distance, seagulls wheeled and cried, soaring upward, swooping to the sea then circling above the land.

Rory had seen the posting in London about the next Atlantic voyage of the HMS *Queen Victoria*. Two weeks hence it would sail from Liverpool. Two weeks meant he would dock at Boston Harbor by Christmas Day . . . should he decide to sail.

His eyes rested on that place at the horizon where the edge of the sea disappeared into the blue gray of the sky. *Oh, Lord,* he prayed, *I feel as lost as a ship at sea, sailing into unknown waters. I thought I knew Yer will, Yer leading. But maybe 'twas me own blind ambitions I was following, not Yer plan atall. I had everything planned meself according to me own dictates. Now everything is lost. At least it feels that way to me.*

Me own brother . . . he paused, his eyes stinging in the wind.

The woman I love . . . he dropped his head in his hands. *And now I don't know which way to turn. To take Eamon's place in the fight for justice and freedom. Or to return to Boston and Olivia.*

Though what if she's changed her mind, Father? What if returning to America is not in Yer plan for either of us?

He looked up, staring again at the sea. If only Olivia had come to him with babies and all, everything would be different. His way would be clear.

As a sudden chill ocean wind whipped over the cliffs, he remembered the words Grandm'am had spoken when she gave him the locket. *"Home is that place in yer heart, that place that God holds fast. Whenever ye worry about finding yer way, lad, look to Him, yer heavenly Da. Look to Him who made ye. For 'tis He who holds ye fast. 'Tis He who will see ye home."*

"Father," he prayed, "help me find my way. Help us both find our way home."

IX

As Christmas approached, Olivia threw herself into a plan to give her little charges the most joyous Christmas that could ever be imagined. Not by showering them with presents but by showering them with love. The little ones' joy might help her forget double heartaches that weighed in her heart like two cold stones: her alienation from her parents and Rory's sudden and silent departure.

She fell into step beside Eliza one day at Trinity Settlement House as they walked down the hall to the dining room. "How would you like to help me put on a Christmas Eve celebration for the children?"

"For Maddie, Katie, and Keara?"

"Plus a few others I have in mind." She grinned. "A few dozen or more."

Eliza stopped and raised a brow.

Olivia laughed. "Actually, I was thinking about contacting our benefactor."

"You can't possibly mean Smiling Joe."

She grinned. "I mean exactly that." Then she sobered. "I'll need help, but I would like to put on a Christmas Eve celebration—here at Trinity—for all the children he might help us find in Charlestown. . . . " She frowned as the ideas came almost faster than she could explain them. "I don't mean just those who are orphaned or alone. But even those from big families who can't possibly provide Christmas for them."

A wave of nostalgia swept over Olivia as she remembered Christmases at her own home: the scent of pine garlands and burning candles, cranberries with cinnamon and nutmeg bubbling on the stove, plump geese roasting in the oven. "It would be so much better—," she began then bit her lip to keep from adding, *to have it in a real home, in my parents' home—filled with warmth and love, the way it once was.* God had given her these children, her three and those in need in all of Boston, to care for. Daily, she touched them with His love out of her commitment to her Lord. This was no time to feel sorry for herself. Not when so much needed to be done.

She pushed her longing for her parents' approval and acceptance . . . her longing for Rory . . . from her mind. Resolutely she began again. "It would make these little ones so happy to experience a real Christmas. We could decorate a tree, lace garlands around the banisters, bake a dozen geese complete with stuffing. . . . " She grinned at her friend. "What do you think?"

The hallway was crowded, and they stepped to one side to let an orderly push a woman by in a wheelchair. Just as they did, Rachel hurried around the corner, a chart in her hand.

"Walk with us a few minutes," Olivia urged. "Your help is needed."

"You may be sorry," Eliza teased. "And you'd better cancel all other plans for Christmas Eve." She nodded to a new doctor who had just begun volunteering one day a week. When he had passed, she raised a brow of appreciation and giggled.

As they walked, Olivia told Rachel about her plan. She didn't even need to ask before Rachel broke in. "I'll do anything I can," she promised, "including cooking Christmas dinner."

Eliza rolled her eyes and giggled. "As if you can even boil water."

"I'll need help, of course," Rachel said pointedly and smiled at Eliza. Then she paused, her expression serious as she turned back to Olivia. "Why don't you ask your mother and father to join us?" Both Rachel and Eliza had committed to pray with Olivia that the older Endicott-Joneses' hearts would soften toward their daughter. "Christmas is a time for miracles," Rachel went on. "If they would just come, take that one step as a gesture of the season's love and joy, they would see what you're doing here. They would be so proud, Liv." Her eyes softened. "Invite them, Liv. You must try."

Olivia nodded solemnly. "I can't. I know what their answer would be. Just hearing their resounding no would be too painful. I'll wait for them to contact me." She hesitated as her friends exchanged glances. "When that word, that note, arrives, then I'll know it's time to reconcile. Not before." Her prayer every morning and every night was that her mother and father would come to Trinity Settlement House of their own accord. She couldn't imagine it happening any other way.

Rachel let out a whistling breath. "What if that note never comes?"

Olivia didn't want to consider it. She shook her head. "I'll wait . . . forever if necessary."

Eliza snorted. "Wait forever?" She shook her head sadly. "Don't let pride get in your way, Liv."

Olivia felt her cheeks color. "Pride?" She laughed. "They're the ones who need to search their hearts, not me. I'm here, waiting to forgive them if they'll ask."

"What if they don't ask?" Eliza persisted. "What then?"

Olivia drew in a troubled breath, considering the question, as a nurse walked by with an expectant mother. A moment later, the three friends watched another nurse pass, helping an elderly patient walk slowly to her room.

"I'm doing God's work," Olivia said finally, "loving and caring for His children. My parents' hearts are cold. They're in the wrong. It's up to them to come to me, not the other way around."

Again her friends exchanged worried glances. Feeling uncomfortable, Olivia headed down the hall. She was right; she knew she was. And that was that. "We'll talk about our Christmas celebration later," she tossed over her shoulder. And she turned her mind to the little ones awaiting her in the upstairs nursery.

·✧·

"MAMA," KEARA SAID one night a couple weeks later. "I forget the words."

"What words, sweetheart?" Olivia snuggled Keara close with her left arm as Katie plopped down on the opposite side of the small sofa and wiggled her way beneath Olivia's right arm. Across the room in her cradle, Maddie sighed in her sleep. A tiny smacking sound carried toward them as she sucked her thumb.

"Old words," Keara said with a frown and a puckered lower lip. "The ones I used to know."

"Me too," Katie said. "I forget too."

Oliva caught her breath and felt the sting of tears near the top of her throat. For a moment the ache was too severe to speak. There was no one to help them speak Gaelic. Only Rory, and he was gone. "I'll try to help you remember," she said. "At least the words that Rory taught us." She swallowed hard then spoke in Gaelic. "'Tis ye I love," she whispered. "'Tis ye."

The little girls said it back to her; then with their arms around her neck, they smothered her cheeks with wet kisses.

"I miss Mr. Rory," Keara said with a noisy sigh.

"Me too," Katie said and popped her thumb into her mouth. "Me too."

"Me too," Olivia said softly.

Keara sat forward, her eyes suddenly bright. "Maybe he could come to our Christmas party. Then he could tell us the words."

Olivia's heart caught, and for a moment she didn't trust herself to speak. "He's far, far away, Keara. Across the ocean. It would be too far. I'm sorry."

Both pairs of solemn eyes rested on her face. "Tell us the story again," Katie said after a moment.

"The one about Baby Jesus," her twin added.

"And no room in the inn." Katie rose to her knees in anticipation, her sadness over Rory put temporarily aside. She wagged her index finger at an imaginary Mary and Joseph. "There is no room for ye here."

"Not ye, silly," her twin said with a dramatic scowl. "Mama said to say you 'stead of ye."

"I like the way Rory says it," Katie said. "He would say ye."

Keara stood up and put her hands on her hips. "Like this, silly." She lifted her chin, frowned, and wagged her index finger, obviously relishing the role of the stern inn-keeper. "There is no room in the inn. You must stay with the donkeys and cows and camels in the barn."

Olivia laughed. "I think you two know the story better than I do."

"But you tell it better," Keara said, plopping down beside Olivia once more.

"Tell us again," Katie said with a sleepy sigh, "the part about the big 'portant kings."

"On big camels." Keara snuggled against Olivia contentedly. "They saw a star."

Katie giggled. "The camels didn't, silly."

Keara stuck her chin in the air. "They could have."

"Them big kings brung presents." Katie looked into Olivia's face expectantly.

"Brought," Olivia said, "they brought presents."

"The best presents they had."

"Best of all," Olivia said, "they brought their hearts to Baby Jesus. No one asked them to come. No one showed them the way. It was a long, long journey. But they wanted to find the Christ Child and kneel before Him, worship and adore Him. It didn't matter the cost. They only knew they had to make the journey." The children studied her with wide eyes as she went on. "That's why we give gifts of love to each other at Christmas—to celebrate the Baby's birth. To share His love with each other."

She cuddled them closer. "And this Christmas, we're going to share Baby Jesus' love right here at Trinity Settlement House. It will be a glory." Olivia smiled down at the children.

"Like the big kings on camels? Bringing our hearts?" Katie wanted to know.

"And sharing His love with all who come to our party," Olivia said. "Boys and girls from all over Boston."

"Tell us again about the party," Keara said.

Olivia settled back against the sofa and smiled. "We'll cut down the tallest Christmas tree we can find that will fit in the parlor downstairs. We'll decorate with candles and pine garlands and bake gingerbread and roast the plumpest geese we can fit in the oven."

Katie sighed happily. "Tell us again about the Christmas tree."

Keara got up on her knees in excitement. "And the gingerbed."

Olivia laughed and described the tree and candles and little cakes for what had to be the hundredth time this week. The little ones never tired of hearing about the upcoming celebration.

"What about the presents?" Katie asked the same question every night. "The ones for Baby Jesus."

"What will we bring?" Keara said with a yawn.

"An act of kindness for someone else," Olivia murmured to the sleepy twins, wondering how she could teach them what that meant. "Something unexpected, a surprise that will show them your love . . . and the love of their heavenly Father." She fell silent for a moment, considering the words she'd just spoken. When she continued her voice was soft. "Because whatever you do for someone else in Jesus' name, it's as if you are doing it for Him."

But the little ones didn't ask any more questions. Their heads were now drooping sleepily. Gently, Olivia first picked up Keara, carried her to their trundle, then scooped up Katie and laid her down beside her sister. Then crossing the room, she turned up the lamp at her writing table, sat down, and dipped her pen in the inkwell and began to write:

Dear Mother and Father,
    I miss you terribly. You have been such a vital part of my life, and these past few months have been especially painful without you. I know you don't agree with the direction I have taken, and I'm not asking you to change your minds or opinions or even to accept me for who I am and what I do. I just want to say one thing during this season of joy: I love you.
    We are putting together a Christmas celebration for

the children here at Trinity Settlement House and for other little ones throughout Boston. I would love for you to join us on Christmas Eve.

The festivities will begin early because of the young children. If you can find it in your hearts to attend, please arrive by two o'clock in the afternoon, December 24.

Sending all my love, I remain faithfully yours,
Olivia

She folded the letter, placed it in an envelope, and sealed it with wax. It lay lightly in her hand as she considered what she might say in a second missive. With a deep sigh, she set aside the letter to her parents and took up the pen again with a fresh sheet of paper.

Dearest Rory,
I have waited as the weeks passed, hoping for some word from you. I have prayed for you and your grandmother through this time of loss. I wanted to write and tell you of my love. I wanted to ask why you spoke such words of tenderness and love then disappeared across the ocean as if they meant nothing. Yet, something deep in my heart tells me you aren't a man to speak lightly, that you wouldn't speak frivolous, empty words. Still, the questions and deep sorrows borne of missing you fill my heart.

That night—so long ago—I pledged I would wait for you forever. But without word from you, without . . .

The words shimmered through her tears, and she swallowed hard as she remembered the last night they were together, the moonlit walk, their pledges of love and dreams of a future together. She pictured his face, the light in his Irish-sea eyes, the way he combed his fingers through his hair. The touch of his lips on hers.

She dropped her pen to the side of the letter and buried her face in her hands. "Oh, Rory," she whispered, "why do you keep your silence?"

Picking up her pen, she wrote three more lines:

> Because this is the season of giving, I am sending with this letter the most precious gift I have: my love. It hasn't died, Rory O'Kelly. Instead, it burns brighter than ever, even in your absence.

A single teardrop fell on the page, smudging the last sentence. She stared at what she'd written and knew she couldn't mail the letter. She wondered if it was pride or good sense that caused her to change her mind. It didn't really matter. If Rory had wanted to contact her, to ask her to wait for his return, she would have heard by now.

She hadn't, and that was that. Standing, she wadded up the letter and dropped it into the small waste receptacle beside her desk. Then she brushed the dampness from her still-wet cheeks and turned to Maddie, who fussed in her cradle.

Holding the baby always calmed her spirits. Olivia closed her eyes as she rocked her, trying not to think of Rory.

It was impossible.

RORY SAT at a table belowdecks. In the distance the engines hummed. The room rocked as the big ship took the angry swells of the stormy Atlantic. Bracing himself, he took his pen in hand and tried to form the words in his mind. None would come.

How could he ask the woman he loved why she hadn't come to him? His pride, that eejit-*amadain* Irish pride, was in the way. When he sailed into Boston Harbor, he wanted to send her this note, asking for permission to call. He wondered if he would have the courage. What if she said no?

He drew in a deep breath, finally deciding that perhaps a more formal tone was called for, then began to write:

Dear Doctor Endicott-Jones,
    It is with pleasure that I anticipate meeting you again. I remember so fondly our last evening together.

He stared at the words, remembering the beauty of that last night. Remembering the glory of Olivia's presence, the fresh scent of her hair as he held her, the warmth of her arms around his neck, the simple joy of being in her presence . . . the wonder of hearing her say "'Tis ye I love!" in Gaelic.

The lantern above the table swung from side to side as the ship rose with an ocean swell. Rory held on to the table and waited until it steadied itself.

He stared at the letter and knew he would do with it the same that he had done with the dozen or more others he had penned since leaving Olivia. He picked up the sheet and tore it into bits. Minutes later, he tossed them into the wind from the deck and watched as they fluttered into the green gray foam beside the ship.

⁎⁜⁎

During the last days leading up to Christmas, Trinity Settlement House seemed to take on new life.

Olivia arranged for two dozen plump geese to be delivered to the kitchen in time for baking on Christmas Eve morning. Eliza and Rachel were frantically gathering recipes and ingredients from their mothers and friends. Neither one had cooked a meal in her life, but they planned to rise to the occasion with humor and grace.

Olivia enlisted the help of men from church to cut a Christmas tree and set it up to be decorated on Christmas Eve morning.

She invited the children who often visited Trinity Settlement House for meals or medical help to come every afternoon to learn Christmas carols. It seemed even the noisiest wards in the clinic hushed as the sounds of "Silent Night" wafted through the hallways. An air of excitement continued to grow as the twins chattered about popcorn stringing and making paper chains and gingerbread men.

Olivia visited Smiling Joe one week before Christmas Eve. Snow was falling as she stepped from the streetcar in Charlestown. She tried to push thoughts of Rory O'Kelly from her mind as she walked to the Gilded Shamrock.

This was no time for sorrow or disappointment. Not about Rory. Not about the sad silence from her parents since she had sent her letter.

The man was standing near the door as she approached. "Well, now, if it isn't me blue-blooded friend," he said with affection.

"I've come with a request," she said.

"Ah, lass. Already? I sent another draft a month ago."

She laughed. He had been generous almost to a fault. Even his generosity, though, reminded her of Rory. If it hadn't been for his caring words about her, about their Lord, Smiling Joe wouldn't have given a dime. Even worse, he would have taken her children.

"No, this isn't about another bank draft," she said. "It's about something else altogether."

"Ye're soundin' almost Irish, lass," he said before he stepped back to let her pass through the doorway. "Come in, please, and get out of the cold. Tell me what you need."

She stepped inside and told him her plan. Before she had finished he'd gathered others around and asked her to repeat what she needed from them.

Even the barmaid had tears in her eyes. "Can I bring me own lit'l ones, then?"

"Oh yes," Olivia assured her, her heart softening. How harshly she had judged this woman. "How many do you have?"

"Three," the woman said proudly. "And no da to help. He died two years back." She moved closer. "And can we come to help ye out atall? We'd be happy to, the lit'l ones and me." She paused. "Me name is Betsie, lass."

"I'd be honored to have your help, Betsie. And bring your children early too."

By the time she left the Gilded Shamrock, more details were in place. Men volunteered to drive if sleighs could be found, and Smiling Joe said he would arrange for as many as needed. Betsie said she would personally visit each family in the parish and tell them about the celebration.

Another woman, a rather unusual-looking woman with carrot-colored hair and mottled skin, moved from the back of the crowd just before Olivia stepped outside. "You're Miss Endicott-Jones?"

Olivia nodded. "Do you have children who might like to join us?"

The woman laughed. "Mercy me, no! I heard what you're planning and just wanted to meet you for myself." She smiled, keeping her eyes on Olivia for a moment longer, looking as if there was more she wanted to say.

But Olivia dismissed the notion as she headed outside. It was just her imagination.

·⟨⟩·

OLIVIA WALKED BACK toward the streetcar stop with a growing sense of wonder. Snowflakes fell, large and lazy, all around her. She stopped and turned to look back. Gas lamps glowed in the dim light of the late afternoon. Families milled up and down the lane, greeting each other as they passed.

How different this place seemed with its fresh blanket of snow. This was only the third time she had come into the heart of Charlestown, but standing here looking around, she wondered why she hadn't come more often. Not to search for someone or ask for favors as she had before, but to give.

Isn't that what Rory's letter to Smiling Joe had been about? Giving from a heart of love as if to the Lord Himself. Wasn't that what she was trying to teach the twins about the meaning of Christmas love?

Staring at the snow, she was ashamed. There were no borders around love, around compassion. Giving meant going forth, stretching her boundaries in ways she hadn't yet considered. Giving as unto the Lord didn't mean waiting to serve those who came to her.

Olivia trudged to the streetcar stop, her boots crunching in the snow. The next car rattled down the street, and she stepped closer to climb aboard as soon as it halted. But in the quiet of snowfall, she thought she heard someone calling her name.

Frowning, she turned, peering through the falling snow.

"Miss Endicott-Jones," came the call again. "Miss Olivia Endicott-Jones?" A woman's voice floated through the twilight.

Olivia waited as the shadowy figure caught up with her.

The woman pushed back a hood that had obscured her face. "I met you just now . . . well, a few minutes ago. At the Gilded Shamrock."

"Yes, of course," Olivia said, frowning.

"I have something for you. Something I should have brought to you long before now."

Olivia thought she must surely mean a donation for Trinity Settlement House. She smiled, ready to thank the woman.

But instead, the woman pulled a small velvet box from

her pocket. "I found this," she said. "A boy named Quigley O'Kelly was beaten just outside my butcher shop. I brought him in and nursed him back to health. This must have been in his pocket. I sent his clothes home with him when he left but found this soon after."

"Quigley O'Kelly?" Olivia tried to understand why he would have something connecting her to the velvet box.

The woman looked sheepish. "I saw what was inside and wanted to keep it for myself, it being gold and all. So I never told a soul what I'd found. Never went after the lad to give it back . . . or to try to find you."

"Why would you want to find me?"

"There's a letter, written to you. Prettiest letter I ever read."

"A letter?" Olivia was still searching for a thread of understanding. "When did you find Quigley O'Kelly?"

"Must've been September. Early September maybe."

Around the time that Rory left her. Her heart pounded as understanding began to dawn. "You said there's a letter . . . written to me."

"With your name on it."

"And something made of gold, you said."

"Yes."

"Is it . . . ?" She dared not hope. Tears filled her eyes. "Is it a locket?"

"Yes. It looks old. Maybe Irish." She shrugged. "Never seen anything like it." She placed the small velvet box in Olivia's hand. "It wasn't till I heard your name today in the Shamrock that my conscience smote me so bad I couldn't stand it any longer." She smiled gently. "I just hope it isn't too late."

Shakily, Olivia clutched the box and stepped onto the streetcar. The light was too dim to examine the locket, but she pulled it from the box and fastened it around her neck.

Next she drew the folded paper from the box and held it to her heart.

And she wept.

ON MONDAY MORNING, after reading and weeping and reading Rory's letter over and over again, Olivia marched through the glistening snow to the streetcar at the end of the boulevard. She rode the short distance to the harbor, thinking she couldn't get there fast enough, and stepped off the car in front of the agent's office of the Atlantic voyages of the HMS *Queen Victoria*. She booked one-way passage for herself and for all three children.

They would sail for Ireland on Christmas Day.

C · H · A · P · T · E · R

X

BOSTON
CHRISTMAS EVE

RORY STOOD on the deck of the *Queen Victoria* as it
sailed into Boston Harbor. In the approaching
dusk, the gaslights shining through the barren
trees along the waterfront cast a golden glow across a
blanket of new-fallen snow. Farther away, the city lights—
candles and lamplights in windows of cottages and
shops—twinkled, creating the look of a painting. A painting of the perfect Christmas with images of sleighs pulled
by high-stepping horses with jingling harnesses, carrying
laughing children and ma's and da's all bundled together
under thick fur robes.

He turned away, unable to bear the beauty of the
snowy landscape and the images it brought to his heart—
the sleigh that should be pulling the giggling Keara and
Katie and Madeilein Mary safe in his arms. And Olivia,
his love, by his side.

After hours of soul-searching during the voyage, he was certain that he didn't want to hear from Olivia's own lips the reasons she didn't respond to his letter. Oh yes, he understood that her responsibilities were great: her work at the settlement house, the care of the twins and Maddie. He understood and accepted them all. But the fact that she ignored his letter, the money he'd sent for passage, his grandmother's locket . . . those difficulties were sheep of a different flock altogether.

He thought about the night they had spoken of their deep affection for each other . . . and hinted at their intentions for the future. It had all happened so quickly. Once he was gone, perhaps Olivia had realized that she had been rash in declaring her love. That she had been wrong when she had said to him, "'Tis ye I love."

He had replayed the scene in his mind a thousand times, turning it this way and that, but always he came to the same conclusion: how could he, a poor Irish freedom fighter, son and grandson of potato farmers, possibly think in his wildest dreams that the beautiful Dr. Olivia Endicott-Jones could love him?

Faith, it had all been a dream, a beautiful impossible dream. And now—here in Boston on business for the Society of St. George—he would let the dream go. If he did venture to her side of town, it wouldn't be for days, perhaps weeks, to come. It would take him that long to get over losing her.

·⚜·

OLIVIA'S FEET SEEMED to have sprouted wings. She couldn't stop smiling as she flew about the clinic, hanging garlands, cutting out paper chains, stringing popcorn, and singing with the children. Upstairs in the nursery, two large steamer trunks had been packed—the children's clothes and toys in one; her clothes, shoes, and cloaks in the other.

The busier she kept, the easier it was to push to the back of her mind her only sadness: leaving without saying good-bye to her mother and father. She had posted her letter to them weeks ago, hoping that with her expression of love would also come reconciliation. Disappointment filled her heart when a return letter didn't arrive.

Still, she held on to the hope that her mother and father would accept her invitation to the children's Christmas Eve party tonight. Through the busy afternoon she watched the lane in front of the clinic for signs of their carriage.

It was just past dusk when the men from church carried in the Christmas tree and placed it in the reception-room window. The children—all forty-one of them—gathered round. Wide-eyed and with small gasps escaping their lips, they watched as candles were fastened to the branches. The lovely scents of beeswax and pine filled the room, mixing with the fragrance of fresh-baked gingerbread in the kitchen.

Pushing aside her growing disappointment over her parents' absence, Olivia helped the vicar and his wife bring the children by twos and threes close to the tree to hang their paper stars and popcorn strands. When the last ornament was hung, she dimmed the room's lights until only the Christmas tree glowed. The children hushed, awed by the sight of the glowing candles.

She gathered the children near the tree—the smallest ones in front, the taller ones behind—and instructed them to sit cross-legged on the floor. "I have a story to tell you," she said, sitting before them. "And it's the finest story you'll ever hear . . . because it's the story of why we celebrate Christmas with gifts of love—" she glanced up at the tree—"and with candlelight. About the One who is the light of the world."

She paused and looked once more toward the clinic's entrance. Surely they would come! It was Christmas. Didn't they care? Biting back another wave of sadness, she turned her attention back to the story. "First I'll tell you about a baby who was born in a manger many years ago."

"It's a good story," Keara said importantly.

"The camels saw the star," Katie added.

"Huh-uh. It was the big kings that did," Keara said. "They were *riding* on the camels' backs, silly."

Olivia cuddled Maddie, who cooed and babbled as she drew the twins close. As she told the glorious story, punctuated by the twins' exclamations of wonder, the children didn't move their eyes from her face. The room grew silent when she said, "And there was no room for Mary and Joseph in the inn."

A worried *ooh* rose from the children's lips.

When she reached the part about Jesus' birth in the manger and the angels singing to the shepherds, Olivia nodded to the children. Their sweet, baby voices, low and soft, joined her as she sang "Silent Night."

⁕

RORY PAID the landlord of the walk-up, arranging for the same room he'd let before. Trudging up the stairs, he tried to forget it was Christmas Eve. He unlocked the door, stepped in, and tossed his canvas bag on the bed. Then walking to the single window, he glanced out.

Carolers were clustered in the street below, and from time to time a horse-drawn sleigh passed by. This was no time to be alone. Even a dinner of Irish stew with Quigley would be better than moping in this dismal place alone. He grabbed his hat and headed down the stairs.

Standing outside the Boar's Head window, he spotted Quigley in his usual haunt, just two blocks from Smiling Joe's Gilded Shamrock.

Quigley looked up with surprise as Rory approached his table. "Rory O'Kelly, you're back."

"Aye, 'tis me in the flesh," Rory laughed, taking a seat beside his cousin. "Back with a mandate from the Society of St. George itself."

Quigley wiped his mouth with a napkin, frowning. Faith, but he didn't seem glad to see Rory. Instead, he kept moving his eyes away from Rory's sharp gaze.

"Is there somethin' ye're not tellin' me now, lad?"

The boy shrugged. "Not altogether. How are things with grandm'am?"

"She's as full of the Irish spirit as ever . . . especially considering her recent loss." He bent closer to his cousin. "But tell me why ye're so quick to change the subject of what ye're hidin'."

Quigley shrugged and let his gaze drift to the window.

"What happened when ye gave me gift to Olivia Endicott-Jones?"

His cousin stared at him, unblinking, and his cheeks flushed scarlet. "She never got yer gift," he said. "I was robbed that very day. Came upon me in an alley. I never had a chance. The ruffians took it all. . . . "

"The velvet box?"

"Aye."

"The money?"

He nodded and sighed.

"Faith, lad! Why didn't ye write to tell me?"

Quigley shrugged. "Ashamed, I was, to've let it happen. Ye finally let me take on a man's job—and I failed. I couldn't bear to tell ye."

Rory settled back, almost afraid to breathe. His heart pounding, he asked the next question, already knowing what the answer was. "And did ye find Miss Endicott-Jones, by chance? Did ye tell her I had to leave that day . . . that I wanted, desperately wanted, to come to her meself . . . but that there was no time?" The boy had turned pale now. Rory wanted to lean across the table and shake him by the lapels, but he forced himself to breathe evenly, deeply, before he did something he regretted. "Did ye do the right thing, lad, and tell her how it was with me?"

Quigley squirmed in his chair and looked away from his cousin. "Nah," he said in a small voice. "Nah, can't say I did."

Rory counted to ten in Gaelic to keep from overturning the table, the chair, Quigley . . . or all three at once. Then taking a deep breath, he stood. "Well," he growled, "at least ye've told me now." And he turned and walked away.

⚜

"I'M OF A MIND to head to the *Queen Victoria* this very night," Olivia said to Eliza as they helped the children choose their gingerbread men, "so I can be first in line to board." She placed a freshly frosted cookie on a plate for Katie. Eliza did the same for Keara and three older girls standing behind her.

Eliza pulled Olivia aside after the children had trotted to the dining table set up in the waiting room. "We'll miss you, Liv. Do you have any idea how long you'll be away?"

"I'm not certain. Right now, the important thing is to get to Ireland as fast as I can, find Rory, and clear up the misunderstanding between us."

The vicar joined them, an empty plate in his hand. "Did I hear you say that you want to board the *Victoria* early?"

"I don't think it's possible," Olivia said. "She just docked from a crossing. They won't let passengers on before the cabins are cleaned and ready for the sailing."

"Maybe I can pull some strings." He smiled, placing

more gingerbread men on his tray to serve the children. "I know some port authorities, Liv. After the party, I'll contact them. Maybe you can board tonight, get the children settled before you sail."

"Tonight?" As first she smiled, then the reality of her journey, the reality of leaving without seeing her mother and father, settled into her soul. "Thank you," she said tentatively, her heart suddenly heavy. "The children and I will be ready."

Eliza squeezed her hand. "Will you see your parents first? Tell them good-bye?"

Olivia swallowed hard. "They didn't come here tonight. I invited them, told them of my love, but still they couldn't bring themselves to come."

"I know you're disappointed . . . "

"It's deeper than that."

"Forgive them, Liv."

"They haven't asked me."

"It doesn't matter. You must anyway." Eliza smiled gently. "Seven times seven."

Olivia shook her head. "You heard the vicar. There isn't time. I must ready the children and leave tonight."

"You must go to them, for their sakes . . . and for yours."

For a moment Olivia didn't speak. "Perhaps it's better this way. Leaving without seeing them, I mean. Perhaps it will let them know how deeply they've hurt me." She didn't add that it was their fault anyway, all of it. They had brought this upon themselves by their judgmental attitude. By not accepting her as she was. By not seeing the good she was doing in the world.

Her bitterness surprised her, and she was glad her friend couldn't see the new, unsettling darkness that had invaded her heart this night. "I tried," she said to Eliza. "I reached out to them, but they ignored the olive branch." She shrugged. "What else can I do?"

Eliza studied her for a long moment. In the other room, the children giggled and laughed. The vicar had sat down at the piano and was playing Christmas carols.

"You can go to them," Eliza said softly. "You can go now. I'll watch the children."

Olivia started to shake her head, but Eliza touched her arm. "Think what you've taught the children about giving love to others this season." Her expression softened. "God gave us His Son, the greatest sacrifice of all. The greatest gift of all."

Olivia nodded. "Sacrificial love . . . the greatest gift."

"Love isn't easy."

Tears filled Olivia's eyes. "It isn't."

"It will be your gift, even greater than words on paper, to tell your parents—tonight—that you love them."

She thought of their harsh words when last they spoke, their rejection of her calling. Her tears fell as she shook her head again, and her voice was a whisper as she spoke. "I don't know if I can."

Just then Rachel came through the door with a fussing Maddie in her arms. "This little one's had enough Christmas. I'll take her upstairs to bed."

"And I'll get the twins into their nightclothes," Eliza said, exchanging a look with Rachel.

Olivia laughed softly, wiping her eyes again. "And I suppose the vicar has a sleigh outside waiting for me?" It was a conspiracy to see that she had the opportunity to do what she needed to do.

Her friends smiled and exchanged another glance as Olivia let out a sigh. "All right then. If you two will see that when Smiling Joe arrives with the sleighs for the children, they are cloaked and ready, I'll go." She started for the door then turned back. "But mind you, I won't be gone long. I still intend to get to the ship tonight."

BECAUSE IT WAS Christmas Eve, the streetcars weren't running. Rory headed up and down the streets of Charlestown, trying to find transportation to the clinic. Finally, he found a milk wagon and an old plug horse. The milkman said he would take Rory to his destination if he wouldn't mind accompanying the man on his milk route. With a sigh of impatience, Rory climbed onto the bench seat and waited as the milkman flicked the reins over the back of the swayback mare. As the wagon lurched forward, its wheels creaking and sliding on the snowpacked road, Rory settled back, biting his lip. At this speed—and with wheels instead of sleigh runners—it might be dawn before they made it out of Charlestown.

THE HORSE HOOVES clopped along the boulevard, the metal runners of the sleigh singing through the snow. Olivia settled back, deep into thick fur blankets, watching the brightly decorated houses pass by. In the stillness that only a fresh-fallen snow could bring, she closed her eyes. "Give me courage, Lord," she prayed. "I'm scared. What if they refuse to see me?"

It took the sleigh less than an hour to reach the family home on the wide, barren-tree-flanked street. The driver flicked the reins, urging the horse on through the snow. Soon the Endicott-Jones mansion loomed at the end of the street.

At first the house looked dark, and Olivia's heart fell. Perhaps her parents weren't home. But as the horse drew the sleigh closer, she saw in the parlor window a single light. She considered all the Christmas Eves of her childhood when the house had been bright with candles on pine bows. The sight of a single gaslight made her heart ache for the time their home was ablaze with celebration and family love. Now it looked empty and cold. A house without love.

The driver halted the horse. Olivia stepped down from the sleigh and, whispering another prayer for courage, started up the snow-covered walk to the door.

She had just lifted her gloved hand toward the brass knocker when the door opened and her father stood before her. "I saw the sleigh," he said quietly.

"Father?" In the moment of silence before he spoke again, all the harsh words he had said months before—about the Irish, the poor, the disappointment he felt in his only daughter—came rushing into her mind. He had accused her of casting her pearls before swine. He had hurt her deeply with his tight-lipped attitudes. And now she felt every hurtful word in the depths of her heart as if he'd spoken them this minute.

Her eyes filled. When Jesus spoke of forgiveness, He knew the dear price of such an act. Love without condition wasn't easy. Olivia hadn't experienced the extent of such a cost until now. *Father, help me forgive them,* she breathed into the silence of her heart.

"Come in, child," her father said, his voice unnaturally gruff, and he stepped away from the door so she could enter.

As he helped remove her cloak, she asked. "Where's Mother?"

"Upstairs." He hesitated. "There's been an accident."

Her heart caught midbeat. "Mother?"

He nodded toward the stairs. "The doctor's been here twice today—first right after she fell, then again late this afternoon." Olivia hurried to the stairs. As her father marched behind her he continued to explain. "We were—" he hesitated awkwardly, cleared his throat, and started again—"we were . . . ah . . . going to surprise you. We were leaving for your . . . ah, the ah . . . clinic early this morning.

The walk was icy. I should have been paying better attention, helping her across the slickest spots—"

Olivia halted midstep and turned to look into her father's face. "You were coming to the clinic this morning?"

He nodded sheepishly. "Well, you see, it was your mother's idea. To surprise you, to help with the celebration you planned. She wanted to help in the kitchen, said she knew you and your friends wouldn't know how to roast a goose if your life depended on it. We planned to bring James to help me with the tree—"

"You were going to help with the tree?"

He drew in a deep breath. "Yes, Liv." He inclined his head to the room at the top of the stairs. "We have much to say . . . so much, but I think your mother needs to see you first."

Olivia took two steps, then looked back at her father again. "Will she be all right? The fall—was it serious?"

He smiled. "Your mother twisted her ankle. Her foot has swollen to the size of a plump Christmas goose, but the doctor says it's not broken. Says she needs to stay off it for a few weeks."

Olivia picked up her skirts and almost ran to her parents' suite. "Mama?" she cried as hurried to her bedside. "Mama?"

Her mother was sitting up, leaning against a pile of pillows. "I'm so glad you've come, Liv. Oh, how I've missed you." Olivia could see her mother had been crying. "We wanted so to come to your celebration today."

"Father told me."

"We have so much to ask, Liv. But it must start with a single question: Can you forgive us?"

Olivia sat on the side of the bed and reached out for her mother, folding her into her arms and pulling her close. As they embraced, her father stepped nearer and placed his hand on Olivia's shoulder. At his gentle touch, Olivia wept.

C·H·A·P·T·E·R

XI

O LIVIA'S FATHER insisted that he take her to the clinic in the family sleigh. As James flicked the reins and the horse carried them through the snowy night, Olivia couldn't help glancing across the seat and smiling at her father in wonder at all that had transpired. *Thank You, Lord,* she breathed. *Thank You!*

James halted the horse in front of Trinity Settlement House, stepped from the sleigh, and gave Olivia a wide grin as he helped her to the street. A light snow drifted to the ground like fine-sifted powdered sugar as the three pairs of footsteps crunched through the snow.

Her father held his cloak open to shelter Olivia. "Are you sure you're doing the right thing, Liv?" he asked. She lifted a brow, and he grinned as they reached the porch. "Sorry . . . sorry!" He laughed lightly and shrugged. "Your mother and I are still trying to get used to the fact that you're a grown woman and can make your own decisions, good or bad."

Olivia took his arm as they climbed the front steps. "Thank you for caring, but I couldn't be more certain." She paused at the door and looked into his face. "Will you and Mother come to see us someday?"

He looked grieved. "You think you might stay? In Ireland, I mean?"

She touched his arm. "I don't know what the future holds. I only know that my home is with the man I love—if he'll still have me."

With this, her father arched a worried brow skyward. "Still have you?"

She nodded. "There was some confusion. He sent this to me. . . . " She touched the locket that hung over her heart. "It was his grandmother's. But it didn't reach me until just a few days ago. I'm worried about what he might be thinking . . . after all these weeks without word."

"You're leaving without knowing the outcome?" She expected a lecture on the foolishness of such a plan, but instead, her father gave her a tender smile. "Then you'll need our prayers more than ever."

Tears filled her eyes again as she nodded. "Yes, Papa, I will."

Within the hour, the twins were snuggled on either side of Olivia in her father's sleigh. Across from them Maddie lay sleeping in Olivia's father's arms.

A CHRISTMAS TREE blinked and twinkled inside the clinic window, casting its glow across the snowy landscape. Grinning at the sight, Rory told the milkman to halt. The man pulled back on the reins, the wheels skidding in the snow, and directed the old mare to the side of the street.

Rory jumped from the wagon, paid the man, and sprinted to the door, his heart pounding.

He reached to knock then stopped. What if Olivia had changed her mind . . . even without receiving the letter? What if he was too late? What if she thought he had jilted her . . . and had . . .

He stopped his wild imaginings and lifted his hand to knock.

He rapped the brass knocker once, twice . . . three times.

Footsteps approached from the other side and when the door opened, an audible gasp met his ears. "Well, glory be!" Eliza said, her mouth gaping as soon as she'd uttered the words.

"Who is it?" came a call from around the corner. A moment later, Rachel appeared. When she saw him, she seemed too stunned to speak.

Rory tilted his head. Killarney and Carraroe! He'd expected surprise, but Olivia's friends looked as if they'd seen a ghost. "'Tis me. Rory O'Kelly," he said, smiling to bring them ease. "In the flesh, straight off the *Queen Victoria* herself."

"The *Queen Victoria*?" Rachel managed to croak. "The ship that's leaving tomorrow?"

"Aye, the same that docked today," he said. "Tell me, is Olivia in? I'm most anxious to see her. Could ye please fetch her?"

Rachel and Eliza exchanged a glance. "Fetch her?" Rachel whispered. "Oh my."

His heart skipped a beat. "Don't tell me . . . she isn't here? Could it be she's gone to visit her family on Christmas Eve?"

"Well, yes, she did do that," Eliza said, then seemed to come to her senses. "But that was hours ago."

"Hours?" He was growing impatient. "Where is she now then?"

"She's gone to board her ship . . . the same you came in on. First-class accommodations for the children and her—a gift from her mother and father once they found out what she was up to."

"The *Queen Victoria?*" He took a step toward the door. "But it leaves at dawn."

They nodded in unison.

"She's off to England then? Possibly Portsmouth?" He was afraid to dream it was because of him.

"And Ireland." Rachel bit her lip and frowned. He remembered her as being the calmer of Olivia's two friends. She looked anything but calm this minute. "Did you arrive by carriage . . . or sleigh?" she demanded.

"Couldna find a single vehicle for hire—with wheels or runners either one." He laughed, still basking in the wonder that Olivia cared enough to make her way to him. "I came with the milkman whose cart wheels slipped all over the streets. Not an event I'd want to re—" He halted, noticing the merry glance they exchanged.

"Seems you'll have to." Eliza grabbed her cloak from a peg near the door. "That is, if we can catch him."

Rachel snatched her cape from a neighboring peg, and a moment later the three ran down the clinic steps, slipping and sliding in the snow, the two young women still laughing merrily.

Eliza grabbed his hand and pulled him along, with Rachel trailing a few steps behind. Toward the end of the block, they spotted the milk cart through the lightly falling snow.

"Ho there, kind sir!" Eliza shouted, still yards away from the cart. The milkman turned, obviously puzzled, and she gave him another merry shout as they drew nearer. "Halt! I say, halt!"

"We need to hire your cart again," Rachel called, "only this time we'll pay you to let our friend here borrow it for the night."

Rory stepped forward to explain. "Aye, kind sir, if ye would be so kind. 'Tis a matter of love and life and all things joyous—or not!—this snowy Christmas Eve."

The man gave him a toothless grin. "M'pleasure," he said, stepping down. "Only where shall I go this cold night? I'm too far from home. Perhaps you'll drop me by—"

"Not enough time," Eliza said then paused, looking worried. "Unless loved ones wait for your return."

He shook his head. "No one awaits me, lady. Not a one."

"Then it's a bit of a Christmas miracle that you've ended up here!" she exclaimed.

Rachel took one of the old man's arms, Eliza the other. "We've just had a wondrous feast . . . " Rachel said. "More heavenly than you can imagine. Roast goose and plum pudding and squash pie. Potatoes piled fluffy and high and smothered with gravy. Gingerbread, spicy sweet and covered with clotted cream. Come with us and we'll fix you a plate—there's plenty. You can warm yourself by our fire."

"And await my return," Rory added, tipping his head. "I promise."

He looked doubtful. "But my customers . . . "

"Aye, kind sir," Rory shouted with a laugh as he climbed aboard, his heart lighter than it had been in months. "If I triumph in my quest to win a certain young lass's heart tonight—I'll help ye deliver the rest of yer milk bottles meself!" He flicked the reins and urged the horse to move. "'Twill take another Christmas miracle to get you to move faster than a snail, old sawbones," he muttered to the horse.

The mare moved her big head to one side so she could stare at Rory with her round, bloodshot eyes. Snow fell around them both.

"Giddap," Rory said, embarrassed at the pleading in

his voice. He slapped the reins again, which caused the beast to flick one ear, the only movement in a body that seemed to have suddenly turned into a sad, swaybacked, granite statue. "Please," Rory said, feeling desperate. "Please giddap. I'll find ye a carrot, maybe even a lump of sugar before the night's through—if ye'll just put one foot in front of the other. Just move!" He flicked the reins again. Still the horse refused to move.

He set the reins to one side, meaning to step from the vehicle and lead the horse himself. But the minute the reins were loose, the beast took a step forward, then another. And Killarney and Carraroe! If the gladsome creature didn't start moving faster than Rory thought possible.

With a grin, he folded his arms and leaned his back against the bench seat, letting the beast take her lead. The muffled clop of hooves on the snowy Boston streets was better than any music Rory could have imagined. "All right, you win," he said with a smile so as not to upset her again. "But it'll be yer hide and hooves heading for the glue factory if my love's ship sails before we reach the harbor."

⚜

OLIVIA WAS GRATEFUL for her father's help when they reached the ship. Already, tight knots of early passengers, their loved ones seeing them off, and the crew had gathered on the cold, snowy dock. The snow had stopped falling, and pinpoints of bright starlight shone between the clearing clouds.

All three children were asleep. Her father carried Maddie, and James carried the sleeping twins, one in each arm, as Olivia checked with the purser, who confirmed the vicar's request for early boarding.

As soon as the children were settled in their bunks, her

father surveyed the room, giving Olivia some last-minute advice about what to do in case the children got seasick, how to deal with the crew and room staff, and how to behave as an upper-class American in a foreign land.

Rather than taking offense, Olivia was touched by his concern with such details. "I'll be fine, Papa. Truly."

He nodded slowly. "I know you will, child." There was new pride in his eyes. "You're doing a brave thing. I just hope this man's deserving."

She rested her hand lightly on his arm. "He is. Believe me, he is."

After a brief embrace, he was gone, and Olivia was left alone with the sleeping children.

Somewhere in the distance, the clock struck twelve. Olivia smiled to herself and, after rummaging through her tapestry satchel, pulled out her Bible and sat at a small reading table in the corner of the small cabin. She turned up the lamp and opened the well-worn pages to St. Matthew's account of the Christmas story.

But before she began to read, a little voice from across the room chirped, "Is it Christmas Day yet?" It was Katie, who sounded wide awake.

"Almost, sweetheart. But try to go to sleep. We sail at dawn, and I want you to be rested."

"I wanna talk 'bout the camels," Keara said, sitting up and rubbing her eyes. "And the big star."

The little girls padded across the floor and snuggled onto Olivia's lap. "Tell us again 'bout 'em comin' to see Baby Jesus," Keara said.

"How they followed the star," Katie added.

"And followed God's leading," Olivia said, holding the little ones close. "No matter what happened along the way, they followed the love for the Child that God had placed in their hearts."

Katie thumped her chest above her heart. "God put the love here?"

Olivia nodded. "Right there."

"And mine too?" Keara wanted to know.

"Yours too," Olivia said, giving her another squeeze. "He puts love in our hearts—for His Son Jesus and for each other."

The twins leaned against her in sleepy contemplation. Then Keara leaned forward. "Did God put love for Mr. O'Kelly in your heart?"

Olivia smiled. "I believe He did." She laughed lightly as she considered it. "Yes, I know He did."

"Me too," Keara said, settling back with a sigh. "God put Mr. O'Kelly in my heart too."

"Uh-uh, silly," Katie said. "He can't fit. He's too big."

Olivia smiled into their upturned faces. "It's about love," she said. "When God places it in your heart—it will fit just right."

"What if we can't find Mr. O'Kelly?" Keara asked. "What if—"

Katie sat forward, her little brow puckered in thought. "Maybe we need a star."

"But it's snowing," Keara said, looking worried.

"Actually, I saw some stars peeking out from behind the clouds as we boarded," Olivia said. "Ship captains do follow stars. That's how they navigate across the big ocean."

"I wanna see," Katie said. "We'll be followin' stars just like the camels."

"The wise kings," Keara corrected.

It would be cold on the deck, and the girls should be fast asleep in their warm, snug beds. But it was Christmas. Gazing at God's handiwork displayed in the night heavens would be a sight they would remember forever. Olivia nodded her assent, bundled the girls in their warmest clothes, then rang for a staff nursemaid to watch over Maddie as she slept.

With a twin holding each hand, Olivia stepped onto

the deck, weaving around coiled ropes, stacked life rafts, and crew members making preparations to sail.

"There!" Katie exclaimed with awe. "Up there in the sky! Look!"

"Oooh," Keara sighed.

The clouds had cleared, and a spangle of twinkling lights lit the midnight sky. Olivia considered the kings who had followed the star so long ago. She considered the direction they chose—with nothing that charts or science could explain—only a deep heart's desire to find the Son of God.

"Guide us on our journey," she whispered heavenward. "Lead us in the way we should go." Though she had spoken in a whisper, the twins were listening intently as they clung to her hands.

"And lead us home to Mr. O'Kelly," Keara said, her eyes scrunched closed.

"And make him fit in our hearts forever and ever," Katie added with equal fervor.

RORY ARRIVED at the dock just past midnight. The *Queen Victoria* rose before him, shadowy and powerful against the star-spangled sky. With dismay, he realized it was unlikely he would be allowed to board the ship. Here he was, poor Irish, looking for a little family of passengers in first class. He whispered a silent prayer that his Irish charm would sway the crew in charge of the gangway.

"Sorry, sir," said the first seaman he encountered. The big man stood with folded arms in front of the rope barrier at the gangway.

"You gotta have a ticket," said another seaman standing nearby.

"'Tis of the most importance ever," Rory said. "You see, the woman I love and the children she's taken in—

they're all on board, readying to sail to Ireland—where they think I am. Only I am here—as ye can well see."

The first seaman frowned and shrugged. "That's a new one."

The second seaman laughed. "Tuggin' at my heart-strings, it is."

"'Tis the honest truth I'm tellin'—check the manifest if ye don't believe me."

A first mate, older and more dignified in carriage than the two seamen, strode across the dock, planted himself in front of Rory, and studied his face. "What's the trouble here?"

Rory quickly explained again then added, "Would it be allowed if one of you accompany me?"

The first mate finally nodded slowly. "I'll check the manifest to see if the names are there and the cabin number. You wait here."

Heart racing in anticipation, Rory stayed at the deck-side end of the gangway, only a rope barrier keeping him from the one he loved.

It was then he heard their voices carrying down to where he stood, clear as bells in the wintry Christmas night, and ringing of love and joy. The lower, soft voice that he knew from his memory and his dreams, the higher-pitched Irish lilts of two children.

With a yelp, he leapt over the rope barrier and raced toward the ship.

<hr />

KATIE STARED at the dock, a look of silent wonder on her face.

"What is it, honey?" Olivia looked toward where the little girl was pointing.

Keara spoke in Gaelic, causing Olivia to start. It had been weeks since the twins had used their native language.

Katie hopped up and down, calling out in her own lyrical tongue. Olivia started to comment about the glory of hearing Gaelic again when she heard an answering call in the same language.

She turned toward the sound, and her heart caught as she saw a figure making his way toward them.

With a squeal, the twins ran toward Rory. He scooped them into his arms with a shout of joy. Holding them in a tight embrace, he made his way to where Olivia stood rooted to the deck.

"Look to me now," he said to Olivia softly in Gaelic.

The children turned to watch her, wide-eyed and silent, each with one arm wrapped tightly around Rory's neck.

He took a step closer to Olivia, looking deep into her eyes. "I'll be caring for ye now, always and forever."

She had never heard anything more beautiful than this sound, this moment.

"And this is the most important of all," he said. "'Tis something that should be said every day . . . till the end of our lives."

"Aye," she whispered, "I remember."

"'Tis ye I love."

BROWN SUGAR COOKIES
to Warm the Heart

1½ cups sifted flour
½ tsp. salt
2 tsp. baking powder
4 eggs
1 package (16 oz.) brown sugar
1½ tsp. vanilla
1 cup walnuts, chopped
1 cup coconut (optional)

Sift together flour, salt, and baking powder; set aside. Beat eggs until creamy. Stir in brown sugar and continue beating until smooth. Pour into saucepan and cook over boiling water in double boiler (with lid on) for 3 minutes. (I have also cooked the egg and brown sugar mixture in a glass bowl in the microwave for 3 minutes.)

Immediately stir in flour mixture. When mixture is smooth, add vanilla, nuts, and coconut (if using). Pour into buttered 9" x 13" baking dish and bake 30–35 minutes at 350°. Let cool a few minutes before cutting into squares.

Beloved friend,

Memories of home always fill my heart at Christmas-time: helping my mother stir together my favorite cookies while the scent of fresh-baked apple pies fills the kitchen; trudging on snowshoes into the forest with my brother to cut down the perfect Christmas tree; traveling to my grandparents' home, where I giggled with my cousins and, before dinner, listened to my grandfather pray long and earnestly for each of us by name . . . while we little ones peeked through our fingers, fearing the turkey would get cold.

After I had a family of my own, I wanted my children's lives to be filled with their own Christmas memories, at home and at their grandparents', so they would always remember that place in their hearts called *home*. Now, all these years later, my daughters are out of the nest. But their memories are tucked deep inside, and the cycle of homecoming begins anew.

This Christmas I invite you to curl up with a cup of tea and a cookie or two (perhaps made from my mother's recipe), pull out a favorite photo album, and celebrate your memories. Let your thoughts linger on those you have cherished through the years.

Gather them into your heart—for as Grandm'am told Rory, "Home is that place in yer heart, that place that God holds fast." And by phone, by e-mail, by letter—or in person—tell that one you treasure, "You're in my heart today. I love you."

Blessings,

Diane Noble

Diane Noble is the award-winning author of twenty-one titles, including novels, novellas, devotionals, and nonfiction books for women. Her works, ranging from historical fiction to romantic suspense, have won numerous honors and received critical acclaim. A popular speaker and writing teacher, Diane makes her home with her husband, Tom, in Southern California.

Diane's previous novels include *Heart of Glass, When the Far Hills Bloom, The Blossom and the Nettle, At Play in the Promised Land, The Veil, Tangled Vines,* and *Distant Bells.* She has also published two nonfiction books, *Letters from God for Women* and *It's Time! When Your Children Have Grown, Explore Your Dreams and Discover Your Gifts.* As Amanda MacLean, she has written the historical romance novels *Westward, Stonehaven, Everlasting, Promise Me the Dawn,* and *Kingdom Come.*

Diane invites you to visit her Web site at www.dianenoble.com where you can catch up on the latest about her new releases, works in progress, and photo album of Diane and Tom's research travels. She also welcomes letters written to her at P.O. Box 3017, Idyllwild, CA 92549 or through her Web site.

THE
Heart
OF A STRANGER

I dedicate this novella with loving gratitude to my

LORD AND SAVIOR, JESUS CHRIST,
AND TO MY ABBA FATHER,

*whose arms opened wide to receive this prodigal
daughter home. Without Him, I would be nothing.*

A·C·K·N·O·W·L·E·D·G·M·E·N·T·S

MANY THANKS to my critique partners, who helped me at a moment's notice and went above and beyond the call of duty: namely, Tracey, Tamela, Jill, Molly, Paige, and a special thanks to my mom, too. Also a big thanks to Kathy O. for her helpful advice and to Anne G. for her faith in me. I couldn't have done it without any of you.

Thou shalt not oppress a stranger: for ye know the
heart of a stranger, seeing ye were strangers
in the land of Egypt.

Exodus 23:9

I

NEW MEXICO TERRITORY
1 8 8 9

SUSANNAH PRUITT never thought her end would come while standing in the middle of barren wilderness during a fierce dust storm.

Frustrated, she watched the driver scratch his head of thinning hair and try to figure out a way to replace the escaped wheel of the stagecoach. It was a wonder they'd even survived the accident with only the few cuts and bruises they acquired. Although Susannah would have preferred a quick death to the one that in all likelihood loomed before them.

"Susannah." Leslie tugged her sleeve. "I think I hear a rider coming! Mercy, what if it's an Indian come to scalp us?"

"They've been on reservations for years now," Susannah replied, raising her voice over the wind. "Since long before I went to Boston." She felt a bit perturbed by her Northern companion's dramatics. Honestly. Sometimes her older cousin didn't display an ounce of courage or common sense.

Using her flimsy lace-edged handkerchief, Susannah covered her mouth and nose with one hand. The other she clamped to the back of her bonnet. She moved away from the barrier of the stagecoach to investigate, turning full into the storm's fury.

Stinging particles lashed at exposed parts of her body. Blinded by the sudden onslaught, she squinted, eyes watering. She bent into the wind, trying to maintain balance by putting a hand to the stagecoach's rear wheel. Her bonnet flew backward—the ribbons tied under her chin the only thing keeping it from blowing away. For the first time she wished for a pair of spectacles, such as those her cousin wore. Though judging from the way Leslie continually dabbed at her eyes with her handkerchief, they didn't keep out all the dirt.

Leslie was right. A lone rider was headed their way. From this distance it was difficult to see much except a dark shape outlined against the rose orb of the sun beyond horse and rider. Yet as broad as the shoulders were, it had to be a man.

Heart slamming against her ribs, Susannah ducked back behind the stagecoach. She hoped he wasn't an outlaw come to rob them! Her thoughts went to the roll of bills tucked away in her valise and the gold locket that had been her mother's. She grabbed the large oval resting against her bosom and dropped it into the neck of her blouse, under her chemise and out of sight. Oh, if only she had her pa's old six-shooter!

Lifting her lips in a tight little smile, Susannah could well imagine the horrified look Leslie would give if she could read her mind. While in Boston, Aunt Agatha and Cousin Leslie had done their utmost to train Susannah in the arts of being a genteel lady, but too often for their liking, her Western roots popped to the surface. "Her fighting spirit," her father used to call it. He had often said with a chuckle, when her mother was exasperated by yet another of Susannah's antics and threatened to send their daughter back East, "You can take the girl out of the wild, Martha, but you can't take the wild out of the girl."

At the memory, the smile faded, and Susannah scanned the area for a weapon. Spotting a jagged rock about the size of her two fists put together, she wiggled it from the dirt and hid it behind her skirts.

No one would get the best of Susannah Rose Pruitt! Not while she could draw breath. Just let him dare try. . . .

·᳅᳅·

JUSTIN ROSSITER bent his head low, the wind pummeling his back. The gale was unusually strong for this time of year, kicking up dry earth from a summer with little rain. But at least this squall was relatively mild compared to the dust storms that came whipping through the area in springtime.

Holding one hand over his hat, he squinted through clouds of dust whirling through an orange red sky. He was right. Up ahead a lopsided stagecoach sat alone on the plain, like a child's discarded toy. As he drew close, he noticed the front wheel missing. Amazingly enough, the horses were still harnessed to the conveyance, but Justin saw no sign of humanity.

Wondering if he should have backtracked or just continued west, he hesitated and pulled on the reins. The old fear connected with being on the lam crowded his thoughts, before he reminded himself that those days were long gone. Whoever was up there—if there was anyone up there—might need help.

Lightly jabbing his sorrel mare's sides with his spurs, Justin leaned forward in the saddle, as much from curiosity as from the relentless wind blowing at his back. He guided the horse around the rear of the stagecoach and stopped in surprise.

A young woman defiantly stared up at him, as though she'd been expecting him all along. Her hands were hidden behind her. Underneath all the dirt streaked across her pale features and with the tangles of midnight dark curls blown loose around her face, it was hard to tell just what she looked like. Behind her, a thirtyish woman wearing spectacles cowered against the stagecoach door. Her sharp features were thin and much cleaner than those of her younger companion's. A man with salt-and-pepper hair and a long, drooping mustache knelt on the ground at the front of the coach, fingering a cracked hub. He looked up at Justin's arrival, relief, then wariness narrowing his deep-set eyes.

"Evenin'." Justin dismounted slowly, so as not to cause alarm. The sudden respite from the storm in the shelter of the stagecoach took him by surprise, but he kept his bandana tied around his mouth and nose. "You folks need help?"

"We had an accident." The young woman acted as spokesperson for the trio, and Justin again focused on her. She eyed him with suspicion. "We hit a rock, and the wheel went flying off."

Justin glanced at the damage doubtfully. "Don't know much about fixing stages, but I do have some beef jerky and a canteen of water you folks are welcome to share."

"Water?" The young woman licked dust-coated, cracked lips, a yearning glint filling her brown eyes. She swept the back of one hand against a damp lock of hair plastered to her forehead. For the first time Justin saw the lump and cut in its middle. A purple bruise ringed the caked blood.

"Are you all right, ma'am?" he asked. Moving closer,

he offered her his canteen. "Your head, I mean. It looks a mite painful." At least the cut had stopped bleeding, he noted with relief.

She hesitated a short few seconds then whipped her other hand out and grabbed the canteen. A muffled thud sounded from behind her. She pretended not to notice and took several long swallows of water, ignoring the shocked exclamation from the other woman.

Lowering the canteen from her mouth, the girl shot a sheepish look his way. "Well, mister, I've certainly felt a whole lot better. That's for sure." A dimple twinkled in her cheek as she twisted her mouth into a facsimile of a smile.

Justin felt an answering grin tilt his lips. He admired spunk, and this mite of a girl had her fair share.

He watched her pass the canteen to the other woman, who carefully wiped the opening with a spotless white handkerchief before taking a dainty sip, grimacing all the while. The driver was the last to take the canteen. He lifted it a few inches, stopped, glanced at both women, then gave a swift shake of his head and handed it back to Justin.

"Where were you ladies headed?" Justin's gaze sailed back to the girl. At least the wariness had left her eyes, and she no longer regarded him as if he were a grizzly ready to attack.

"A small town called Landis," she said in a husky voice. "We took the train all the way from Boston, then hired this stagecoach to take us the rest of the way."

"Landis. You mean near the Pecos, on a ways down from the Goodnight-Loving Trail? In the New Mexico territory?"

"Where else?"

A pinprick of alarm raised the hairs on the back of his neck, but Justin quickly dismissed her offhand words as queer coincidence. He pulled the brim of his dusty hat low over his forehead. "Well, if you don't mind the company, I'd be right honored to help—or give what help I can under the circumstances. I'm traveling through Landis myself."

His offer produced another shocked exclamation from the older woman. Justin glanced at the stagecoach driver, who'd returned his attention to the broken hub. His scrawny build looked like the wind might break him in two as easily as snapping a twig in half. Justin wondered if he even knew how to handle a gun.

"It's dangerous for two ladies to travel alone in these parts," Justin added, directing his words to the younger woman, who seemed to be the only clear thinker of the bunch. She was the only one who'd spoken, anyway.

A flicker of some unnamed emotion lit her eyes before she slowly nodded. "We appreciate the offer, mister. And we gladly accept."

"Oh, mercy," her companion murmured.

Justin nodded and moved toward the stagecoach driver to see how he could help. Even if the girl had refused him, he wouldn't have left these people stranded in this remote wilderness. From what he remembered, the nearest town was a half day's ride or more. Still, Justin was pleased that the young lady seemed to favor his company.

"What seems to be the problem?" He hunkered down beside the driver.

"Cracked clean off." The man looked up. "Cain't understand it. Stage was in good shape when we left the station. Still, I reckon it'd be easier to tie down a bobcat with a piece of string than it would be to fix this here wheel."

Justin nodded. "Shall we tell the ladies?"

"Weell now, if you don't mind, I'd be much obliged if you'd be the one to take care o' that."

Susannah stood in the circle of four, trying not to let her gaze wander to the stranger as they discussed their options. She hadn't been able to see much due to the red bandana that still covered the lower portion of his face, though the wind had died down a short time ago. Yet what she'd seen, she liked.

His wheat-colored hair grew several inches past the collar of his buckskin jacket and blue denim shirt, which was a shade darker than his eyes. A dusty brown cowboy hat was hooked low over his forehead. She could see the angles of his cheekbones above the bandana, since the cloth had slipped to the end of his long, straight nose. Tall and lean, he looked strong, the perfect escort to take them across the desolate plains and into Landis. Home. Just in time for Christmas, a little more than four weeks away.

"Then it's all set." His low voice sent tingles dancing up Susannah's spine. "We'll make camp here tonight, since there's not much daylight left. And tomorrow we'll ride."

"Without a sidesaddle?" Leslie looked indignant. "That's preposterous!"

"I'm sorry, ma'am. I'm afraid you'll have to make do with my saddle." His sky blue gaze roamed Susannah's way, and her heart tripped. "And you can ride behind her. You're small and the saddle seems wide enough."

Susannah shook her head. "The weight would be too much for your mare, and we still have quite a distance to go. I'll ride one of the stage horses."

"Bareback?" Leslie's gloved hand flew to her mouth. "You can't do that!"

"And why not? I've ridden that way before, when I was younger. Besides, this is an extraordinary circumstance. Wouldn't you agree?" Susannah looked at the stranger, her brows lifted.

He returned her stare, his eyes soft with something close to surprised admiration. Suddenly embarrassed, she averted her gaze.

"Your companion's right, miss," the stagecoach driver answered. "Them horses ain't broke for ridin'. Likely if you tried, you'd get thrown a long ways, with your head split wide open—easy as a melon."

"Mercy," Leslie murmured, her eyes going large behind the spectacles.

The stranger cleared his throat, and Susannah looked his way again. He glanced at each one of them in turn. "There won't be any riding of any stage horses. This isn't the time or place to try and break them in. The ladies can take turns with Star—my mare. One can ride, the other can walk, and they can switch whenever the need arises."

Somehow he'd taken charge of their motley group, but Susannah didn't mind in the least. Judging from the relieved reaction of the driver, neither did he. This young man, who'd come riding up out of nowhere, exuded a strength and confidence that reassured. Susannah knew they'd be safe in his care.

In one fluid motion he mounted his horse and grabbed his shotgun from the saddle. "I best go try and find some dinner before it gets dark," he explained before clicking his tongue as an order for his horse to proceed.

Susannah watched him ride away, the setting sun casting rose tints on his tall, erect form. A sharp jab in her ribs made her draw her breath sharply. She turned to face a frowning Leslie, who'd come up beside her.

"Honestly, Susannah. Do stop gawking at the man, and try to behave like a lady," Leslie scolded under her breath. "And the way you guzzled from that canteen earlier was horrendous. No lady slurps when she drinks her water. If Mother had seen you, after all we've tried to teach you, she would have had a conniption. . . ."

"Yes, Leslie." Susannah turned a deaf ear to yet another of her cousin's tiresome reprimands and moved to fetch her shawl.

⚜

SOON AFTER DARKNESS blanketed the land, Justin approached the disabled stagecoach, relieved to see the welcome glow of a campfire. Silently, he commended the driver for making the blaze and abandoning further efforts to fix the broken wheel. The air was rapidly cooling and the heat would be welcome. At least he showed some sense.

Justin watched the young woman come into view as she turned the corner of the coach. As before, her bonnet dangled from its tied ribbons to the middle of her back, exposing her mass of dark hair. Much of it hung loose, though some curls had managed to stay anchored to the top of her head. Arms full of sagebrush, she moved toward the flames and tossed the dry vegetation onto the fire. It blazed upward with renewed fury, coming dangerously close to her skirts. Justin increased his horse's pace.

"Looks fine," he said when he'd drawn near enough to be heard. Useless pieces of the stagecoach burned in the flames. "I imagine that's all the fuel it'll need, though." He smiled at her, then dismounted and held out a dead jackrabbit. "It's not much, but I reckon it'll tide us over 'til morning."

Consternation crossed her features, but she nodded and took the offering by the ears. Staring at it, she bit her lower lip as though uncertain.

Sudden realization hit Justin, and he removed the rabbit from her grasp. "What say I take care of cooking this? You look plumb tuckered out."

Relief flashed in her eyes as they flicked back to his. "Thank you."

"My pleasure." He continued to stare. As close to her

The Heart of a Stranger | 163

as he stood, he noted that the firelight caused her eyes to glow an unusual pale brown—the color of gingersnaps. And as velvety soft as a doe's coat, with a fringe of coal black lashes surrounding them. He'd once known someone with eyes like that, and her hair had been just as shiny and dark.

"Guess I better see to our meal," he said hoarsely, turning away.

As he skinned the rabbit, he wondered how it was that she didn't know how to cook. He'd thought all girls possessed that knowledge by the time they started wearing long skirts. Then again, she was from Boston, and Justin had heard that the ladies in the East were refined, with maids in their homes taking care of the work. Seemed like such a waste—them "refined" women frittering their lives away with nothing better to do.

Justin found a sharp stick to pierce the meat and returned to the campfire. He sank to the ground, stretched his arm across one upraised knee, and held the stick with the rabbit over the flames. His gaze returned to the girl, and he watched her for some time.

She sat primly beside her female companion, who suddenly turned and whispered something to her. After a moment, the young woman turned her head his way. Again their gazes locked. This time she broke the connection, a flush reddening her cheeks beneath the streaks of dirt.

Pulling his hat low over his forehead, Justin stared at the rabbit beginning to brown. What was wrong with him? He had entirely too much looming in his uncertain future to sit here and gape at a woman.

He sucked in his upper lip, wondering what his pa would do once he discovered the prodigal had returned. Would there be any kind of welcome? Or would Pa cast him out, as Justin deserved? He knew he had a lot of nerve returning to Landis after all he'd done. But deep down, Justin knew Landis was where he must go. He had unfinished business there.

⚜

SUSANNAH ATE the last bite of her cooked rabbit, barely resisting the urge to lick her fingers afterward. She'd been famished and never realized rabbit roasted over a simple campfire could smell or taste so good. It was easily ten times better than the countless ways her aunt's fancy French chef had prepared rabbit in Boston.

As she'd done throughout the meal, when she knew he wasn't looking, Susannah glanced at the stranger. The bandana now circled his neck, but it was too dark to see much of his face. In the light of the dying fire she could just make out the outline of a strong jaw and the hollows beneath his cheekbones.

"I'll return shortly," Leslie murmured for Susannah's ears alone.

I wonder where she plans to find an outhouse in this wilderness, Susannah thought wryly. Seeing apprehension cloud her cousin's features, she softened. "Would you like me to go with you?"

"Certainly not!" Leslie's color rose, her expression mortified. "Actually, I'd rather you stay by the fire and make certain *they* remain here while I'm gone." She sent a brief nod in the direction of the two men sitting across from them.

"All right," Susannah agreed, hesitant. "If you're sure." She trusted their escorts—apparently far more than Leslie did—and wasn't certain her cousin should wander off alone, especially since she was such a greenhorn to the West. However, Susannah was fourteen years Leslie's junior, and she knew Leslie wouldn't appreciate any suggestions from her young cousin, no matter how prudent.

Once Leslie moved away, Susannah's gaze again

The Heart of a Stranger | 165

zeroed in on the stranger. This time she was shocked to find him watching her. Suddenly nervous, she swiped the back of her hand across her forehead, wincing as she made contact with the bruised lump.

He frowned, grabbed his canteen, and stood to his feet. Her heart jumped when he closed the distance between them and lowered himself next to her. The pulse in the hollow of her throat pounded out a rapid beat, and she stared into the low fire, forcing herself to breathe. The crackle of the flames grew almost deafening as the seconds crawled by.

From her peripheral vision, she watched him untie the bandana from around his neck and tip the canteen over a portion of the cloth. Curious, she turned her head his way.

He hesitated then offered a semi-embarrassed smile. "That cut needs cleaned. You don't want it to get septic."

The fire's glow softly illuminated his face underneath the hat, and she could only stare as she took her first good look at their rescuer. His defined features held a fierce yet oddly gentle beauty, like that of a warrior angel. His pale blue irises were rimmed with a thin circle of darker blue. She drew her brows together in confusion. Those eyes . . .

"We shouldn't waste the water." She forced the hoarse words past numb lips.

"Don't worry about that. There's a creek not far from here. We'll stop by it in the morning."

He lifted the wet bandana to her forehead and dabbed at the cut. She couldn't prevent a painful hiss from escaping. A V appeared between his golden brown brows.

"Sorry," he said. "I'll try to be more gentle."

She nodded, staring at the tan column of his neck, the wavy ends of his light hair just covering his shoulders— anywhere but at his face.

"Would you think me too forward if I asked your

name?" His voice came low, soothing, as if trying to veer her thoughts from the stinging pain.

"No, of course not. It's Susannah."

The pats of the cloth came slower then stopped altogether. But he didn't move away.

Moments later she felt the wetness firmly swipe along one cheek, and she looked up in surprise. His eyes were intense, strangely uneasy. He stared at each of her features in turn as he slid the moist bandana across the other cheek, her jaw, her chin, her nose—his actions coming faster as he wiped away the caked dirt covering her features.

The bandana fell to the ground between them. With shaky hands, he smoothed back her thick, tangled hair, revealing every inch of her heart-shaped face to his close scrutiny.

Stunned speechless, Susannah remained immobile, terrified of what was coming, yet oddly expectant too. But he didn't kiss her, as she'd thought he might.

Eyes going wide, he drew in a soft whistling breath through his teeth and jerked his hands away from her face as though her skin had scorched him.

She blinked in confusion.

Before either of them could say a word, a horrified scream ripped through the night.

II

"Leslie!" Susannah exclaimed, eyes widening.

Justin shot to his feet at the same time she did. He grabbed his Colt .45 from its holster and hurried in the direction of the scream. "Stay by the fire," he tersely ordered over his shoulder when he heard the rustle of skirts and crunch of her footsteps behind him.

"I'm not waiting there alone."

"The driver will stay with you."

"No, he won't. He's gone."

Justin ceased his rapid gait and spun around. Alarmed, he scanned the camp. She was right. The driver was nowhere. He must have slipped off when Justin had been so absorbed with Susannah. "Listen, Susie, I'm not sure what I'll find. You'd best stay by the fire where it's safe."

Surprise lit her eyes at the slip of his informal use of her name, but she didn't comment except to shake her head. "Who's to say that I won't be in danger there? I don't have a weapon to defend myself, except for that silly old rock."

"Rock?"

She blushed but didn't comment.

Frustrated, Justin clamped his teeth together, suddenly remembering just how stubborn she could be. "All right then. Stay close behind me, and don't make a sound."

Together they moved around the rear of the stage-coach. Justin could sense her warmth at his back. Her breath came soft but rapid to his ears, and she practically melded herself to him, leaving little space between. When she stumbled and her hands flew to his shoulders, he couldn't help but feel the shiver of pleasure her touch brought. Crouching, trying to ignore the woman behind him, he stared into the thick darkness, waiting for his eyes to adjust. He stopped and put his hand back to prevent her from treading on his heels and knocking him over.

In the distance he could see the dim silhouette of a couple locked in embrace. Shock propelled him upright and he holstered his gun. His boots pounded the earth as he raced toward them. Clamping his hands on the stage-coach driver's bony shoulders, he wrested the vile man away from Susannah's companion, throwing him to the ground. Justin stooped to grab a handful of the man's checkered shirt and pulled back his fist, ready to strike.

"Oh, mercy me!" the lady cried. "Don't harm him!"

Her emphatic words effectively stilled his actions. Baffled, Justin swung his head her way. He couldn't see her blush in the dark, but could tell that she'd raised her hands to her cheeks in embarrassment.

"Leslie," Susannah said, out of breath as she hurried toward them. "What happened?"

"Some horrid creature skittered across my boot, and I screamed," the woman said, her tone remorseful. "It's too dark to tell what it was, but I think it might have been a lizard! Mr. Hadley came to my rescue, and I'm afraid, in my relief, I—I threw myself into his arms." The admission came low.

"Really?" Amusement tinged the disbelief in Susannah's voice. "How unusual."

The woman straightened and adjusted the bodice of her traveling outfit. "Yes, precisely. This day has been filled with abnormalities of every sort. Now, if you will excuse me, I wish to return to the campsite where it's safe." She glanced around the dark plains. "Reasonably safe, that is."

Once she bustled away, Justin released his hold on the stagecoach driver's shirt. He awkwardly rose to his feet and held out the same hand to help Mr. Hadley up from the ground. The middle-aged man took it but brushed Justin's stilted apology aside with a shake of his head.

"No need for that, son," he said, his tone cordial. "Had I been in your boots, I likely woulda done the same." His gaze went to Susannah, who hadn't stopped looking at Justin; then he again glanced Justin's way. "Weeell," he said, fixing his hat upon his head, "at least the weather is clear and not too awful cold. Ought to be right nice to sleep under them stars. Night, folks."

"Night." Justin could feel Susannah eyeing him, but he didn't look at her. Now that he knew who she was, it would be best for him to hightail it out of here as fast as possible. Still, he couldn't leave an old man and two helpless women alone on the plains to fend for themselves.

The outlandish thought of Susie Pruitt being helpless almost made Justin smile. She might have spunk, but when it came to wilderness living of this sort, he knew she was unprepared. Especially if she'd been living in Boston for any length of time. Why had her ma sent her to Boston, of all places?

"Mister?" she said, her voice curious.

Justin stiffened. He turned in her direction, thankful for the moon behind him. His face was in shadows while her lovely features, now clear of dirt, were highlighted in the pale glow.

How had he not recognized her when he'd first come upon the stagecoach? True, she'd grown up quite a bit. Six years was a long time, and the memory of her face had faded in his mind with the passage of years. Yet considering all they'd shared, he would have thought he would have known his Susie at a glance. Obviously, she hadn't recognized him either, and Justin planned to keep it that way.

"Ma'am?" he asked, his voice low.

She tilted her head curiously. "I still don't know your name. I can't go on calling you 'mister' forever."

"Sure you can. I don't mind."

She crossed her arms over her chest and gave a protesting little sound, clucking her tongue against the roof of her mouth then letting out an exasperated breath as she'd done when they were kids. "That's hardly a way to address a person," she argued. "Especially someone as considerate and helpful as you've been to us. At least tell me your surname so I may address you properly."

Justin soberly eyed her. "Just call me Friend, if you'd rather do that." He moved away, thinking of the incongruity of such a name. Had Susie realized who spoke with her, she would have had a more appropriate label for him, he was certain. Such as Enemy or Traitor or Fiend.

Sighing, he pulled the brim of his hat lower over his brow. "Best come along back to the campsite," he tossed over his shoulder. "Besides lizards, there are plenty of critters that like to run wild over these plains at night. Critters like coyotes and snakes, just to name a couple."

"Snakes?" she echoed in a weak voice. He heard her quick footsteps catch up to his. "You're right. We have a busy morning ahead and should get a good night's sleep."

At the decisive words she used to mask her dread of the reptiles, Justin couldn't help but throw her a sideways grin. "Yes, ma'am. That we should." Yet Justin had a feeling that the night ahead would provide little sleep for his weary soul and restless mind.

·⚶·

THE SHARP REPORT of a gunshot startled Susannah awake. She sat bolt upright from her cramped position on the stagecoach seat. Her gaze went to Leslie, who lay curled on the opposite bench. She'd often found it strange that her nervous cousin could sleep through any type of disturbance. Susannah pushed aside the stiff black curtain that had been rolled down over the stagecoach window.

Through the narrow opening she could see the sky had lightened to a deep periwinkle blue. There appeared to be no sign of trouble in the area. Susannah reasoned that the stranger must have found them breakfast. Face going warm at the thought of him, she smoothed back her tousled curls, glad the uncomfortable pins were gone. However, she'd forgotten to braid her hair last night, and it was a hopeless mass of tangles. Retrieving a comb from her reticule, she tried to tame her wild locks, but finally gave the feat up as impossible and resolved to go without piling her hair in its customary pins. Leslie would be horrified, but in such conditions there was little else to do.

Deciding to keep on the woolen dress she'd pulled over her traveling suit for warmth, Susannah emerged from the stagecoach and looked toward the low campfire where the men had slept. Both were gone, and she noticed the horses had also disappeared. She hurried to the other side of the stagecoach to check there.

"Mornin', ma'am," Mr. Hadley said as he bent, sharpening a stick with his pocketknife.

"Where are the horses?" Her words came out as puffs of fog in the chill air.

"I let 'em go early this mornin' an' they took off for parts unknown. Seemed right happy about it too. If horses could smile, I reckon they was smilin'. But don't you worry none; they'll know how to take care of themselves 'til my boss can make arrangements to round 'em up again. They're new to the run, but there's a fair chance they might've even headed back to the station."

Only a fair chance? Susannah frowned and absorbed that bit of information, uncertain if his decision to let the horses loose was a wise move. Still, she was glad they were running free and no longer restricted. She lifted her gaze to the vast scope of shadowed plains.

Large tumbleweeds lazily rolled along in the distance, the gentle breeze that pushed them nothing like the harsh wind of the previous day. A narrow band of pink covered the eastern horizon, and above that, filmy clouds swirled in rose, gold, and violet. Far away a bird of some sort let out a screech, and Susannah could see its black form etched across the sky. In Boston there was snow this time of year. Here, in this untamed wilderness, the seasons knew no bounds.

"Where's the stranger?" she asked, trying not to sound too interested.

"Right here, ma'am."

At the familiar voice, her heart gave a little jump and she whirled to face him. He regarded her from the rear of the stagecoach, his eyes steady, though for a moment Susannah thought she detected wariness there as well. A dead wild turkey hung from his hand.

Inexplicably nervous, she covered the few feet between them and grabbed the bird, needing something to do. "I'll take care of that," she murmured without meeting his eyes. It had been years since she prepared food, and she hoped she still possessed some knowledge in that area.

"You'll need this," the stagecoach driver said, handing her the stick when she walked past him.

The stranger said nothing, and Susannah was grateful when he made no move to follow her to the campfire. Something about him made her feel jittery inside, as though something within had been knocked out of kilter and was banging around, demanding to be let out. That would explain why her pulse rate escalated so, her face grew hot, and her heart thudded like a frisky colt when he drew close. Whoever *he* was.

She blew out a frustrated breath and set about her preparations with grim determination. With each reddish brown feather she plucked from the bird, her thoughts about the identity of the stranger grew more dismal. A sudden notion made her straighten and look toward the stagecoach in the direction she'd last seen him. Suppose he was a wanted man? That would explain his hesitancy in revealing his name. Should she share her suspicions with Mr. Hadley?

Yet later, as the meat cooked and the morning sun spread its golden warmth over the land, chasing away part of the chill, Susannah ousted that idea. He was just too nice to be an outlaw. Of course, she'd once thought Justin just as nice, and he had fooled them all.

Now why did she have to go and think of him?

Biting the inside corner of her lip to quell the tears, Susannah inhaled deeply. A charred odor invaded her nostrils, and her horrified gaze lowered to their breakfast. It had passed the tasty brown stage and at some point had moved to crusty black.

"Oh no!" Quickly she withdrew the weighted stick and wrinkled her nose at the result of her pathetic effort. Hearing footsteps rustle in the grass, she darted a glance over her shoulder, her defenses starting to rise at the scorn she was likely to receive.

The stranger offered her a tentative smile, and her heart gave a sudden lurch. That smile . . . what was there about that crooked, boyish smile that tugged at the trappings of her mind? Confused, she turned back to the fire.

"You okay?" he asked, coming around to the other side. "Oh," he added when he saw her burnt offering.

"I think I need a refresher course," Susannah tried to joke, telling herself the lonesome prairie was making her see things that weren't there.

"Don't feel bad," he said, studying the blackened bird. "We can peel away the outside and eat what's underneath."

She said nothing, only focused on the face under the cowboy hat. Without the bandana, in the light of day, he looked suddenly familiar. But who . . . ?

His gaze lifted to hers, and his smile disappeared as rapidly as it had come. "I need to check on my horse," he said and moved away. "Once we eat, we'll head on out. You'll have to travel light—no trunk. Just take what you've absolutely got to have."

Long after his words faded, Susannah continued to watch his retreating form.

SHOTGUN IN HAND, Justin walked alongside Star, with Susannah's cousin riding stiffly atop his horse. Hours ago, when they started out, Miss Leslie tried sitting sideways in his saddle, though she wore a split skirt, but she kept slipping so she had grimly resorted to riding astride. Mr. Hadley took up the rear, and Susannah walked on the other side of the horse, an arrangement that satisfied Justin just fine.

His relief was short-lived, however, when he heard

quick footfalls crackling behind him in the short prairie grasses. He tensed, doubting it was Mr. Hadley who sought his company. When Susannah came up beside him, he continued to stare ahead to the far-off mountain range.

"Mister," Susannah said pensively, as though she'd been giving what she was about to say a great deal of thought, "I don't recall you telling us where you were headed. Just that you were traveling through Landis. Yet to my recollection there isn't much on the other side but outcroppings of steep rock. In fact, Landis is a ways off the trail or from any other town for that matter. It seems strange that you'd want to go there."

Susie was smart. Justin would give her that. She always was as quick as a whip.

He debated telling an out-and-out lie, then disposed of that idea. Once they arrived in Landis, she would know. Besides, he was tired of deceit, had taken part in it for years. Now that he'd "gotten religion," as the sheriff at the jail so recently put it, he had to learn not to stoop to old habits. Uneasily he wondered if shielding his identity from her was a form of deceit, then reckoned he was only trying to keep the peace for as long as was humanly possible. Still, he wasn't sure how to respond without giving too much away.

He sent her a sideways glance and spoke through the bandana he used to cover the lower half of his face. "Well, ma'am, actually I'm heading to Landis too. I know some people who live on the outskirts of town."

"Really?" Her tone was more than curious. It was downright probing. "And who would that be?"

"Just a couple of ranch hands," he said evasively.

Exasperated, she blew out a short breath. "Well, that could be just about anyone. Landis is a cattle town."

"Yes'm. So I heard."

A split-second pause. "So, are the people you're going to visit there relatives or friends?"

He stiffened. "Both, I suppose."

"Really? And do they have a name?"

"Susannah! Would you come here a moment, please?"

At Leslie's sharp command, Justin barely refrained from blowing out a hearty sigh of relief. Susannah muttered something under her breath. "Yes, all right," she called back. Her gaze again went to Justin. "Well, mister, I hope you have a nice visit with your folks. People should be with the ones they care about at Christmastime. Don't you agree?"

Justin gazed at her a moment longer; then he roughly cleared his throat and set his sights ahead to the waving parched grasses of the prairie. "Yes'm. That they should."

· ❦ ·

AFTER A WHISPERED and heated discussion with Leslie about the rights and wrongs of conversing with strange men, Susannah retreated to her original spot in a huff, walking next to Star on the other side of the stranger. Leslie simply didn't understand, though Susannah had tried her utmost to enlighten her.

All morning long snippets of previous conversations with the stranger had floated to Susannah as they tramped over the plains, as well as the memory of his odd reaction to her last night when he wiped the dirt from her face. Susannah had come to the decision that it was her place to find out just who "Mister" was. Mr. Hadley didn't seem to care, and Leslie was too proper to do anything about it. Some things simply didn't make sense concerning the stranger. Nor had Susannah totally ruled out the possibility of his being a wanted man—nice or not. One way or another she'd have to grill him, without his realizing it, of course. And she'd have to do it without Leslie around to interfere.

Her gaze went to the hazy mountains in the distance.

Above the rounded peaks a thick cloud bank had formed, promising rain. Though rain was a welcome sight on the prairie, Susannah hoped the clouds wouldn't head this way just yet. To arrive at her sister's home looking like a wet, bedraggled hen wasn't Susannah's idea of a proper homecoming. She couldn't imagine plodding over a vast, muddy plain, with each step a struggle, as her mother had done when she was a child in a wagon train. It was bad enough that Susannah had to leave her Saratoga trunk behind, though she remembered to grab her wad of bills and stuff them into her purse, after which she changed into a long-sleeved blouse and split skirt, offering Leslie her spare. Her cousin had eyed the item with distaste but, with Susannah guarding the stagecoach door as Leslie had done for her, Leslie had changed into more appropriate riding clothes.

When the sun was directly overhead, they came to a creek sparsely fringed by scraggly looking trees. Relief melted through Susannah as she sank to the ground beside the sparkling water. She removed her bonnet and fanned her flushed face for several seconds, then discarded the stiff hat. Anxious for a drink, she bent low, cupped her hands into the brook, and brought the refreshing, icy cold water to her parched mouth.

"Don't bend over too far, ma'am," the stranger said, a trace of teasing in his voice. "The reptiles in these waters are powerful hungry from what I hear. You might prove too tasty a morsel for them not to sample."

Susannah froze, her gaze fastened to the ripples forming circular patterns on the silver gray water. Yet it wasn't the stranger's warning that addled her, but rather the words themselves. Slowly, she lifted her head and looked at him.

"What did you say?" she asked, her voice hoarse.

The smile gradually slipped from his eyes. "Don't rightly reckon I remember." He stroked a hand along his horse's muzzle and let the sorrel step forward to drink its fill. Leslie had dismounted and stood under the bare branches of a tree, out of hearing distance. Daintily she sipped from the canteen while Mr. Hadley talked to her.

Focusing her attention on the stranger, Susannah rose, smoothing her wet hands down the sides of her wool skirt. "Then allow me to enlighten you; you warned me not to bend over too far or the snakes might mistake me for lunch and take a bite out of me."

"Did I say that?" He seemed really interested in something in his saddlebags.

"Not in those exact words—no. Actually those were the words that someone I once knew said a long time ago."

He stiffened, and his movements stopped for a short few seconds, before he began refastening his saddlebag. "Well, ma'am, I guess it's a fairly common phrase at that."

"I don't recall ever hearing it before. Except for six years ago, that is." Her eyes narrowed as she stared at his buckskin-clad back and the tufts of wheat blond hair escaping from under the brim of his hat. "The person who told it to me made it up. He knew I didn't like snakes and thought it fun to tease me."

The stranger continued fiddling with the saddlebags, frustrating Susannah. Why wouldn't he look at her?

When he finally did turn around, his eyes were steady. "Well, now, ma'am, I reckon young'uns sometimes tell fibs in the hope of gaining others' approval. I guess your little friend musta heard that saying from someone and thought it a nice turn of phrase, so he decided to take credit for it."

Susannah crossed her arms. "How come you wear that bandana around your face?"

"Pardon?"

"The bandana. Around your face."

He coughed. "Well, the fact is I was sick a few weeks

back. The dust makes my throat scratch and I start coughing."

"The dust storm is long over. And we're standing in a sea of grass—hardly any dirt like there was where we left the stagecoach." She swept her arm out to the side, encompassing the area. "It's a clear day with little breeze to it. Warmer than I remember these parts to be—but beautiful."

He intently looked at the sky above. "Yes, ma'am. That it is. We should be grateful it ain't snowin' yet. Cattle can freeze to death in cold weather. Stupid critters don't know no better than to stand stock-still in the snow 'til someone comes along and brings 'em in."

Susannah blew out an irritated breath. It certainly hadn't been her intention to divert him to the topic to which he'd so smoothly moved. Too smoothly in her opinion. She watched him eye the heavens as though he'd never seen blue skies with white clouds before.

"Mister . . ." She hesitated, wondering how to frame her words. She wanted him to prove to her that the crazy idea brewing inside her head and bubbling around since this morning was totally unfounded. "What did you say the last name of your kin was?"

He remained silent, his gaze never breaking loose from the sky.

"Mister?"

"Jacoby," he said suddenly, looking her way. His eyes were sober. "Their last name is Jacoby."

"Oh." Susannah wondered why her heart should feel as if it were plummeting to her toes in disappointment. She was relieved he'd proven her wrong. Not distressed—relieved! She certainly wouldn't have been happy had he proven her right.

Forcing a smile, she picked up her bonnet from the ground and tied it beneath her chin. "I don't think I've heard of them. They must've moved to the area after I left.

I've been in Boston for well over three years." She fidgeted, suddenly uncomfortable. "Well, I'll leave you be now."

"Why'd you go to Boston?"

She'd only taken a few steps when the stranger's soft query stopped her in her tracks. Surprised he would ask such a thing and wondering why he should care, Susannah spun to face him.

He cleared his throat, looking uneasy. "I mean, you seem like you're much more at home out here on the open prairie than you ever would be in a highfalutin, stuffy place like Boston," he added lamely.

She allowed a small grin and walked closer to him. "Well, you're right about that. And since I was so nosy asking you all those questions, I suppose turnabout is fair play. I went to live with my aunt shortly after my mother died. It was her desire that Aunt Agatha try to make a lady of me before it was too late."

The expression in his eyes softened. "I'm sorry to hear about your ma."

"Yes, well, after my pa was killed, she was never happy." Susannah felt uncomfortable with the way he was staring at her. As though he was genuinely sorry and not just saying it to be polite. "My mother always said they were a matched set, so when the fever struck her that winter, she was ready to go be with him."

He didn't say anything, just kept looking at her with those incredibly sad blue eyes.

She cleared her throat. At this rate she'd be bawling on his shoulder before long, and that was one thing she was determined not to do. She forced a giggle instead. "You're right when you say I don't fit into a place like Boston. I'm afraid Aunt Agatha and Cousin Leslie never did teach me to become a real lady, much to their regret. Cousin Leslie is forever correcting me about something. Pa always said I was his spirited little filly, and, well, I guess I am at that."

The stranger's eyes gentled, and the expression in them became mesmerizing, drawing her in. If his eyes were twin pools, she would have drowned.

"I think you're quite the lady, ma'am," he said faintly. "Quite the lady."

Peculiar warmth coursed through Susannah's insides, tempting her to abandon all decorum. She suddenly wanted to take the few steps that separated them and have him hold her in his arms. She wanted to jerk that annoying bandana away from his face and cup his lean jaw in her hands. She wanted to stand on tiptoe and tilt her mouth to his. . . .

Heat singed her face, and she looked away. Such thoughts were hardly a lady's thoughts! Where had they come from?

"We best be going if we're going to make it to that town by nightfall," she murmured, her gaze going to the plains they had yet to cross.

She sensed the stranger stare at her a moment longer before turning to his horse. "Yes, ma'am. I reckon we had at that."

C · H · A · P · T · E · R

III

BEFORE THEY CONTINUED their journey, Justin separated himself from the group and found a quiet spot farther down the creek. Pulling off his hat, he held it by the crown and bowed his head.

"Well, Lord, I reckon me telling Susie that half-truth wasn't the right thing to do—was it? And not something You'd abide, I'm sure. Even if saying it meant keeping the peace between us a little while longer." He lifted his gaze toward the line of distant mountains—hazy purple against a turquoise blue sky.

The name Jacoby had been his mother's maiden name, so in a sense it was a family name, one Justin hadn't reckoned on Susannah knowing. And he'd been right. Yet the trickery he'd used in deceiving her—even if it was for a good cause—must be wrong. That would explain why the guilt continued to gnaw a hole in his gut, making Justin feel almost physically ill, as though he'd gotten ahold of a rancid hunk of beef.

He never dreamed Susannah would remember the taunting words he'd spouted as a youngster. In fact, he hadn't remembered them himself until she confronted him about it. When he'd seen her kneeling by the creek, fixing to take a drink, the teasing warning about reptiles just slid off his tongue quicker than roping a cow.

Justin shook his head. The woman had a mind like a lariat's noose, the way she locked on to that phrase. It was a good thing for him that her amazing memory halted at words and didn't include faces, though he, too, had changed in six years. Life as an outlaw had carved into him a somberness that reflected on his lean face, had whipped his lanky boyish frame into the muscular toughness of a man's, and had impressed on him a silent nature so different from the happy-go-lucky clown he'd been in his youth.

Though some of the new traits were welcome, the price he'd paid for them had been steep. He wished he could have those days back to do all over again. Had Justin known the future, he never would have had the fight with his pa that led him to sneak from the ranch one night to join Mitch and his gang. For some, betrayal came easy. For Justin, the bait that lured him away from family and friends had been the promise of his share in stolen gold.

"Mister?"

Her sweet voice coming so abruptly from behind caused his heart to leap. He turned, his manner guarded.

Susannah smiled shyly. "Leslie and I are ready to depart."

Justin averted his eyes from her shining face and set his hat on top of his head. "Then I reckon we better head on out."

He strode up the short embankment toward Star,

thankful to see Susannah's cousin already perched stiffly in the saddle, though she was frowning. Helping her mount the first time had been a chore, one Justin wasn't keen on repeating. Obviously the woman had never ridden a horse—at least not one with a regular saddle— and wasn't in favor of accepting any man's help if it meant he had to touch any part of her in the process. The result was almost humorous, though frustrating, with her sliding every which way when she tried to mount unaided. Seeing Mr. Hadley beside Star now, his jaw rigid, Justin gathered by the expressions on both his face and Miss Leslie's that the stagecoach driver hadn't put up with any of the woman's nonsense and likely had lifted her bodily onto the saddle.

Justin withheld a chuckle and led his small party onto the prairie. He tensed when Susannah fell into step beside him, but relaxed when she began talking about her surroundings and didn't toss out probing questions.

Though most women's mindless chatter grated on his nerves, Susannah's sweet voice played like a soothing melody to Justin's heart. She talked, not expecting him to answer every few minutes and prove he was listening, like most other womenfolk did. As a result, his ears became attuned to her words, and he even responded to her when he felt inclined to do so.

"It's good to be going home," she said, once they were well into their trek. Lifting her arms out as though to encompass the plains, she released a heartfelt sigh. "Oh, how I missed the West and its wide-open places! I don't see it as a Great American Desert, as the travel books say. Why, there's so much more here than a sea of dirt and grass. There's an abundance of colorful wildflowers in spring and endless blue sky with white, cottony clouds— and majestic mountains painting the horizon. Snow-topped ones and tabletop ones—even ones made of volcanic rock. A huge diversity!"

Grinning, Justin threw her a sideways glance. "Maybe you should write one of them there travel books."

"Maybe I should at that." She smiled. "Lucy—my sister—is a writer. She's even sent some of her work to a magazine company, though she uses her initials and not her full name. Pa once told her that he didn't think the men around these parts would take kindly to a woman writer, since her stories weren't what's expected of a woman to write. They were more adventuresome—about staying alive in the wilderness and tough issues like that." Susannah frowned. "It doesn't seem fair, when one stops to think about it. Women often have the best way of putting things into words, so why shouldn't they get credit for their hard work?"

Justin remained silent since the question was far removed from his territory. Except for several years of primary schooling under stern Mrs. Pritchard, Justin had received no formal education. He'd been just fourteen when he joined the gang.

Susannah gave a little toss of her head. "Well, anyway, it'll be wonderful to see Robert for the first time—he's my nephew. And, according to Lucy's letters, quite the little spitfire." She chuckled. "Much like his aunt, I expect. I just wish I wouldn't have had to leave his Christmas present behind in the stagecoach. But it was much too bulky to carry with me—an actual model of a Union Pacific railroad car, with little bench seats inside—the cutest thing! Still, he's only three, so maybe it was a bit old for him. Aunt Agatha always said I had impractical ideas."

Justin looked her way and frowned. "You're limping."

A darker pink stained her cheeks, heightening her already flushed face. "I'm all right."

"No, you're not. You should ride Star."

"It's these shoes," she explained, not looking at him. "Boston boots weren't designed for walking over the plains—but I can make it. Let Leslie ride. She's been feeling poorly since this morning."

Justin halted and faced Star. "Miss Leslie," he called, "do you think you can handle traveling the rest of the way on foot?"

"I said I was fine!" Susannah fumed behind him.

"Miss Susannah's shoes are paining her, and if she keeps up her limping we won't get very far very fast."

Leslie gave a rigid nod. Mr. Hadley pulled on the reins as he walked alongside. The horse stopped. With much difficulty and slapping the stagecoach driver's hands away, Leslie dismounted—almost tumbling to the ground. Quickly she straightened and smoothed her skirts.

Beneath the bandana, Justin grinned then turned to Susannah. The fire leaping from her eyes could have branded him.

"I don't like people overriding my wishes and thinking they can decide for me," she clipped out, hands on her hips. "I received that kind of treatment for the past three years from my aunt and cousin—but I won't take it from you! Understand, mister? I said I can walk just fine, and I meant it."

"Miss Susannah," Justin replied calmly, as though they were discussing nothing more significant than the fine weather, "if you don't hightail it over to Star right now and get up on that horse, I'll have no choice but to carry you over there—kicking and screaming like a bawling calf, if I have to."

Her eyes widened incredulously; then a self-assured expression swept across her face. "You wouldn't do that. You're only bluffing."

"Try me."

Susannah stared at him, her brows drawing together with indecision. Justin could almost hear the inward battle raging in her mind, as to whether to believe him or not. She couldn't see his grim mouth, since the bandana hid that, but he was certain the stalwart determination radiated from his eyes. He could be just as stubborn when the need arose. And he wasn't about to deal with two obstinate women today.

She opened her mouth to argue, stopped, then closed it as though she finally realized that fighting him was a lost cause. "Fine. I'll ride your old horse. But I don't need your help in mounting!"

Justin watched her stomp-limp over to Star. With the ease born of a lifetime in the saddle, she placed one button-up, heeled boot in the stirrup and swung her other leg over the horse. Firmly ensconced atop the mare, she sat as stately as a queen and stared down her nose at him. "Satisfied?"

"Very," Justin said, grinning and glad she couldn't see it. He averted his attention to the landscape ahead and hoped that no delays kept them from reaching Landis. At the rate they were going, he didn't need to worry about any secret leaking out to break the peace. Justin had seen that look in Susie's eyes before and knew this was far from being over.

·⚜·

BY THE TIME they entered Grenada, a dusty, small town, the globe of the sun shimmered crimson as it settled between far-off mountaintops. Susannah was thankful the rain cloud she'd spotted earlier that afternoon had long ago drifted in the other direction.

A string of buildings glowed deep rose from the day's waning light and faced one another across a wide dirt road. Obviously it was one of many cattle towns in the West, designed to lure cowboys who rode through while transporting cattle in their charge—if the saloon on the right and the painted ladies lingering outside on the upper balcony were anything to go by. Susannah grimaced and looked to her left. Two men leaning against the rail on the opposite boardwalk tipped their hats to her, their expressions anything but respectful. She averted her gaze to the dusty street ahead.

"Hey, pretty boy," one of the women called down to the stranger. "Why not rest your heels up here with me for a while?"

Susannah noticed the stranger didn't pay attention to the woman, a fact that satisfied her greatly, though she didn't want to delve too deeply to figure out just why his response should matter. Riding atop Star had cooled off her disposition as well as made a marked improvement on her feet, and she had to admit she was grateful for his thoughtfulness. Even if he had been a bit mulish; but then, so had she.

They stopped in front of the hotel—next door to the saloon, Susannah noticed with dismay. The Jezebels hadn't stopped their taunts and giggles. The redheaded one leaned far over the rail, her low-cut blue gown leaving little to the imagination. "Hey, handsome, I promise you won't be disappointed if you come up and visit me for a spell."

The stranger spared her a fleeting look before he turned toward Susannah, ignoring the woman's invitation. "I'm not sure how much a stay here is, but I might have enough to get you ladies a room—"

Susannah cut him off. "Not to worry, mister." She held up her wrist with the reticule dangling from it. "I have enough for two rooms. One for Leslie and me. One for you and Mr. Hadley."

The stranger shook his head. "Thank you kindly, ma'am, but I can't take your money."

"After all you've done for us, I insist."

"No, ma'am. It don't seem proper, but thank you just the same."

"I agree," Mr. Hadley inserted, his gaze straying to the women above. "We can't be takin' a lady's money. We'll manage."

Leslie frowned and cleared her throat. Mr. Hadley had the grace to look away from the balcony, his expression abashed.

"I'll just see to it that you ladies are settled before tending to business." The stranger looked from Leslie to Susannah. "Need some help?"

"No. I can manage." Frowning, she dismounted, somewhat painfully. It had been a while since she'd ridden on a man's saddle, and the inside of her legs felt chafed. She didn't want to think about what "business" the stranger needed to tend to, and she certainly hoped it didn't have anything to do with what was going on next door.

They entered the hotel. The pleasant fragrance of lemon mixed with cedar was strong and inviting. Near the desk, a fair-haired child sat in a strange-looking cane chair with one large iron wheel on each side. A thick woolen blanket covered her legs, and a crochet hook dangled from her hand with something filmy on its end. Dusky mountain blue eyes twinkled at them from a pale face. She didn't look more than twelve, if that.

"Hello," she said with a smile. "Welcome to Grenada. If you're in need of rooms, my mother will be down shortly to check you in."

Relieved by the enormous difference between this sweet-faced child and those of the "welcoming committee" next door, Susannah moved closer. A lump of emotion clogged her throat when she realized the girl was crippled. "What are you crocheting?" she asked softly.

The girl held up a flimsy scrap of ivory. "Isn't it pretty? It's a snowflake. I've made nine already, and I hope to make three more before Christmas comes. I want to hang them on the tree Mother promised to get."

Susannah fingered the lace doily, as fragile as the child's face and form. "It's beautiful."

Her sincere praise earned her another wide smile. "I'm Amelia. What's your name?"

"Miss Susannah. And with me is my cousin Miss Leslie, and Mr. Hadley, our stagecoach driver, and—" she broke off, uncertain how to complete the introduction.

The stranger stepped forward and put out one lean hand. "Just call me Mister," he said quietly.

The girl shook his hand then giggled. "That's a funny name to call you, but I don't mind if you don't. How come you wear that bandana around your face, Mister? Do you have an ailment like I do? That's why I have to sit in this chair," she said on a little sigh, wrinkling her nose. "My legs don't work right anymore."

"Amelia," a wavering voice came from the stairs. A pretty woman continued her trek down the steps and approached, the lines creasing her mouth and forehead evidence of the trials she'd encountered. Her fair hair and features were a match to the girl's, though her own smile was wobbly. "That's enough, child. You mustn't bother the guests."

"Amelia's no bother," Susannah intervened. "I enjoyed talking with her."

The woman beamed. "I'm Helen Larson. Can I help you folks?"

"The ladies need a room for the night," the stranger said. "And you wouldn't happen to know if there's a stage due through here any time soon?"

Helen shook her head. "I'm sorry. I don't. Grenada is small, as I'm sure you've noticed. We don't get a lot of visitors—just your usual cowhands and the like."

The stranger didn't seem happy to hear the news, and Susannah wondered if he wished to be rid of them. The thought didn't sit well with her, and she frowned when he looked her way. He stared at her a moment then cordially declined Helen's invitation to join them for supper. Pensive, Susannah watched him stride to the door, Mr. Hadley in his wake.

⋅°⚬⟨⧫⟩⚬°⋅

WHILE SUSANNAH SOAKED her throbbing feet in a tub of warm salt water that Helen had brought up and squeezed a cold compress against the lump on her forehead, she tried not to think of the stranger's whereabouts. What difference did it make to her if he visited those painted women next door? He was nothing to Susannah, and there was certainly no reason she should feel such distress at the distinct possibility that he had gone over there.

Determined to corral her wandering thoughts, she forced her gaze away from the wall facing the saloon and looked over the simple but tidy room she and Leslie were given. An inviting, colorful, patchwork quilt decorated the iron bedstead on which Leslie rested, and a lace doily lay under the kerosene lamp on the bedside table. Amelia's handiwork? Susannah smiled when she thought of the friendly little girl.

Once her feet stopped stinging, Susannah replaced her detestable fashion boots, grimacing all the while, and joined Helen and Amelia downstairs for the meal. Leslie stayed in bed, complaining of feeling poorly. The stranger and Mr. Hadley were also absent, surprising Susannah. She'd been sure they would change their minds. A good home-cooked meal was difficult for a man to turn down, and Susannah wondered why both men had done just that.

At Helen's invitation, Susannah accompanied the Larsons to the keeping room for coffee. Amelia charmed Susannah with her humorous stories and infectious smiles. The child yawned twice, but didn't seem to want to leave. Susannah noticed how tired she looked, and her skin seemed paler now. Only after her mother insisted she get some rest did Amelia sigh and agree. Once Helen came back from wheeling the child to her room, she sank to a chair, her expression grave, as though she could no longer keep up any pretense of being cheerful.

"Amelia's such a dear child," Susannah said, knowing it must be hard for Helen to know that her little girl would never run and play like other children.

Tears sprang to the woman's eyes. "Forgive me." She withdrew a handkerchief tucked inside her sleeve and dabbed under her lashes with the embroidered square cloth. "Every day with her is a blessing from the Lord. I wake up each morning, dreading it might be her last."

Susannah gasped. "Surely you don't mean that Amelia is going to . . ." She couldn't finish the sentence.

Helen nodded. "It was a year ago when Amelia had the accident, but she hasn't improved much. She only seems to get weaker instead of stronger."

"How did it happen?" Susannah asked gently, not sure she had any business in knowing, but curious none-theless.

Helen paused a moment before answering. "She was walking along a high rock with her friend Beth. Amelia slid and fell into the creek. Beth's uncle was supposed to be watching them, but, well, he was drunk, and Beth couldn't rouse him, so she dragged Amelia from the water herself." Helen stopped to softly blow her nose. "By the time Doc got there, Amelia had been lying on the bank a long time, soaking wet, which Doc said worsened her condition. I forget all them fancy words he used when he spoke about her case, but he did say she would always be a cripple and I should just be thankful she was alive."

Helen sucked in her lower lip as though trying to stem the tears. "But I know it's only a matter of time. First I lost my husband, and now I'm losing my child."

Susannah wasn't sure what to say to console the distraught woman and spoke the first thing that came to mind. "I certainly hope that drunk got the justice he deserved!"

Amelia's mother smiled, a sad sort of smile. "At first I felt that way too. But Sam Greer was steeped in grief. That's why he was drinking. He'd recently lost his wife and son in childbirth. When he sobered, he felt terrible about not being there for Amelia."

Helen picked lint off her skirt, her manner pensive before she peered at Susannah again. "I'm not sure why I'm telling you all this. I don't often unburden myself to strangers. But I've learned it takes a whole lot more effort to hate than it does to forgive. The days are too short and special to waste on getting steeped in bitterness and despising people for the mistakes they made. The hours we have left are too precious and golden to waste on anything like that."

The woman's words resounded in Susannah's head as she tried to sleep that night, and they revisited her the next morning while she readied for their departure. She moved downstairs, Leslie behind her. Susannah was surprised to see the stranger crouched in front of Amelia's chair. The child and the man appeared to be engrossed in a serious discussion, judging from his sober features. It was then that Susannah realized his bandana was missing.

A stair creaked, and he turned his head to look up. A powerful current sizzled through Susannah. She was certain he also felt it with the way he continued to stare at her. Yet before she could descend all the way to ground level, the stranger stood and moved toward the door.

"Good-bye, Miss Susannah," Amelia said, her eyes bright. "It was a pleasure having you and your friends stay. If you ever come this way again, be sure to stop back by."

"I will." Susannah smiled. "I had a lovely time. You're a magnificent hostess, Amelia."

Her words earned her a dazzling smile. Susannah suddenly hoped she would see this child again, though she hardly saw such a thing as being possible. On impulse, she hugged Amelia, then quickly moved to the door, blinking back tears.

⋅⚜⋅

JUSTIN SCANNED the quiet town just waking up with the dawn. He knew he would mentally chew on what the girl had told him, later when he had the time. He wasn't sure what had drawn him to talk to her while he'd waited for Susannah and Leslie to come down. Something about her shining face and earnest eyes, so young yet so old, had spoken to his soul. The wise words that had spilled from her childish lips seemed to come from a source who knew no time, as though she weren't the one doing the talking at all, but rather One was talking through her.

Confused with the incident and feeling as if he'd just had some sort of spiritual encounter, such as happened to those souls in the Bible, Justin stepped off the wooden boardwalk.

Susannah exited the hotel. Justin tensed, hoping he hadn't made a mistake. Remembering his bandana, he slipped it over his jaw. She halted, staring at the dark mare beside Star.

"I thought you might need your own horse," he explained, motioning to the new addition. "I was even able to locate a sidesaddle for your cousin, though they had only one at the stables. You'll have to continue using mine."

Her expression softened then became suspect. "I thought you barely had money for a room. You didn't win at the gaming tables next door to get this, did you?"

Justin frowned. Trust her to remember his words concerning his scant finances. "No, ma'am. I didn't do anything that the Good Book warns against."

Surprise lit her eyes at his reference to the *Holy Bible.* "How'd you get it then?"

He released a heavy breath, knowing she wouldn't let up until she had the truth. "I traded my shotgun for it."

"Your shotgun?"

"It's all right," he hastily assured. "I still have my peacemaker." He patted the handle of his Colt, now snug in its holster hanging from the gun belt around his waist.

She cocked her head, measuring him. "I don't know much about prices, Mister, but it seems like you got a mighty good deal. A shotgun for a horse *and* a woman's saddle?"

Exasperated, Justin hooked his thumbs into his belt. He wished she'd just stop talking and mount up. "I threw in a few other things besides. The owner warned me the horse is a little high-strung—but I figured since you handled Star so well that it shouldn't be a problem. And the sidesaddle I got for your cousin is worn, but it'll do."

Susannah regarded him with a soft approving look— one that warmed Justin clear down to his boot tips. "Well, it was mighty nice of you, Mister. Truth to tell, my feet still ache something awful, so I'll gladly take you up on your offer—this time."

When she threw him a saucy grin, Justin's heart skipped a beat. Did she realize how appealing she was? Much more attractive than the painted saloon women who'd tried to arouse his interest since he'd first come to Grenada.

Last night Justin thought about getting a room at the hotel, but figured it best to save his money and instead bedded down in the hay next to Star. Then, too, he considered it wise to avoid Susannah whenever possible.

Thankfully the man at the stables hadn't charged him extra. Justin didn't know where Mr. Hadley had bunked. Nor did he consider it his business to ask.

Leslie loudly cleared her throat, and Susannah looked away from Justin. She moved toward the mare and stroked its muzzle, putting her face close and murmuring something Justin couldn't hear. The horse shook its head up and down, as though agreeing. Susannah quickly set her foot in the stirrup of Justin's saddle and mounted the mare with ease.

"I think I'll call you Midnight," she said to the horse, whose ears flicked backward as though eager to hear her every word. She fondly petted its neck. "Your coat is as rich and dark as a late-evening sky without stars. That is, I'll call you Midnight if your new master agrees."

"Fine by me, ma'am," Justin said, though he had no intention of keeping the mare. He didn't need two horses.

As they rode from town and left the buildings' shelter, a chill wind blew against them, making Justin thankful for the two extra blankets he'd also acquired to add to the other three. He wouldn't be surprised if a norther blew in sometime soon and dumped a few inches of snow on the ground. He only hoped any change in the weather would wait until after they reached Landis. Too bad there hadn't been a stagecoach available for the women to continue their journey.

As he strode between the mares, his gaze frequently went to Susannah. Her thick tangle of dark curls bounced against her back with each of the horse's steps. Her eyes were bright as she stared toward the mountains, which were growing larger and more apparent though they were still a long ways off. She really did handle a horse well, and Justin sensed her desire to prod the animal's sides and urge Midnight into a wild run. The thought made him grin.

When the fireball of the sun had arced to the west,

they stopped to eat a portion of the jerky in Justin's saddlebags. While they ate, he moved away from the group, sensing Susannah watching him the entire time. Soon they were on their way again, much to Justin's relief, since she'd switched her attention to the scope of prairie ahead. They'd only gone about a mile when Midnight suddenly reared, letting out a frightened whinny.

"Whoa, girl!" Tenaciously, Susannah clutched the black mane, having lost her slight hold on the reins. The horse reared a second time. Susannah went tumbling to the ground with a shocked cry, echoed by Leslie's terrified scream.

"Susie!" Justin yelled.

Seeing the danger, he retrieved his Colt, aimed it in her direction, and rapidly fired two bullets into the snake coiled beside a clump of rocks—ready to strike only feet away from her prone form. Holstering his gun, he rushed to Susannah's side and dropped to the ground. Blood ran from her temple into her hair near the lump she already had on her forehead.

Justin fought down panic as he gently drew her upper body into his arms and held her tight. "Susie!" he commanded, his face close to hers, his voice desperate. "Honey, open your eyes and tell me you're okay. Don't you dare go dying on me! Please, Susie—*open your eyes.*"

Her eyelids fluttered open, but the brown orbs looked cloudy. She drew her brows together in confusion as she tried to focus on his face. Before Justin could recover from the strong emotion that quaked through him, she lifted trembling fingers and gently tugged his bandana down.

"Jus . . . tin," she whispered, letting her hand fall back to the ground.

Alarmed, he watched her eyes roll back in her head. Her eyelids closed and she went limp in his arms.

IV

PAIN.

Excruciating . . . horrible . . . pain.

Susannah grimaced as she came to. Her head throbbed, each beat pounding the inside of her temples and heightening the hot sting along her scalp and forehead.

And cold . . . intense, dreadful cold rising from the uncomfortable ground to ruthlessly pierce her bones. Something weighty covered her from her shoulders to her boots, but it didn't remove the chill beneath. Shivering, she opened her eyes and saw sky. Sky that was slate gray, without stars or moon. Drawn to a flickering glow, she turned her head and saw a campfire. A knife blade of pain immediately sliced through her temples and she groaned, squeezing her eyelids shut.

"Susannah!" Leslie rushed to her side and took hold

of her limp hand. "Thank the merciful Lord you've returned to us! I was certain you were dead."

"Have . . . water?" Susannah croaked, not even trying to form a complete sentence. The effort was too great.

"Lift her head so's I can give her a drink." Mr. Hadley put one knee to the ground next to Susannah's shoulder and placed the canteen to her lips while Leslie raised her head. Water dribbled down both sides of Susannah's mouth as she gulped the cold liquid. Some went down the wrong way, and she coughed.

"Whoa there, missy. Not so fast." Mr. Hadley jerked the container away. "Now that you've come back to the land of the living, you sure don't wanna choke to death first thing. That tumble you took plumb scared our friend over there outta his wits. Ain't never see'd a man's face turn so white—like the underbelly of a lizard, it was. Thought he'd like to keel over."

"Our friend?"

Leslie lowered Susannah's head, and Susannah tried to think. There was something she knew she should recall, but the memory skirted the fringes of her woozy mind.

"The stranger who helped us after the stagecoach took a spill. You remember that, don't ya? He says you hit your head purty hard and mistook him for someone else. Says you weren't making a lick o' sense afore you blacked out. Shook him up real bad," Mr. Hadley explained.

Sense? Nothing made sense yet.

The crunch of rocks caused Susannah to turn what little focus she had upward, past Mr. Hadley. The stranger stepped in front of the campfire, his face in shadows.

"It's good to see you awake, ma'am." His voice was low, steady. If he had worried about her, he hid it well.

"What happened?" Susannah asked.

"You took a bad fall. Your horse threw you when you came across the snake."

"Snake?" she whispered in horror.

"It's dead," he said quickly. "How are you feeling?"

The pain started to jab behind her eyes, and Susannah closed them again. "Not good. My head . . ." She let her words trail away as she put her fingers to the lump on her brow and winced. Even slight pressure hurt.

"Really, Susannah. You must rest and cease this talking," Leslie chided, pulling the blankets that covered Susannah up to her neck. "Mother always says a good dose of sleep cures all ills."

Scratchy wool irritated Susannah's chin, and she rolled her head to one side. The action brought a fresh surge of pain. She winced then lay motionless. The pounding began to ebb, though it didn't completely disappear. Her mind and body felt so heavy. All thoughts faded as she drifted back into a world of darkness. . . .

·⚜·

A WAVE OF PANIC washed over Justin when Susannah moaned, and he looked at her prone form. He didn't know much about sleep curing all ills. What he did know was that she needed a doctor. And soon.

Since she'd been thrown from the horse, every minute that passed was connected with strings of prayers to the Almighty, spurred on by Justin's anxiety that he might lose her. He felt bad telling the others she'd mistaken him for someone else, but the last thing he needed was for her to learn the truth now and refuse further aid from him. In frustration, Justin removed his dusty hat and slapped it against his thigh. He felt so helpless.

When he'd fired the shots that killed the snake, the mare spooked and galloped off in the direction they'd come, leaving them with one horse again. Justin built a fire, and they'd laid Susannah on a blanket close to it, piling on the others, save for the one Miss Leslie kept wrapped around her shoulders. Still, there must be something more he could do. If only God would show him what.

"That's a right nasty cut she's got on her head," Mr. Hadley said, coming up beside Justin. "I'm afraid it may go septic if it ain't tended soon. And if that little gal don't get some doctorin', she could take on a fever besides. Specially in this cold night air."

The man wasn't telling Justin anything he didn't know. Worry twisted his stomach in tight knots, but he kept his manner calm. "Best we can do is wash out the dirt with water, as Miss Leslie's done. If Miss Susannah's better come morning, we'll put her on Star and head on out. To my recollection, Landis is almost a two days' ride. So we'll backtrack and take Miss Susannah to the doctor in Grenada."

Hadley's expression looked doubtful. "In the shape she's in, I sure don't see her up and around anytime soon. Don't you think mebbe you should ride ahead of us and fetch the doc?"

Justin gave a faint nod. "I'd thought of that, but I'd rather not leave you without a horse or weapon, in case you should come up against more troubles." He hesitated and touched the handle of his peacemaker. "Know how to fire one of these?"

"Ya mean straight?"

Justin withheld a groan. He couldn't leave this man in charge. What if something happened to Susannah while he was gone for the time it would take to reach Grenada, find the doc, and come back? And Justin sure didn't plan to put himself in the precarious position of being left behind and trusting Hadley to get help either.

Aggravated with the situation, which seemed to grow worse by the minute, Justin slapped his hat on his head and turned his attention to the woman who stood shivering on the other side of the fire. "Crawl under them covers, Miss Leslie, and get up close to her. That'll help keep you both warm."

She seemed about to protest, her mouth opening as if she would refuse, but she closed it, nodded, and did as Justin directed. Susannah moaned again.

"I don't wish to hurt her," Leslie called out, alarmed.

"You can't hurt her any more than she's been hurt already. Just keep her warm."

Needing time to think, Justin moved away from the fire and toward Star. He stroked the mare between her eyes and lowered his hand to her muzzle. "I'll get you into a snug barn with some fresh hay soon, girl. I promise. But as soon as it's light enough to see, I might need you to do some pretty hard ridin'." Star softly snorted into his palm, as though agreeing to his terms.

Still, a band of unease tightened around Justin's chest. "Lord, I can't go and leave them alone on these plains for a day, unprotected." He raised his face to the sky. "How will the womenfolk survive under Hadley's care? And Susie—what if she takes a turn for the worse? Will Hadley know what to do?"

I will be here with them.

As soon as the swift thought came, bringing with it a measure of comfort, something cold and wet struck the bridge of Justin's nose. He brushed it away and peered hard at the dark sky. Alarmed by what he thought he saw, he spun toward the fire. In the glow above the yellow blaze, faint dots of sparse white drifted through the air.

Snow.

His decision was made.

⚜

SUSANNAH SENSED brightness behind her closed lids and opened her eyes, immediately wincing at the dazzling sunshine that bathed the place in white. Once her vision adjusted and she became more alert, she noticed she lay under a downy quilt on a soft mattress. Her head didn't ache as badly as before, but something stiff covered her brow. Putting her fingers to it, she discovered a cloth wrapped around her forehead.

"Oh—you're awake!" a girl's delighted voice exclaimed from nearby. Susannah moved her head on the pillow to see Amelia sitting beside the bed. The girl smiled and rotated her chair to face the door, her hands moving the huge iron wheels. "I must tell Mother. She'll want to know." Before Susannah's sleep-dazed mind could formulate a response, Amelia glided out.

Curious about how she had ended up back at the Larsons' home, Susannah surveyed the tiny room. A doll with a painted china face and wearing a fashionable dress with a bustle sat on a table next to a flowered porcelain pitcher and a washbasin near the opposite wall. Practically all the furnishings in the cheery room were cream colored or poppy blue.

Helen whisked in. "Oh, good! Everyone's been so worried. How are you feeling?"

Susannah smiled. "Rested. My head doesn't hurt as much as before." She lazily stretched then inched up to a sitting position, grateful that her movements caused no pain. "How long have I been here?"

"Four days."

"*Four days?*" Susannah repeated, eyes widening. No wonder she felt so rested!

"You came down with a fever shortly after you got here. That nice young man rode hard to fetch Doc, and they brought you back in Doc's wagon. You woke up a few times, but were never all that clear—talking feverish—though we were able to feed you some broth.

Do you remember any of that? You kept asking for someone named Justin."

Justin!

Helen's words jolted Susannah's dormant memory. After six years, Susannah had seen the face of the boy she'd once known. It had been reflected in the face of the stranger—who'd held her tightly in his arms, called her "Susie," and begged her not to die.

"Are you all right?" Helen asked anxiously.

Susannah yanked the quilt away from her and swung her bare feet to the cold floor. "Where are the others?" Sudden weakness hit, and she clutched the edge of the mattress.

Helen's hands went to Susannah's shoulders and gently pushed her back against the pillow. "Now, now. You mustn't get up. Not until the doctor checks on you again. And don't you worry about your friends. Doc felt it best that you have your own room. To make it easier on everyone, we put you on the main floor, here in Amelia's room. Your cousin is resting upstairs, and that nice young man is at the creek. At least that's where he told me he'd be. I'm not sure where Mr. Hadley is." Helen eyed Susannah as though still uncertain. "I'll heat you up some broth. You must be hungry."

Politely Susannah thanked the woman but said nothing more. When the opportunity first presented itself, Susannah resolved to dress and slip out of the hotel. She felt well enough, a little dizzy perhaps, but that was to be expected after being bedridden. The broth would give her the added strength she needed for the walk to the creek. Ever since the stranger had come into her life, Susannah felt on edge, curious, plagued by the possibility that she knew him somehow.

Her lips thinned as angry thoughts took hold and made her blood boil.

Now she was certain she did.

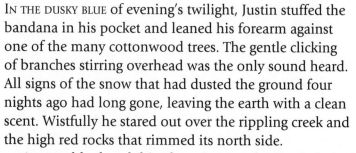

IN THE DUSKY BLUE of evening's twilight, Justin stuffed the bandana in his pocket and leaned his forearm against one of the many cottonwood trees. The gentle clicking of branches stirring overhead was the only sound heard. All signs of the snow that had dusted the ground four nights ago had long gone, leaving the earth with a clean scent. Wistfully he stared out over the rippling creek and the high red rocks that rimmed its north side.

A peace blanketed this place. A peace that Justin lacked and yearned for.

The child's words from the morning they'd first left Grenada drifted to him as if steered by the cool breeze: *"You can't go on blaming yourself for something you did when you weren't so smart and didn't know no better, Mister. Especially since God's forgiven you. Because if you keep blaming yourself, that's like saying God's forgiveness isn't good enough."*

Justin wasn't sure why he'd told Amelia about hurting his loved ones by running away and breaking the law. Her counsel to him afterward had disturbed him as well as given him fodder for thought. Yet he couldn't seem to release his burden of shame. Nor did he deserve to.

Worse, Susie's feverish ramblings left him little doubt that she'd recognized him. After she'd continually whispered his name two nights ago, Justin panicked and would have left town then. He wasn't ready for a confrontation, though he knew that day would inevitably arrive. Still, he'd stayed in Grenada, needing to know she would be okay. This morning Doc had given Justin the good news that her fever had broken. It was time to go. . . .

"Justin."

Hearing his name spoken so loudly after weeks of not hearing it at all made him turn without thinking.

With her hands curled into fists at her sides, Susannah

stood close, having come up behind him while he'd been woolgathering. Her face almost matched the color of the white bandage around her head, and her eyes seemed to crackle like burning coals.

He swallowed hard, trying for ignorance. "Ma'am? You shouldn't be out of bed yet—"

"Don't you 'ma'am' me!" She stepped forward and pushed hard against his chest, making him trip a step backward. "'Yes, ma'am,' 'No, ma'am,' 'I reckon so, ma'am'—oh!" Furious, she gave another hefty push to his chest, causing him to stumble back against the tree trunk. "How could you, Justin Rossiter? How could you not tell me who you were? Did you really think I wouldn't find out?"

Justin gave up any pretense. "I did it to keep the peace."

"Peace?" she shouted, then stomped on his boot.

The action hardly hurt with the soft slipper she wore. Her limbs quivered, proof she was still weak, but her anger, along with the look of betrayal he saw in her eyes, gave her the determination of a wounded wildcat. Without warning, she swayed, and he reached for her.

"Susie—"

"Don't touch me!" She slapped his hand away and put her palm to a nearby trunk to steady herself. "Why'd you do it, Justin . . . why?"

"I told you. To keep the peace."

"I'm not talking about that," she snapped impatiently. "I'm talking about what you did to my pa. To me." She added the last softly, and her anger seemed to drop away as tears glistened in her eyes, causing his heart to wrench.

Her fury he could stand. He deserved it. But her misery he couldn't abide.

"Please, Susie, don't cry."

"Why shouldn't I cry?" Her words came out rushed. "You and I were the best of friends. I'd even hoped that someday—" she abruptly stopped, then started again, her words more quiet this time—"you took my heart with you when you ran off like you did, Justin. And then, as if that wasn't enough, you killed my pa when you and your gang held up that train. You just stood there and shot him dead."

Justin gasped. "Susie—no! Let me explain, and then you'll never have to see me again, if that's what you want—"

"I'll tell you what I don't want." She glared at him. "I don't want to hear anything you have to say—now or anytime in the future. And you're right when you say I never want to see you again. I shall despise you for what you did 'til the day I die! You'll never be anything more to me than an unwelcome stranger—do you hear, *Mister*?"

Tears streaming down her pale cheeks, Susannah whirled and raced for Star. She grabbed the reins and, with the agility of someone born to the saddle, mounted the horse in one swift move.

"Susie—get down from there!" Realizing her intent, Justin rushed forward to stop her. "You'll hurt yourself. You're not fit enough to ride."

"Get away from me!" She fought him off, lashing out at him, then plunged her heels into the horse's sides. "Ya!" she screamed.

Star shot off like a reddish brown bullet heading for the barren plains.

S USANNAH HICCOUGHED back a sob. She wouldn't cry. It did no good. Besides, as cold as it had gotten, the tears likely would turn to icicles on her lashes. At least she'd had the foresight to grab her woolen shawl before leaving the hotel.

Star plodded over the night-encased land lit up by a glimpse of a near-full moon. The partial orb glowed through hazy strips of clouds that floated across an ink dark sky. Stars sprinkled the heavens, but they didn't shed much light. Circular forms of yucca plants thickly spotted the ground yet could barely be seen. Knowing that their swordlike blades could inflict damage, Susannah carefully guided Star.

With a quick swipe of her wrist under her eyes, she brushed the tears away, never letting go of the reins. She was so tired, so cold. Her wound had started to throb, and the itch was about to drive her crazy.

Rubbing the bandage with her fingertips, she peered ahead. She didn't want to admit it, but she was lost . . . alone . . . on the dark, high plains. And it was all *his* fault.

Her nose ran from the chill air, and she sniffled and rubbed it. Okay. Maybe it was partly her fault, too, for not thinking clearly. Justin deserved every bit of the wrath she'd dealt him, but she should've returned to the hotel, instead of taking Star and fleeing for the plains. If she had maintained a sensible head, as Leslie was always scolding her to do, she'd be snug under a warm eiderdown quilt right now.

A coyote gave a mournful howl, the sound seeming to come from directly before her. Susannah yanked on the reins, bringing the horse to a stop. She had no idea where she was going, but she wasn't about to present herself as the main course for a wild animal's dinner.

A shotgun sure would come in handy about now, though Susannah wasn't sure she possessed the strength to lift one and aim. She thought of her sister, Lucy, and her nephew. Come Christmas, would they be mourning her loss? Would she still vainly be roaming these forsaken plains, trying to find her way home?

Where am I, God?

Another long howl went up, and Star gave a frightened whinny.

"Shh. It's all right, girl." Not wishing to be thrown a second time, Susannah leaned forward and stroked the mare. A surge of light-headedness hit, and she grabbed Star's mane to keep from falling. When the weakness passed, she slid off the saddle, deciding it might be better to walk. Something sharp pricked through her stocking, making her calf sting. Jerking her leg away, she craned her head to look over her shoulder. She had lowered her foot next to a yucca plant.

"Of all the—" Susannah bit off her incensed words,

scrunching up her face in an attempt not to cry. She found a clear spot to step down and let go of the saddle. Her pa had always commended her for her spirit and tenacity. Well, now wasn't the time to give up. "Come on, Star," she said, pulling on the reins to turn the horse in a different direction.

After a time of cautiously picking her way along the ground, Susannah stopped and surveyed the dark gray land with its oddly shaped black silhouettes, hoping to spot a welcome lamp in a distant window. The moon peeked out from behind the clouds, but nothing looked familiar. She was so tired. Maybe she should rest. No, on second thought, if she sat down she might not get back up.

"Well, Star." Her voice rang loud in the emptiness. "I wish I knew where we were. Since God watches over sparrows, though, He must be watching over us too." Hearing the firm words helped to dispel some of the fear and kept her going. She continued the one-sided conversation until Star whinnied.

A horse's answering whinny came from nearby.

Susannah stopped in surprise, her gaze darting over her shoulder. The dim form of a rider moved toward her and dismounted several yards from where she stood. Even in the scant light she could tell it was Justin.

Overjoyed to see another living soul on two legs, no matter who it was, Susannah dropped the reins and rushed toward him. Relief spurring her on, she threw her arms round his waist and pressed her face to the soft buckskin covering his chest. Fresh tears wet her lashes. Seconds passed before he lifted his hands to her back.

Susannah drew in a soft, shaky gasp. His touch brought home the reality of the present and the reason she'd fled in the first place. Hurriedly she retreated a step, away from his warmth. Again feeling the chill, she wrapped her arms around herself and lightly cleared her throat. "Thank you for finding me," she mumbled, uneasy.

Justin didn't reply, only looked at her. He turned and grabbed a blanket from his saddle.

She wished he would say something, anything—even to scold her for running away—but he kept silent as he stepped close to her, wrapped the coarse material around her shoulders, then brought the folds together under her throat. Susannah's heart gave a little jump when he didn't move his hands away, and she looked up at his shadowed face, uncertain.

Swiftly he released his tight hold on the blanket and moved toward Star. Susannah watched while he brought the horse to her and waited. She placed her foot in the stirrup and mounted, and he did the same with the horse he'd ridden.

As Justin led the way back to town, Susannah gripped the reins tightly, her mind traveling down a different path. She should hate him, as she'd told him she would, but she couldn't. Each time Susannah tried to harden her heart against him, a fond memory from their childhood surfaced to haunt her. Then, too, he had saved her life, yet again.

Justin had been her only love since the day they'd first met when he was six and she was four. He'd given her a bite of his licorice stick after she fell down at the church social and scraped her knee. He was the boy she had hoped to marry. But that boy had run away from Landis a week after she turned twelve. Three years later, she'd been told that Justin shot her beloved pa.

Why had he done it? What had changed him so?

The pain in her head became unbearable, burdened by despair's added weight. Knowing it was likely her questions never would be answered, Susannah focused on the present and determined to forget that she had once known a boy named Justin.

"GONE? HE'S GONE?" Susannah sat up in bed and stared at Helen, absorbing the shock of the woman's words. Amelia sat in her wheeled chair a short distance away.

"Yes. He left before daybreak." Helen regarded Susannah from the doorway. "He said to tell you that he learned a stage would be through here soon, and he left money for tickets for you and your cousin. Mr. Hadley will be accompanying the both of you to Landis."

Susannah barely heard Helen's explanation. Justin had abandoned them? He'd left without saying a word? Even more upsetting was the fact that she actually cared he was gone. She should be grateful that she no longer had to look at him instead of disappointed to be without his company. What was wrong with her?

Helen fidgeted, obviously uneasy. Susannah managed a tepid smile. "Thank you for all you've done—and for the slippers too. They're much more comfortable than those horrid boots."

"I'm glad. Truth be told, I'm not sure why I bought them. No reason for a body to own two pairs of shoes." Helen wiped her hands down the sides of her apron. "Well, I best be getting supper on. Do you feel up to eating with us? We're having company."

"Company?"

"Sam Greer will be joining us." A hint of rose tinged Helen's skin.

Susannah was astonished that Helen would allow the man indirectly responsible for Amelia's physical condition into the hotel, much less invite him to her dinner table, but she managed to hide her surprise. "Thank you. I'll be there."

Once Helen walked off, Amelia spoke. "Are you upset that your friend left without you?"

Susannah studied the girl. Childlike curiosity shone

from her dusky blue eyes. "To be honest, I'm not sure how I feel," Susannah admitted.

"Mister was mighty worried when you took off on Star like you did. He came running into the hotel all upset and asking if there was anyone we knew who could loan him a horse. It was a wonder the blacksmith found that mare close to town the other day—the same mare Mister bought when you first left Grenada. He sold it back to Mr. Abuelo to get money for your stagecoach tickets."

"Really?" Frowning, Susannah rubbed a finger along the short nap of the blanket.

"Yes. I've never seen someone so worried over a person like Mister was over you."

"He has a name," Susannah snapped, weary of hearing about 'Mister.' Realizing she was being harsh, she looked up and softened her tone. "His name is Justin Rossiter. But he's certainly no friend of mine."

Amelia's eyes and mouth opened wide, as though she'd been struck with sudden insight. "You're the girl he hurt, aren't you? The girl from Landis."

"He told you about me?" The bridge of her nose burned as Susannah felt tears rush forward. She blinked them back. Why had Justin spoken to this child of such things? What had he hoped to gain?

Amelia nibbled on her bottom lip, evidently hesitant to speak. "Miss Susannah, please don't be angry with me for saying this. And if I'm being impertinent, like Mr. Dawson the storekeeper always used to call me, I'm sorry. But you can't keep thinking on those days. Because the bad feelings will eat you up alive if you do."

Amelia clutched the wheels of her chair and guided it closer. "I know Mister is really sorry he hurt you. He didn't say exactly what he did, though it must have been bad. But he did say he wanted to try to make it up to you and his pa any way he could."

"Impossible!" Susannah stubbornly raised her chin. "His greed destroyed my family. I can never forget that."

"But, Miss Susannah, if you hold on to the anger it will just make you sick." Amelia put one small hand to her bodice. "In here. That's what happened to me. For months I was so mad after what happened. Especially at Mr. Greer. It wasn't until I forgave him that I felt good again. He's even become our friend—and is taking me and Mother in his wagon to find a Christmas tree!" The girl's face glowed as she added the last bit in excitement. She calmed and settled back in her chair. "Truth is, Miss Susannah, you need to forgive Mister. Else you'll never feel quite right inside again. And if I'm being impertinent for saying so, well, then I'm sorry. But sometimes words are in need of being said, as Mother often tells me."

Susannah's gaze went to the china doll on the table. The painted eyes stared back, vacant. Susannah felt just as empty. Just as hard. She didn't see how she could release the resentment of so suddenly losing her pa, then her ma—or even that she wanted to. Yet to tell Amelia that, after all the child had suffered, didn't seem right either.

"I read in the Bible each morning," Amelia said after a short time elapsed in silence. "Today I read the verse that talks about being a new creation in Christ—and that the old is gone and the new has come. I don't know how bad Mister was before, but I see how nice he is now. Why, he prayed for you every day when you were sick with the fever."

The words surprised Susannah, and her eyes darted to Amelia.

She nodded in emphasis. "He knelt right there beside the bed and begged God to spare you. He's different than he was, Miss Susannah. Can't you just give him a chance to prove it?"

The child's soft words tugged at the chains around

Susannah's heart. Yet the links were strong, forged by years of pain and bitterness, and she only looked away.

·⚜·

Justin sat on horseback atop a hill and stared at the small but adequate spread sprawled out in the wide, grassy valley below. The shallow waters of the Pecos flowed past, about a hundred yards behind the main house. The bunkhouse and connecting cookhouse had weathered and were shabbier than he remembered. A ranch hand was patching up its roof. To the south, Justin spotted another cowhand doing the menial chore of chopping wood.

Home. He'd finally arrived.

Ignoring the sick feeling in the pit of his gut, Justin prodded Star with his boot heels and guided the horse down the path. Images of his last day with Susie came to mind. She'd always fill a spot in his heart, and he doubted any woman would ever take her place. But he sure couldn't blame her for despising him for the mistakes he'd made. Would his pa feel the same?

As he drew near, both ranchmen stopped what they were doing to stare. Justin lifted his hand in greeting. They didn't respond.

When Star reached the main house, the door swung open, and a wiry man in a checked shirt and dirty trousers stepped onto the porch. A beaten sombrero covered his head, but it didn't look half as worn as the sunburned face beneath, its jaw covered in white whiskers. Where was the tall, proud man with the stern features and corn yellow hair? Still, despite the changes time had wrought, Justin knew this man.

He pulled on Star's reins. The sick feeling climbed to his throat, scalding it. "Pa?" Uncertain, he slowly dismounted. "It's Justin."

The man stood stock-still and stared, his features blank

Christmas Homecoming | 218

with shock, but his pale blue eyes shimmered with something suspiciously close to tears. Or maybe it was a trick of the sun's dying light?

"Justin," his pa said faintly after numerous seconds had passed, "you've changed. Growed taller."

"I was fourteen when I left, Pa. I'm a man now."

"A man." The reply came quietly.

Justin waited for the cursing and criticizing to start. When it didn't, he only stared. His pa had evidently changed in both looks and manner. Justin wouldn't have believed the change if he didn't see it with his own eyes. What had happened in the six years he'd been gone?

"I'm a free man now," Justin went on, his voice strangely hoarse. "I helped the sheriff catch the gang I rode with."

"You get religion?"

"Something like that." Justin took a few steps closer but stopped at the foot of the porch stairs. Only four wooden planks separated the two men, but right now the gap seemed greater than the distance across the widest canyon. "I was wrong to run away, Pa. I came to ask your forgiveness."

His pa's eyes softened as if he were recalling a memory. "Manuela taught me about forgiveness. And religion." He uneasily cleared his throat. "Manuela's my wife."

His *wife?* Justin tried to absorb the startling news, certain the shock must be apparent on his face.

His pa took a couple of quick steps forward. "Just 'cause I took me on a new wife don't mean you ain't welcome." Emotion softened his coarse voice. "You're my only boy. My blood. And if you want to talk forgiveness, it's probably as much my fault as yours that you joined up with that band o' desperados in the first place. I never paid you no mind. I was always too busy with other things goin' on to listen to a young'un in them days—"

"No, Pa—don't." Justin was shaken to see just how

much his pa had changed. The Clive Rossiter of old would never have acknowledged any shortcomings. "It was my hankering for money that got me in the fix I was in. At the time all I wanted was to be well-to-do— to show you I could make it big without you or your ranch. But I don't want gold or wealth no more. I just want to come home."

The weathered face, beaten by years of regret, crumbled. "You are home, Son. I don't have a whole lot left, but you're welcome to what I got."

Dampness sprang to Justin's eyes and he blinked hard. Trying to swallow over the lump lodged in his throat, he forced his booted feet to traverse the chasm, up the stairs. Eyes shining with what Justin could now see were tears also, his pa clapped his hands over Justin's shoulders, then stared at him a little while longer—as though still not believing he was truly there—before grabbing him and pulling him into a tight embrace.

·❈·

SUSANNAH EYED the crocheted snowflake hanging in Lucy's sitting-room window. Amelia shyly had presented Susannah with the early Christmas gift on the afternoon she'd left Grenada. The girl was so precious, and Susannah prayed nightly for her to receive a miracle.

Often Amelia's wise words found their way into Susannah's thinking, as did the words Helen spoke to Susannah on the first night she stayed at the hotel: *"It takes a whole lot more effort to hate than it does to forgive,"* Helen had said. *"The days are too short and special to waste on getting steeped in bitterness and despising people for the mistakes they made. The hours we have left are too precious and golden to waste on anything like that."*

Since she'd arrived in Landis eleven days ago, Susannah frequently stared out the sitting-room window and remembered all Justin had done for them on the trip home. That person had been so kind, so selfless—nothing like the image of the cruel outlaw her mind had formed these years. Susannah fidgeted in her chair, also remembering the sorrow in Justin's clear blue eyes . . . the regret in his quiet voice when she'd confronted him by the creek.

Forgiveness. Such a simple word carrying with it such a heavy weight. *Lord, why is it so difficult to let go?*

Susannah frowned. She knew she must forgive Justin, no matter what he had or hadn't done, because the Bible commanded it. Because God wanted it. Still, she resisted. . . . She knew she didn't hate Justin, though she wasn't sure if she exactly liked him either. Actually, she had no idea how she felt about Justin Rossiter.

"Susannah, you're in that daze again. Maybe you should go lie down and rest. Is your head paining you?"

Snatched from her musings, Susannah looked away from the crocheted snowflake and plucked the last puffy white kernel from her lap. Feigning a smile, she glanced at her auburn-haired sister. "My head's fine, Lucy—has been all week. And I wouldn't trade stringing popcorn with my nephew for a week's worth of sleep. Hand me another bunch, Robert, honey. If we're going to get this strand finished by Christmas, we should hurry. It's only a few days away, you know."

"Kiss-mas!" The towheaded three-year-old turned from the sawbuck table and grinned. His purple-stained lips, chubby cheeks, and small fingers glowed a delicious shade of huckleberry.

"My pie!" Lucy shrieked in dismay, throwing aside the shirt she was stitching.

"Oh, mercy," Leslie softly exclaimed from the corner of the cozy room that acted as both sitting room and kitchen.

Susannah couldn't help herself—she laughed. Her chuckles made the boy laugh too.

"Robert funny!" he squealed, clapping his hands together.

"No," his mother corrected. "Robert naughty! That pie was for Christmas dinner. I only have two jars of huckleberries left, but now I suppose I'll have to bake another." She cleaned his hands and mouth with a damp cloth. "One thing's for certain—there'll be no more pie for you, young man."

"Oh, Lucy. He didn't mean anything by it," Susannah defended the boy with a smile Robert's way. "He's too young to know better."

From where she sat knitting in the spindle-backed rocker across the room, Leslie cleared her throat in disapproval and peered at Susannah over her spectacles. "Lucy is Robert's mother. She knows what's best concerning him."

Susannah barely managed to curb the irritated words that wanted to pop out. She was grateful to her cousin for all she'd done for her while she was injured, yes, and even had come to admire the woman for showing some courage during their long trek across the plains. Yet Susannah wondered if Leslie would ever stop correcting her.

Lucy sighed. "I just wish his father were alive. Robert has been such a handful lately."

"Well, I'm here to help and so is Cousin Leslie—at least until spring. That's why I came home."

"Of course," Leslie murmured, her needles clicking in the corner. "I shall help in any area that I'm needed, Lucy."

"I'm thankful for the both of you." When Lucy finished cleaning Robert, she gave a light swat to his backside. Robert scampered toward the fireplace, not far from where Leslie rocked in the rocker, and quickly took up interest in his wooden blocks.

Lucy looked Susannah's way. "You know, this reminds

me of the time you and Justin ate half the pecan pie Mother baked, not knowing it was for the church social— then you tried to whip up another so she wouldn't notice." Lucy laughed. "The kitchen was a-shambles. Neither of you had any idea what you were doing. There were eggshells and nutshells in the bowl, and you must've put in ten cups of flour and just as much sugar! I reckon you were five and Justin was seven. Do you remember that, Susannah? Ma was near hysterical when she walked in and saw the mess, and Pa tanned both your hides but good. Mine too, for not keeping a better eye on the two of you."

Susannah didn't want to talk about any memory connected with Justin. "Don't you think the stew is ready? It certainly smells ready. The corn bread is probably ice-cold by now."

"You only took it out of the oven a few minutes ago." Lucy gave her a curious look but went to the black stove and lifted the iron lid off the pot, giving the contents a quick stir. "He's home, you know—Justin. I hear he's no longer a wanted man—though from the way I saw folks treat him, you'd never know he's been pardoned. Mrs. Hughes snubbed him when he came into her general store and wouldn't wait on him. She just turned her back and walked away."

"Good for Mrs. Hughes," Susannah mumbled.

"What?"

"Nothing." Susannah pricked her index finger and yelped. She stuck the injured fingertip in her mouth and sucked the bead of blood away.

"Justin's pa almost lost his ranch not long after you left for Boston. Did you know that? First we had that awful drought, followed by the worst winter ever. Horrible! Dead cattle everywhere. The newspaper I worked for called it the Great Die-Up. That was a bad time for everyone. Mr. Rossiter particularly had his share of troubles. His manager of ten years just up and quit on him in the spring, and then a sheepherder moved onto the adjoining land. There's been problems ever since. Cattlemen and sheepmen don't mix, you know."

Lucy stopped talking long enough to put the wooden spoon loaded with chunks of beef and red chile peppers to her mouth for a taste. "I've felt sorry for Justin's pa; at least he has his son back. And of course he has Manuela. She's really such a dear. Still, Clive Rossiter was all set to sell the ranch. But I hear now that Justin's home, they're giving it more time to see how things go."

Susannah released a frustrated sigh.

"Did you say something?" Lucy asked, turning her head.

"No—and could we please stop talking about Justin?"

"I thought you two were friends. He did help you get home. In fact, I was even thinking we might invite him over for supper one night soon, to show him our gratitude."

"*Gratitude?* How can you say such a thing? After what he did to our family, I'm surprised you'd even mention his name in this house!"

At Susannah's shout, Robert looked up from playing. Leslie also glanced their way. As if realizing the conversation wasn't meant for young ears, she rose from the rocker and picked up Robert, taking him outside.

"What do you mean, Susannah?" Lucy laid down her spoon and stared at Susannah. "What do you think Justin did?"

"I don't mean anything." Susannah busily set to work on the popcorn string. "Forget I even brought the subject up."

Lucy took a seat beside her and fixed her with a steady gaze. "But you did bring it up, and I want to know why. Did you hear something? Your face is going pink, and it always does that when you're upset."

Realizing that trying to change the topic would be futile once Lucy got that look, Susannah gave up any pretense of working on the popcorn. Frowning, she faced her sister squarely. "All right then. Why didn't you or Mother tell me it was *Justin's* gang who robbed the train Pa took?"

"So that's it," Lucy muttered. It was a while before she spoke again. "I always knew you'd learn the truth some day, as inquisitive as you are. But Ma didn't want you to know then. She took special pains to prevent you from finding out."

"But why?"

"You were still pretty young and grieving so for Pa. She didn't want you to suffer any more than you already were. We couldn't keep from you the fact that Justin had become an outlaw—but Ma was determined you weren't to be told that he was part of the gang that shot Pa. She wanted you to forget Justin. And I reckon she hoped that if his name weren't mentioned, you'd lose all memory of him. But you never did forget, did you?" Lucy shook her head with a sad little smile. "You two always were so close. I remember that first year he left how you used to climb the hill in back of the cabin every day and stand there for hours, looking out over the land, hoping he'd return."

"Well, those days are long gone," Susannah muttered, upset by the memory. "How could you even think I'd be friends with the man who pulled the trigger and shot our pa down in cold blood?"

"*What?*" Lucy sat up straighter. "Who told you that?"

Susannah blinked, confused by her sister's tense reaction. "Roy Smothers did. Before I left for Boston. That's when I first learned that Justin had been on the train. And had killed Pa."

"Why, that low-lying snake . . . I knew he was sweet on you, but I never reckoned he'd stoop so low as to tell you such a bald-faced, out-and-out lie." Lucy muttered something under her breath. "So that's what you've thought all these years? That Justin shot our pa?"

Susannah dumbly nodded.

"Susannah," Lucy said patiently, "Justin didn't shoot Pa. He tried to save his life."

"Tried to save his life?" Susannah's hand jerked, her fingertip knocking against the point of the needle. She barely felt the prick this time. "How do you know?"

"Months after Pa's death, Ma received a letter from a passenger who'd ridden the same train. He chronicled everything. Turned out he's a reporter for a Colorado newspaper—the same one I now send my fiction pieces to—and he made it abundantly clear that it was the leader of the gang who shot Pa. He related more besides. More about Justin."

"More about Justin?" Susannah parroted, feeling as if her brain had somehow disconnected from her body and floated away. She focused on the crocheted snowflake in the window and remembered Amelia's words about giving Justin a chance. The child always did have such faith in him. "Do you still have the letter?"

"Yes."

"What more did he relate about Justin? I want to see it."

Lucy eyed her a long moment, then shook her head. "Not yet. If you're ready to let go of your preconceived notions, Susannah, and want to learn the truth about Justin—and I think it's high time you did—then you know who you need to talk to. And it isn't me. Nor will you find all the answers in that letter either."

Rising, Lucy went back to her stew, leaving Susannah in a tizzy of frustration.

How could she speak with Justin after all that had happened between them? And yet, concerning all she'd learned today, how could she not?

No longer hungry, she set down the popcorn string and went into the room she shared with Lucy. Five minutes later, dressed in her riding clothes, Susannah pretended not to see the satisfied smile on her sister's face as she headed for the door.

C·H·A·P·T·E·R

VI

J USTIN FORKED another mound of hay toward his
father's bay stallion and received a soft whinny of
approval for his effort. From a stall close by, Star
snorted.

Justin grinned. "Stop your bellyaching and eat. I gotta
take care of all the livestock now. Not just you."

Lax winter months often whittled down the number
of cowhands, so the few men left at the ranch were no
surprise. What had been a surprise was Pa's statement
that he didn't plan to hire the others back come spring
and that he'd decided to sell the place. Yet after two
weeks' worth of persuading, Justin had finally convinced
his pa to reconsider. At least Pa still listened to him,
though no one else would except for Manuela. But Pa's
Mexican wife understood little English. She was kind to
Justin, though, treating him as if he were her son, and it

didn't take Justin long to figure out why his pa had married her.

Justin sobered as he finished his chore. He'd expected snubs from the townsfolk. That had come as no shock. But when Mrs. Hughes refused him service and turned her back on Justin when he tried to buy supplies to repair some barbed-wire fences, he saw how deep the town's loathing for him went—as if he were a reeking skunk that had wandered onto their property. Justin even recalled spotting two frowning ladies wrinkle their noses in disdain and move closer to the building when they passed him on the boardwalk. Things were bad—and not just the fences—but like he'd told Pa last night, with a lot of hard work and a helping hand from above, they'd manage.

Cold blew at Justin's back, ruffling the hair at his nape. Curious, he turned to see who'd joined him.

Susannah stood in the open barn door, her expression undecided. The wind had whipped roses into her cheeks and lips. Strands of dark hair had come undone from her braid and floated around her face. Her eyes sparkled from her ride, as if bits of glossy topaz shimmered inside them.

"Hello, Justin."

He could only stare. His voice seemed paralyzed, as it had been on the night when he'd found her on the plains. That memory still made him ill from the panic she'd caused him. While he'd frantically searched for her, Justin vowed he would leave once she was found, since she so obviously despised him. He'd implored God to show him where she was. To suddenly hear her voice talking to Star that night had been an answer to his prayer.

To hear it now was a miracle.

She hesitated then moved toward him, the hay crunching under her boots. When the gap between them closed to less than a yard, she stopped. "I came to ask you something." Her hands went to the sides of her riding skirt, clutching and releasing the smooth brown hide. "I wouldn't listen before, but I want to know now . . . how'd my pa get killed?"

Justin's eyes slid shut. *No, Susie, not that . . . anything but that.* Weeks ago in Grenada, he'd been prepared to tell her. Now that he was home, he only wished to blot that day from his mind and never think on it again.

"Please, Justin . . . Mother never told me the details. Lucy says it's because I was too young and upset. But . . . but I need to hear it now. From you."

Resigned, he opened his eyes then quickly averted his gaze, unable to look at her sweet face. She deserved the truth. All of it. *Dear God, help me.*

"We jumped the train not long after it left the station," Justin began slowly, somehow finding his voice. "Mitch was in an ornery mood. It didn't take much to push him over the edge." He cleared the huskiness from his throat, seeking the strength to say the rest. "When your pa refused to hand over his money, Mitch got mad and put a gun to his head. I didn't want any part of it. Robbing was one thing, but killing was another—at least that's what I thought then. I yelled at Mitch to stop and grabbed him round the neck, but he broke loose and we got into a brawl. I fell. Before I could get up, he aimed the gun at your pa and pulled the trigger."

As he quietly said the last words, Susannah made a little choking, sobbing sound. Justin looked at her. Tears trickled down her cheeks. She appeared as fragile as a reed that might break any minute when assaulted by a merciless squall.

He ducked his head in shame. "I'm sorry, Susie. I sure didn't know your pa would be on that train."

Silence stretched like a thick barrier between them.

"Roy told me you shot Pa," she said at last. "I should've known better than to believe him, but I was confused. I mean—I didn't know what to believe. I never would've thought you'd hook up with a band of outlaws in the first place. Not the Justin I knew . . ."

Her choked words, full of question, ran roughshod over his heart, and he quickly lifted his head. "I loved your pa, Susie. I never would've harmed him. You gotta believe me!"

Justin hesitated, not sure if she cared to hear the rest, but he felt the need to purge his soul. "After that day, I kept riding with Mitch 'cause I felt like nothing more than a no-account varmint. I wanted out, but I was scared. I was still pretty young—and he was bigger and meaner. I figured if I ran, he'd come after me. Later, after I filled out some and had gotten taller, I stayed with the gang 'cause I figured there was nothing left for me by then."

"But why did you join up with him in the first place, Justin? That's what I don't understand."

He heaved a sigh. "I met Mitch when him and his boys came riding through town. At the time they weren't that well-known. I was sitting on the stoop outside the saloon—angry with Pa—and Mitch saw me. He talked to me about opportunities and gold and getting rich. I listened. I'm sorry I ever did."

She regarded him sadly. "I remember how hard it was for you to get along with your pa. I should've been a better friend and helped you. Maybe then you wouldn't have run away."

"No." Justin swiftly moved forward, the self-condemnation in her words leading him to take a solid hold of her upper arms. "None of it was your fault, Susie. None of it."

She was quiet a moment. "What made you finally decide to leave the gang?"

He released his tight grip on her and moved a few feet away, toward the closest stall. "I didn't leave. I was caught. The sheriff was a God-fearing man who read his Bible aloud in the jailhouse. While we waited for the circuit judge to come around, I listened from my cell and remembered my ma and her strong faith. Something clicked inside. After that, the sheriff and I talked quite a bit. Later, he offered me amnesty if I'd help him catch Mitch and the boys. I did."

Susannah stared at him, her eyes moist. Without warning, she stepped close and wrapped her arms around his waist in an affectionate but quiet hug.

Totally dumbfounded, he stood motionless.

"I've missed you, Justin," she whispered. "And . . . and I do forgive you. For everything. Thank you for trying to save Pa."

Before he could collect his scattered thoughts to respond, she released him and hurried from the barn.

⁕

ON THIS MILD Christmas morning Susannah and Lucy, each holding one of little Robert's hands, hurried through the double doors of the modest church. A beaming Leslie followed in the company of Mr. Hadley, who'd slicked himself up for the occasion and slathered on a good amount of bay rum.

He had surprised the women when he'd sent off for their belongings left behind in the wrecked stagecoach, then personally brought their trunks to the door. Leslie had been beside herself ever since, acting less like a dour spinster and more like a giddy young girl. Better yet, she hadn't corrected Susannah once in the past forty-eight hours.

Susannah looked over the one room that usually smelled of chalk dust from school sessions held during the week; with Mr. Hadley's hair tonic, it was difficult to get a whiff of much else. The place was packed with men and women dressed in their Sunday-go-to-meeting clothes. Most sat on benches along the wooden floor.

When she spotted Justin, Susannah frowned. He sat alone in the center of a front bench. People loudly whispered while eyeing him, and some made their disgust known by the appalled expressions on their faces.

Lucy claimed her usual bench. Instead of following her sister, Susannah released Robert's hand, compressed her mouth with purpose, and marched to where Justin sat. He looked sharp in a pair of tan trousers and his buckskin jacket, a clean white shirt, and a black ribbon tie. His hat lay on the bench beside him, and his wheat blond hair was combed back.

Surprise filled his eyes when he looked up at Susannah, and he hurriedly stood to his feet.

"May I sit beside you?" she asked with a smile.

A few benches behind them, Susannah thought she heard Leslie's horrified gasp of "Oh, mercy." And she was sure she heard Mr. Hadley chuckle.

Justin's clear eyes shone with gratitude, then something warm that made Susannah's stomach give a little flip. "Please do," he said.

Once everyone was seated, Pastor Phelps moved to the pulpit and opened his Bible. "Welcome, friends. What a joyous day to celebrate this blessed Christmas, the anniversary of our Savior's birth." He paused, adjusted his half-moon spectacles, and looked out over the congregation with a paternal smile. "Please turn to number forty-six in your hymnals."

From all over the room, pages began to rustle. Susannah took a deep breath for courage and raised her hand. "Pastor Phelps? Before we start with the singing, may I say something?"

A shocked chorus of murmurs rippled through the room. The silver-haired preacher lifted shaggy brows in puzzlement but nodded. "Of course, Miss Pruitt. If you feel that what you have to say is beneficial to all present, then you may speak."

"Thank you." Knees suddenly wobbly, Susannah stood and faced the townspeople. Her former schoolteacher, Mrs. Pritchard, glared at her with disapproval, as did several other matrons. The men frowned, but their expressions were curious. The children looked on, round-eyed and aghast.

Susannah cleared her throat and focused on the opposite wall. "I'm triply blessed to be here today, to celebrate this Christmas with you. Most of you know what happened to my cousin and me during our travels home. Once by accident, once by unforeseen circumstances, and once by my own stupidity my life was endangered. Each time, a man came to our aid, giving little thought to his own well-being. He came to us a stranger—and easily could have left us on the plains, defenseless, a number of times. But it just wasn't in his heart to do so."

Susannah briefly looked down at Justin. He stared at her in disbelief, his mouth agape.

"Some of you may have heard that it was Justin Rossiter who shot my pa. Well I'm here to tell you it just isn't so." She sought out a face in the crowd and, finding it, narrowed her eyes. Roy Smothers coughed and looked down. "For years I believed that lie. But I finally decided not to rely on gossip any longer, thanks to my sister and a precious child in Grenada, but instead to 'incline my ear to the truth,' as Pastor Phelps says we're to do. Frank Carstairs is a journalist who was riding on the train and documented the incident. I recently read a letter he wrote to my mother months after Pa was shot. Mr. Carstairs described Justin as 'an awry but benevolent soul in a band of black-hearted thieves.' Justin tried to save my pa's life. He didn't kill him."

The congregation stirred, and loud whispers circulated the room.

"All that aside," Susannah said more loudly to make herself heard, "we talk about our need of a savior, and on

Christmas we thank our Lord Jesus for coming to the earth to take our sins away and being that Savior. But who are we to say if a person is worthy of that gift or not? Is there a one of us who's truly perfect? Didn't the Lord die for *all* mankind?"

Susannah caught Mrs. Hughes's haughty stare and steeled herself to continue. "Justin did wrong by robbing those trains and such, yes, but he asked God's forgiveness. And my Bible says that if a person repents of his evil deeds, God will show him mercy. Now I know for us mortals it's often hard to forgive—I had trouble with that too. Still, if God's forgiven someone like Justin, who's strayed and come back to Him, shouldn't we do the same? Especially on Christmas Day?"

Emotion unexpectedly clogged her throat and she cleared it, blinking the sudden wetness from her eyes. She caught Lucy's gaze. Her sister was smiling at her. As was Leslie.

Susannah's mind went blank from the shock of her cousin's obvious approval. "Well, I . . . I suppose that's all I have to say. Thank you for listening." Hurriedly she turned and took her seat next to Justin. Quiet permeated the room.

She stared at the lap of her blue poplin skirt, only beginning to realize what she'd done. She'd just stood up and told off the entire town.

Justin's warm, calloused palm closed over the back of her hand where it rested on the bench. Startled, she looked his way.

Admiration filled his eyes, which shone a clear, intense blue, reminding her of a western sky. "You're somethin' else," he whispered.

Heat flooded her face, and Susannah focused her attention frontward. Pastor Phelps dabbed at his eyes with a kerchief, ran the cloth under his nose, then stuffed it back in his coat pocket and smiled. "Thank you, young lady. I doubt I could have expressed the sentiment any better." He looked at the congregation. "Now, if you will all please stand, let us lift our voices in one accord this glorious Christmas morn as we sing one of my personal favorites, 'God Rest Ye Merry, Gentlemen.'"

Though her weak contralto sometimes resembled a frog's croak, Susannah sang as lustily as the others. Justin held the hymnal for both of them, his rich baritone pleasing to the ear. While they sang the last stanza, gladness streamed through Susannah at the words, and she felt as buoyant as a snowflake dancing in the breeze.

> *Now to the Lord sing praises,*
> *All you within this place,*
> *And with true love and brotherhood*
> *Each other now embrace;*
> *This holy tide of Christmas*
> *All other doth deface.*
> *O tidings of comfort and joy, comfort and joy;*
> *O tidings of comfort and joy!*

Glancing at Justin and catching his attention, Susannah smiled. She put her arm through his and gave it a happy squeeze. Surely there couldn't be a finer Christmas than this one!

❖

WHILE PASTOR PHELPS told the story of the night Christ was born, Justin cast covert glances at Susannah. He couldn't get over how she'd taken on the whole town on his behalf, and he loved her all the more for it. She had grown into a fine young woman and deserved a husband of whom she could be proud. Justin yearned to be that man, but such a hope seemed as far-reaching as the

North Star. Likely, he always would be branded an ex-outlaw and judged for his past.

When the pastor dismissed everyone, Justin was taken aback by the number of townsfolk who approached his bench. A few of the greetings sounded stiff, but no one was downright rude. In the confusion of three women talking to him at once, Susannah disappeared.

What seemed eons later but must have been only minutes, Justin managed to respectfully detach himself from the buzzing group of women and hurry to the sunny outdoors. Blowing out a relieved breath, he slapped his hat on his head.

As he reached the bottom step, Susie appeared by his side. "Justin! I'm so glad I caught you. Lucy asked that I invite you over for Christmas dinner. Mr. Hadley bagged a turkey and we're having a veritable feast. He even managed to find a young piñon pine to cut down for a Christmas tree. Do say you'll come and join in the frivolity."

"Blessed Christmas, Susannah," Mrs. Blakely, the seamstress, called out from nearby.

"Interesting speech, Miss Pruitt," the stout Mr. Blakely added.

Pink tinged Susannah's skin. "A blessed Christmas to you, Mr. and Mrs. Blakely." She looked at Justin. "Well? Can you come?" Her big, ginger-colored eyes sparkled with hope.

Staring at her shining upturned face framed in the blue bonnet, Justin almost considered asking if he might court her. "Pa was feeling poorly this morning. I should be getting back so I can take on his chores."

"Oh, dear. I hope he's not ill."

"No, nothing serious. His joints are acting up again."

She wrinkled her brow. Her dark lashes fanned down, then upward. "In that case, couldn't you just drop by for an hour?"

"Merry Christmas, Susannah . . . Mr. Rossiter," a young

woman greeted as she trundled past, her freckled face aglow with curiosity.

"Merry Christmas," they both replied.

Justin looked at Susannah. "Can I talk to you in private for a minute?"

Her smile was quick. "Sure."

She accompanied Justin across the dusty street to where Star was tied to a hitching post. Justin glanced around to make sure they were alone, then pulled his bandana from his pocket and stuck the cloth in her gloved hand. Her expression curious, she studied the wadded red material then him.

"Open it," he prodded.

She did so and gasped. "Pa's pocket watch."

"I took it from Mitch's saddlebag one night when he was drunk. I'd always hoped someday I could give it to its rightful owner—you. Your pa would have wanted you to have it, Susie. I planned to give it to you in Grenada before I left, but well . . . I forgot. Merry Christmas."

She fingered the curlicue engraving on the front of the shiny gold metal disk, her face working as though she might cry.

Justin felt suddenly awkward. "Susie?"

"This is the best Christmas I've had in a long while." Her voice was choked.

"Susannah!" Lucy called from her wagon across the street. "Are you coming?"

Susannah looked up at Justin. "You're a wonderful man, Justin Rossiter. And I do hope you change your mind about sharing Christmas dinner with us."

Abruptly she placed her hand on his jaw, stood on tiptoe, and pressed her soft lips to the opposite corner of his mouth. Justin stiffened in amazement. Susannah took a quick step backward. They stared at one another a few rapid heartbeats longer, until she whirled around and dashed for Lucy's wagon.

Justin put his fingers to where she'd kissed him and watched her go. That she'd forgiven him boggled his mind. That she thought him "wonderful" and had kissed him left him speechless. For the first time since they were reunited, hope flickered at the prospect of a future together.

⁛

SUSANNAH SET THE DISHES in the washtub and glanced toward the sitting room, her gaze going past the others and across the room to the lone window. The golden ball of the sun teetered beyond a low hill, near the Pecos, leaving behind a gilded shimmer that covered both land and trees.

Christmas dinner with the family had gone well. Both Susannah and Lucy had been shocked but pleasantly surprised when a giddy Leslie announced her acceptance to Mr. Hadley's marriage proposal while the older man sat beside her and embarrassedly cleared his throat from time to time. They planned to marry in the summer, and by the looks of things, Lucy would soon follow their lead. She had invited a cowhand from the Rossiter Ranch to eat with them, and Paulo had yet to take his eyes off a bubbling Lucy.

Paulo's boisterous laughter now filled the room. Susannah sighed, restlessness prickling her like the needles of a pine tree. She had offered to wash the dishes herself so the men could court their ladies and she could separate herself from the group for a while to think. Justin had acted so odd after the church gathering, with his weak excuse as to why he couldn't share dinner with them. Then, after he'd given her Pa's pocket watch, she had acted recklessly by following her heart and kissing him. She shouldn't have done it. The astonishment in his eyes had told her that, and she certainly didn't want him to think her brazen!

Tenderly she touched the small bulge she'd placed underneath her corset by the locket, near her heart, until she could find a suitable chain for the watch. She smiled when she thought of Justin's selfless gesture in risking his life to take back from Mitch what belonged to her. Amelia and Lucy were right. Justin had changed for the better. His actions to rectify past mistakes were apparent to all. He'd become a man of strong moral fiber. A man Susannah would be proud to walk beside for the rest of her days.

Catching a glimpse of movement at the window, she redirected her gaze outside. Her heart gave a little thump against her fingers. Head lowered, hands in his pockets, Justin slowly moved between a shrub and his horse, looking for all the world as if he was about to change his mind and leave. Hurriedly Susannah wiped her damp hands on her skirt and rushed to grab her shawl from its peg.

"I'll be back in a minute," she tossed over her shoulder. She stepped over Robert, who happily played with the railroad car she'd given him, and headed out the door, closing it behind her.

"Justin!" She hurried over the brown grass toward him. The air had chilled and held a bite to it. She pulled her shawl more tightly around her shoulders.

He turned from his horse, his expression almost sheepish. "Hello, Susie."

"Hello." Nervous, she stopped a few feet in front of him, remembering her resolve to be less forward. She smiled demurely. "I'm so glad you changed your mind and came to visit us. We've already eaten, but there's plenty of turkey and other fixings left over. I can get you a plate, if you'd like."

"Thanks, but I can't stay." Perspiration glistened on his face, and he pulled off his cowboy hat to wipe his brow with the back of one long sleeve. His sweat-dampened locks shimmered red gold in the burgeoning sunset. "I just came to bring you a letter. Mrs. Dreyfus caught me after church and asked me to give it to you. She tried to catch you, but you'd already left. It came yesterday, and she felt it might be important. It's from Helen Larson."

Susannah wrinkled her brow. Church had been over more than six hours ago. What had taken him so long to get here?

He took the letter from his saddlebag, gave it to her, then replaced his hat. A few awkward seconds elapsed. "Well, give my best to your family."

"Wait!" Heart pounding erratically, as much from the dismay of him wanting to leave as from the excitement of receiving an unexpected letter, Susannah stepped forward to stop him, then again remembered her decision to be demure and halted in her tracks. "Won't you stay while I read it? There might be a message in it for you."

He hesitated, then nodded.

Suddenly fearing bad news, she slowly tore into the post. Justin moved closer, as though sensing her thoughts. She scanned the curvy script and laughed.

"Oh, Justin—Amelia's better! Listen: 'I praise God each day for the improvement I've seen in Amelia. She's still confined to her chair but is quite pert and doesn't tire as easily. Her lips and cheeks have pinkened some, and she seems happier, if that's possible. Most likely because Mr. Greer and I plan to get married in the spring—'" Susannah abruptly stopped reading, her words choked.

"Susie? You okay?"

"Of course I'm okay." Trying to act as if she didn't care that apparently every eligible woman in the New Mexico Territory had plans to marry the man she loved, except for Susannah, she studied the letter and smiled. "Amelia added a note at the bottom. It's addressed to both of us. It reads: 'Dear Miss Susannah and Mr. Justin, remember—'"

She stopped when she caught sight of the next two

lines. Tears stung her eyes. She couldn't have voiced the words if she tried.

Justin took hold of the other side of the letter. "'The heart of a stranger is never far from those who love him most,'" he solemnly continued to read where she'd left off. "'And those who love him most see past outside flaws to the true heart of the stranger. Sincerely, your friend from Grenada, Amelia Ann Larson.'"

Justin looked up. "That little gal is something else. It's as though she can see straight through to a person's soul." His soft gaze locked with Susannah's for mind-numbing seconds then uneasily drifted away. "Well, I suppose I should head on out now."

Susannah gripped the letter hard. "Yes . . . all right. I suppose you should." Not wanting to again make the mistake of acting when she shouldn't, she turned her back to him.

"Susie?" He touched her elbow. "What's wrong?"

All resolve to be reserved disintegrated, and she faced him. "How can you even ask that question, Justin? I'd thought things were finally right between us. But they're obviously not."

"I wouldn't go as far as to say that."

"Wouldn't you? Then how come you treat me as if I had the plague?"

"I didn't mean to—"

"You can't seem to wait to get out of here."

"If you'll just settle down and listen."

Susannah opened her mouth for a burning retort then stopped. Anger and impetuosity had gained her nothing but problems when Justin had tried talking to her in the past—and she certainly didn't need more problems. She forced herself to calm. "All right. Talk."

He seemed taken aback. "You mean it?"

"Yes. And it had better be good."

His eyes glimmered with amusement. "All right . . .

truth is, I didn't feel I had the privilege to see you 'til I could show you—and everyone else—that I've changed. I know God forgave me—and that you and your family and my pa forgave me. But it took me some time to forgive myself, as strange as that may sound. I felt ashamed for the misery I'd caused. Then in Grenada, Amelia said something that stuck to me like a burr. And this note here just makes what she said that much stronger. Like God underlining what He showed me through that little gal."

His voice caught. "She told me that if I kept punishing myself for past mistakes, that's like saying God's forgiveness isn't good enough. And she's right. I've been reading through Ma's old Bible since I've come home, and that's also helped me to grab hold of some truths. But, Susie—" he put his hands to her shoulders—"I want to prove to *you* that I could be the man you described at church this morning. A man worthy of your love and trust. 'Til that time, I don't feel I have the right to come calling."

Her heart seemed to melt. Though his last words came out as a statement, she could hear the underlying question beneath them, and she was more than ready to allay his doubts. "Oh, Justin. You showed your fine character throughout our entire journey home, the way you took such good care of us. Is that the only reason you've been acting so peculiar?"

"Well . . . no."

Susannah stiffened, and Justin tightened his hold, as though afraid she might run. "A little over two weeks ago, in Grenada, you told me you despised me and never wanted to see me again. Remember? Then today you stand up for me in church, and later tell me I'm wonderful and kiss me." He grinned. "What's a man to think? I've been riding for hours, trying to sort it all out."

Discomfited, Susannah dropped her gaze, then shyly looked up at him through her lashes. "Well, Justin,

I've heard it said that a person *can* change if given the chance."

He laughed, sending her heart soaring. "Is that a fact, now?" Dropping his hands from her shoulders, he wrapped his fingers around hers, instantly serious. "And what about your heart, Susie? Can you learn to love this stranger?"

"I think you already know the answer to that," she whispered. "But you're no stranger, Justin. Not anymore." Her cheeks felt as if they were roasting. "And I don't want you to become one, either, by making yourself scarce."

"Oh, sweet Susie, that's just what I'd hoped to hear." With a boyish grin, he gently tugged on her hands, pulling her a step closer.

She felt suddenly breathless at the roguish gleam now lighting his eyes. "What are you doing?" Her voice came out sounding funny.

"Something I've had the hankerin' to do since I first set eyes on a feisty gal who tried to make a campfire on the plains—and almost set her skirt afire doing it," he teased in a low voice. "A dirty, brave slip of a gal who faced down a stranger in the middle of a squall, hiding nothing more than a rock behind her back for a weapon—"

"You knew about that?" she squeaked.

He nodded.

"All right, Justin, I know I was pathetic, but can you do me a huge favor and forget that day?" Susannah tried to tug her hands from his, but he tightened his hold, refusing to let go. "You always did love to tease me. If it wasn't about snakes, it was something else." Still, she was only half exasperated. He was talking to her like old times, and that made Susannah giddy with relief. Silently, she thanked God for restoring her best friend to her.

"Ma'am," Justin drawled, "you are anything but pathetic." His smile grew wider as he slowly drew her closer. "Brave. Bold. Beautiful. But in no way pathetic."

His light, affectionate words made her face grow even hotter. "So what's this hankerin' you've had since you first saw me?" she asked quickly.

He pulled her the last several inches toward him. "This," he murmured, then lowered his head and gave her a tender kiss.

Swiftly she took in a little breath, feeling strangely dizzy and happy—and gloriously alive.

He moved away a fraction. "Maybe I don't have the right to ask you just yet," he whispered, his breath sweet on her lips. "I can't promise life'll be easy hitched up with a man like me. But I love you, Susie. Always have. Always will. Marry me, and be my wife."

The proposal she had so longed to hear and thought she never would caught Susannah off guard, and she yanked her head back to fully stare.

His clear blue eyes were warm. Mesmerizing. Sincere.

"You mean it?" A smile spread across her face. Pulse racing with joy, she looped her arms around his neck. "You love me and want to marry me?"

"With all my heart."

"Oh, Justin, I do love you so!"

Justin slid his strong arms about her waist, and swung her round and round, sending Susannah into a whirlwind of laughing bliss. Once he set her down, he again lowered his mouth to hers, effectively showing her—in a most delightful way—that Justin Rossiter was indeed a man of his word!

CHOCOLATE CHIP PECAN PIE

Here is a family favorite of a chocolate lover's version of the pecan pie that Justin and Susannah attempted to make when they were children. I hope you have better success than they did! Enjoy—and Merry Christmas!

> 1 cup sugar
> 3 eggs, slightly beaten
> 1 tsp. vanilla
> 1 cup pecan pieces
> ½ cup presifted flour
> 1 stick melted margarine, cooled slightly
> 6 oz. pkg. semisweet chocolate chips
> ¼ cup sweet, flaked coconut (optional)
> frozen, deep-dish pie shell

Mix ingredients and stir until blended. Spoon into the unbaked pie shell. (You can easily double the recipe and make two pies—since the pie shells usually come in packages of two.)

Bake at 350° for about 40 minutes, until crust and top are golden brown and center of pie is set. Cool 30–45 minutes and serve with whipped cream.

Dear friend,

In writing Justin and Susannah's story, I felt drawn to a truth that I believe God dropped into my heart. Forgiving others is often a hard concept for people to bear. Yet, to a great many people, forgiving oneself seems impossible. Why is that? Why do we tend to judge ourselves so harshly, when the One who is the orchestrator of all mercy has already forgiven us our sins? God casts our sins into the depths of the sea, as the prophet Micah tells us, and that means He forgets them completely. Not only does God forgive us for past mistakes we've made—He makes the decision to *forget* them as well. What an awesome God we serve!

If you, like Justin, are fighting self-condemnation— or perhaps you're dealing with issues similar to Susannah's and are battling with the idea of forgiving someone who's hurt you—then my prayer for you this Christmastide is that you, too, will choose to release past mistakes into the sea of forgetfulness . . . and let them go forever.

May this Christmas season be one of everlasting joy and peace for you, a time of new beginnings and new blessings as you focus upon the One who loves you most.

God bless you and keep you safe in His love—

Pamela Marie Griffin

 Pamela Griffin is a native of central Texas and divides her time among God, family, and her writing ministry— in that order. She is a multipublished author of Christian romance and believes a story should not only enter- tain the soul but also minister to the spirit. Once a prodigal daughter herself, with the blessing of having a prayer warrior for a mother, Pamela is now on fire for the Lord and gives Him the glory for everything she is today.

Pamela welcomes letters written to her in care of Tyndale House Author Relations, P.O. Box 80, Wheaton, IL 60187-0080 or by e-mail at words_of_honey@cowtown.net. She also invites you to visit her Web site at <http://members.cowtown.net/PamelaGriffin>.

To my wonderful parents,

JAMES AND ELEANORA DALY.

*Thank you for your earthly example
of unconditional love.*

A · C · K · N · O · W · L · E · D · G · M · E · N · T · S

THANK YOU to the rest of the "Lucky 7": Edwina Columbia, Nancy Plisko, Chris Kraft, Jane Sabo, Debby Conrad, and Peggy Musil.

A special thank you to June Lund Shiplett, who started it all.

I

HOLLY LAKE, MINNESOTA
1891

JOSEPHINE PATTERSON watched as Raymond Rawlings, Esq., carefully lifted the wire-rimmed glasses from his narrow nose. Removing a white linen handkerchief from the breast pocket of his jacket, he proceeded to wipe the right lens with slow, deliberate movements.

She knew he was stalling. She'd been a child of ten the last time she was in Holly Lake twenty-five years ago. As an adult she hadn't wanted to return to her hometown, hadn't wanted to face the memories of the past. And she had no intention of remaining in Minnesota one minute longer than necessary.

"Mr. Rawlings, my time is valuable," she said, adjusting the delicate Irish lace at the cuffs of her satin dress. "I didn't come all the way from Washington, D.C., to sit and watch you clean your glasses. Your letter specified I be here on December 20 at 2:00 P.M. It is now 2:10."

She pinned him with a pointed look. "Shall we get on with it?"

He cleared his throat and replaced his glasses. "I apologize for the delay, Mrs. Patterson. We'll commence with the reading of your grandmother's will shortly."

Josephine frowned. The man was trying her patience. "Not shortly, sir. I must insist you begin this meeting now."

"Mrs. Patterson, we cannot start until all the parties concerned are present."

"All parties? I am my grandmother's only living relative. There *are* no other parties—"

"Sorry, I'm late!" The door to the attorney's office flew open, and a tall, burly man rushed in. "Bill Nords's horse threw a shoe right as I was supposed to leave. That mare has always been difficult to shod. Set me back a few minutes." Noticing Josephine sitting in front of Mr. Rawlings's desk, the man whipped off his weather-beaten hat and held it by the brim with his two massive hands. "Excuse me, ma'am," he said, nodding at her. "I didn't realize Ray had company."

Josephine eyed the brawny man with disdain. Despite the chilly weather, he wore no coat, and dark streaks of perspiration ran down the front of his blue chambray shirt. His damp, carrot-colored hair lay plastered against his head, and the strong smells of sweat, horse, and smoke accompanied him as he entered the room. The words *common laborer* passed through her mind.

Mr. Rawlings gestured to the wooden chair next to hers. "Have a seat, Ben," he said in a friendly manner.

The man obliged, and the odor became more pungent as he lowered his bulky frame onto the overly small chair. Josephine stiffened, resisting the urge to pull a scented handkerchief from her reticule.

"Mrs. Josephine Patterson, this is Benjamin Akers. Ben, Mrs. Patterson is Wilma's granddaughter." Mr.

Rawlings took a thin sheaf of papers off the pile on his desk and adjusted his eyeglasses. "We are now ready to begin. 'This is the last will and testament of Wilma Bernay Redmond—'"

"Wait just one minute," Josephine interjected. A shot of alarm coursed through her as she looked at Benjamin Akers, who appeared every bit as surprised by her presence as she was by his. "I don't understand why he has to be here for this."

A slow smile crept over the attorney's face. "You will, Mrs. Patterson. Soon, you will."

BEN GLANCED over at the woman sitting next to him. The words *true lady* crossed his thoughts. He'd never seen anyone dressed in so much finery. Lace dripped from her throat and wrists, pristine white against the shiny green fabric of her dress. A small hat in the same color perched atop a mass of thick, auburn ringlets.

His eyes dropped to her pale hands folded tightly in her lap. Glittery rings adorned two slender fingers—one stone bright red, the other bright green. Emeralds and rubies. He'd never seen any up close before. He thought the jewels were almost as pretty as the woman wearing them.

"Mr. Rawlings, you may not read my grandmother's will in the company of a stranger," she said, her tone clipped.

Rawlings started to speak, but Ben interrupted. "Miss Patterson, I knew your grandmother very well. Wilma and I have—I mean had—been friends for a long time."

Josephine gave him a look that could freeze the Mississippi. "That's *Mrs.* Patterson," she corrected in a thin, reedy voice. "And I could only imagine what kind of a friend you were to my grandmother. She was an old woman managing a farm alone, with no one to protect her from opportunists such as yourself."

Ben felt his anger rise. And a few minutes ago he'd actually thought this woman was pretty. He suddenly pitied poor Mr. Patterson. "Mrs.—"

She fluttered a bejeweled hand at him in dismissal, turning her attention to the lawyer. "I don't have time to argue about this. You may proceed, Mr. Rawlings."

Rawlings looked at them both oddly. If Ben didn't know any better he would have thought the man was trying not to laugh. Ben didn't see anything funny about the situation at all.

"As I said before, 'this is the last will and testament of Wilma Bernay Redmond,'" Rawlings began as he read from the document. Most of what he was saying didn't make much sense to Ben, just a bunch of jumbled legalese from what he could tell.

A stab of pain pierced his heart at the thought of Wilma, who had taken him and his girls into her home shortly after his wife, Mary, had died. Wilma had been a grandmother in every sense of the word to his five young daughters and a source of strength to him as well. A month had passed since the dear Wilma's death, but he still couldn't believe she was gone.

He cast a quick sideways look at Mrs. Patterson. Her lips were pressed firmly together, and she rapidly twisted a ring on one of her fingers back and forth as Rawlings continued to read. His earlier irritation with her dissipated slightly. Anyone could see she was strung tighter than a barbed-wire fence.

Looking down at the crushed hatband in his clenched fists, Ben knew exactly how she felt.

Rawlings stopped reading and laid the paper aside. He looked at them both. "I don't need to explain to either of you that Wilma was a wealthy woman. Her husband, Peyton, had left her with a prosperous farm. Because of her sharp business sense, she was able to almost double her wealth since Peyton's death."

Josephine leaned forward in her seat. "Yes, yes, I know all this," she said impatiently.

Ben silently prayed for patience as the attorney slowly picked up another piece of paper. *You sure can draw a moment out, Rawlings.*

"This is a codicil Wilma recently added to the will. The generous monetary gifts to the church and school will not change, but she altered the disbursement of the farm property." Rawlings peered down through his glasses and began to read. "'Redmond Farm shall be divided equally between Josephine Redmond Patterson and Benjamin T. Akers. The sale of any parcel of land will not occur unless both parties are in mutual agreement to the terms of any future offers.'"

Ben slumped back in the chair, stunned. He hadn't expected this at all. "She said she was leaving it to me," he mumbled.

Josephine sprang from her seat. "I knew it!" she said, her voice growing shrill. She shook an accusing finger at him. "You dastardly man. How dare you take advantage of an elderly, addled woman?"

Ben jumped up and stared her down. "Addled? Now wait one blasted minute, Miss High-and-Mighty. If you'd bothered to visit your grandmother every once in a while, you'd know that a kinder, more intelligent woman couldn't be found in all of Minnesota."

"That's Mrs.—"

"Pardon me—*Mrs.* High-and-Mighty."

Her delicate nostrils flared. "I won't allow it, you gold digger. Do you have any idea who I am?"

"No, but I'm sure you'll tell me."

"Do you recognize the name Henry Patterson?"

Ben searched his mind, but the only Henry he knew was Henry Flint, who owned the livery where Ben worked while his daughters were in school. "Can't say that I do," he admitted.

"Henry Patterson, of the Washington, D.C., Pattersons? Are you really so backward that you haven't heard of the most well-known political family in Washington?"

He flinched at the insult. "I suppose Henry is your husband. Lucky him."

A shadow passed over her face, so swiftly he nearly missed it. "Yes, Henry was my husband," she said, tilting her chin in the air. "He passed away two years ago."

Ben immediately felt contrite. He knew the heartache of losing a spouse. How he'd grieved for his Mary when she died three years ago giving birth to their youngest daughter, Missy. The pain had almost been too much to bear. Only by leaning on Jesus had he been able to work through his grief and discover the peace he now felt at knowing Mary was home. "I'm sorry for your loss, ma'am," he said to Josephine, genuinely sincere.

She blinked, and he thought he detected a slight tremble in her chin. Then just as abruptly the movement stopped, and she shot him an icy glare. "Spare me your false condolences, Mr. Akers. Unlike my grandmother, I'm not as easily taken in. And despite my widow status, I'm still very well connected in Washington society."

She turned to Rawlings. "You will be hearing from my attorney shortly. That codicil isn't worth the paper it's written on."

"Does this mean you are planning to contest the will?" Rawlings asked, lifting a graying brow.

She snatched her reticule from the floor. "Indeed I do. I will get what I deserve, Mr. Rawlings." She glared at Ben. "And so will you." Breezing past him, Ben caught the scent of her flowery perfume as she took her coat from the stand. "Good day, gentlemen," she said, walking out the door and letting it slam behind her.

The two men stood in silence for a moment before Rawlings spoke. "She's quite a lady, wouldn't you say?"

Ben ran his hand over his face. "I can think of a thing or two to call her," he said, shaking his head, "but Lord forgive me, *lady* isn't one of them."

❧

JOSEPHINE SLAMMED her hotel-room door shut. Jerking out the pin that held her hat to her hair, she threw the small satin chapeau down on top of her bed and took a deep breath. She tried to stem the panicky sensation threatening to overtake her. She needed a clear head, needed to think. She couldn't allow herself to lose control.

Absently she worked at the ruby solitaire on her left forefinger. It was one of the many gifts Henry had given to her over the years to buy her silence. Reminder trinkets, he'd called them, as if she'd ever forget her responsibilities as a prominent politician's wife. Be gracious to society, smile for the reporters, and turn a blind eye to her husband's numerous liaisons.

Initially she'd hated herself for accepting his bribes, for silently supporting his adultery. At one time she would have traded all her jewels, furs, and imported European clothing to have a faithful, loving husband. But material wealth was all she'd gleaned from her loveless marriage. Now it was all she had.

No, it was all I used to have, she thought. Henry had been more secretive in his business dealings than in conducting his personal affairs. She'd been shocked to learn the mountain of debt he'd left behind after his death. Poor investments as well as a hidden gambling habit had left her virtually penniless. It had taken many months for Henry's creditors to decipher his crooked accounting records, and during that time she hadn't found a way to pay them back. Now they were after her, demanding money she didn't have.

With renewed frustration she recalled how the Patterson family had turned its back on her, spreading rumors that it was her lavish spending habits, not Henry's, that had forced her into bankruptcy. Unwilling to risk a scandal, they'd separated themselves from the situation and refused her pleas for help. And she had outright lied to Mr. Akers about her Washington connections. The society that had embraced her when she was Senator Henry Patterson's wife shunned her now that she was his widow. What she needed was a miracle.

Then she'd received word of her grandmother's death, and despite herself, she knew her miracle had come.

Josephine walked over to the window and stared out onto the dusty street below. From the second floor of the Granger Hotel, she had a view of the entire town. It had grown quite a bit since she'd been sent away to live with her spinster Aunt Millicent in Washington twenty-five years ago. The post office, livery, and church were new. Several men and women were walking on the wooden boardwalk, heading toward Piper's Mercantile. A horse-drawn wagon rolled down the street in the opposite direction, its driver tugging the collar of his greatcoat closer to his neck to ward off the cold air.

As she watched the man, an unexpected wave of pleasant childhood memories washed over her: Winter had arrived, and Christmas was just a few days away. It had been her grandmother's favorite holiday, and as a young girl, Josephine used to love helping her decorate the farmhouse and bake dozens of shortbread cookies. Her grandmother had always had a way of making Christmas extra special.

She turned away from the window and pushed the happy thoughts from her mind. Reminiscing about her childhood in Holly Lake wouldn't solve her problems. The profits from selling Redmond Farm would.

She had been counting on that money. What had possessed her grandmother to give half of it to Benjamin Akers? Although Josephine had accused him of duping Grandmother out of her property, she had a hard time believing it. With his red hair, clear blue eyes, and a face full of freckles, he looked more like an overgrown schoolboy than a smooth swindler. And the genuine way he'd offered his sympathy to her, as if he truly empathized with the death of her husband, caused further doubt to creep into her mind.

Still, was it possible he had been threatening the elderly woman in some way? That had to be the only explanation. Grandmother wouldn't have voluntarily given part of the farm to an outsider. It had been her wish that Redmond Farm remain in the family.

Josephine ignored the pang of guilt that suddenly assailed her. She *had* to sell the farm; there was no other option. And whatever emotional attachment she felt to the land and to her grandmother had been severed long ago. Selling the farm was business, and she had to take care of business as soon as possible.

If only she could figure out what to do about Mr. Akers.

II

W ITH THE BACK of his fist Ben wiped off the sweat
pooling on his brow. Adjusting his grip on the
hammer, he raised it high and slammed it
against the glowing horseshoe he held against the anvil.
Red and gold sparks flew around him as he continued to
pound and shape the metal with deliberate, rapid strokes.
Within minutes the horseshoe was finished, and a hissing
sound filled the air as he plunged the hot metal into a
bucket of cold water.

"You're still here?"

Ben looked up to see Henry Flint walk into the smithy.
"Making up for the time I was gone today, sir," he
explained, reaching for the bellows. He'd been employed
as a blacksmith at Flint's Livery for only two weeks, and
working late seemed a small sacrifice. He couldn't afford
to lose his job. Employment was hard to come by in
Holly Lake.

Flint shook his head. "Don't worry about it, Ben. You've worked hard this afternoon, and we're all caught up. It's nearly dark. Go on, pick up your girls and head home."

Ben nodded with relief. Daggers of pain pierced his aching shoulders and back as he put his tools away, intensifying as he thought about all the chores waiting for him back at the farm.

The sun had dipped low in the horizon by the time Ben hitched his horse to the wagon and headed toward the O'Briens'. When he arrived at the modest clapboard home, he quickly jumped down from the wagon and went to retrieve his daughters, eager to see them after such a long day.

Four young girls ran toward him all at once when he entered the O'Briens' front door. "Daddy!" they cried as he scooped up the two youngest into his arms and planted a kiss on each tender cheek. Missy and Beth responded by tightly hugging his neck.

"We missed you, Daddy," Beth said against the collar of his coat.

"And I missed you too, darlin'. And Missy and Katy and Livvie," he said, nodding to the other three.

"What about Abby?" nine-year-old Livvie asked.

Ben nodded toward Abby, who was standing apart from the group. Abby was twelve years old; he knew she thought herself too old for such displays of affection. It saddened him, but he understood. She was growing up. "Yes, I missed Abby too," he said, winking at his golden-haired daughter. His heart melted when she gave him a small smile.

Faye O'Brien appeared from the back of the house with her arms full of coats, bonnets, and mufflers. "Abby, help your father bundle the girls," she said, sidestepping her two younger sons, who were playing a game of checkers on the wooden floor in front of the hearth. "It will be a cold ride back to the farm."

Putting Missy and Beth down, Ben took some of the clothing from Faye's arm. "You don't know how much this means to me, Faye," he said, kneeling in front of Katy. He began to wrap a scarf around her neck. "Watching Missy during the day and the rest of the girls after school, along with your three boys. I just wish I could afford to pay you more."

"Stop speaking nonsense, Ben," Faye said, buttoning up Beth's short red coat. "The girls are no trouble at all, and besides, your Abby is a big help."

"You're an answer to prayer all the same. At least you'll have a break now that the school's closed for winter. Oh, sorry, sweetheart." He tugged the dark woolen cloth away from Katy's nose. "Better?"

"Yes," Katy replied, her smile revealing a wide space where her two top teeth used to be. "I can breathe now." She scrunched up her tiny freckled nose. "But, Daddy, you smell bad!"

"Katherine Leigh!" Abby scolded. "What a rude thing to say."

"Your daddy works very hard, young lady," Faye added, giving the seven-year-old a stern look. "You should mind your manners."

Ben laughed and tapped his daughter on the nose. "Nothing wrong with your smeller, little one. But you're right. I reckon I could use a bath tonight after the chores are done."

Within moments the Akers family was ready to go. "Make sure you have plenty of firewood laid in," Faye said as Ben opened the door and sent the girls to the wagon. She rubbed her arms as the crisp cold air entered the room. "A bad winter storm's coming soon. My Casey says he can feel it in his bones, and he's rarely wrong about these things."

"Thanks for the warning, Faye," Ben said, despite being skeptical about her husband's prediction. Two years ago

Casey O'Brien's bones had predicted that a huge flood would wipe out the town of Holly Lake. That spring had been the driest anyone could remember.

"Casey's gone to Piper's to get some supplies," Faye continued. "He's positive we'll be snowed in for days."

"Well, let's pray that doesn't happen." Ben tipped his hat.

Faye gave him a dubious look as she waved good-bye.

Ben climbed up on the wagon seat and signaled to his horse Old Bay. The younger girls chattered to each other in the bed of the wagon while Abby sat next to him in the front seat. The evening light grew dimmer as they made their way to Redmond Farm, located a couple of miles south of town. They'd have just enough time to finish the chores and eat dinner before bedtime.

As he listened to the clopping of Old Bay's hooves against the dirt road, he thought about the meeting in the attorney's office. He had forced his disappointment and confusion over Wilma's will from his mind while he was at work; losing his concentration at the forge could have serious consequences. But with his horse leading the way home, he let his mind drift back to his conversation with Ray and the irritating Mrs. Patterson.

In the three years he'd known Wilma, she hadn't once mentioned her granddaughter. He could see why. It was hard to believe that the two women were related. Wilma had been a warmhearted, generous woman who always had a kind word to say about everyone. Josephine Patterson was the complete opposite. He'd never met a woman with a sharper tongue. And now he had to share half of Redmond Farm with her. What had Wilma been thinking when she added that codicil?

"Father?" Abby said, breaking into his thoughts. "Is everything all right?"

Ben looked at her, her features barely visible in the faded light of the evening. She was the image of her mother, having inherited Mary's pretty blonde hair and fair skin. But the pale sprinkling of freckles across the bridge of her nose was obviously from him.

"I'm fine," he answered. "Why do you ask?"

"You've been very quiet, and you haven't asked me about my day." She paused. "Does it have something to do with your meeting at Mr. Rawlings's office?"

Ben nearly dropped the reins. "How did you know about that?"

"I'm sorry, Daddy," she said sheepishly. He noticed she suddenly forgot that she'd insisted on calling him "Father" a few weeks ago. "I overheard you praying about it this morning. I didn't mean to eavesdrop, but when I went to your room to tell you breakfast was ready, your door was open. You were praying so loudly I couldn't help but hear you."

He chuckled. "It's all right, Abby. Maybe that will teach me to shut my door next time." Sobering, he went to reach for her hand only to decide against it. He wasn't sure how she would respond to the gesture. Words would have to do. "I did have a meeting with Mr. Rawlings, and unfortunately it did not go well. But I don't want you to fret about it. With a little thinking and a lot of prayer, I'll figure something out."

"Will we have to move again now that Grammie Wilma is gone?" Abby asked softly.

He didn't miss the note of worry in her voice. "I hope not. But I do know that God has a plan for us, and we have to trust Him. He'll take care of us, Abby-girl. Hasn't He always?"

"Yes."

"And He will this time too. Good, home at last." Ben steered the horse toward the house. "Take the girls in and get supper started while I put up Old Bay and finish working out here." He brought the wagon to a stop in front of the house, thinking about how much he counted on his oldest daughter. She'd been forced to grow up and take on the household responsibilities her mother used to do. "I'm sure I don't tell you this enough, Abby, but thank you."

Ben caught the flash of a smile. "You're welcome, Father," she said, jumping down from the wagon.

Back to "Father" again, Ben thought, sadness settling over him as he watched the girls go inside. His throat constricted as he thought of how much he loved them. They'd been through so much, the death of Wilma being only the latest in a string of tragedies that had shadowed their lives. They deserved some lasting happiness.

After putting up the horse and wagon, he went to the barn to check on the livestock. Soon after moving in with Wilma he had taken over managing the farm, but since her death he'd been forced to take a job in town. While Ray had assured Ben that he and his daughters could live in the farmhouse indefinitely, he legally didn't have access to Wilma's money until after the will was read, and he couldn't run the farm and take care of his daughters without an income. He had assumed that reading the will would be just a formality, especially in light of what the elderly woman had told him the night she died.

"Redmond Farm is yours, Ben."

"Shh . . . Wilma, don't talk like that. You'll pull through this—"

"No, I won't. You know that as well as I do. You and the girls have been a blessing to me, as dear to my heart as if you were my kin. I've always wanted a houseful of children, and the Lord saw fit to give them to me. Just not in the way that I expected. God's ways are not ours, Benjamin. Never forget that."

Ben leaned against the doorway of the barn, his heart growing heavy as he recalled that night, remembering how she simply faded away after she'd spoken. And how true her words were. Once again he faced an uncertain future, this time finding himself in partnership with a woman who was about as pleasant as a pit full of rattlesnakes.

He lit a lantern and placed it on its hook in the barn wall, the thick scent of the animals in their stalls surrounding him. Filling the dented tin buckets with cut oats, he wondered what Josephine's plans were for Redmond Farm. He wouldn't be surprised if she wanted to sell it. A fancy society woman like her hardly seemed the type to settle for running a modest farm in Minnesota. As for him, he would never sell, not to anyone. He and his daughters had made their home here, and he had no intention of letting go of his share of the land.

With a weary sigh he finished feeding the stock. If God's hand was in all of this, Ben was having a hard time seeing it.

⋅☙⟐❧⋅

"MRS. PATTERSON, I must admit I'm puzzled." Raymond Rawlings gestured for Josephine to sit in the chair in front of his desk. "I thought your attorney was handling this affair."

Josephine didn't answer him. She'd spent a sleepless night turning her problems over and over in her mind, unable to come up with a solution to her dilemma. Out of desperation she'd come to Mr. Rawlings's office as soon as it opened this morning. But now that she was here, she didn't know what to say. Yet she had nowhere else to turn.

She began to pace the width of the room, the dull sound of her heels against the wood floor echoing through his cramped office. Her hand flew up to the lace at the collar of her dress. "It's stifling in here," she said, fanning herself with her fingers.

"Why don't you sit down—"

"I don't want to sit!" The shrill tone in her voice halted her steps. She realized she was on the verge of hysteria.

Mr. Rawlings stood. "Mrs. Patterson, sit down, please. I'm sure we can discuss this situation calmly."

Numbly she went to the chair and sat. He returned to his seat and looked at her. The kindness she saw in his creased gray eyes gave her the encouragement she needed. She told him everything, not sparing even one humiliating detail.

"I sympathize with your plight," he said gently when she'd finished speaking. "But I'm afraid my hands are tied. The codicil is legal and binding, and I can't change it. Even if I could alter it, I wouldn't. It's what your grandmother wanted."

He cleared his throat after a lengthy pause. "If I may be so bold, Mrs. Patterson, I couldn't help but notice the fine quality of your clothing and jewelry. Perhaps the funds from selling a few pieces might assuage your creditors a bit."

Josephine balked. "You're suggesting I pawn my possessions? I couldn't possibly do that." She wouldn't admit to the man that she'd brought everything she owned with her to Holly Lake. After the bank had threatened foreclosure on her residence in Washington, she'd dismissed the servants and closed up the house. Her jewels, furs, clothing, and a small amount of pocket change were all she had left to her name. To sell them off would be admitting defeat, and she wasn't defeated . . . yet.

"I don't understand why my grandmother would do this," she continued, keeping her focus on the business at hand. "Why would she divide her legacy this way?"

"I'm afraid that information is confidential."

"Then what am I supposed to do?"

"I don't have an answer for you. This is something you and Ben are going to have to work out between yourselves."

She clenched her fists. "I should have known better than to come here. Will you at least tell me where I can find Mr. Akers?"

Mr. Rawlings checked his pocket watch. "I imagine he's arrived at Flint's Livery by now," he said, snapping the gold lid closed and slipping it into the pocket of his vest. "But I would suggest you wait to talk to him after work. The forge is no place for a lady."

Josephine disagreed. "Time is of the essence," she said, standing up. "I assume I can at least trust you to be discreet, Mr. Rawlings. I'd rather not have my name bandied about by the town gossips."

"Please, call me Raymond. I can assure you our conversation will be kept confidential." He stood and walked around his desk, then met her eyes. "Not only that, but I'd be happy to help you with any legal matters that may present themselves while you're here in Holly Lake."

His offer took her off guard, but only for an instant. "I will not accept charity," she said.

"No, no, you misunderstand me," he explained hastily. "Naturally I would expect appropriate reimbursement. I'd simply be willing to postpone my fee until you were financially solvent."

Josephine considered his proposal. Although she left Washington without a word to anyone, it was conceivable that Henry's creditors would eventually try to track her down. Perhaps she would be in need of Raymond Rawlings's services in the future. "All right," she agreed. "As long as you keep a record of any expenses you may incur on my behalf."

"Of course." He smiled, and she felt some of her tension drain away. He'd become an unexpected ally.

Raymond escorted her to the door, then took her cloak and hat from the rack. "I know this situation is difficult, Josephine, but Ben is a reasonable man, and

I'm confident the two of you will be able to come to a mutual agreement about this. My prayers are with you both."

Prayers! she thought with disgust, taking her fur-lined wrap from Raymond's hand. What good were useless prayers? As a child she'd believed in prayers, thought that if she prayed long enough and hard enough, God would grant her wishes. She'd believed it with all her heart.

But she wasn't a child anymore, and God had stopped listening to her long ago. Since leaving Holly Lake she'd managed to live without God, and she would continue to do so.

"Don't waste your breath," she told Raymond, wrapping her cloak tightly against her. "Prayers are for people who don't know any better."

"Your grandmother believed in the power of prayer."

"My grandmother was a fool." Whirling on her heel, she rushed out of Raymond's office.

A blast of cold air slammed against her face as Josephine stepped onto the boardwalk and headed toward the livery. Unbidden tears started running down her hot cheeks. She wiped them away with the back of her hand.

"Blasted wind," she muttered before swallowing the lump lodged in her throat.

III

U PON ENTERING the livery office, Josephine furrowed her brows as the strong aromas of hay and manure reached her nose. While not exactly repugnant, the earthy scents were definitely overpowering. They were a stark contrast to the more human smell of city living that she was used to.

In the corner of the office a thin, waspish-looking man sat at a wooden desk. He turned around in his chair as she approached.

"I'm looking for Mr. Benjamin Akers," she said.

"He's back in the smithy." The man rose. "I'm his boss, Henry Flint. Is there something I can do for you, ma'am?"

"You can tell me where the smithy is."

"Behind the livery—wait, you can't go back there!"

"I'll only take a minute of his time," she reassured him as she walked out of the livery office. With hurried steps she went around the building, heading in the direction of a small lean-to, which she assumed was the smithy. Thin trails of smoke wafted from beneath a dilapidated roof, and the sound of metal clanging against metal reached her ears. As she neared, she saw Benjamin bringing down a hammer onto an anvil with strong, powerful strokes while a fire blazed in the hearth nearby.

"Mr. Akers!" she called out.

But the man was totally focused on his task. Josephine watched, mesmerized, as he continued to pound on a piece of metal he held between a pair of huge iron tongs. Even beneath the faded red shirt he wore, she could see the muscles of his arms and shoulders rippling with every movement. He worked quickly, with strength and skill.

Only when he had stopped hammering did she remember why she was there. Cupping her hands around her mouth, she yelled louder this time. "Mr. Akers!"

Startled, he jumped and the tongs slid from his grasp. The metal objects fell to the ground with a clatter, and Josephine saw that the still red-hot horseshoe had narrowly missed landing on his foot.

"What—?" He looked up in angry astonishment at Josephine. "Woman, what are you trying to do, burn off my foot? Don't you know any better than to interrupt a blacksmith when he's at work?"

For once Josephine found herself at a loss for words. "I-I . . ."

"Now look at it!" he shouted, pointing at the horseshoe. "It's ruined; I'll have to start all over." He bent over and picked up the tongs, then retrieved the warped shoe. He laid the objects on top of the anvil, irritation flashing in his eyes. "Well, Mrs. Patterson, what's so important that it couldn't wait?"

Regaining her composure, she began to speak. "Mr. Akers, I've come to discuss the terms of my grandmother's will."

"I thought Ray explained the terms just fine," he said, wiping his soot-covered hands on the front of his leather apron.

"Perhaps he did to you. But I believe there is a problem." She paused, measuring her words carefully. "I've been told you're a reasonable man."

"I like to think so." His expression softened slightly.

"Then you must realize this whole thing is a misunderstanding. My grandmother would never have given one acre of Redmond Farm to anyone outside the family."

"True," he said. "But then again, I'm family."

Family? What is he talking about? "Mr. Akers—"

"Ben," he interjected.

"What?"

"Call me Ben. Seems that since we're sharing the farm now we might as well dispense with the formalities."

"Out of the question. I insist that we refer to each other properly."

She watched as a grin slowly spread across his face. "Does that mean I can't call you Jo?"

"Certainly not!" she said, ignoring the way his smile caused her heartbeat to accelerate.

"Too bad." He winked at her, all evidence of his earlier anger having disappeared. "I think Jo suits you. Much better than Josephine. Josephine's so . . . stuffy."

Her blood pressure rose a notch. This man with the giant body and boyish face could turn on the charm when he wanted to. By the heated flush that spread across her cheeks, she realized she wasn't immune to it. How annoying. "Mr. Akers, I came here to discuss a serious matter with you. It's imperative that we settle this situation now."

"All right," he said. "How do you propose we do that?"

She was relieved to see he finally took her seriously. For a moment she'd glimpsed a side of Benjamin Akers she didn't want to deal with. "I'm prepared to give you a fair offer for your share of the property."

He cocked his head to the side and looked at her for a long moment.

She shifted her feet under his scrutinizing gaze. Despite the frigid temperature of the midmorning air, her wool cloak seemed much too warm. "Mr. Akers? Did you hear what I said?"

"I heard you, Mrs. Patterson." Then he abruptly turned from her and picked up the bellows. "Wait a minute while I tend to this fire. Can't let it burn out."

"I think you'll find my offer most generous," she said over the din of the whooshing bellows.

She watched him as he continued to work. His clothing was simple homespun, his shirt worn thin at the elbows, the fabric straining against the broad expanse of his back. His apron covered the rest of his clothes, but the part she could see was stained with dirt and grime. No doubt the small amount she could afford to offer him would seem like a fortune to a man of such meager means. Besides, what would a blacksmith do with all that land?

When the fire burned brightly again, he stepped toward her, looking down into her face. "Before we go any further with this, I need to know one thing," he said, his eyes holding hers intently. Then they darkened, becoming the deepest shade of blue she'd ever seen.

Josephine licked her lips, which suddenly felt dry. "What?" To her dismay, she'd squeaked out the question. Her heart started to beat in triple time. Why was she allowing him to have such an effect on her?

"What?" Josephine said a second time. "What is it that you want to know?"

Ben blinked. What *was* it that he wanted to know? He'd forgotten completely, so entranced he'd become by the woman standing a few inches in front of him. From far away Josephine Patterson was a beautiful lady. But up close, where he could see the flawless texture of her skin, the natural pink tint of her lips, and the sparkling green of her eyes, she was nothing short of perfection. With every breath he took he smelled her perfume—a sweet, feminine scent that seemed very out of place amidst the smoke and soot of the smithy.

Finally he regained his senses. "Before I agree to any offers, I want to know what you plan to do with the land."

She averted her eyes. "That's none of your business."

"Oh, it's very much my business. As I recall, the will states we have to agree on all the terms of future offers. I'm not selling my share of the farm without knowing what's going to happen to it."

Thrusting her hand into her reticule, she fished out a slip of paper. "Here," she said, shoving it at him, effectively changing the subject. "I'm sure you'll find the amount more than sufficient."

Ben took one look at the number written on the paper, threw his head back, and laughed. Was she serious?

Her face turned the shade of a holly berry. "Mr. Akers, I fail to see what you find so humorous."

"Humorous?" he sputtered, raising the paper up in the air. "Is this a joke?"

"No," she returned. Her pretty lips pursed into an unattractive frown.

His laughter faded. "My share of the property is worth four times this much." His gaze narrowed. "I suspect you already know that."

"What I know is that I've given you a fair offer," she said, the words coming out in a weak rush. The fact that she refused to look him in the face told him she was lying. "I can have my attorney draw up an agreement within the hour."

"An hour? Washington attorneys work that fast?"

"Mr. Rawlings is now my legal representative."

"Well, if that don't beat all. First you insult my intelligence by trying to cheat me out of my property, and then you turn around and do it with my own lawyer." Ben shoved his fingers through his hair. "You've got gall, Josephine. I'll give you that."

"So you'll accept the offer?" she asked, her eyes lighting up with hope.

"No. I may be a simple man, but I'm not stupid." He moved near the hearth and dipped his finger into a tiny pile of ashes that had settled away from the heat of the fire. Flipping the paper over, he smeared out an equally low counteroffer.

She balked when he handed her the paper. "You can't possibly believe I'd sell my portion for that price."

"Didn't think so." He took the paper from her hand, crumpled it into a ball, and tossed it in the fire. Then he turned to her and eyed her squarely. "Honestly, it wouldn't make any difference if you offered me the moon. My share of Redmond Farm is not for sale."

All color drained from her face. "You can't mean that."

"Yes, I do. I've made my home there, me and my—" He stopped midsentence, suddenly not wanting to mention his daughters to Josephine. He remembered the comments from some of the townsfolk when Mary had died.

"Poor Ben Akers, having to raise five girls alone."

"Don't see how the man does it."

"It's not fair, a young woman like that cut down in her prime, leaving her husband with a passel of children."

"What those girls need is a mother."

No, he didn't want his daughters involved in this. They'd been through enough. But mostly he didn't want Josephine's pity.

He needn't have worried. Her expression was filled with ire, not pity. "You've already moved in? But that's my grandmother's house!"

"It's half mine now," he reminded her calmly.

She let out a cry of frustration. "This is ridiculous! We can't split a house down the middle any more than we can divide a farm in two. I ask—no, I *demand*—that we come to an agreement about this right now."

Obviously Mrs. Josephine Patterson of the Washington, D.C., Pattersons was used to getting her way. The woman was sputtering like a near-empty teapot. If the circumstances were different, he might have found her behavior amusing.

He could tell she was desperate. For some reason she wanted the farm and wanted it quickly. That she wasn't willing to tell him why made him even more suspicious of her motives—and more determined to hang on to his part of the inheritance.

"Everything all right back here?"

Ben looked over Josephine's shoulder and saw Henry Flint approaching, his expression stern. "Everything's fine here, sir," he said, moving over to Josephine and placing his hand underneath her small elbow. "Mrs. Patterson was just leaving."

"Let go of me," she whispered through gritted teeth.

"I'm not going to lose my job because of you," he said, barely moving his lips as he spoke. He pushed slightly against her elbow. She tried to wriggle free, but he held on fast.

"This conversation is not finished," she muttered, then turned her attention to Henry. "Thank you so much, Mr. Flint, for letting me speak with Mr. Akers. We had some pressing business to take care of." She gave Flint a disarming smile. "Would you mind escorting me back to your office? I would love to hear how you got started in the livery business."

His boss's thin cheeks turned pink, and Ben knew it wasn't because of the cold weather. "I'd be delighted to tell you the history of Flint's Livery, ma'am." He offered her his spindly arm, and with one fluid movement she was out of Ben's grasp and into Henry's. "I've been in business here in Holly Lake for nearly twenty years," he said as they walked away, leaving Ben to return to his work.

But instead of going back to the forge, he stood at the edge of the smithy and watched as they disappeared into Flint's office. The woman was a complete mystery—filled with fury one minute, calm and collected the next, easily charming his normally unflappable boss. Ben could only guess what would happen if she ever used those charms on him.

No, he knew what would happen, and the thought stirred a tiny spark of emotion he'd thought had died long ago.

C · H · A · P · T · E · R

IV

S ETTLING HERSELF into the uncomfortable sidesaddle,
Josephine signaled to the roan she'd borrowed from
Flint's Livery. The owner had been most generous
in offering it to her for free, instead of charging his normal fee. Like Raymond Rawlings, Josephine felt she'd
found a friend in Henry Flint. The knowledge gave her
a small measure of comfort.

Smoothing the folds of her crimson-colored skirt, she
tried to remember the last time she'd ridden a horse. As
a senator's wife she'd had the privilege of having a driver
take her anywhere she wanted to go. In Holly Lake she
was forced to find her own transportation.

She grasped the reins and steered the horse in the
direction of Redmond Farm. Today was Saturday, and
she had learned that Benjamin had the day off. She'd
been dissatisfied and highly disheartened at the way their

discussion had turned out yesterday morning. After consulting with Raymond and doing some figuring of her own, she managed to come up with a little more money to offer Benjamin. Christmas was three days away, and she wanted the matter settled before then.

Hopefully he'd been exaggerating when he said his part of the farm wasn't for sale. It still irritated her that he now lived in the same house she'd once lived in. He truly seemed to consider himself a part of Wilma's family, which of course was absurd. Yet she couldn't help but wonder what made him believe that.

Continuing down the uneven dirt path that led away from town, she drew her cloak closer to her body. The sky had taken on an ashen hue, and throughout the morning the temperature had steadily dropped. Small white puffs blew from the horse's nostrils and mouth as well as from her own. Every breath felt like shards of glass penetrating her lungs, and she shivered against the biting wind that cut through her clothing like newly sharpened shears. She'd forgotten how harsh December weather in Minnesota could be.

However, there were many memories she hadn't forgotten, and their images were growing sharper in her mind the longer she stayed in Holly Lake. She looked upon the familiar scenery as she traveled to the farm, remembering the times she and her grandmother would come to town to sell eggs and butter and to buy supplies.

Josephine had always looked forward to those trips, to going to Piper's Mercantile and seeing the large oak barrels filled with flour and sugar, the multicolored bolts of cloth that brightened the store, and the canisters that overflowed with penny candy. Before they headed back to the farm, her grandmother would let her choose one of those candies. She'd always selected a peppermint stick, savoring the sweet, sticky confection on the wagon ride home.

How loved she'd felt as a child, living on Redmond Farm with her grandmother. She didn't remember her parents, who'd died when she was a baby. From that time on Grandmother had been her mother and her father, teaching her how to bake and sew, how to milk the cows and churn the butter. Her grandmother had been a woman of infinite patience and energy—never tiring of Josephine's endless questions, never resentful that she had to raise another child after she'd already raised her own. For almost ten happy years, Josephine had felt the secure comfort of a loving home.

Then her grandmother had sent her away.

Josephine's eyes burned as she gripped the reins. The same questions that had plagued her since that day twenty-five years ago still whirled in her mind now. *Why, Grammie? What did I do wrong? Why did you send me to Washington with Aunt Millicent?*

She knew she was torturing herself, for her questions had no answers. Her mother's sister, Aunt Millicent, had arrived on the farm and taken her away, telling her that her grandmother didn't want the burden of a child anymore but never explaining why. Josephine had hated living with her selfish, bitter aunt, and she'd sent numerous letters from Washington to Holly Lake, begging, pleading to come back home. She'd never received a reply to a single one.

With a hard jerk Josephine slapped the reins against the horse's side, urging it into a full gallop. She didn't care that the frigid wind burned against her cheeks, that her hat had fallen loose from its ties, or that her limbs were stiff with cold. Any sensation was preferable to the pain searing her heart.

Faster and faster she pushed the mare on, and within minutes she saw the farm come into view. Determination filled her as she sped toward the farmyard. She would take care of this once and for all. She would get her property, sell the farm, and return to Washington, ridding herself of the painful memories forever. Then she could start building a new life on her own terms.

Suddenly she saw something dash out in front of her horse. Horror seized her when she realized what it was. A child! She didn't have time to wonder where the girl had come from, only time to react. With all her might Josephine pulled back on the reins. "Whoa!" she shrieked as the horse reared up. The leather straps slid out of her grip, and she screamed again as she flew into the air. A sharp pain pierced her head when she landed on the ground.

Then everything went black.

⚜

BEN'S HEART stopped as he watched the scene unfold before his eyes.

He'd dashed out of the barn just in time to see the accident. The other girls were inside the house, but Missy had wanted to go with him to milk the cows. He hadn't realized she wasn't by his side until he'd heard the sounds of a horse galloping and a woman's ear-shattering shriek.

When he saw how close Missy had come to being trampled, his blood ran cold. The rider had restrained her horse and barely missed his baby girl, saving his daughter's life. Helplessly he'd watched as the horse threw the woman, who landed on the ground with a sickening thud.

Missy's frightened wails spurred him into action. "Abby! Come quick!" he hollered, running toward Missy, who was now sitting at the edge of the barnyard sobbing uncontrollably.

Abby rushed out of the house and down the porch steps. "What happened?" She looked to Missy. "Is she all right?"

Ben fell to his knees in front of Missy, cupped her tiny

face, then slid his hands swiftly over her body. "She seems okay. Take her in the house and make sure."

Abby hurriedly scooped up the child in her arms. "Go back inside," she ordered her other sisters, who were crowded at the edge of the porch trying to find out what all the commotion was about.

Ben rushed across the yard to the fallen woman. Shock surged through him when he realized who she was: Josephine Patterson.

She lay still, way too still. *Dear Jesus, please, no! Not another death. I can't bear to see another woman die.* He prayed fervently as he laid his head against her chest, letting out a deep breath when he heard the faint beat of her heart. *Thank You, Lord, thank You.*

Gently he checked for broken bones. With relief he saw that her limbs looked normal, not twisted or broken. Then he noticed the thick trickle of blood that oozed from a deep cut on the upper corner of her forehead. She'd struck the edge of a sharp rock.

Carefully he lifted her from the ground, cradled her wounded head against his chest, and carried her into the house. Ignoring the curious questions of his children, he took Josephine straight upstairs to Wilma's room and laid her on the soft feather bed.

Abby appeared in the doorway. "What can I do to help?"

Ben glanced at her. "Send Livvie up here with a clean rag and a pitcher of water. Is Missy okay?"

"She's fine. Scared, but fine. I'll send Livvie right away."

When Abby left, he turned his attention back to Josephine. He sat down on the bed next to her, disconcerted by the pale color of her skin and her bloodied head. Anger warred with the worry inside him. Foolish woman! Why was she riding that horse so fast? Didn't she know how dangerous that was? But he knew if Missy hadn't run out in front of her, Josephine could have easily slowed her animal to a trot, then to a safe stop. Guilt surged through him. If he'd kept a better eye on his daughter, this woman wouldn't be lying unconscious right now.

He stood at the sound of footsteps entering the room. A white porcelain pitcher wavered in Livvie's hand, and she held several strips of cloth in the other. "I brought more than one, just in case," she explained.

Ben yanked off his coat and took the water from her. It splashed over the sides of the nightstand basin as he hastily emptied the pitcher.

"Is she dead, Daddy?" Livvie asked, her voice trembling.

"No, honey, she's not dead. She's going to be fine." Josephine's wound worried him, despite his reassuring words. But he didn't want to alarm his sensitive daughter, who'd been known to burst into tears if she so much as accidentally stepped on a spider. Of his five girls, Livvie had taken Wilma's death the hardest, and he didn't want to upset her further by hinting that Josephine might not recover.

"Hand me one of those cloths," he said, forcing a neutral tone. He dipped the cloth in the cold water, wrung it out, and cautiously dabbed at the cut on Josephine's forehead. He'd have to fetch the doctor as soon as possible. But first he must stop the bleeding.

"Can I say a prayer for her?"

Touched, Ben looked at Livvie. "How about we pray for her together?"

"Okay." She kneeled next to Ben while he continued to tend to Josephine's wound. Screwing her eyes shut, Livvie prayed. "Dear Jesus, please take care of this pretty lady. She's hurt bad, and I don't want her to die. Will You heal her? I know You can, because You can do anything. In Jesus' name, amen."

"Amen," Ben echoed. He lifted the cloth and saw that the flow of blood had stopped. He picked up a clean cloth and laid it over the cut. "I have to go into town and get Dr. Winger, Livvie. I need you to stay with Mrs. Patterson. Can you do that for me?"

The young girl hesitated; then she lifted her chin and nodded, her red corkscrew curls bouncing against her shoulders. "Yes, I can."

"That's my girl." He covered Josephine's legs and torso with one of Wilma's colorful patchwork quilts. He started for the door when Livvie's voice stopped him.

"Daddy, do you think Jesus heard our prayer?"

He cast a glance at Josephine's prone form. She was beautiful, even with the makeshift cloth bandage on her head, her auburn hair spread wildly over the goose-down pillow. He realized what he wanted more than anything was for this woman to be healed. "Yes, Livvie. We have to believe He did."

V

J OSEPHINE STRUGGLED to open her eyes. Her lids felt heavy and gritty; her body ached all over. She let out a tiny cry as she tried to move her head.

"Thank God," she heard a deep voice say.

With great effort she turned and saw Benjamin Akers sitting in a chair a few feet from the bed. "What are you doing here?" she asked shakily.

"You don't remember?"

"No."

"You've had an accident," he said, leaning forward in the rocking chair. "Dr. Winger was here a little while ago; he examined you and bandaged up your head. He said you'd be all right once you woke up."

"I don't feel all right," she said. "I feel like I've been run over by a locomotive."

Benjamin's mouth tilted in a half smile. "Nothing so serious as that. You were just thrown from your horse."

"Thrown from my horse?" Suddenly she remembered the incident clearly. Her horse galloping at top speed, a young girl running in front of it—

"The child!" she cried, sitting up straight. "What happened to the little girl? Is she hurt? Is she . . . ?" Josephine felt a throbbing pain run through her head. She brought her fingers to her forehead, touching the stiff bandage there. "Oh . . ."

Benjamin immediately came to her side. "Shhh," he said soothingly as his arm encircled her back. "Missy's fine, thanks to you. Lay back now. You're in no shape to be sitting up. It's a miracle you didn't break any bones."

She let him ease her back down on the bed. When the room stopped spinning, she took a moment to scan her surroundings. It didn't take long for her to realize she was in her grandmother's room.

The bedroom was small and sparsely furnished but cozy. The big feather bed took up most of the space, along with a small oak wardrobe, the matching nightstand, and the hand-hewn rocking chair Ben had been sitting on. Several samplers—Bible verses hand stitched years ago—hung in simple wooden frames on the wall.

Everything was exactly the way she'd remembered it, as if she'd stepped back in time. The only thing different was the huge man hovering over her, concern etched on his features.

"Can I get you anything?"

She started to shake her head, but any slight movement brought the pain back again. "No. How long have I been unconscious?"

"Almost eight hours."

"What?" She cast a glance at the window and saw the blackness of the night through the frosty pane of glass. Again she tried to sit up. "I can't stay here. I have to get back to the hotel."

His hand was gentle but firm against her shoulder. "You're not going anywhere. Doctor's orders. You're to stay in bed for the next two days."

"But what about my things? I can't possibly remain in the same clothes for that long."

"I'm sure we can find something of Wilma's for you to wear," he replied.

"No!" she blurted before she noticed the odd look on Ben's face. "I mean . . . I have some valuable items in my suitcases. I don't want anything to happen to them."

"If you're worried about thieves, don't be. I can't remember the last time we had any criminal activity in Holly Lake." He paused. "But if you tell me what you need, I'll go get it for you in the morning."

"I need it all," she said quickly.

"All right. I'll take care of it," he said, his tone low and reassuring.

Josephine relaxed slightly, watching him reach for the rocking chair and drag it closer to her bed. The wood creaked when he sat down on it, and he looked uncomfortable in the too-small chair. A long awkward silence stretched between them before he spoke.

"Thank you," he said finally.

"For what?"

"For saving Missy's life."

Josephine scowled. "I nearly killed her. I should have never ridden the horse that fast."

"And I should have kept a closer eye on my daughter."

She blinked in surprise. "That little girl was your daughter?"

"My youngest."

"How many children do you have?"

He ticked off their names on his fingers. "Abigail's the oldest. She's twelve. Olivia is nine, Katherine seven, Bethany's five, and Melissa turned three last month."

She looked at him in disbelief. Five daughters! She'd

assumed he wasn't married. "Where's your wife?" she asked, closing her eyes. She could only imagine how upset the woman must be with her right now.

"She passed away three years ago," he said quietly, his voice tinged with sadness.

Her eyes flew open. Suddenly she saw Benjamin Akers in a new light.

⚜

JOSEPHINE DESPERATELY wanted to leave Redmond Farm.

More than twenty-four hours had passed since the accident. Her head ached and she felt sore everywhere else, but she didn't care. Doctor's orders or not, she wanted to collect her things and return to town. The last place she wanted to be was in her grandmother's farmhouse, especially this close to Christmas. She'd never expected to be stuck here.

It hadn't taken her long to figure out Benjamin's situation. A widowed father with five young children to care for. Her grandmother living alone in the sprawling house. Benjamin's earlier claim that he was a part of her grandmother's family. She didn't have to be a genius to put the pieces together. She knew the Akers family had been living at Redmond Farm for a while.

Josephine picked at a loose thread on the quilt. Her grandmother had opened her home to a family of strangers, and she had formed enough of a bond with Benjamin to bequeath him half the farm. But why only half? Wilma Redmond hadn't wanted anything to do with her own granddaughter for twenty-five years, and she had a houseful of potential heirs living with her at the time of her death. Why bother to give Josephine any of the inheritance at all?

She sighed. She tried to ignore a pain in her heart that was more agonizing than the one in her head. But she couldn't, not when reminders of her grandmother surrounded her. How ironic that Benjamin would choose this particular room for her recuperation.

Throwing the cover off her lap, she slowly sat up. The room spun, but only for a moment. She looked at the stack of luggage in the corner of the bedroom. Benjamin remained true to his word. That morning he had retrieved her bags from the hotel before he and his four younger daughters attended church services, leaving the oldest girl behind to keep an eye on Josephine. He had explained to the manager what had happened, even paying a visit to Henry Flint and taking back the horse she'd borrowed. Early that afternoon Benjamin had set down the suitcases and asked her if she needed anything. When she told him no, he'd left so she could get some sleep.

Then she'd met his oldest daughter, Abigail. When the pretty young girl had brought her a light breakfast, Josephine noticed her blue eyes were kind, hinting at a young lady wise beyond her years.

But that was hours ago. Josephine felt stronger now, so she gingerly swung her legs over the side of the bed. The sooner she was up and around, the sooner she could ask Benjamin to take her back to town. When she managed to stand on slightly unsteady legs, she glanced out the window. By the cloudy, grayish sky it was difficult to determine the time of day, but she guessed it was late afternoon, plenty of time for him to take her to the hotel. With slow steps she crossed the room to her stack of luggage and bent over to undo one of the clasps. She couldn't wait to get out of her dirty, wrinkled dress and into a fresh one.

A deep burst of pain penetrated her skull, and the floor spun beneath her. Before she could stop herself, she fell to the floor.

A loud stomping sound reached her ears as she

struggled to sit up. She turned to see Benjamin burst through the door. "Josephine! What are you doing out of bed?"

"I . . . I needed something . . . ," she said, staring at him until his face came back into focus.

With two long strides he was at her side. "You should have called for me or Abby. We would have gotten whatever you needed."

"I wanted to get it myself," she told him weakly. Placing her hands on the floor on both sides of her body, she tried to get up. But the returning dizziness coupled with the long folds of her dress made it impossible.

"Steady," Benjamin said, grasping her around the shoulders. In one swift motion he lifted her in his arms as if she weighed no more than a porcelain doll.

Josephine felt breathless, and it wasn't because of her injury. She looked up at him, his face so close to hers she could see the tiny lines creased around his eyes, and if she wanted to, she could count the freckles on the bridge of his nose. Instead of the offensive odors of sweat and dirt, she breathed in the clean scent of bay-rum soap.

For a brief instant she felt the bizarre urge to lay her head against his shoulder. A part of her relished the sense of safety she felt at being wrapped in his powerful arms, so different from the cold embrace of her late husband.

But the feeling evaporated when she saw where he was taking her. "I don't want to go back to bed!" she protested. "I demand you put me down this instant."

"Stop squirming," he replied, tightening his grip. "And stop acting like a child. The doctor said you were to rest, and I aim to see that you follow orders."

"Please," she said, her voice trembling, "I-I can't stay in this room."

Benjamin halted, giving their surroundings a brief

glance. Then he looked at her, and his expression changed. "This was Wilma's room," he said quietly, as if more to himself than to her. "I should have realized . . . you're still grieving." Sadness contorted his features. "We all are."

Josephine didn't try to correct his assumption. But in that moment she realized something as well. Benjamin Akers had genuinely cared for her grandmother. His grief was evident in his eyes, in his tone of voice. She could tell that his feelings ran deeper than that of gratitude toward the woman who'd taken his family into her home.

"You can stay in my room," he said suddenly.

She sucked in her breath. "Mr. Akers, I hardly think that's an appropriate solution—"

"Hold on there, Mrs. Patterson. Don't jump to conclusions. I'll sleep on the settee in the sitting room tonight."

She didn't miss the twinkle in his eye as he spoke, and she had to admit she was glad to see his melancholy fade. "Well, I suppose it will do," she agreed with reluctance.

Benjamin laughed heartily. "I'm glad you approve." He smiled at her, and she became acutely aware that she was still cradled in his arms.

"I must be getting heavy," she said softly.

His smile faded. "Not at all, Josephine," he replied, his voice low and husky. "I do believe you fit in my arms quite well."

C · H · A · P · T · E · R

VI

J OSEPHINE TUGGED her grandmother's quilt closer
around her shoulders, savoring the words Benjamin
had spoken to her over an hour ago: *"You fit in my
arms quite well."* A rush of warmth passed through her, a
sensation she'd never experienced before, especially not
with Henry. *What is happening to me?*

She tried to attribute the unfamiliar emotions to the
bump on her head, but that was merely an excuse. She
felt drawn to Benjamin Akers. And that posed a serious
problem.

"Tea, Mrs. Patterson?"

Josephine looked up into yet another freckled face
framed by brilliant red hair. Since Benjamin had brought
her downstairs to the sitting room and settled her in a
chair in front of a warm fire in the hearth, she'd been
waited on hand and foot by his daughters.

This one looked to be about ten years old. Josephine plumbed her memory. "Are you Olivia?" she asked, reaching for the china teacup and its matching saucer.

The girl beamed. "Yes, ma'am."

Josephine was quite pleased herself that she'd remembered the child's name. "Thank you, Olivia." She took a sip of the tea, which was tepid and over sugared. "Delicious," she said, unwilling to hurt her feelings.

"I made it myself."

Josephine smiled. "I can tell."

"I'm so glad you're well again. Jesus heard my prayer after all."

Frowning, Josephine lowered her teacup. She started to question Olivia, but the girl gave her another heart-stopping smile and scampered off into the kitchen.

"The girls bothering you?" Benjamin asked as he entered the room, a huge load of firewood stacked in his arms. He still wore his coat and hat, and his cheeks were as rosy as apples. Snow dusted the shoulders of his coat.

"Not at all," she replied, steadying the teacup in her lap. "They're quite charming."

Benjamin smiled proudly. "Now that's something we can agree on. They're remarkable girls." He laid the wood next to the hearth. "If you'll excuse me, I need to hang up my things." With long easy strides he headed out the sitting-room door.

Josephine stared into the flickering flames of the blazing fire, its warmth providing comfort to her body but not her soul. Confusion ruled instead. She shouldn't be here, not with Benjamin and his family. And certainly not in her grandmother's house. She felt like an outsider, yet legally she had a right to be here.

Then why didn't she feel like she did?

She looked down at the teacup in her lap. The china was creamy white in color, with delicate pink roses hand-painted on one side. The saucer was rimmed with matching blossoms. She remembered the tea set, a cherished heirloom passed down through generations of the Redmond family. As per tradition, it would have been given to Josephine as a wedding gift. But of course it hadn't.

Her hands gripped the sides of the cup. She was losing perspective here. She couldn't allow the allure of Benjamin Akers and his sweet daughters to derail her. The accident had been enough of an interruption.

The heavy tread of Benjamin's boots against the wooden floor of the sitting room brought her out of her thoughts. He held a steaming mug of fragrant coffee and sat down on the chair opposite her. The tin mug looked as fragile in his large, strong hands as her china teacup did in her slender ones.

"Looks like Casey O'Brien's bones might be right after all," he said cryptically.

"What?"

"O'Brien predicted we'd have a huge snowstorm," he answered. "Said he felt it in his bones. Trouble is, his bones usually send him mixed messages." He smiled, sipping his coffee. "He could be right this time, though. Snow's really starting to come down."

Josephine tore her gaze away from his face, which seemed to become more handsome to her by the second. No more distractions. "Mr. Akers, we need to talk."

"There you go again."

"Pardon me?"

"You're starting up with that 'Mr. Akers' claptrap. What will it take to get you to call me Ben? or at least Benjamin?"

"Does it really matter what I call you?"

"Yes, it does." His eyes locked on to hers, and this time she couldn't pull away.

"Daddy?"

Josephine turned to see a little girl, a tentative expression on her cherubic face. Her body was partially hidden behind the frame of the doorway, and she quickly averted her eyes when Josephine looked directly at her.

"Come in, honey," Benjamin said, holding out his free hand. "It's okay."

The girl scurried in and climbed onto her father's lap. He set his coffee mug on the floor beside the chair and cuddled her in his arms. She immediately whispered in his ear. He nodded in reply. "You're right, Beth, but it's impolite to whisper in front of other people. If you have something to say, sweetheart, say it so Mrs. Patterson can hear."

Beth flushed a shade of red that closely matched her hair and shook her head briskly.

"You'll have to pardon her manners," said Benjamin. "She's more than a little shy." As if to prove her father's statement as true, Beth buried her head in his broad chest. "Go along, little one. Help your sisters get supper ready."

She quickly complied. After she'd been gone a few moments, Josephine couldn't stand it anymore. "Well, what did she say?"

He cleared his throat, and she thought she detected a slight blush on his face. "She said you're a very pretty lady."

Again the odd sensation flowed through her, not so much at the words, but at the way he looked at her as he said them.

Yes, she was definitely losing perspective.

DINNER WAS COLD, but that was to be expected. It was Sunday, and the meal had been prepared the night before because working was prohibited on the Lord's Day. Glancing at the plate of cold ham, potato salad, and bread and butter, Josephine's stomach began to growl. She hadn't been this hungry in days.

Laying her napkin in her lap, she picked up her fork and aimed it at her potato salad, when she heard Benjamin speak from the opposite end of the long oak table. "Dear Lord, thank You for this day . . ."

Josephine set down her fork and immediately bowed her head.

". . . for the abundant food set before us and for all the blessings You have bestowed upon our family. . . ."

Blessings? Josephine tried to count her blessings but came up empty-handed. And what did Benjamin have to be so thankful for? He had lost his wife, then his benefactor, and now he was left to raise his five daughters alone.

"We ask that You continue to have Your hand upon us, guiding our thoughts and actions. . . ."

Her stomach growled loudly. Would this prayer never end? She peeked at his daughters, sure that they would be squirming in their seats by now. But every one of them, from the oldest to the youngest, sat obediently still, with her head bowed and eyes closed. Devoutly still.

"Bless this food and the hands that prepared it. In Jesus' name, amen."

Finally! She lifted her fork again, only to be thwarted by one of the girls.

"On Sundays we always say what we're thankful for, Mrs. Patterson," Katy said, giving her a gap-toothed grin. "What are you thankful for?"

"Katherine Leigh!" Abigail admonished. "Mrs. Patterson is our guest. You shouldn't put her on the spot like that."

"But since she's our guest, shouldn't she go first? That's what Grammie always said. Guests go first." Katy shot her sister a satisfied glare.

Josephine suddenly felt six pairs of eyes on her. What was she grateful for? Being deprived of a happy childhood? Being coerced into a loveless marriage by her status-seeking Aunt Millicent? Being rejected by her grandmother? Being forced into desperate financial straits by her late criminal husband?

No, she had nothing to be thankful for.

"Girls, why don't we do this later," Benjamin said, picking up his fork. He gave Josephine an empathetic look, as if he understood what held her back. "I don't know about you, but I'm starved."

The meal continued in relative silence, and Josephine was again impressed with Benjamin's daughters. No, they weren't perfectly still or quiet and Benjamin had to warn Missy twice about being seen and not heard, but overall they behaved like little ladies. After having had her own experiences with the bratty behavior of some of the children of Washington's elite families, she had to give Benjamin and his late wife credit for raising their children well.

When everyone finished eating, Abby rose from her chair. "Livvie, it's your turn to help me do the dishes. Katy, you and Beth clear the table."

"What 'bout me?" Missy asked with eagerness.

"You can clear your own cup and dish, little one," Benjamin said before he pushed back his chair. "I have to settle the stock in for the night," he said to Josephine. "Won't take me too long. Will you be all right until I get back?"

"Yes," she said. "You really don't have to be so concerned about me."

"Because you're fine, right?"

She paused, surprised at his response. "Yes, Mr. Akers. I am perfectly fine."

He studied her for a moment. "Why don't I believe that?"

She sensed he was referring to something other than the bump on her head. It bothered her that he could read her so well. "I don't care what you believe," she retorted. "And while I appreciate you and your family's hospitality, we still have the matter of the farm to discuss."

"We can talk about it when I get back," he said.

"We'll talk about it now!" she shouted. She shut her eyes against the sharp pain in her head. When it passed, she opened her eyes and felt her stomach drop beneath the shocked stares of Benjamin's daughters.

"Girls, finish clearing the table," Benjamin said, glowering. His eyes never left Josephine as his daughters grabbed the rest of the dishes and scurried from the room. "Perhaps we should go to the sitting room and talk, Mrs. Patterson," he gritted out as he stood from the table. "Do you need assistance?"

Feeling like a reprimanded child, she looked away and shook her head. Without another word Benjamin stalked out of the room, the heavy tread of his large work boots thundering ominously against the floor. Swallowing, Josephine moved to follow him, knowing she'd overstepped her bounds.

Entering the sitting room, she quietly slipped into the chair near the fire. Benjamin hunkered down in front of the hearth and threw a thick log on the flames as if it weighed no more than a toothpick. She could sense that the fire wasn't the only thing blazing in the room. When he turned his hot, stormy eyes on her, she knew she was right.

He rose and walked toward her. "I would appreciate it if you would treat me with a little respect in my home," he said, his voice low and controlled. "Especially in front of my daughters."

A snide comment about the house being only half his came to mind, but Josephine quickly extinguished it as she looked up at him. Although he was more than twice her size and obviously angry, she didn't feel threatened by him. Once again she found herself comparing this man to Henry, whose volatile temper and harsh words had cut her to ribbons more than once during their marriage. Not for an instant did she believe Benjamin would hurt her. Yes, he definitely deserved her respect.

"I'm sorry," she said, sincere. "I shouldn't have yelled at you like that. It won't happen again."

The anger instantly melted from his features. "Well," he said, skimming his fingers through his thick red hair, "that wasn't the response I expected."

"Bracing yourself for another argument, were you?"

He flushed, making him appear more boyish than usual. And more appealing. "Yes," he admitted, taking a step back. "I guess I was."

Josephine let out a weary sigh. She was tired of it all, tired of fighting everything and everyone. It seemed she'd been fighting for most of her life.

To her surprise, Benjamin knelt in front of her. "As soon as I take care of the stock and get the girls to bed, we'll talk. About the farm . . . or anything else you want to discuss." His blue eyes locked on to hers for an instant, seeming to peer straight into her soul.

For that split second in time she felt completely exposed. Yet instead of wanting to hide from him, she had a strong desire to tell him everything, to share every painful aspect of her life.

But she couldn't do that. He had enough to deal with raising five daughters alone. He didn't need to hear about her problems as well.

He rose to his feet and smiled. "I'll be right back. Don't run off now."

She let out a flat chuckle, despite the despair that was creeping over her. "Where would I go?" she joked weakly as he walked out of the room.

Indeed, where else would she go? Whom could she turn to? Staring at the flickering flames that danced in the old hearth, she knew the answer.

No one.

CHAPTER

VII

A FTER HE'D RUSHED through his chores and hastily tucked the girls in bed for the night, Ben went to the kitchen, intent on fixing a cup of tea for Josephine. Reaching for the kettle, his hand stopped in midmotion. How many times had he done the exact same thing for Mary? She'd always enjoyed a cup of hot tea before bed on cold winter nights.

He closed his eyes. He still thought of his deceased wife often, but the images of her had been less sharp lately. Instead his mind swirled with visions of a feisty woman who was as much of an enigma as she was beautiful. But tonight he'd been given a small glimpse beneath her frosty exterior. For the shortest of instants he'd seen her wounded soul. *How can I help her, Lord?*

His prayer caught him by surprise. When had she become so important to him? His concern for Josephine

Christmas Legacy | 307

went beyond her physical well-being, beyond settling their dispute. For some reason he wanted to reach out to her, to discover what she harbored inside that could have brought such anguish to her eyes.

Grabbing the teakettle, he filled it with water and lit the stove, his thoughts wandering back to Mary. He found himself comparing her to Josephine and shaking his head. The two women couldn't be any more different—Mary, shy and soft-spoken, had possessed a solid will and a strong faith in Christ. He detected the same inner strength in Josephine but doubted she had faith in anything.

A tiny twinge of guilt shot through him, as if his comparing Josephine to Mary made him unfaithful to his wife's memory. He dismissed the emotion as unfounded. He had loved Mary and would love her for the rest of his life. What he felt for Josephine . . .

What did he feel for Josephine exactly?

The piercing sound of the kettle's whistle brought him out of his musings. He prepared the tea, poured himself a lukewarm cup of coffee, and headed for the sitting room.

The fire cast a soft glow around the room, accompanied by the faint smoky smell of burning oak logs. He moved toward Josephine, who had her back to him. When he reached her, his mouth formed a faint smile. She was sleeping.

He crept around her chair, setting her teacup on the small wood table next to her before easing himself into the chair on the opposite side of the hearth. The room was quiet, except for the low crackling of the fire and the faraway howl of the wind, which had picked up considerably in the past hour.

Ben took a swig of his coffee, then leaned back in the chair and looked at the lovely woman seated across from him. Gone were the lines of strain that always tugged at the corners of her mouth and eyes. Josephine in repose was the picture of peace. He wished she could find that peace when she was awake.

Closing his eyes, he began to pray. *Be with her, Jesus. You know her hurts; You understand her pain. But does she know You? Does she realize that You are here for her?*

"Why didn't you wake me?"

At the sound of her low murmur, he opened his eyes and watched her shift uncomfortably in her chair. Her posture was again ramrod straight, the serene expression now replaced with tense awareness.

"I didn't want to disturb you," he said. He gestured to the table beside her chair. "There's a cup of tea for you if you'd like."

She nodded and picked it up, her delicate hands cupping the fragile china. "I must say, your daughters have been most attentive," she pointed out, peering into the liquid. "This must be the third cup of tea they've brought me today."

"That's not from them. It's from me."

Her gaze flew to him. "You . . . made this for me?"

"Yep," he answered, hiding his grin at her stunned expression.

Again she stared at the cup. "I-I don't know what to say."

"Well, thank you would do," he teased, stretching out his long legs and crossing them at the ankles.

"Yes . . . thank you," she said gravely, her eyes meeting his.

The pain he saw in them tore at his heart. Uncrossing his ankles, he leaned forward in his chair. "Josephine, what's wrong?"

"Nothing," she said, turning her attention to the fire. "I'm fine."

"We both know that's not true. I wish you'd stop saying it."

"And I wish you'd stop doing that!" she shot back, looking at him again, anger contorting her features.

"Doing what?" he asked, confused.

"Acting like you know me." She placed her teacup on the saucer with a loud clink, the dark liquid splashing over the sides. "Like you can see deep inside me," she said, her voice cracking on the last word.

Ben sensed her defenses crumbling, revealing a layer of raw vulnerability beneath. "What I can see is that you're hurting," he said gently. "And I want to help you. If you'll let me."

She hesitated, and for a moment he thought she might open up to him. But it didn't take long for her to rebuild her fortress. "You can help by selling me your portion of the farm."

He fell back against his chair. Back to that again. He had promised they would discuss the farm, and she was holding him to it. "I already told you, my half isn't for sale." His eyes dropped to her hands and watched as she twisted the ruby ring on her finger back and forth in an anxious movement he now knew well.

"What would I have to do to get you to change your mind?" she asked, desperation coloring her tone.

Ben eyed her squarely. "Tell me why you want it so badly."

He waited while she considered his request, fascinated by the internal struggle he knew she was battling. Why couldn't she trust him? Then he realized he hadn't given her a reason to.

"When my wife passed away, I thought the world had ended," he said, setting his coffee cup down on the floor. "She died giving birth to Missy." He clenched his fists at the memory, even though the pain had dulled over the years. "There I was with four young daughters and a newborn to take care of and no family around to help. Then your grandmother stepped in."

"Why are you telling me this?" Josephine asked, uneasiness filling her eyes.

"Because I want you to know why this place means so much to me. That I'm not withholding it from you out of spite. Wilma took us in, treated me and my girls as if we were part of her own family. I had already been working for her as a hired hand for a few months, after we had moved here from Ohio. She opened her house and her heart to a broken man and his daughters. She helped lift us back on our feet." He looked at Josephine, willing her to understand what he was trying to say. "Her home became our home too."

Josephine bit her bottom lip, apparently taking in everything he'd told her. "Did she ever mention me?" she finally said in a childlike whisper.

"No."

"I see." Slowly she rose from the chair, her hand briefly touching her temple, as if warding off the pain, before she dropped it to her side. She turned and faced the fire.

Ben got up and moved to stand behind her. He tried to convince himself he went to her out of concern for her physical condition, in case she became dizzy and lost her balance again. But he failed. Deep down he knew he wanted to be near her, close enough that if he reached out his hand a few inches, he could touch the glossy auburn curls she'd pinned up earlier that morning. It shocked him how powerful his desire was to do just that.

It took all of his inner strength to keep his hands still, to return his focus to their discussion of the farm. Then an idea suddenly occurred to him. "Josephine," he said, "I think I might have a solution."

When she didn't turn around, he stepped to her side and glanced at her profile, which remained impassive. "I figure you're planning to sell the land, right?" he began. He took her silence as confirmation and continued. "What if you sold it to me? I couldn't buy your half outright, but we could work out some kind of payment plan. I can get Rawlings to draw up a contract to make it legal and binding."

Ben started to warm to the concept. Yes, this might work after all. "That way you wouldn't have to worry about finding a buyer for half of the property, and you'll know the farm will be in good hands. What do you think?"

She turned to him, the movement deliberate, calculated. "If you refuse to sell me your portion of Redmond Farm, I shall be forced to bring legal action against you."

Ben felt like he'd been punched in the gut. "What? I just gave you the perfect solution to our problem, and now you're threatening me?"

"It's not a threat, Mr. Akers. It's a promise. I am my grandmother's blood kin. This farm is rightfully mine." She paused, not masking the resentment in her eyes. "*All mine,*" she emphasized.

He couldn't believe what he was hearing. "After everything I've told you, you're not even willing to consider my offer?"

"No."

"So it's your way or no way. Even if it means that me and my daughters lose our home."

She turned her face from him and looked at the fire again. "That's not my problem," she said quietly.

Powerless to stem the fury burning within him, Ben exploded. "Of course not!" he shouted, unaffected by the way she flinched at his words. He spun away from her and began to pace the length of the room, not caring if he woke his daughters or not. Then he halted his steps. "Do you have any children?" he asked.

A long pause. "No."

"Now why doesn't that surprise me?" he sneered. "I'm sure children would have put a dent in your Washington social life." From the slight slump of her shoulders he saw he was cutting deep, but it didn't matter. "I bet you're incapable of caring for anyone but yourself," he added viciously, no longer feeling compassion for whatever pain he thought he'd seen in her. Any woman who would try to evict children from their home had ice water running in her veins.

She turned around and walked toward him, squaring her shoulders. "I want to leave in the morning," she told him, her words and expression empty.

"I'll be happy to take you to town," he retorted, allowing her to pass.

She moved a few steps past him, picking up a small oil lamp from the table by the door. The yellow flame flickered ominously beneath the cloudy glass shade. Spinning on her heel, she turned and faced him. "Not that it's any of your business, Mr. Akers, but I'm barren," she said, her green eyes suddenly shiny and wet. She blinked several times. "I can never have children."

For the second time that evening Ben felt his breath knocked out of him, followed by a wave of remorse that left him speechless. Dumbfounded, he watched Josephine leave the sitting room, the eerie howling of the wind outside pounding in his ears. His harsh words— both spoken and thought—came charging back at him, each one causing him as much pain as he knew he'd caused her.

C · H · A · P · T · E · R

VIII

S WALLOWING HARD, Josephine struggled against the sharp pain that choked her throat as she shut the bedroom door. She leaned back against the sturdy oak, resolving not to waste her tears on Benjamin Akers. He didn't deserve them.

How could she have been so wrong about him? She had truly believed Benjamin would never hurt her, yet with a few words he'd shattered her feelings as if they were made of thin glass.

Why had she told him she was barren? Although she had long ago accepted that she couldn't have children, she felt like a fool for divulging such a personal weakness—and a weakness it was, one that Henry had thrust in her face time and time again. The last thing she wanted from Benjamin was his pity. She knew she already had his disdain.

With stiff movements she took a few steps into the room, the dim flame from the lamp she held illuminating her surroundings. She stopped as she noticed her suitcases stacked neatly against the side of a large wardrobe, courtesy of Benjamin. In spite of her turbulent emotions, she appreciated his thoughtfulness. For an instant she considered moving back into her grandmother's room, but changing rooms again wouldn't make any difference. She felt trapped either way. One room assaulted her with the past, while the other taunted her in the present. Neither gave her hope for the future.

The roaring wind shrieked through the gaps in the window sash, filling the room with bone-numbing cold. Josephine turned up the lamp and set it on the bedside table, then wrapped her arms around her shoulders and walked to the window. Her heart sank at the sight of the furiously swirling snow that blew against the pane of glass. A blizzard. *Perfect.* An unpleasant shudder passed through her body. There was no way she could leave Redmond Farm tomorrow.

Unable to stand by the freezing window any longer, she quickly changed into her nightgown, twisted her hair into a thick braid, and walked to the massive four-poster bed in the middle of the room. *His bed.*

She didn't want to get into it, but the fatigue and cold that consumed her body were winning out against her will. Reluctantly she lifted the bulky layers of quilts and blankets and slid between the smooth sheets. She felt her spirit sink lower as she turned down the lamp.

She didn't know which distressed her more: that he considered her to be selfish and uncaring or that she suspected he was right.

Her options now seemed more limited than before. How she wished she'd never come out here, never met Benjamin's sweet daughters, never allowed herself to become attracted to the man who turned out to be much more complex than the simple blacksmith she'd assumed him to be. Despite his sharp words slicing her to the quick, she couldn't deny her growing feelings for him. And she couldn't bear the thought of him and his family being cast from their home.

But what about *her* home? Even if she accepted Benjamin's offer, the proceeds from selling only half the farm wouldn't be enough to settle the accounts. The situation seemed impossible.

A sudden creaking sound drew her immediately out of her thoughts. She sat up and turned the lamp on low in time to see the top of a white nightcap dash by the foot of the bed.

"Missy?" Josephine whispered as the young girl ran to the side of the bed. Her wide, frightened eyes were visible even in the low lamplight. "What's wrong?"

"I'm scared," the child whimpered. "The house is movin'."

"That's just the wind," Josephine said, giving her a small smile. "It's not going to hurt you."

Missy remained standing, visibly shaken. "Can I sleep wif you?" she asked, her arms outstretched.

Josephine was stunned. "Don't you want your father? He's right downstairs, on the sitting-room settee."

The little girl simply shook her head. "I wanna sleep wif you."

"Oh, dear." Josephine wasn't sure what to do. But when Missy started shaking from the cold air, she didn't hesitate further. "All right," she said, pulling back the covers and shifting to the center of the mattress. "But just for a short while."

"Us too?" chimed three more voices from the foot of the bed, startling Josephine. She stared at Olivia, Katy, and Beth, all dressed in white nightgowns and matching nightcaps, each with red ringlets flowing over their shoulders. All of them had sheepish expressions on their faces, and Josephine knew why.

"Are all of you scared too?" she asked. The girls nodded vigorously. Josephine had no choice. She pushed back the bedcovers. "Climb in."

Soon the four girls and Josephine were snuggled beneath the warm covers. That Benjamin's daughters didn't have a problem sharing a bed with a strange woman struck her as odd, but it sent a cascading flow of unfamiliar maternal warmth through her.

"Beth, turn down the lamp," Josephine instructed the young girl nearest the bed table. "Unless you think Abby might join us soon."

"Nope," said Olivia as the room was plunged into darkness again. "She can sleep through anything." She paused. "You're good with names, just like Grammie Wilma. She learned our names right away."

"Isn't everyone good with names?" Josephine asked.

"No," Katy, who was lying next to Josephine, piped up. "Our teacher, Mrs. Ratliff, still can't remember Beth's name."

"That's because Beth never says anything," Olivia countered, not unkindly. "She's so quiet no one knows she's there."

"I'm here," Missy said through a yawn.

"So am I." Josephine could barely discern Beth's shy whisper.

"Is it true Grammie Wilma was your Grammie too?" Katy asked, sounding as if she would be awake for a while.

"How did you know that?"

"Daddy told us before we said our prayers. He said that you were Grammie's granddaughter. Did you used to live here too?"

Josephine gripped the edge of the quilt. "Yes . . . when I was a little girl."

"Then how come you weren't here when we came?"

"Because I went to live somewhere else."

"Why?"

Josephine cringed. "Aren't you tired? Your sisters are already asleep."

Katy turned on her side toward Josephine. "No, I'm not tired. The wind woke me up. It sure sounds creepy, doesn't it?"

"Yes, it does."

Relieved when the child didn't say anything else, Josephine closed her eyes, assuming Katy had fallen asleep. They flew open at the child's next remark.

"Daddy likes you, Mrs. Patterson."

"Oh, I don't know about that," she said, disguising how Katy's simple words affected her. Even if he had felt something for her at one time, she'd destroyed it earlier this evening.

"It's true," Katy said in a sleepy voice, the tone counteracting her earlier claim that she wasn't tired. "He looks at you the way he used to look at Mama, all moony-eyed."

Moony-eyed? What did *that* mean? And why did the very idea of Benjamin looking at her that way play havoc with her heartbeat?

Katy nestled her slight body closer to Josephine. "I like you too," she whispered in a faint voice.

The child's heartfelt admission tugged at Josephine. The children's presence had a calming effect on her, even as the ferocious wind made the rafters of the house tremble. As she lay sandwiched among Benjamin's charming daughters, it wasn't too long before her problems dimmed in her mind and a welcoming sleep came over her.

"Mrs. Patterson!"

Abby's frantic voice awakened Josephine. She turned and looked at the blonde-haired girl standing by the side of the bed, alarmed by the worried expression on her face.

"It's Father," she said, lowering her voice as she looked at her sisters' sleeping forms. "He hasn't come back from the barn this morning."

Josephine looked past Abby to the window. Grayish light streaked through the snow-splattered pane. "What time is it?"

"Eight o'clock. I didn't want to wake you and the girls." Abby looked slightly puzzled as she glanced at the four small mounds underneath the covers. "They usually sleep with Father when there's a storm." She wrung her hands. "I've been up since dawn, but he wasn't in the sitting room when I came down. I figured he was checking on the stock early. Mrs. Patterson . . . he hasn't come back."

"I'm sure he's fine," Josephine said, maneuvering gingerly around Katy and Beth before her bare feet hit the cold, hardwood floor. "He's probably waiting in the barn for the storm to let up."

"For three hours? Daddy's always starving in the morning. He never misses breakfast." Abby lost her grown-up demeanor as her voice lowered to a frightened whisper. "I'm afraid something has happened to him."

Josephine padded to the window, only to see a blanket of white through the glass. She strained to discern where the barn *should* be, but to no avail. Panic enveloped her as she remembered a story from her childhood about a man who had frozen to death in a blizzard— his body had been found only a few feet from his house. The thought of Benjamin losing his way in the blinding snow sent slivers of ice racing down her spine.

"I'm sure he's perfectly all right," Josephine reiterated to Abby as she turned from the window, her forced enthusiasm more for her own benefit than for the young girl's. "Go downstairs and I'll wake up your sisters. We'll join you in a little while, and your father will probably be back by then."

Abby seemed relieved. "I'll start frying the eggs," she said, then hurried out the door.

Josephine woke the four girls and sent them to their rooms to change. Stripping off her nightgown, she quickly slipped into a dove gray dress, her fingers fumbling over the tiny pearl buttons. But it wasn't the chill of the bedroom air that made her fingers shake as a sour lump of worry settled in her stomach. *Please, Lord, let him be all right.*

She stilled, her fingers touching the top button at her collar. Had she just *prayed?* The words had come to her mind unbidden, silently spoken as if she had been used to praying all her life. In reality she couldn't remember the last time she'd said a word to God, other than to blame Him for the shambles her life had become. Yet for some reason buried deeply inside her heart, she knew the best thing she could do for Benjamin was to pray.

Swiftly she buttoned the last button, put on her shoes, and rushed downstairs. Entering the kitchen, she was greeted by the aroma of freshly baked biscuits and frying eggs, as well as the sight of four little cherubic, freckled faces already seated at the kitchen table. Abby, her back to Josephine, was manning the stove.

"Good morning, Mrs. Patterson," the children said in unison as they burst into a fit of giggles.

"Good morning, girls," Josephine said, her mouth forming what she hoped was a cheerful smile. She moved over to Abby and touched her shoulder. The girl shook her head briefly, biting her bottom lip as she returned her attention to the eggs bubbling in the iron skillet.

Feeling a tug at her skirt, Josephine turned to see Katy standing behind her. "Where's Daddy?" she asked.

"Doing the morning chores," Abby snapped, not looking at her sister. "Go sit down."

"But he's missing breakfast," Katy pointed out. "We should wait for him."

Abby spun around, brandishing a wooden spoon. "You do as I say or you'll go to your room without your own breakfast!"

Katy's bottom lip poked out. "I'm telling Daddy that you're yelling at me. He'll get you for being so bossy."

Seeing the hateful glare Abby directed toward her younger sister, Josephine intervened. "Come sit with me, Katy, and let Abby finish breakfast. I'm sure your father will join us soon." The words were wearing thin, but she had to continue her reassurances. It was bad enough having one of Benjamin's daughters worrying about him. She didn't know if she could handle the five of them fretting at one time.

When breakfast was served, Benjamin still hadn't come in from the storm. Realizing all five girls were looking at her expectantly, she licked her dry lips. "Does anyone want to say grace?" she asked, surmising that prayer before mealtimes was a habit in the Akers' household.

"Daddy always says grace," Katy volunteered. She shot Abby an annoyed glance. "And I still think we should wait for him."

Abby remained silent, gripping her fork so tightly her knuckles were turning white.

"Katy, I imagine your father is busy making sure all the animals are staying warm in the storm," Josephine said, hoping to diffuse the tension at the table.

"Blizzard," Olivia corrected. "That's a blizzard outside. . . . We learned about those in school." Her blue eyes widened. "What if Daddy's lost in the blizzard? What if he can't find our house?" She paled, jumping from her seat and dashing to the window. "What if he freezes to death?"

Instantly the younger girls burst into tears, following Olivia to the white-encrusted window. Amid the wails and laments for their missing father, Josephine looked helplessly to Abby, the girl's own accusing look wet with unshed tears.

Josephine had never felt so out of her realm. How did one reason with four hysterical girls? Miraculously, the answer came to her immediately. "Girls! Come sit down this instant!"

The crying ceased as they turned to look at her. Something in the tone of her voice must have reached them, for they obediently went to their chairs, sniffling and wiping their faces with their sleeves.

"As I've said before, your father is fine. He's taking care of his stock, just as a good farmer should, and when he's finished he'll come back inside." She gave each daughter, including Abby, a stern look. "In the meantime you'll have breakfast and finish up your chores. And no more crying! Is that clear?"

Everyone nodded, and Josephine felt a rush of relief run through her. "Now, who will say grace?"

Silence.

"Anyone?" she asked, hoping one of them would volunteer.

"We want you to say it," Katy said, the rest of the girls nodding in agreement.

Josephine swallowed. "I-I'm not very good with prayers," she mumbled.

Katy ignored Josephine's comment. "Let's hold hands, like Grammie used to do," she said, slipping her small hand into one of Josephine's, while Missy tucked her tiny one into the other.

Again trapped unwittingly by Benjamin's daughters, Josephine relented and closed her eyes. "Dear Lord . . . um, thank You for this . . . ah, plentiful food." Despite being certain that God had never heard a less eloquent prayer, she pressed on. "Bless the hands that prepared it." Pleased that she remembered part of Benjamin's prayer from last night, she continued more confidently. "And be with our thoughts and . . . um, actions. In Jesus' name—"

"Wait," Olivia interjected. "Aren't we going to pray for Daddy?"

Josephine smiled at her, then bowed her head again. "And, Lord, we ask that You be with Mr. Akers. Bring him home safely—"

As soon as the words left her mouth, the door flew open, and a strong blast of frigid, snow-filled air raced through the room. In the doorway stood a hulking figure, seemingly frozen in place. Josephine watched in shock as the girls instantly jumped up and ran to their father, reaching him as he crumpled to the floor.

JOSEPHINE PLACED the hot-water bottle at the bottom of Benjamin's feet. "Feeling any warmer?" she asked, tucking the thick patchwork quilt around him.

"Getting there," he murmured, sinking deeper into the covers. "I still don't know how you and Abby managed to get me into this chair. I was stiff as a log."

"We're a lot stronger than we look," she said, glancing up at him. Her heart suddenly leapt in her throat at the sight of him gazing down at her with his soft blue eyes. Disconcerted, she rose from the sitting-room floor. "Do you need anything else?" she asked, vexed at the hoarseness in her voice.

"No."

"Are you sure? I could put another log on the fire."

Benjamin's lips tipped in a wry smile. "Really, Josephine, I'm warm enough. I'm even starting to feel my fingers and toes again."

Thank God. She had feared the worst when she and the girls rushed over to where he had fallen on the kitchen floor. Fortunately he hadn't lost consciousness, but he was too cold to move on his own. Somehow she and Abby had helped him to the sitting room; removed his frozen gloves, boots, and outer clothing; and stoked the fire until it blazed. His cheeks were red and raw from the blowing wind, but amazingly he seemed to be unharmed, in spite of nearly getting lost in the blizzard.

"I should have strung a rope," he muttered.

"Pardon me?"

"A rope. Between the barn and the house. I could have used it as a guide, and I wouldn't have gotten disoriented. But I could still see the barn when I went out this morning. By the time I finished the chores and headed back to the house, I couldn't see my hand in front of me."

A tremor of fear passed through her at the thought of how close he'd come to freezing to death. If he hadn't been able to find the farmhouse . . .

"Daddy!" Katy scampered into the sitting room and pounced on her father.

"Young lady," Josephine warned sternly, "your father needs to warm up, and he needs his rest."

"I'll only be here a minute," Katy insisted. Turning to Benjamin, she said, "It was amazing, Daddy. We were all so worried about you, but Mrs. Patterson started to pray, and as soon as she asked God to bring you home, you came in the door!"

Surprise registered on Benjamin's face. "You . . . prayed for me?"

A warm flush crept to her cheeks. "It wasn't exactly like that."

The little girl spoke animatedly, as if she hadn't heard a word Josephine said. "It was a miracle, just like the ones in the Bible."

Josephine's face went hot. "Hardly a miracle," she mumbled.

"I don't know about that," Benjamin said, then turned and looked at her. "I was close to giving up on ever finding the house. I was so cold, and the snow was blinding me so I couldn't find my way back to the barn. I kept wandering, holding my hands in front of me, hoping . . . *praying* I'd feel something solid." His eyes met Josephine's and held them, Katy momentarily forgotten. "Then suddenly my hand touched the latch on the door."

Gooseflesh rose on Josephine's arms beneath the sleeves of her dress. She rubbed them with her hands. "Well, the important thing is that you're safe," she said, unable to tear her gaze from his. She watched as his eyes darkened, irresistibly drawing her into them.

"Do you mean that, Josephine?" he said quietly.

"Of course she means it, Daddy," Katy said, throwing her small arms around his neck. "We're all happy that you're safe."

Josephine quickly averted her eyes, busying herself by smoothing imaginary creases from her skirt. "If you don't need anything else, Mr. Akers, I'll see if I can help Abby in the kitchen." Her eyes flicked to his, and she was bemused to see the disappointment in them. Before he could reply, she started to leave the room but stopped when she heard Katy speak.

"Daddy, what about Christmas?"

Christmas! Tonight was Christmas Eve, and Josephine had been so wrapped up in all her problems she had forgotten about the holiday.

"Christmas will come just as it always does, Katy," Benjamin said.

"But what about the play? We always go to church on Christmas morning to see the baby Jesus story." Her voice was filled with chagrin. "I was supposed to be an angel this year."

"I don't see how we'll make it to church tomorrow, unless this storm lets up," he said. Turning halfway around, Josephine watched him cup Katy's chin in one massive hand. "Don't you worry. I promise we'll do something special to celebrate the day."

"But it won't be the same," Katy huffed. "After church we always have a big dinner, and then we go home and open presents."

"Katy, honey, the play, dinner, and presents are all nice things, but they aren't what Christmas is about. We must remember the real reason for our celebration—the birth of our Savior." The glowing firelight reflected the fatherly tenderness in his eyes. "I'm sure whatever way we decide to honor our Lord, it will be special to Him."

Josephine felt like an intruder, but she was incapable of walking away. Benjamin's obvious love for Katy—for all his children—and their love for him plucked a chord in her heart she hadn't been aware existed. The empty hole in her soul seemed to grow larger the more time she spent with the Akerses. How she longed for the security and closeness they represented.

"Now run along," Benjamin said, giving Katy a smile. She immediately followed his order and dashed past Josephine and out of the room. Josephine moved to follow her.

"Don't go."

She hesitated, caught off guard by his words.

"Come sit with me, Josephine."

Again she paused, even more confused. His tone had taken on an intimate quality she'd never heard from him before.

"Please."

Unable to resist further, she went to him. As she sat in the chair opposite his, he tossed off the blankets and rose from his seat, dragging his chair closer to her. "I've always thought these chairs were too far apart," he said softly.

A sensation hotter than the blaze in the hearth burned inside her at his proximity. The inner flame was fanned when he reached for her. She gasped as he took her hand in his own. "Mr. Akers, this is hardly appropriate behavior, especially with your daughters in the next room!"

Instead of becoming annoyed with her, he laughed. "Oh, Josephine, you're something else. You hide behind that propriety of yours, using it as a shield to keep everyone at bay." He entwined his fingers with hers. "But I know there's more to you than perfect manners and proper decorum. And I'm going to say this for the last time . . . it's *Benjamin.*"

Staring at their hands joined together, she tried to think straight but found it impossible, not when she could feel his calloused flesh against her smooth palm. The roughness of his skin, a testament to the hard work he did in dedication to his family, caused a tingling sensation along her fingers.

"Mr. A—Benjamin," she said, nearly choking on his name, "you should be under those blankets. You don't want to catch a chill." When she dared to look at his face, the smile he gave her nearly melted her bones.

"Saying my name wasn't so hard, was it?" he asked. "Besides, sitting here in front of the fire . . . with you . . . is all the warmth I need."

If her cheeks were any hotter, they would have burst into flame. Was he *flirting* with her? What brought this on? Last night he couldn't wait to be rid of her.

His smile faded as if he had read her mind. "I owe you an apology," he said, rubbing his thumb across the top of her hand. The movement was so natural she wondered if he was aware of doing it. "I should have never said the things I said to you last night. I lost my temper and I hurt you, and . . . well, I'm truly sorry for that."

Josephine didn't know what to say. His sincerity was obvious in the softness of his eyes, in his gentle caress of her hand. For a moment she allowed herself to be carried away on the wave of safety he instilled. Yet she knew it wouldn't last. "Apology accepted," she said stiffly, tugging her hand away from his.

"Josephine," he said, undaunted by her withdrawal, "I can see the pain in your eyes. What is causing you such heartache?"

Suddenly she felt as if she were standing on a precipice, teetering on the edge. Her list of agonies seemed endless . . . hopeless . . .

His penetrating gaze kept her in place. "It's all right; you don't have to say anything. But if you can't tell me, then tell God." He clasped both of her hands in his. "Give your burdens, your pain, to Him. He understands them all, and He can help you through them."

A sharp stinging assaulted her throat. "How can you be so sure?"

He tilted his head and smiled. "Because I know it firsthand. When my wife died, He was there for me, dulling the pain. And when your grandmother died, I leaned on Him then too. Even now, with an uncertain future, I trust He'll be there for me—and my girls. He always has been."

She dropped her eyes and looked at the fire. How she wished she could have his confidence that God would bring peace to the turmoil that raged inside her like the blizzard winds outside the farmhouse. But it couldn't be that easy. Could it?

Lightly he touched her chin with his finger, turning her face back to him. "Let me pray for you, Josephine. Just as you prayed for me." Before she knew what was happening, Benjamin bowed his head and spoke.

She sensed a flicker of peace at his soothing petition to God on her behalf. But it disappeared as guilt seeped in, distorting his words until she no longer heard what he was saying. While Benjamin prayed with skill and conviction, her prayer had been a few halfhearted sentences said to appease five worried daughters. Regardless of what

Katy thought, it had been mere coincidence that her father had opened the door when he did. It certainly wasn't because God had been listening to a weak prayer from a woman who had turned her back on Him.

"In Jesus' name, amen." Raising his head, Benjamin looked at her expectantly. The hope she saw in his eyes dimmed as he continued his scrutiny. She had failed even him.

IX

I FAILED HER, he thought. *I can't reach her.*

He watched Josephine jump up from her chair as if the legs were on fire. "I should check on the girls," she said, grabbing the discarded quilts and hastily arranging them on his lap. "I'll have Olivia bring you a cup of coffee later."

"Josephine—"

"I really must go." Before he could say anything else, she left, the long gray skirt of her dress flaring around her ankles as she exited the room.

Sinking back in his chair, he tugged the blankets closer, feeling colder without her presence. He stared at the fire, second-guessing himself. Had he made a mistake by praying for her? He should have known to tread carefully where Josephine was concerned. Perhaps he'd been too familiar with her, but he couldn't help himself. There had been a connection between them, one that had nothing to do with farms and lawyers and winter storms but had everything to do with a man and a woman.

He could no longer deny his feelings for her, and he found he didn't want to. Underneath her pain and confusion was a woman with a vibrant, if dormant, heart. He saw it in the way she related to his daughters, treating them with respect and care. That quality alone would be enough to win his affections. Still, he sensed there was more. But it would take God to break down her walls and bring it out.

His mind could only imagine what made her guard herself so fiercely. He more than suspected it had something to do with her late husband. Could Wilma have been involved as well? Difficult as it was to believe, he didn't dismiss the possibility. Josephine's reluctance to discuss her grandmother, even in passing, couldn't be ignored. Until she decided to trust him, all of it would remain a mystery.

If she decided to trust him. He surmised that Josephine wasn't used to trusting anyone.

So what should I do, Lord? I care for her, but I can't show it. For whatever reason she won't turn to You. And there's still the situation of the farm to settle. We're nowhere close to meeting eye-to-eye on that. And what about Christmas? I haven't done a thing about the holiday.

Mary had always taken care of the celebration, and after she died Wilma took over. He'd been so busy working at the smithy that he hadn't had time to do something special for the girls. A sense of defeat came over him. *I admit it, God—I don't know where to go from here.*

Then the words he'd spoken to Josephine minutes earlier echoed in his thoughts: *"I trust He'll be there for me—and my girls. He always has been."* What right did he have to give her that advice, when he wasn't following it himself?

Closing his eyes, he began a new prayer. *I lay my burdens at Your feet, Jesus. . . .*

It was time for him to do some trusting of his own.

IT CONTINUED TO STORM well into the afternoon. After lunch Benjamin, exhausted from his morning ordeal, went upstairs to take a nap. He had tried to rest on the settee, but it was almost laughable to watch him attempt to adjust his large body into a comfortable position on the too-small sofa. Josephine figured he hadn't gotten much sleep there the night before either.

After cleaning up the noon-meal dishes, the girls stared forlornly out the kitchen window at the whirling snow. "It doesn't even seem like Christmas," Katy groused.

"There's no pine boughs decorating the sitting room," Olivia added with a frown.

Even Abby was disgruntled. "We don't have a Christmas turkey either."

They voiced several more complaints before Josephine's head started to throb. "Girls, that's quite enough. Come sit back down at the table."

Within moments they were all seated, looking at her in expectation. *Now what?* their gazes seemed to ask, and the same sentiment echoed in her head. They were waiting for her to direct them, but she didn't know what to do next. She glanced apprehensively around the kitchen, then spied her grandmother's wooden rolling pin.

"When I was a little girl, I used to help my grandmother make shortbread cookies for Christmas." Surprised that she could speak of her childhood so freely and encouraged by the girls' piqued interest, she continued. "We made dozens of them in all different Christmas shapes."

"She did that with us last year," Olivia said, the

excitement growing in her voice. "We made wreaths and candy canes and stars—"

"Don't forget the crosses," Katy reminded.

"I know, I know." Olivia tossed her an irritated look. "Lots of crosses. Grammie had us make them so we would remember the reason why Jesus was born. She and Abby rolled out the dough, and we cut them out."

"Can we do it again?" Katy asked, practically jumping out of her seat.

In a voice a little louder than a soft breeze, Beth asked, "Please?"

Abby looked to Josephine. "Grammie didn't write the recipe down, but I think I remember how to make the dough."

"She didn't write any of her recipes down," Josephine said. "Half the time she didn't even measure the ingredients." She paused as memories of her and her grandmother baking together invaded her mind. She bit her lip. As long as she was in this house she would never escape the reminders of her past.

Affected by the eager expressions of Benjamin's daughters, she shoved the thoughts out of her mind and looked to Abby. "I'm sure between the two of us we can figure it out."

Two hours later, they were all up to their elbows in flour and sweet cookie dough, while three dozen shortbread cookies cooled on the kitchen table. Several of the candy canes had misshapen hooks, and two of the stars were suspiciously missing points. The pale yellow crumbs covering Missy's chin betrayed her crime, but Josephine pretended not to notice.

"Now what can we do?" Olivia asked, brushing the flour off her hands. "We can't go out and fetch pine boughs. It's snowing too hard for that."

"I still wish we could go to the play at church," Katy said, her lips forming her familiar pout. "I was supposed to be an angel, you know." Then she suddenly brightened. "We could have the baby Jesus play here!"

"Here?" Josephine asked.

"Why not here?" Abby countered, her blue eyes showing more enthusiasm than Josephine had seen her express before.

"My doll could be Jesus," Olivia offered.

Abby gathered up the tin cookie cutters. "And we have our costumes for the church play."

"I don't know about this," Josephine said. *Costumes? Baby Jesus?* "What would your father say?"

"We could surprise him!" Olivia said, bouncing up and down. "He can be our audience."

Katy's upturned mouth suddenly frowned. "How are we going to practice without him finding out?"

"We'll have to find a way to distract him." Abby turned to Josephine. "Right, Mrs. Patterson?"

Unnerved at the young girl's knowing look, Josephine started to protest but changed her mind when she observed the happiness evident on the children's faces. "All right," she said, relenting. "I'll keep your father occupied." *Somehow.* "But before you do anything else, we must clean up this mess from the cookies."

Never had she seen a kitchen cleaned so quickly. Afterward, the two youngest girls brought out some paper and began drawing donkeys and halos, while Olivia, Katy, and Abby brought out the costumes. Satisfied that the girls had everything under control, Josephine left and entered the sitting room.

She added another log to the fire and folded Benjamin's discarded blankets, laying them neatly over the narrow settee. Standing alone in the room, memories of Christmas Eves spent in Washington came pouring over her. First with Aunt Millicent, who used the holiday as an excuse to host elaborate social functions, then with Henry, who had insisted that they attend all

the society Christmas parties under the ruse of being
a happy couple.

From the time she'd left Holly Lake, Christmas had
been a holiday she dreaded. Now, with the girls' faint
chatter in the background, she found herself looking
forward to tomorrow and their surprise. She was sure
Benjamin would love whatever they did.

The sound of muffled footfalls on the ceiling above
alerted her that he was about. Determined to fulfill her
promise to the girls, she rushed out of the sitting room
and headed upstairs to intecept him.

They met in the hallway just outside her grandmother's bedroom. His tousled red hair hung in his eyes,
and the familiar flooding of warmth he elicited every
time she was close to him returned once again.

Positioning herself between him and the staircase, she
effectively blocked his way. "I trust you had a nice rest?"
she asked, hoping she sounded more at ease than she felt.

He peered down at her. "Yes, I did. Thanks for asking."
He feathered his hand through his hair in what she realized was an attempt to straighten it. Her eyes followed his
action, her own fingers tingling at the thought of them
running through those thick locks. The direction her
thoughts had taken stunned her.

Disquiet lit his features. "Do you feel all right?" he
asked.

"Of course," she answered quickly, weaving her fingers
tightly together. "Why do you ask?"

"You look flushed." He placed his hand against her
cheek, his touch searing her skin. "You don't feel feverish."

Eager to put more distance between them, she moved
backward. But she lost her balance as she missed the step.

Benjamin's arm shot out and grabbed her waist. "Care-
ful," he said, pulling her toward him. "Don't want you
taking another tumble now."

Pressed against his solid body, Josephine actually did

feel faint. While part of her wanted him to release her, she suspected she'd probably swoon right down the staircase if he did. Embracing Benjamin wasn't exactly what she'd had in mind when she'd agreed to keep him away from the kitchen. "We seem to be finding ourselves in these . . . compromising situations," she said awkwardly.

"Now why do you suppose that is?" He tightened his hold and, with a smile, inclined his head toward hers. "Maybe we've been brought together for a reason," he whispered.

"What possible reason could that—" Her breath caught as she felt his lips brush hers. "Benjamin, what are you doing?"

In the shadows of the upstairs hallway she could barely discern the mischievous look in his eyes. But it was there. "Kissing you," he said calmly, as if it were something he did every day.

"I know that," she said, trying to sound annoyed but finding it difficult with the sensation of his mouth still lingering on her lips. "I hardly think this is—"

"Appropriate. I know." The desire faded from his eyes as he dropped his arm. "For once, I agree with you." Uncharacteristic tension filled his face, as if he were struggling with some inner emotion. "I think I'll go down and check on the girls," he muttered, starting to move past her.

"Okay," she mumbled, still trying to sort out what had just happened between them. Then she remembered her promise to Benjamin's daughters. "I mean no!" Her hand latched on to his muscular forearm. At the questioning lift of his brow, she lowered her voice. "I checked on them a short time ago. They're fine."

"Thank you for doing that." His expression softened, and he glanced at her hand on his sleeve. She snatched it back. "Then I'll go put another log on the fire," he said, giving her an odd look.

"Why don't you come up to the attic with me instead?" she offered, saying the first thing that popped into her head in her desperation to keep him from descending the stairs.

"The attic?" He now looked completely confused. "Why would you want to go up there?"

She panicked. Why did she mention the attic, of all places? Thinking quickly, she searched her mind for an answer. "Because I . . . oh yes . . . if I remember correctly, my grandmother's Christmas decorations are stored up there," she said, relieved that she'd come up with a sensible response.

Benjamin nodded. "I put them up there for her last year."

Josephine steered him away from the staircase. "I think it would be nice to decorate the house for the girls, don't you? Let them have a little Christmas cheer, even in the middle of a blizzard."

"I think it would be very nice." The warmth in his eyes surrounded her like a velvet cloud. "You never cease to amaze me, Josephine." He turned and went back into her grandmother's room. He came out a few seconds later, holding an oil lamp in one hand and a thin piece of metal in the other. "The key," he said, placing it in her hands.

Josephine ascended the stairs to the attic while Benjamin followed. Turning the skeleton key in the lock, she opened the door and flinched at the draft of cold air that greeted her. The wind continued to blow fiercely outside as they entered the room. Benjamin placed the lamp on an oval table and turned it up. Light flooded the small area.

She breathed in the faintly familiar musty scent of abandoned clothing and furniture. As a child she had been allowed to play in the attic on warm spring days and cool fall ones. She recalled how thick ropes of dried flowers, fruits, and vegetables used to hang suspended from the rafters like holiday decorations. Except for the absence of those, the attic looked exactly as she remembered.

"I think I put them over here," Benjamin said, walking to the back of the room. "I'm sure they're in one of these trunks, but I can't remember which one."

She caught sight of a large black trunk in the corner of the room. "I recognize that one," she said, moving toward it. Curious, she brushed a light coating of dust off the lid with her fingers, then opened the latch.

Shock coursed through her as she peered inside. It was filled with little girls' clothing. Kneeling, she picked up a play dress made of light green lawn, recognizing it as her own.

Clutching the dress to her chest, she swallowed hard. Years ago Aunt Millicent had insisted that she pack sparsely for her journey east, claiming that there was limited space on the train for luggage. Josephine had even been forced to leave some of her belongings behind, believing her aunt's empty promises to send for them.

With one hand she sifted through the garments: dresses, petticoats, bonnets—all in various sizes, from infant to young girl. Why had her grandmother kept these things? If she hadn't wanted anything to do with her, why hang on to her outgrown clothing?

Josephine's hand delved deeper into the trunk, until her fingertips touched something that felt like yarn. Dropping the small dress, she used both hands to bring forth the object. Her heart squeezed when she saw what it was. Her rag doll.

"Josephine?"

She looked up to see Benjamin standing next to her. Turning her face from his, she stared at the doll again. "Grandmother made this for me when I was seven," she said, touching one black button eye. "She made one for me every year, until . . ."

He laid a comforting hand on her shoulder as he knelt beside her; then he reached out and gently extracted the doll from her hand before gesturing to the contents of the trunk. "These things are all yours?" he asked.

Nodding, Josephine sat back on her heels. "Why did she keep them all these years?" she whispered, more to herself than to him.

The question hung between them. After a few moments of silence, Benjamin said, "Tell me what happened between you and Wilma."

It wasn't a question or a demand. She took it for what it was, an opportunity to voice what she'd kept hidden deep inside for so long.

"My grandmother raised me from the time I was an infant, after my parents died," she said, running her finger against the worn leather of the trunk. "When I turned ten, my mother's sister showed up from Washington, D.C. I remember her and Grandmother talking in hushed voices a lot, especially when they thought I had already gone to bed. I assumed Aunt Millicent was just staying for a visit, but a few days later my suitcase was packed and she took me back to Washington with her."

"Did Wilma tell you why?"

"No. On the train ride my aunt explained that my grandmother was tired of raising me alone. She said Grandmother had already raised my father, and now her child-rearing years were over. Since Aunt Millicent was my only other living relative, I had no choice but to go with her."

Josephine rose and walked toward the middle of the room. "She was wealthy and provided me with a good education, made sure I learned all the rules for proper behavior, and insisted I associate with only the *right* sort of people. It was at one of her Christmas parties that I met my husband."

"It sounds like everything worked out for you," Benjamin said.

She whirled around. "You don't understand. I *hated* living with her. She was a mean-spirited woman who didn't care anything about me, other than what I could do for her. She treated me no better than a servant in her home, threatening me if I didn't keep up the appearance of a pampered girl to the outside world." Josephine took a deep breath, shaking inside at the memory. "When I came of age she used me as bait, tossing me out into a sea of sharks, hoping I'd lure a prize catch."

"Did you?" he asked quietly.

"*She* thought so."

Benjamin frowned. "Why didn't you tell Wilma any of this?"

"I tried to," Josephine said. Hating the catch in her voice, she forced back her tears. "I wrote her letters, sometimes every day. For two years I begged to come home. I missed the farm dreadfully." She began twisting her ring as she glanced down at the floor. "She never wrote me back."

Benjamin stood, shaking his head. "That doesn't make sense. I can't imagine Wilma Redmond turning her back on anyone, especially family."

Josephine lifted her chin, meeting his gaze. "She did. Aunt Millicent told me she'd mailed my letters herself."

"And you believed her? Did it ever occur to you that she might have lied about mailing them?"

"The thought crossed my mind," Josephine admitted. But only after she'd become an adult had she entertained the possibility. As a child she'd believed everything her aunt had said. However, none of that mattered now. "Even if she didn't send the letters, my grandmother never tried to contact me."

"Maybe your aunt kept her from doing so."

Josephine's anger flared. "Why are you defending her? I'm the one who was wronged!" She turned away. "I shouldn't have told you any of this."

Instantly he was at her side. "I'll admit I can't explain why you were sent away," he said, guiding her to face him. "But I am glad you told me about it. I know you're hurt and angry, and you have a right to be." He drew her against him. She melted into the solace of his strong embrace, grateful for his understanding.

He rested his chin on the top of her head. "You can find the peace you're looking for, Josephine," he said, his soothing voice breaking the silence.

She didn't reply. Instead she closed her eyes, the steady thrum of his heartbeat a comforting cadence in her ear. Peace was here, in Benjamin's arms. She needed nothing else.

But he wasn't finished. "Let your anger toward Wilma go."

His words hit her like a blast of chilling wind. She jerked back from him. "How can I?" she spat. "After what she did to me—after what she's done to us now?"

Benjamin's jaw clenched. "What has she done to *us*?"

"She's ruined our lives!"

"No, she hasn't."

"Yes, she has! Don't you see? Because of her neither one of us can move forward. We're stuck in an impossible situation."

"Nothing is impossible with—"

"God, right?" she said with venom. "Do you know how many times I heard Grandmother say that? I used to believe it too. Well, even God can't fix this mess."

"How can He?" Benjamin asked accusingly. "You've already hardened your heart against Him."

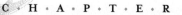

H OW DARE YOU say that to me?" Josephine's green
eyes turned to cold stones. "You assume too
much."

"I'm not assuming anything." Ben struggled to keep
his tone controlled. He knew he risked firing her temper,
but the words had to be said. He couldn't stop now, no
matter how much he wanted to take her back in his arms
again, to kiss her with all the passion and longing he felt
inside.

"Your bitterness is eating you alive," he said, straining
to keep his voice steady. "Wilma's gone. Does it really
matter anymore why she did what she did?" He reached
down and caressed her cheek with his palm. "Let Jesus
help you heal," he murmured.

Tears pooled in her eyes. His heart cracked as each one
slid down her delicate cheeks. "Why should I?" she said,

moving to escape his touch. "Where was He when I needed Him? When I prayed every night for someone to come and take me back home? Where was God when Henry—" She stopped, color draining from her face.

A thin blade of alarm pierced him at the sight of her pallor. "When Henry what?"

Immediately she turned away but not before he saw the dark pain in her eyes. Quickly she moved to the trunk and tossed her belongings inside.

"Don't shut me out, Josephine," he said, going to her.

She closed the lid of the trunk, keeping her back to him. After a pause she spoke. "Did you love your wife?"

He was caught off guard by her question, but he answered her truthfully. "Yes, I did. We had twelve wonderful years together."

Her hands briefly went to her face; then she turned to him, her eyes dry. "Then she was a lucky woman. Some of us aren't as fortunate." She lifted her chin, her expression closed. "If you'll excuse me, I feel a headache coming on."

He glanced at her wound, knowing her claim was an excuse. Her injury was healing, as she had removed the white bandage earlier in the day. "Josephine, don't go. Stay. Let's talk about this."

"Please give your daughters my regrets," she said, moving past him and heading for the door. "I won't be joining them for dinner."

"Josephine, wait—"

Before he could say anything else she was gone.

⁂

THE HOUSE was quiet. *Too* quiet.

Josephine stared into the darkness of the room, unable to sleep. The blizzard had subsided earlier that evening, and now the wind was no longer audible outside the sprawling farmhouse. She found herself wishing the noise would return. Perhaps it would drown out the deafening thoughts echoing in her head.

Benjamin's image replayed over and over in her mind—memories of his soothing embrace and tender kiss conflicting with his accusing words. How she could love someone so much and still want to throttle him was beyond her comprehension.

Yes, she loved Benjamin. But loving him was pointless. She would keep her feelings for him locked deep inside her heart, her *hard* heart, as he would say. Once again she'd managed to destroy whatever affections Benjamin had held for her. Surely their conversation in the attic had taken care of that.

How long she lay there tossing and turning in Benjamin's big feather bed she didn't know, but she was weary of it. Picking up her lamp, she headed downstairs, moving quietly as not to wake Benjamin or his daughters.

When she entered the sitting room, her breath caught. Benjamin had brought down the Christmas trunk after all, and apparently he and the girls had decorated the room earlier in the evening. White crocheted snowflakes and cranberry garlands adorned the mantel. Dark velvet ribbons were tied on every piece of furniture, some in neat bows while others were fashioned into lopsided loops.

Josephine recognized her grandmother's two Christmas quilts draped over each of the chairs on opposite sides of the hearth. She touched one of them, running her hand over the faded red-and-green fabric softened by age. It was decades old, having been stitched by her great-grandmother. Another family heirloom.

Placing her lamp on the table, Josephine sank down in the chair, her emotions a whirlwind. She felt adrift on a sea of pain and confusion, lost and without an anchor. A silent cry escaped from the depths of her soul. *Help me, Lord. Help me.*

The light in the lamp flickered, and she reached to turn it up. Her eyes widened at the sight of a worn leather book lying next to the lamp's base. Her grandmother's Bible. She surmised that Benjamin must have been reading it before retiring for the night.

But why would he read her grandmother's Bible when surely he had his own?

Josephine stared at the book for a moment before picking it up. *Grandmother believed all the answers were in here. Benjamin does too.* She skimmed her palm across the cracked leather cover. *Does it hold any answers for me?*

With a deep breath she let the volume fall open. She read the first verse that came into view, from the book of John: "Let not your heart be troubled: ye believe in God, believe also in Me."

It sounded so simple. She craved freedom from her troubled heart, and she longed for a faith in Christ like Benjamin had. Lifting the Bible from her lap, she thumbed through it, reading a passage here, a Scripture there, unsure of what she was looking for but absorbing every word. Then suddenly she knew what she had to do.

Setting the Bible aside, she sank to her knees. "Forgive me, Lord," she whispered, her words thick with unshed tears. She closed her eyes. "Please take this pain away. Help me turn it all over to You. I put my trust in You alone."

Opening her eyes, she frowned. Had He heard her prayer? By the heaviness still covering her soul, she wasn't sure. She started to rise, but a small, round wooden object lying on the floor caught her attention. She picked it up. Missy's wooden top.

Josephine glanced around the room. Abby's unfinished needlework lay on the small end table by the settee, one of Beth's blue hair ribbons draped across it. Two school slates had been left on the couch. Benjamin's half-empty coffee mug was still on the floor by his chair.

Signs of the Akers family were everywhere in the room

and throughout the house. Rising from the floor, Josephine instantly felt a quiet peace flow over her. Benjamin belonged at Redmond Farm. It was his home . . . his family's home. Suddenly the question of her future no longer plagued her. All that mattered was Benjamin—and that he and his daughters received the legacy they deserved.

She would make sure of it.

⚜

CHRISTMAS DAY dawned clear and bright, sparkles of brilliant sunlight reflecting like diamonds off a white blanket of snow. The blizzard was over.

Bleary-eyed from lack of sleep, Ben trudged through the ankle-deep snow as he returned from doing the morning chores. He hadn't slept a minute last night, Josephine weighing heavily on his mind and his heart. The anguished look in her eyes when she'd mentioned her late husband still haunted him. She deserved to be cherished, not rejected. Henry Patterson had been a fool. Ben's gloved hands fisted at the thought of the man harming her in any way.

Sent away by her grandmother. Unloved by her husband. Ben could only guess at the depth of pain Josephine suffered. He knew God would help her. Yet he also knew that it was up to her to open her heart to her Savior. As much as Ben wanted to take away her sorrow, he couldn't.

Lord, help her. And help me too. We both need You so much right now.

⚜

JOSEPHINE LOOKED up as Benjamin entered the kitchen, stamping his boots in the doorway to shake off the powdery snow. She caught his gaze, and her heart beat in

Christmas Legacy | 347

triple time, even as she felt sorrow creeping over her. But she shoved it away for the sake of his family.

"Good morning, Benjamin," she said, striving for a cheerful tone. She set down the last plate on the table, forcing a smile. "And Merry Christmas."

A look of surprise briefly colored his expression before he returned her smile with a wonderful one of his own. "Merry Christmas, yourself," he said, his blue eyes holding hers.

"Daddy, take off your hat and come sit down." Katy bounced over to her chair and pulled it out, the legs scraping sharply against the wood floor. "It's time to eat."

Whipping off his hat, he tossed it onto a peg and shrugged off his coat. He sat down at the table and looked at his plate. "Where did the fancy dishes come from?"

"Mrs. Patterson suggested we use Grammie Wilma's china this morning," Abby said as she placed a stack of steaming hotcakes in front of him.

Josephine brushed by him as she laid a platter of crisp bacon in the center of the table. She jumped when he laid his hand lightly on hers. Her eyes met his questioning look. She knew what he wanted to ask. "I'm fine, Benjamin," she said, her smile genuine this time. "For once, everything is all right."

A sharp knock at the front door had her snatching her hand away. Benjamin glanced at her one more time before rising from his chair. "Who could that be?" he wondered aloud as he opened the door.

"Merry Christmas!" Raymond Rawlings greeted cheerfully. "Sorry to arrive on your doorstep unannounced, but I heard about Mrs. Patterson's accident from Henry Flint day before yesterday. Unfortunately the storm prevented me from coming to check on her before now." He stepped into the kitchen and smiled. "You're looking well, Mrs. Patterson. I'm glad to see your injury wasn't too severe."

"Yes, I was very fortunate. Benja—Mr. Akers and his daughters have taken excellent care of me."

"Why don't you join us for breakfast, Ray?" Benjamin asked, offering to take the attorney's coat.

Raymond removed his hat. "If you're sure it won't be an imposition."

Benjamin hung it on an empty peg. "Of course not." Then he turned to Josephine. "That is, if you don't mind."

Josephine suddenly realized how fortuitous Raymond Rawlings's arrival was. A tiny wave of relief flowed through her. "Not at all," she said, gesturing to the plates piled high with food. "We have plenty."

Breakfast went by quickly, the girls struggling to contain their excitement during the meal. After the breakfast dishes were cleared, Olivia and Katy each grabbed one of their father's hands.

"Come on, Daddy. We have a surprise for you," Olivia said, giving his arm a tug.

Katy pulled on his other hand. "It was *so* hard keeping it a secret."

Benjamin flashed Josephine a knowing look. "So you've all conspired against me," he teased, standing up.

"What does *kinspired* mean?" Missy asked.

"Never mind." Abby ushered her out the door.

When they were all seated in the sitting room, the girls unveiled their surprise. Benjamin's delight in his daughters' amateurish attempt to tell the Christmas story was evident. From the hand-drawn donkey to the yarn-haired Jesus, their play was charming.

Tears misted Josephine's eyes as the girls took their bows. *I will miss them so much.*

"Excellent performance, young ladies!" Raymond said, giving them a standing ovation. "And if you'll allow me, I have a little surprise of my own." He slipped out of the room and left the house, returning with his arms full of packages.

"Presents!" Katy squealed and ran to Raymond, nearly knocking the slim man over in her enthusiasm. Josephine watched as he doled out several gifts wrapped in brown paper and twine.

When the presents had been distributed, Benjamin walked over to him. "You didn't have to do this, Ray," he said solemnly.

"I know."

Benjamin clapped him on the shoulder. "I thank you for it, and as soon as I'm able I'll pay you back."

"No need," Raymond protested, looking at the children. "Those smiles are payment enough."

The younger girls made a fuss over their new dolls, while Abby carefully drew on her new white gloves, touching the delicate tatted lace at the wrist. "Thank you, Mr. Rawlings," she said, the other girls echoing their gratitude.

"You're welcome. Now, I must be off. Mrs. Rawlings is expecting me back shortly." He headed toward the kitchen.

Josephine rushed to stop him. "Wait," she said, placing her hand on his arm. "Can . . . will you take me back with you?"

The entire room fell silent.

Katy jumped up, her doll forgotten. "You're leaving, Mrs. Patterson?"

She nodded slowly. "It's time for me to go."

"But we don't want you to leave!" The four younger girls ran to her, and she knelt in front of them.

And I don't want to go. But she had to. "The storm is over and my injury has healed," she said gently, fighting against the lump in her throat that threatened to choke her. "There's no reason for me to stay."

Abby approached her, chewing on her bottom lip. "Will we ever see you again?"

Josephine met each girl's tearful gaze. "I don't know.

But I want to thank you for allowing me to stay in your home and for your impeccable hospitality." She rose from the floor and gave them a wobbly smile. "Your Grammie Wilma would have been proud of you." She turned to Raymond. "Would you be so kind as to wait for me to pack? I'll only be a few minutes."

"Of course." Raymond's formerly jovial look had completely vanished. "If you're sure this is what you want to do," he added.

Her brows furrowed at his cryptic reply. Why would he question her leaving? "Yes, Mr. Rawlings, I'm sure." She looked to Benjamin. "May I speak to you privately?"

Benjamin nodded, his lips forming a grim line. They left the sitting room and walked to the hallway, stopping by the staircase.

She faced him, holding up her hand when he started to speak. "The farm is yours," she said.

His eyes widened. "What?"

"When I get back to town I'll have Raymond draw up the contract."

"We don't have to do this now," he said quickly. "We can wait. We'll decide on a price together. . . ."

"There's no price. I'm giving you my half of Redmond Farm."

His mouth dropped. "I don't understand. Why would you—?"

"Because it's the right thing to do. And because I *want* to. This is your home, you said so yourself. It just took a while for me to realize that you and your daughters belong here."

"Josephine, be reasonable. You can't give up your inheritance."

"I can . . . and I will." Although she knew it would increase the pain building in her heart, she closed the distance between them. Unable to stop herself, she pressed her palm against his cheek, her hand looking tiny and pale against his tanned, handsome face. "Let me do this, Benjamin. I finally understand what you've been trying to tell me. I know now I have to trust God . . . with everything."

Tearing her gaze from his, she spun away from him, grabbed her skirts, and flew up the stairs before his stricken look made her change her mind.

C·H·A·P·T·E·R

XI

BEN RETURNED to the sitting room, still trying to make sense of what Josephine had said. The room was silent except for his daughters' sniffling.

Rawlings sprang from his chair. "Did you convince her to stay?" he asked, concern etching his features.

Ben simply stared at him. "She gave me the farm," he said dully.

Rawlings sucked in his breath. "She *gave* it to you?" He whipped off his spectacles and began polishing them frantically with his handkerchief. "Well, this is a most unusual turn of events. Not what Wilma had in mind at all. And what of Mrs. Patterson now? How will she manage without an income?"

Rawlings's words broke through Ben's shock. "What are you talking about?"

The attorney shoved his glasses back on and began to

pace. "This was not how things were supposed to turn out," he mumbled as if Ben wasn't there. "I tried to tell Wilma her plan was far-fetched, but she wouldn't listen."

"What plan? And what about Josephine's income?"

Rawlings halted. "I shouldn't say any more. Attorney-client privilege. Then again," he said as Ben shot him a menacing glare, "I can make an exception in this case. The circumstances certainly warrant it."

"The point, Ray," Ben insisted. "The woman I love is about to walk out of my life. I don't have time for all this lawyer talk."

"You love her, Daddy?" Katy asked from the other side of the room.

Ben prayed for patience. "Yes, honey, I do, but I need to talk to Mr. Rawlings right now." He turned back to Rawlings. "I want an explanation."

· ⟡ ·

THE BEDROOM DOOR flew open, and Benjamin went straight to Josephine. "You're not going anywhere."

Josephine's hand flew to her chest, her heart racing like a herd of wild horses. "How dare you burst in here and scare the life out of me?"

"I dare because I have to." He grasped her shoulders, his huge palms covering them completely.

"Get your hands off me!" she demanded, though her tone didn't match the force of her words. Instead, she sounded breathless, the intensity of his gaze preventing her from breathing properly.

"No. Not until you listen to what I have to say. I know all about Henry, Josephine. The affairs. The debt."

She felt the color drain from her face. "How?"

"That's not important right now. What's important is your future and the future of Redmond Farm." He let go of her shoulders and claimed her hands. "Marry me,

Josephine. We'll keep Wilma's legacy in the family, and the profits from the farm will take care of your debts."

Marriage? Images of a life with Benjamin swirled in her mind. Of being a mother to his five precious girls. Of being a wife to a man she loved more than life itself. Of living in a house that she'd never wanted to leave in the first place. She'd have it all.

But she wouldn't have what she needed the most. His love.

She pulled her hands from his grip. "I can't marry you, Benjamin." Each word slowly ripped her in two, and her eyes burned as she turned away from him. Carelessly she tossed her expensive clothing into her Saratoga, clothing she intended to sell along with her jewelry when she returned to Washington. The material things that had meant so much to her before last night were now insignificant. The proceeds from the sale of them would be enough to satisfy the creditors for a while. She would trust God to take care of the rest.

Ben came up behind her. "Josephine," he said, his voice laced with pain. With gentle fingers he turned her toward him. "Why?" he whispered.

Tears spilled down her cheeks as she closed her eyes. *Father, help me. Help me make him understand.* She looked at him. "I married for convenience once, Benjamin. It nearly destroyed me. I won't do that again."

His pained expression faded, replaced with understanding. "You think I don't love you? Is that why you won't marry me?"

She nodded, unable to speak.

Cupping her chin, he smiled, its warmth penetrating straight to her soul. She looked into his eyes, and instantly she knew what he felt for her before he spoke the words.

"I love you, Josephine."

She melted against him. Her heart soared as the doubts she'd had about his feelings for her disappeared.

He grinned. "So . . . when do you want to get married?"

She paused. One issue remained unsolved. "What about children?" she asked, despising the fact that she couldn't be whole for him. "You don't mind marrying an imperfect woman?"

Benjamin released her and cradled her face in his hands. "I hate what Henry did to you," he lamented. "Everything about you is perfect, sweetheart, and I plan to spend the rest of my life proving that to you." He lowered his lips to hers and kissed her tenderly.

"What about my girls?" he asked after they parted. "Do you think you could learn to love my daughters?"

She gave him a slow smile. "I already do. And my answer to your proposal is yes."

With a yelp of joy he swung her up in his arms, holding her tight. When he set her down, she nestled against his chest. After a few moments he said, "There's something you should know."

She looked up at him. "There is?"

"I had a talk with Ray downstairs. He told me the whole story about Wilma and your aunt. Millicent wanted you to come to Washington for a monthlong visit, and seeing as you were her only living relative, Wilma couldn't refuse. But one month turned into two and then three. Ray said Wilma wrote you several letters, but you never replied."

Josephine was stunned. "I never received them," she said quietly.

"Finally Wilma did hear from Millicent—Millicent's attorney, actually. She threatened Wilma with legal action if she tried to contact you again." Benjamin traced Josephine's cheek with his fingertip. "Wilma didn't want to put you through that so she agreed to stop writing to you.

"But she never stopped loving you. She had Ray hire a private investigator to send back reports about your life in Washington. After your wedding, the reports included newspaper clippings about your new marriage." A cloud passed over his face. "Later they also included . . . other things."

"Henry's affairs and his gambling," Josephine supplied.

Benjamin nodded. "She knew how unhappy you were, and she wanted to make things right. According to Ray, that's why she split her inheritance between us." He gave her a knowing smile. "Seems she thought we were well suited for each other."

"So all this was some grand plan my grandmother concocted?"

With a small chuckle he replied, "Appears that way, although I never would have pegged Wilma for a match-maker." He sobered and tightened his hands around her waist. "But you won't find me complaining about it."

"Neither will I," she replied, amazed by what her grandmother had done. "She really did care about me."

"She never gave up on you, Josephine."

"Neither did God."

Benjamin kissed her again. "As much as I'd like to spend the rest of the day alone with you in this room," he said, a wicked twinkle in his eye, "we better head downstairs before Ray begins to wonder what's happened to us."

"Oh yes," she agreed as he dropped his arms and led her to the door. "We wouldn't want to appear improper, would we?"

He laughed. "Never."

When they reached the bottom of the stairs, Josephine halted. She looked up at Benjamin, feeling a sudden attack of nerves. "What if the girls don't want this?"

He took her hand and gave it a reassuring squeeze. "There's only one way to find out."

Hand in hand they walked into the sitting room. Benjamin's daughters took one look at them and came running. Josephine spied Raymond sinking into a chair as if relieved. "Does this mean what I think it does?" he asked.

"If you're asking whether she agreed to be my wife," Benjamin said, "then the answer is yes."

"Really?" Katy threw her arms around Josephine's waist. "You and Daddy are getting married?"

Josephine reached out and tentatively stroked Katy's hair. "Is that okay with you?" she asked, looking at all the children.

"Yes!" they all said at once, each of them trying to hug her at the same time.

"This is the best Christmas ever!" Olivia exclaimed.

A joy unlike any Josephine had ever known consumed her. *Thank You, Lord. This is more than I dared hope for.*

Benjamin put his arm around her and drew her close. "Welcome home, my love," he whispered in her ear.

"You're a little late," she said, smiling as she leaned into him. "I've been home all along."

IVY DALY'S SHORTBREAD COOKIES

One of my favorite Christmas memories as a child was making my nana's shortbread cookies. She would travel from Michigan to Arkansas to visit us at Christmas; and my brother, sister, and I would help her make the cookies. We decorated them with red and green sugar, but you can use any decorations you like. I hope you enjoy them.

By the way, Nana is ninety-five and still going strong!

> 1 cup sugar
> 1 pound butter at room temperature
>   (no substitutes)
> 4 cups all-purpose flour

Cream butter and sugar together until well mixed. Add flour, 1 cup at a time, beating between additions. The dough will be stiff.

On a floured surface, roll dough to ⅛-inch thickness (or thicker if you want). Cut out cookies with cookie cutters and place them on an ungreased baking sheet. Prick with a fork 2–3 times.

Bake at 350° for 8–12 minutes. Cookies should be barely brown at the edges, and they will be soft when removed from oven. Let cookies sit on the cookie sheet for 1–2 minutes; then transfer to a cooling rack. Decorate as desired.

Dear friend,

Trust. It's a simple, five-letter word, but its meaning is anything but simple. There are many people in our lives to whom we offer the gift of trust—our spouse, our families, our friends. However, trusting others is oftentimes difficult, especially if, like Josephine, our trust has been betrayed by those closest to us.

Yet there is One whom we can trust implicitly. He will never betray us in our time of pain, never forsake us in our moment of need. We can put all of our trust in a little baby born under the most humble of circumstances so long ago. An infant, who became our Savior and gave His life for mankind. Once we trust in Jesus, He will heal our hurts and our hearts and make us whole again.

I wish you and your family a blessed and wonderful Christmas season.

Peace,

Kathleen Fuller

Kathleen Fuller was born in New Orleans, raised in Arkansas, and now lives near Cleveland, Ohio. A former special education teacher, she and her husband, James, live on a small farm with their three young children.

Kathleen's previous HeartQuest novella, "Encore, Encore," is included in the anthology *Chance Encounters of the Heart.* Her short stories have appeared in several on-line publications, including *lovewords, Short Story Magazine,* and *Short Story Writer's Showcase.*

Kathleen welcomes letters written to her in care of Tyndale House Author Relations, P.O. Box 80, Wheaton, IL 60189-0080, or you can e-mail her at kathy@the-fuller-family.com.

Turn the page for an exciting
preview from Robin Lee Hatcher's next
HeartQuest book,

CATCHING
KATIE
ISBN 0-8423-6099-9

Available in early 2004 at a bookstore near you.

B EN FROWNED as he read over his editorial for the third time. It was boring. The words were as dry as dust, pure and simple. With a sigh he dropped the papers onto his desk, then leaned back in his swivel chair and rubbed his eyes with his knuckles. He wondered if he was ever going to get it right.

Staring at the ceiling, he allowed his thoughts to drift once again to Katie. Only three more days and she would be here. And it was about time, too.

His mother feared that Katie had been gone so long they wouldn't recognize her, but Ben knew that was impossible. He would know Katie no matter how long she stayed away. Eleven years hadn't dimmed his memories of her.

He remembered the little girl with the thick black braids reaching to her waist and the enormous brown eyes that had seemed too big for her face. He remembered the tomboy, often dressed the same as he was, in shirt and trousers, scabs on her knees, scrapes on her hands. He remembered the girl who could swing a baseball bat as hard as any boy in Homestead and who was absolutely fearless as she raced her horse alongside the train. He remembered his childhood pal in a hundred different ways, and all of them made him smile.

Katie Jones was unforgettable.

Grinning, he rose and walked to the large plate-glass window. Main Street was quiet, as usual. Just the way he liked it. But even he had to admit he missed the way Katie could liven up a town. Nobody else was so full of ideas or mischief. She'd gotten Ben in plenty of hot water when they were kids, but he'd always forgiven her. He couldn't help but forgive Katie anything.

Yes, it was going to be great having Katie home again. But she wouldn't be here until Friday's train pulled into the station, and in the meantime he had an article to write for the next edition of the paper. Reluctantly he returned to his desk.

As he sat down, he stared at the editorial. It hadn't changed itself in the last few minutes while he'd been daydreaming. It was still boring, boring, boring. He picked up his pen, promising himself that he would finish it, even if he had to sit there until the wee hours of the night.

Maybe if he added a paragraph right here, and then—

"You're working late, Mr. Rafferty."

He glanced up, surprised someone had entered without him knowing it. The hinge on the front door was badly in need of oiling and creaked abominably whenever it was opened.

The woman smiled. "Haven't you a welcome for an old friend?"

Ben stood. "Katie?" He knew his expression must border on the ridiculous.

"Have I changed so much?"

Had Katie changed? *Yes!* When had she become a woman? A beautiful woman? And despite the flecks of mud on her cheeks and clothes, she *was* beautiful. She hadn't been beautiful before, had she? Ben didn't think so. She'd just been Katie.

A frown replaced her smile. "Well, for pity sake, say *something.*"

He moved from behind his desk, stepping toward her, studying her face for some sign of the gawky schoolgirl he'd remembered. Her eyes were the same luminous dark brown, but they no longer seemed too big for her face. Her complexion was smooth, her skin the color of honey. She was still tiny, a good foot shorter than he was, but she was noticeably more curvaceous than the girl he'd left behind. The braids were gone, he suspected, but he couldn't be certain because of the broad-brimmed hat and scarf she wore.

"Have I *really* changed so much?" she repeated.

"I can't believe it's you."

Her dazzling smile returned. "It's me all right, Benjie." Then, without warning, she threw herself into his arms and kissed him on the cheek as she hugged him tightly. Her laughter warmed the office like a fresh ray of sunshine. "Oh, Benjie, it's so good to see you."

Suddenly he laughed with her, all else forgotten. "It's good to see you, too." He set her back from him, his hands still on her upper arms. "How did you get here? You're not expected until Friday."

"I arrived in Boise City yesterday and decided to drive up. My motorcar is out front."

"You *drove?*"

"All the way from Washington. I've been following the Suffrage Special on its tour of the West in the Susan B."

"The Susan B?"

Katie took hold of his hand and drew him toward the door. "She's my Ford touring car. I named her for Susan B. Anthony. Come take a look at her."

This was Katie all right. Leave it to her to be the first valley resident to own an automobile. Leave it to her to motor clear across the country, and to blazes with the convention that said a woman didn't do such things.

"There she is." Katie waved an arm toward the Model T Ford parked in front of the *Homestead Herald* office. "Isn't she scrumptious?" She squeezed his fingers as she turned toward him. "Will you drive out with me to the Lazy L? I'm sure Papa will loan you a horse to get back to town, and I'd love to talk with you awhile. It's been so long since we've seen one another, and I want to catch up on all the news. Letters aren't the same as hearing things firsthand." She stepped closer, and he caught a whiff of rosewater.

When he was twelve and Katie just shy of eleven, Ben had kissed her. They'd been up on the ridge near Tin Horn Pass, and she'd said she didn't know what made grown folks want to get married, but maybe it had something to do with kissing since her father was always kissing her mother. She'd wondered what all the fuss was about, so they'd decided to find out. Afterward they'd decided kissing wasn't anything special. Certainly nothing they'd cared to try with each other again.

That was a long time ago. Ben had kissed more than a few girls since then. Now he found himself wondering if Katie had discovered, as he had, that kissing wasn't so bad after all.

"Say you will, Benjie. Please?"

Memories of Katie saying those same words rushed over him—*Say you will, Benjie. Please?*—and he knew it was useless to argue. She would get her way before she was through. It had always been so between them.

He nodded. "Let me get my hat and lock up."

⊱━┈•◦❖◦•┈━⊰

While Ben was inside, Katie let her gaze wander the length and breadth of Main Street. She was surprised by the emotions she felt at the sight of her hometown. She hadn't thought she wanted to return to Homestead, to leave her friends and the intense activities of Washington for the quiet sameness of Idaho. Yet now that she was here, she was glad.

She heard the door close, and she glanced at Ben as he stepped up beside her.

Homestead might not have changed much, but the same couldn't be said for Ben Rafferty. He'd grown tall, and his shoulders were amazingly broad beneath the cut of his suit coat. The angles of his face had sharpened, matured. The boyish good looks had more than fulfilled their promise in the man he'd become. The color of his hair—which brushed his collar, begging to be trimmed—had darkened to a rich shade of gold, and she thought it a shame when he placed his hat on his head, hiding it from view.

"Ready?" he asked, glancing down and meeting her gaze.

She felt a sudden embarrassment, as if she'd been caught doing something inappropriate.

"Katie?"

She saw a teasing good humor in his dark blue eyes, and her embarrassment vanished. This was Benjie. This was her dearest friend in the world.

"I'm ready," she answered.

Ben took hold of her arm and guided her toward the passenger door. "Mind if I do the driving?"

She cast a dubious look in his direction.

"I *know* how to drive, Katie. I went to college, too."

It was on the tip of her tongue to tell him she never allowed anyone else to drive her motorcar, but his next words caused her to swallow the argument unspoken.

"You wouldn't withhold the pleasure from me, would you?" He ran his fingers along the side of the door. "It's been a long time since I've had the opportunity."

"Of course you may drive her, Benjie. Anytime you wish."

Grinning like a schoolboy, Ben reached inside the automobile and pulled the latch, then opened the door with a flourish and assisted Katie onto the running board and into the Susan B. When she was settled and the door once again closed, he went around to the driver's side, reached in, and set the levers. He whistled a tuneless melody as he walked to the front of the motorcar and gave the engine crank a hefty turn. Without a trace of her sometimes temperamental behavior, the Susan B sprang to life.

Straightening, Ben shot Katie a look of pure joy before returning to the driver's side, where he vaulted over the stationary door and settled onto the seat behind the wheel. A few minutes later the two of them were well on their way to the Lazy L Ranch.

><+>-0-<+><

Ben had forgotten how much he enjoyed driving an automobile. Homestead had a way of making one forget there was a whole other world beyond this valley and the surrounding mountains. Maybe it was good to remind himself of that fact every so often.

Overhead, dusk splashed the smattering of clouds with shades of pink, announcing the coming of night.

"The headlamps are electric," Katie said softly.

Her voice drew Ben's gaze in her direction. She was holding her hat with one hand while the fingers of her other hand fiddled with a button on her duster. He wondered if she was nervous about going home.

Hoping to distract her, he asked, "It hasn't changed much, has it?"

"Homestead?" She shook her head. "No. Not much."

"Surprised?"

"No. Not really." She smiled. "Tell me about the newspaper."

"Nothing much to tell. It's still a weekly. I do everything but the typesetting. Harvey Trent does that. Harv's the best typesetter west of the Mississippi. He used to work for the *Idaho Daily Statesman*, but I lured him away." He chuckled, remembering how hard it had been to convince the man to move to Homestead. Ben had succeeded only after Harvey started sparking Esther Potter, the proprietress of Zoe's Restaurant.

"Do you write all the articles and columns?"

"Yes."

"It must be a great deal of work. Week after week. Maybe you should hire a columnist to help you."

"A columnist?" He had a niggling suspicion.

Katie met his gaze and flashed him another smile. "Don't you think a woman's column would be of interest to your readers? Of *course* it would be of interest. Women read your newspaper, too. Don't you think they would enjoy a column from a woman's perspective?"

"And who would write this column?" As if he didn't know.

She twisted on the car seat, then leaned forward, touching his arm. "Oh, Benjie, there is so much they need to hear. Do you know how fortunate the women of Idaho are to be able to vote? But so many waste that right. It's a right that should be exercised, but they throw it away, leaving it up to men to decide what happens in our country. If only we could make them see—"

"*We?*" He allowed the automobile to roll to a stop.

Katie's eyes danced with excitement. "Yes. *We.* Don't you see how much good we could do? You own the newspaper, and I have so much to share about my work. I've met some of the most distinguished and gifted women in the country. Even now they're calling upon women voters of the enfranchised states to—"

"Hold up a minute, Katie."

Her expression sobered.

Ben searched his mind for the right words. It wasn't that he didn't support suffrage for women. He did. A woman's vote was as valid as any man's. But he wasn't certain Homestead—or the rest of Idaho, for that matter—was ready for Katie's firebrand variety of women's concerns. Katie never did anything halfway. She would stir up a hornet's nest in no time.

And there he'd be, smack-dab in the middle of it.

Visit www.HeartQuest.com for lots of info on
HeartQuest books and authors and more!

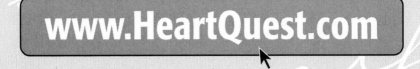

Coming Soon

JANUARY 2004

Catching Katie
Robin Lee Hatcher

Patience
Lori Copeland

HEARTQUEST ANTHOLOGIES
Stories of the Heart

Visit www.heartquest.com

HEARTWARMING ANTHOLOGIES FROM HEARTQUEST

Chance Encounters of the Heart—What could be more romantic than a chance encounter with your one true love? Let these delightful stories by Elizabeth White, Kathleen Fuller, and Susan Warren surprise you with unexpected love. In "Will and a Way," old acquaintances Will Fletcher and Zoë Hancock never expected to run into each other in a busy airport. But as their travel plans are thrown into confusion, they find their hearts taking flight toward a completely unexpected destination. "Encore, Encore" finds talented violinist Annika Goran having just been given her dream opportunity: she will be concertmaster and soloist for the Moreland Chamber Orchestra's upcoming European tour. But when she almost sits on Josef Gemmel's priceless Stradivarius, she finds that more than her dreams may be at stake. And in "Measure of a Man," the last person Calli Deane expects to see trapped in an elevator in Siberia at 2 A.M. is Peter Samuelson—the man who broke her heart. Now she is swept into the past and drawn toward a future she never expected.

A Victorian Christmas Collection—Now available in one volume, four delightful Christmas novellas from beloved author Peggy Stoks: "Tea for Marie" (originally published in *A Victorian Christmas Tea*); "Crosses and Losses" (originally published in *A Victorian Christmas Quilt*); "The Beauty of the Season" (originally published in *A Victorian Christmas Cottage*); and "Wishful Thinking" (originally published in *Prairie Christmas*).

Letters of the Heart—What says romance more than a handwritten letter from the one you love? Open these historical treasures from beloved authors Lisa Tawn Bergren, Maureen Pratt, and Lyn Cote and discover the words of love that hold two hearts together.

A Victorian Christmas Keepsake—Return to a time when life was uncomplicated, faith was sincere . . . and love was a gift to be cherished forever. These three Christmas novellas will touch your heart and stir you to treasure your own keepsakes of life, love, and romance. Curl up next to the fire with this heartwarming, faith-filled collection of original love stories by beloved romance authors Catherine Palmer, Kristin Billerbeck, and Ginny Aiken.

Sweet Delights—Who would have thought chocolate could be so good for your heart? A cup of tea and a few quiet moments are all you need to enjoy these tasty,

HEART
QUEST®

calorie-free morsels from beloved romance authors Terri Blackstock, Elizabeth White, and Ranee McCollum. Each story is followed by a letter from the author and her favorite chocolate recipe!

Prairie Christmas—In "The Christmas Bride," by Catherine Palmer, Rolf Rustemeyer can hardly wait for the arrival of his Christmas bride, all the way from Germany. You'll love this heartwarming Christmas visit with friends old and new from A Town Called Hope. Anthology also includes "Reforming Seneca Jones" by Elizabeth White and "Wishful Thinking" by Peggy Stoks.

A Victorian Christmas Cottage—Four novellas centering around hearth and home at Christmastime. Stories by Catherine Palmer, Debra White Smith, Jeri Odell, and Peggy Stoks.

A Victorian Christmas Tea—Four novellas about life and love at Christmastime. Stories by Catherine Palmer, Dianna Crawford, Peggy Stoks, and Katherine Chute.

A Victorian Christmas Quilt—A patchwork of four novellas about love and joy at Christmastime. Stories by Catherine Palmer, Peggy Stoks, Debra White Smith, and Ginny Aiken.

HEART QUEST®

CURRENT HEARTQUEST RELEASES

HEART
QUEST.

MOVING FICTION

OTHER GREAT TYNDALE HOUSE FICTION

- *Safely Home,* Randy Alcorn
- *The Sister Circle,* Vonette Bright and Nancy Moser
- *Out of the Shadows,* Sigmund Brouwer
- *The Leper,* Sigmund Brouwer
- *Crown of Thorns,* Sigmund Brouwer
- *Looking for Cassandra Jane,* Melody Carlson
- *A Case of Bad Taste,* Lori Copeland
- *Child of Grace,* Lori Copeland
- *Into the Nevernight,* Anne de Graaf
- *They Shall See God,* Athol Dickson
- *Ribbon of Years,* Robin Lee Hatcher
- *Firstborn,* Robin Lee Hatcher
- *The Touch,* Patricia Hickman
- *Redemption,* Karen Kingsbury with Gary Smalley
- *Remember,* Karen Kingsbury with Gary Smalley
- *Winter Passing,* Cindy McCormick Martinusen
- *Blue Night,* Cindy McCormick Martinusen
- *North of Tomorrow,* Cindy McCormick Martinusen

- *Embrace the Dawn,* Kathleen Morgan
- *Lullaby,* Jane Orcutt
- *The Happy Room,* Catherine Palmer
- *A Dangerous Silence,* Catherine Palmer
- *Fatal Harvest,* Catherine Palmer
- *Blind Sight,* James H. Pence
- *And the Shofar Blew,* Francine Rivers
- *Unveiled,* Francine Rivers
- *Unashamed,* Francine Rivers
- *Unshaken,* Francine Rivers
- *Unspoken,* Francine Rivers
- *Unafraid,* Francine Rivers
- *A Voice in the Wind,* Francine Rivers
- *An Echo in the Darkness,* Francine Rivers
- *As Sure As the Dawn,* Francine Rivers
- *Leota's Garden,* Francine Rivers
- *Shaiton's Fire,* Jake Thoene
- *Firefly Blue,* Jake Thoene
- *The Promise Remains,* Travis Thrasher
- *The Watermark,* Travis Thrasher